MASQUE

Also by F. Paul Wilson and Matthew J. Costello
MIRAGE
Available from Warner Books

MASQUE

F. PAUL WILSON AND MATTHEW J. COSTELLO

ASPECT®

WARNER BOOKS

A Time Warner Company

Aspect® name and logo are registered trademarks of Warner Books, Inc.

Warner Books, Inc., 1271 Avenue of the Americas, New York, NY 10020

Visit our Web site at http://warnerbooks.com

 A Time Warner Company

Printed in the United States of America

First Printing: April 1998

10 9 8 7 6 5 4 3 2 1

Library of Congress Cataloging-in-Publication Data
Wilson, F. Paul (Francis Paul)
    Masque / F. Paul Wilson and Matthew J. Costello.
      p.   cm.
    ISBN 0-446-51977-4
    I. Costello, Matthew J.   II. Title.
PS3573.I45695M37   1998
813'.54—dc21   97-34571
                                                                     CIP

Book design by H. Roberts

To the cast and crew of the Sci-Fi Channel's *FTL NewsFeed*
for faithful and brilliant service during the years 2142–2146

This one's for you

"We have discovered the secret of life."
Francis Crick

"We control the secret of life."
Teresa Goleman

The fat man breathed hard as he stood in the vast valley between two empty black buildings, their struts and columns exposed like the skeletons of giant prehistoric creatures felled by spears and left to rot.

At least they're rotting slowly, he thought. Enough of the buildings remained to house thousands of outsiders.

The fringe of the jumble. Glom control ended miles back, but this urban wilderness was no freezone. Nothing here but miles of desolate, burned-out buildings. Was there a more dangerous place? Dark as interstellar space, with only eerie glimmers of light speckling the buildings, lights fueled by outsiders, who could see him . . . watch him.

They'd know he was alone. They'd think he must have come from the warm heart of the jumble, from one of the gloms. He might have weapons, he might have a splice card or a credit chip—as good as metal.

Wrong on all counts, but they could do things to him . . . things he wouldn't let himself imagine.

He stopped and listened.

He heard yelling, the voices faint at first, then swelling, growing more excited. Good, he hadn't lost them. He licked his lips, scanned the ragged walls to either side, and started moving again.

The fat man reached a corner, the curb worn to a nearly smooth bump. Other skeletal buildings stretched away in the distance.

And now he saw them. Five figures chasing one. He'd followed them from the westernmost stretch of Flagge Glom, through the warren of outsider camps that girded its boundary and clung to its perimeter like remoras on a shark, looking for scraps—food, trade, people.

The fat man had followed the five as they hunted this lone mime.

Now he edged closer to the flank of one of the buildings, but not so close that a noose could snake out and pull him into the stench and darkness.

Still, he couldn't let the men see him . . . and he had to get closer.

Who were these five? Hunters, out to nab the mime for a bounty? A mime bolts into the jumble for some reason, and the hunters are called out. Happens all the time. The mimes never get very far.

They all know better, but desperation sometimes overcomes good sense.

Or maybe the five were Sibs. In which case the mime was doomed. Sibs blamed mimes for all their problems: Mimes caused the Great Collapse . . . mimes took all the work, leaving nothing for real humans . . . mimes degraded the Brotherhood of Man.

So let's kill them all.

They'd tear the hated mime to pieces, and that would be the end of it.

The fat man didn't have the stomach to watch that. Getting stuck watching a street mimefight was bad enough.

One of the little aphorisms, the official wetphitti that filled the Ocean, suddenly popped into his mind. *It's a good world, and it's getting better all the time.*

Sure it is—and the gloms only want peace and harmony for the whole world.

Uh-huh. And I've got one of the finest transit tube systems in the jumble I can let you have for a very reasonable price.

The fat man inched close to the next corner. Beyond it he saw older buildings, even some TwenCen ferro-concrete monsters squatting in the dark, worn to crumpled heaps that didn't deserve the word "building." Fires dotted the cavelike openings.

The wind bit him . . . supposed to hit freezing tonight. Bad news for anyone without an energy allotment, which meant just about everyone outside the gloms.

The mime was yelling. The fat man couldn't make out the words. Not yet. He backed closer to the cold concrete of the building, pressing himself tight. The five thugs, whoever the hell they were, could just as easily turn and come for him. And nothing would save him if they realized he'd been following them.

Another few feet. He heard the mime screaming, yelling in frustration.

Then something snapped out of the darkness and looped around the fat man's throat. He managed to slip a hand inside the noose before it pulled tight. He fought a surge of panic as he imagined the grizzled figure on the other end of the coil. He hoped his attacker was alone. His life could be over in seconds if he wasn't.

The fat man's free hand slid up to the inside of his belt as he fumbled for his pulser—and came up empty.

The noose tightened further and tugged him back toward the darkness. He clenched his teeth.

The mime's yells and screams seemed to mirror what was happening to him.

Where was his weapon? Had he dropped it, racing after the mime and his hunters? Had he somehow missed the clatter of its fall?

He grabbed the cable with his free hand and yanked on it, putting his considerable weight behind it. His girth had its drawbacks most days, but tonight it gave him an advantage. A human bag of bones tumbled out of the shadows and sprawled on the pavement.

The fat man took advantage of the slack in the cable to make another swipe at his belt, and now he felt it, right where it was supposed to be. He pulled out the weapon and placed the muzzle against the poor creature's scabby scalp.

"Sorry, brother," he whispered. "I know you're desperate, but that's no excuse."

He pressed the trigger and his attacker crumbled as an ultrasonic pulse jellied his brain.

"Peace, brother," the fat man whispered, feeling a little sick as he secured his weapon.

He looked back to the street corner.

Mute! The mime had moved, and his pursuers had followed. He couldn't see them, couldn't hear them anymore. Might all be over by now and the risks of this midnight run would have been for nothing.

He moved as fast as his mass would allow, trying to land lightly on his feet, but mainly concerned that he might miss what was happening.

The fat man found them around the next corner. He stopped only a few meters from where they clustered in the center of what had once been a street, encircling their prey. The trapped mime, in male masque, still in his teens, cried out, his voice echoing off the cold walls rising around them.

"No . . . please!"

"Steady there, clown boy," one of the pursuers said. "We keep telling you, we're not going to hurt you."

The mime kept turning, studying the men. The fat man saw something in his hand. Not a weapon. If he had one he could have used it on them when they were chasing him. No, it looked like a blade . . . a chunk of something sharp.

So why aren't they killing him? Why are these five men standing there, trying to talk to him?

"Flux, mime!" one of the men said.

"Yeah! We want to see you change."

The mime turned in a slow circle, looking as confused as the fat man felt. What was this all about? If they were Sibs they'd have killed him already. And radical Imagists probably would have done the same thing—though True Shape preachers in the Ocean claimed that they only wanted "eternal freedom" for the poor freaks.

And hunters simply would have slapped a collar on the terrified mime and dragged him back to his owner and eventual death in the Arena.

So who were these men, what were they doing?

That was what the fat man was supposed to learn. Those were Okasan's instructions. Watch for any strange antimime activity, anything out of the ordinary.

But the fat man was uneasy now. This was a little too far from the ordinary.

"Go on, hit a mutin' template, mime. Give us a show. Let's see what you got."

The mime scanned the angry faces. He looked like some dumb animal being asked to do a trick but knowing he'd get a beating instead of a treat when it was done.

One of the men pulled out a weapon—a full-size version of what the fat man carried. That model pulse gun could be programmed to knock someone out for ten minutes or punch a hole in a steel wall. Standard issue for glom security forces.

The mime stood wide-eyed and wobbly, certainly as scared as any human the fat man had ever seen. His instincts urged him to help, do something to even the odds. But he could only watch, then tell Okasan what he'd seen.

"Hit your button," a voice barked.

And now the mime, resigned, nodded.

Why so reluctant? the fat man wondered. No big thing. Probably nothing the mime hadn't done fighting in the Arena. Or if he were an agent, he might flux a few times a week.

Why so nervous now?

The mime spoke. "I know you've done something to me. What did you—?"

"Shut up," one of the men barked.

The mime's eyes reflected the scant light as he looked around.

The fat man too looked around. He wondered if the thousands in the twisted steel nests were watching.

One of the men in the circle took a step closer. "Quit stalling, copycat!"

And that was when the fat man noticed something strange about the mime's eyes. A sadness there, something like resignation. His hand fumbled over his abdomen, opening his interface slit, removing the template seated there. He looked around the circle again, blinked.

Then began to flux.

His features shifted, the flesh rising, doughlike, as if released from the skeletal structure below.

And then a hissing noise. One of the men in the circle, close to the mime, moved to his right, blocking the fat man's view. More hissing, then a terrible low dull moan, a sad animal sound, the cry of something dying, that rose suddenly to a shrieking bellow. An awful sound, like what must have come from—what did they used to call them?—slaughterhouses.

What the hell is this? he thought. What's happening? If only I could *see*.

The shriek devolved into a sickening gurgle, and then he heard a thick, wet sound as something smacked against the pavement.

The fat man backed away, trying to move slowly but wanting to be *out* of this place. His right foot kicked against a stone and it clattered a few inches away.

He kept his eyes on the circle of men. Had they heard that? No. They still encircled the mime, who remained hidden from view. And they fell silent, as if the brutality that defined their existence was being sated by what they were witnessing.

The fat man backed away a bit more, then turned and retreated at a brisk walk. And when he thought he'd gone far enough, he pushed himself into his best approximation of a run, heading back to the more civilized areas of the jumble.

And along the way he kept scanning the buildings for those flickering lights, watching for anyone who'd risk coming for him. He kept his pulser in his hand.

As he moved, he struggled to understand the significance of what he had seen—and *not* seen.

A mime had been tracked and trapped—but not killed—simply forced to go into flux. But something had happened. Something lethal.

But what?

One thing the fat man did know: Neither he nor anyone else outside that circle had been meant to witness that. And his life would be worthless if he spoke publicly of what he had seen here tonight.

But he'd tell Okasan.

Okasan would understand. Okasan would explain. Okasan knew everything.

INTO THE WOODS

"Your lordship, it's time now. Come, please . . . you don't want to miss your meeting, Lord Tristan. Mr. Cyrill will be waiting."

Tristan opened his eyes.

Blue . . . his one-room compartment was lit in soft blue tones, almost as if it were underwater. Tristan had never seen any of the world's seas firsthand, and yet . . .

The name Cyrill brought him to full alertness as Regis prattled on.

"He expects you in less than a quarter hour, Lord Tristan, and you *know* how he hates to be kept waiting."

Tristan slid out of the bed and Regis retreated. As soon as his feet hit the floor, the room changed color. The blue light shifted, warming to a burnished orange while a few spots in the room started glowing with a lean white light.

The bubblescreen array he'd been watching last night still floated at the end of his bed.

Tristan glanced at them now, an arrangement of his favorite antique vids, nearly all of them black and white. The absence of color seemed to make them more real, as though they came from a different world, a planet without color, but filled with emotion, filled with people he cared about.

His world had color. No emotion, no beliefs, no people—but lots of color.

Tristan walked closer to the floating screens.

The vids were frozen at key scenes, moments that particularly interested Tristan. A man stood on a small town's bridge, giant snowflakes flying in his face. Should he jump or not? Was his life really meaningless?

How could it be? Tristan thought. With a wife and children, and that great town filled with people who loved him?

The next image made Tristan smile. A man named Rick sat at a table, a cigarette in one hand and a drink in the other, talking to the most beautiful woman in the world.

Who just happened to walk into his club.

Tristan reached out and pushed his hand through the image, and the flat black-and-white image danced on his hand.

He wished he could step into that world.

He shook his head. This was dreaming. Looking at these vids, dreaming about a world that probably never was.

"Access my newsfeed, Regis."

"Oh, there's nothing there that you'd be really interested in, your lordship. And you *are* running late."

"Play it," Tristan said, thinking he *must* set aside time to reprogram his PDA.

This English butler thing was getting old. He'd picked up the idea after watching all these old vids, the black-and-white flatties; he'd thought it would be fun to have his own butler. But in real life, day after day, it got pretty muting annoying.

Before this reprogramming Regis had been an elderly cardinal, addressing Tristan as "Your Holiness."

Fun . . . for a while.

Everything got annoying. Or boring. Especially when your life was so circumscribed. The mime warren had every amenity . . . except freedom of movement. No mime could leave the warren unless his Roam Grid was cleared by the glom.

Tristan could only look at the tantalizing holovisions of places so different from the gloms. There were jungles, lush and crazily green, filled with mottled snakes that hid in the trees and odd little mammals with dark, haunted eyes. What a wonderful thing to actually go to *them*, he thought. Or imagine the mountains, the tremendous jagged peaks. *Imagine* climbing up those rocky cliffs, feeling the hard stone, the icy wind.

Tristan *could* imagine it. And that made this life, this imprisonment, so much harder.

But today he'd get out and travel, if only in the man-made world of the glom. Yes, today would be a good day.

He turned and saw his reflection in the large glistening mirror against one wall. His features were blank, with flat cheekbones, a rudimentary nose, a slit for a mouth, his irises nearly white. His smooth naked body stood slim and pale, with no sexual organs.

He took a step toward the mirror. His templates lay on the counter, including the new ones Cyrill had sent over.

A ball of light materialized in the air behind him as Regis began to run his personal newsfeed.

"Lord Tristan, I do wish you'd forego today's—"

An announcer's voice cut Regis off.

"A new wave of antimime violence is sweeping the freezones."

Tristan glanced at his PDA. "Still trying to shelter me, Regis?"

Then he turned back to the holo. Sure, he thought, anything could happen to a mime in the freezone. *Without a glom behind him, a mime was as good as dead.* The gloms hammered that one home.

The bubble filled with solid-looking images of a pair of running mimes. The pursuing crowd screamed at the escapees, their yells filling Tristan's apartment.

"Kill the copycats! Kill the freaks!"

Sibs on the prowl . . . he wondered how many of them were roaming the jumble.

Some of the screaming crowd carried weapons—sticks, stones, knives. So primitive. Revulsion crawled through Tristan's gut, still he kept watching, fascinated. Something so primal about the scene, almost like a racial memory.

But mimes had no race.

In the globe, the mimes turned a corner. The robocams followed, recording the incident from above and behind, dumping the images into the Ocean for anyone to watch, to enjoy over and over, to alter, to add to their favorite vid collection.

Simply one more set of images to play with.

The announcer's voice, incongruously matter-of-fact, described the obvious.

"We are tracking two escaped mimes who have been ID'd by a Sibs local. The crowd is rushing to make quick work of the two runaways."

"Lord Tristan, you really should hurry. Mr. Cyrill expects you—"

Tristan raised a hand.

The mob caught up to the two mimes and flowed over them like a tide of rushing water. Fists rose, shiny blades glinted even in the murky morning light—silvery at first, then red. The camera lingered. Sure . . . not much different from the Arena . . . just more entertainment, another show.

The announcer's head floated above the mayhem.

"We asked someone from the crowd if he had any remorse over attacking and killing those defenseless mimes."

Suddenly the holobubble filled with a florid, moonlike face, brutal and belligerent. Tristan took an involuntary step backward.

"Why should we? Damn things aren't human, and yet the genetic freaks take work away from us, the *human* family. You steal our jobs, you pay the price. Every dead mime frees a job for a real human." He raised his fist. "The Brotherhood of Man—Sibs forever!"

"Lord Tristan," Regis said, "you have less than seven minutes now. I suggest that you—"

Tristan said, "Off." The bubble responded by collapsing on the face, crushing it out of existence.

It doesn't concern me, Tristan thought.

No, the only concern he had was the assignment he'd been training for. It began today.

Tristan turned back to the mirror. He picked the two four-centimeter disks off the countertop. Both flexible, slightly translucent, with a feel almost like callused skin. But the first was a single piece, a typical ROM template from Cyrill—the starting point for the new assignment.

The other was something new, with a removable seal: Kaze Glom's writable template. But that was for later. Right now he needed to activate the ROM template.

Male or female? he wondered. Let's see what they've cooked up for me.

He reached down and ran his fingertip along his lower left abdomen, dividing the skin there and opening a six-centimeter slit. He inserted the new disk, then ran his finger back over the opening. The slit disappeared without a trace.

And now the flux began. He braced himself as the interface wetware began reading the code on the disk, digitizing it and bioelectrically transmitting the sequence data to the nuclei of his cells. Any second now, he'd—

There! He felt the familiar rush as his mDNA began responding to the new genetic code. His cells, one by one at first, then in cascades of billions—brain cells, blood cells, nerve cells—began copying it, mimicking it.

He'd prepped for this, loading up on nutrients—carbohydrates and amino acids—last night.

It was all a physical process . . . only physical changes.

At least, that was what everyone who worked with mimes liked to believe.

But Tristan wasn't so sure about that.

He looked up at the mirror. His face was already changing, as a rugged chin began to jut, and his eyes took on an eggshell blue tint.

Good-looking masque, Tristan thought. Wonder who the donors are . . . or were.

Assignment masques were almost always composites, bits and

F. Paul Wilson

pieces assembled and tailored to the specific needs of the task at hand. Unless of course you were supposed to impersonate a real person.

An ache grew in his bones as his body began to stretch. Now came the painful part as the skin pulled and cells struggled to keep up with the rapid changes. If he checked his neuronet he knew his personal readouts would show respiration and pulse accelerating crazily, as if out of control. He'd heard stories of mimes who died after too many fluxes.

Only stories.

Sweating, groaning, he leaned against the wall. He breathed heavily, noisily, grunting as he gave birth to this new body.

When he could open his eyes, the first place he looked was his groin.

I'm a male today. Not that it mattered.

Not that it mattered. That was what he told himself.

But over the years he'd found that he tended to think of himself as a "he"—a good indication that his source DNA had probably started out with a Y-chromosome.

He looked down at his hands—good, strong fingers, muscular forearms.

Slowly the pains subsided, and he took a good look at his reflection.

This is who I am today.

Not bad. Straight brown hair, clear blue eyes, strong jaw, lean, well-muscled physique. He smiled. Nice teeth.

"You handsome devil," he muttered. The line, the way he said it . . . stolen from another old vid.

Finally, a standout phenotype. The template he'd been given for his last assignment had turned him into a stoop-shouldered, weasel-faced woman. He'd hated every second in *that* masque.

He felt his energy sagging after the flux. He needed a little pick-me-up.

"I'm afraid that you don't have any time for breakfast, your lord-ship," Regis told him.

"I'll eat during the conference."

"Your *lordship*! That would be insulting."

Tristan ignored him. He walked through Regis and emerged on the other side—just to make a point. I may be a mime, he thought, but at least I'm solid.

More than you could say for a Personal Data Avatar. And a damned annoying one at that.

I may be property, but at least I own you.

Tristan took a jump from the closet, pulled on the one-piece outfit, and waited as the smartfabric adjusted its size to his new body. Usually he wouldn't need clothes to meet Cyrill in the Ocean. He could sit here buck naked and appear in jeweled armor at the meeting. But he didn't know how much time he'd have before starting the assignment.

And he did know that Cyrill wanted to see the new phenotype.

"Scan me," he said.

"Yes, m'lord."

Laser flashes fanned from the wall unit, enveloped him for an instant, then winked out. His new image was ready to dive into the Ocean.

"Lord Tristan," Regis said. "I'm getting a message. Mr. Cyrill is arriving in the ice box. He'll expect you to be there, waiting!"

"I know, Regis." He grabbed a concentrate tube and glanced at the officious Regis who wore a properly worried expression. "I know, and thanks."

Tristan enjoyed making Cyrill wait.

He blinked his right eye twice, then his left eye once, activating his neuronet. He'd programmed it to jack him into Cyrill's supersecure virtual meeting room in three seconds.

Two.

One.

"I'm diving, Regis. Stay out of trouble."

"Lord Tristan, I would never—"

Tristan's compartment dissolved in a brilliant flash. A swirl of rainbow colors, thunderous music, an instant of vertigo.

CHAPTER 2

Welcome to the Ocean. Where if you don't learn how to swim . . . you drown.

Tristan raised his real hand and saw his virtual hand move. A quick jab, and he was at the door to the virtual room. No swimming today. No surfing. The address for the meeting room was preset.

The ice-house door stood before him, looking like rich, intricately carved wood. Only someone cleared to meet with Cyrill could pass. Tristan pulled on the latch and it swung open, as real as any door he'd ever seen.

Inside, he noted that Cyrill had chosen a starship motif—a vast control room with a panoramic view of interstellar space.

Cyrill stood by one of the huge ports, gazing out at the swirling galaxies . . . his back to him.

Immediately, Tristan could tell that he wasn't happy.

The virtual door gently shut behind Tristan with an equally authentic sounding "click." And still Cyrill didn't turn.

"You're late, Tristan."

"I hit a lot of crosscurrents."

Now Cyrill turned. He was dressed in a gray corporate suit that matched the muted colors of the room and his brilliant white hair. Of course, Tristan had no idea if Cyrill really looked like this. Maybe it was a look he adopted just for Tristan . . . maybe he had a different avatar for each mime agent he handled.

"Humor, eh? I didn't know mimes were given to humor."

"Blame it on my wardrobe."

"Speaking of which . . ." Cyrill looked him over. "Nice pheno. That new template looks good on you."

"I hope it's been well scrubbed," Tristan said.

Cyrill raised his eyebrows and took a step closer to Tristan in the virtual room.

"Scrubbed? What—? Oh, come now, Tristan. Don't worry. You can't get psychseep from a composite."

"I do."

"So you've told me, but all the experts say it can't be."

"Maybe I'm just extra sensitive."

"Perhaps. And perhaps that's what makes you a top agent. If so, embrace it."

"Maybe," Tristan said slowly, "that explains my sense of humor."

"That or too much free time. Too many hours floating among the old vid islands in the Ocean when you're not on assignment. You've been catching up on centuries of bad media." Cyrill fixed Tristan with his gaze. "Don't worry about seep from this template. It's been designed to encompass the particular characteristics and attributes you will need on the first leg of your assignment—"

Just like every other template you send me, Tristan wanted to say, but told himself to be patient.

"—the assignment that's going to earn you Selfhood."

Tristan nodded. Right. That was the goal. He had to keep reminding himself: Selfhood. That's what I get at the end, when all this is done. If I live.

"So, let's get to it, eh? As you've no doubt guessed from your VR training sessions, Kaze Glom has an extraordinary assignment for you."

As Cyrill turned away, Tristan noticed his handler's holoimage sweep through his own, like two ghosts bumping in the night. The breach of virtual etiquette—acting as if someone wasn't there—made Tristan feel a bit edgy.

But two could play that game. He took a quick squeeze from the concentrate tube and swallowed while Cyrill's back was turned.

He knew from the months of planning and training sessions that this assignment was going to be very big.

And, if promises were kept, his last.

Cyrill made a small rectangular holobubble appear in their virtual space. Its chamber filled with the 3-D image of a huge structure, rising impossibly high, a hundred bony fingers pointing up to space.

"You know this place?"

Of course, thought Tristan. Who wouldn't? "It's Flagge's Citadel."

"Correct. The center of power for Flagge Glom."

The Citadel reminded Tristan of an old vid he'd seen . . . a place called Oz. Except Oz was green and wonderful. The Citadel was a hopelessly dark place. A black hole from which no light escaped.

The solid-looking image stopped turning, and then the view zoomed closer.

"The Citadel . . . Flagge's impenetrable heart." Cyrill smiled. "Filled with mysteries. A veritable treasure trove of secrets."

"Which no one but the Flagge inner circle will ever see," Tristan said.

Now Cyrill's smile broadened. "Some would say, Tristan, that its defenses are impenetrable."

He's playing with me, Tristan thought. Teasing me. Talking about Selfhood, and now—

"But we know that to be untrue."

Tristan rubbed his chin, feeling the unfamiliar contours.

"And you see," Cyrill said, "that's your assignment."

Tristan looked away from the chamber. Cyrill wasn't smiling anymore.

"You're going in there, Tristan. Into the Citadel."

Tristan felt his stomach tighten. "*Now* who's joking?" he said.

"No joke," Cyrill said, shaking his head. "Think about it: Hundreds of people pass through it every day. Moving in and out without a problem—"

"Sure. Because their genomes check out. But someone from our glom?"

"Trust me, Tristan. It can be done. You're going to do it."

"How?" Tristan's gut tightened further.

All those VR training sessions, all those virtual Datacenter environments, the virtual merging with a holographic datameister, learning the routines, mimicking his movements step by step . . . but he'd never dreamed he'd be going in *there* . . . to Flagge Citadel's datacenter.

"Listen carefully." The chamber shifted to a flyby of the Flagge Quarter, a self-contained megalopolis within the jumble. And at its center, the giant Citadel. "You know that Flagge has surrounded its nerve center, the aptly named Citadel, with superior counterintelligence equipment."

Tristan wondered why Cyrill said this as if it were unique to Flagge. He knew damn well it was SOP for Kaze Glom too. For all the gloms.

"But suppose you were to pass through the perimeter defenses and actually enter the heart of Flagge, enter the Citadel?"

Cyrill paused. The more Tristan looked at him, the more he was sure that the real Cyrill or whatever his real name was, would bear no resemblance to this "elder statesman" of Kaze Glom.

"What would you find in the Citadel? Only the finest ICE anywhere, whether you were trying to enter the system from the outside, from the Ocean, or through the structure itself, the automated defenses would identify the intruder and terminate him, her, or it." Another grin. "Immediately."

"So, it can't be done. We all know that."

"Don't worry, Tristan. I see what you're thinking . . . that maybe we consider you expendable. That could not be further from the truth. But I spoke to the *bosu* himself—"

Another pause. The bosu. The head man. Kaze Glom CEO Kennedy Otari, one of the two most powerful people on the planet.

"—I told the bosu there was only one mime agent for this mission . . . and that was you."

Normally such a rare compliment from Cyrill would have buoyed him. But here, now, in this place, staring at the image of the Citadel, it gave him a sinking feeling.

"I'm listening."

"No system is perfect. Flagge Glom has an Achilles' heel. Flagge has dissidents in its midst, some of them quite high up. And we have moles who are working with these dissidents. It's all a very complex arrangement that started well before your incept date, Tristan."

"And—?"

"We can get you in."

Tristan stared out the nearest port at the wheeling galaxies. A stunning effect. It took millions of years for a galaxy to rotate. In here it happened in minutes.

"And once you're in, you simply follow the procedures you've been learning. You get to the Datacenter, access datasphere 87342J, and bring back a sample from that dear little cat's eye to me."

A model of a datasphere appeared in the floating chamber. A tiny yellow ball, no bigger than a molar, its smooth surface marred only by a slim crescent slit. A universe of information was transcribed on the RNA of the virus it hosted.

Viruses had become indispensable. No matter what ICE was deployed, information accessible from the Ocean was always vulnerable.

Only data with an isolated, dedicated reader was safe; and doubly safe when, between readings, the data was stored off the reader, inaccessible, locked away until needed. *Never* put online. All the secrets, the programs, the routines stored on the RNA in the cat's eye remained safe and secure.

Especially if the cat's eye was buried in the Citadel.

He shrugged. "Nothing to it. I'll be back in time for lunch."

Cyrill's smile was tiny, pinched. "More humor. Very good. But this is a very serious matter."

"What makes this cat's eye so important?"

"Oh, not much. Not much at all . . . except its virus is encoded with all of Flagge's long-term goals and how they will achieve them. All safely hidden in that tiny sphere: Flagge's one-, two-, three-, four-, and five-year plans." Cyrill laughed. "It's the damned golden goose of the Flagge empire."

"If they learn of the breach—and they probably will—won't Flagge simply change their plans?"

"So much the better! All their plans, all that groundwork will go into the void. We'll know every strategic move they had planned, both here and Off-World. It will be a major blow to Flagge Glom, a calamity, and an incredible boon to Kaze Glom. Mind you, Tristan, I'm not talking about a mere advantage here. What you do on this assignment could end the glom wars. Flagge will drop out as a major player."

"But isn't that going to happen anyway?" Tristan said. "I mean, Kaze's writable template is going to revolutionize mime technology. Flagge hasn't got anything even close to that, and they're probably years away from developing anything like it."

"True. They don't even know such a thing as a writable exists. It's so advanced that even if they stole one, they don't have the technology to copy it."

"Exactly my point. Kaze's going to *own* the mime market by next year."

"That's the assumption, yes, but markets are fickle. Who knows what they'll be like next year? Sampling that cat's eye will be the coup de grâce. Flagge will have to merge with Kaze."

"A world without glom wars," he said softly. "It won't seem right."

"We've been engaged in our war since the Collapse. A long time. But this will end it. One glom—ours—taking control. Imagine the effect on the Mars Base, the moon colonies!"

Tristan had started thinking about the reality of the assignment. It still seemed impossible. And he didn't believe Cyrill's talk of a merger. Kaze Glom would use the cat's eye to destroy Flagge Glom.

But that was fine with him.

After all, Kaze Glom was his home. And Flagge wouldn't be the first glom he'd helped kill. How many now? The first had been Lexor, back when he was just starting out. He'd apprenticed on that one, and when Kaze had absorbed it, he'd been rewarded by a move up to full agent status. Rapalan had been next, then Mertex. And each destroyed glom was quickly absorbed into the conqueror's territory. The predators grew larger . . . and fewer.

So many. But never one so big as Flagge. How wonderful to retire at the top of your game.

He wouldn't miss Flagge. No one would.

"And trust me," Cyrill said. "You will walk in and walk out. I've got all the arrangements made, we'll—"

The room flashed with a brilliant white light, as if the link, the connection between Tristan and Cyrill in this virtual space, was breaking up.

But that wasn't the problem.

Another flash, and suddenly a new link, a new connection . . . a new presence.

Amazing! Someone was invading Cyrill's ice house—breaking through Kaze Glom's best intrusion countermeasure electronic fences, and kicking down the virtual door.

Tristan stared in awe as the new entry's holoimage took shape. The points of light coalesced into the form of an old woman dressed in a shabby robe, with a shawl over her head, looking like a pathetic beggar from the freezone.

A beggar who could crack top-grade ICE.

The image of the woman struggled to maintain focus. She began to speak, but the audio devolved to a scratchy hiss.

Tristan overcame his shock and turned to Cyrill. His handler was frantically accessing his own neuronet, alerting Kaze's Electronic Intrusion Security.

Then Tristan turned back to the woman. He sensed no hostility, no threat from her. And his initial shock turned to wonder at how she got into this supposedly secure room.

She stared back at Tristan.

Her voice changed from a hiss . . . to speech. And she was speaking to him.

"—*speak to you.*"

Tristan shook his head. She might look like some pathetic freezone freeloader, but her voice had an unusual quality. She moved closer.

"*You didn't hear me?*" The voice was now clear, the transmission unhindered. "*I am Okasan. And I must speak to you.*"

The word *OKASAN* appeared above her head in wavering script; an ideogram hovered below her feet.

Okasan! Tristan had heard the name, the *myth* of Okasan. Other mimes whispered a story about a woman who was the mime savior, a woman who rescued mimes and gave them their freedom. Tristan always thought it was a tale borne from the hopelessness of the Arena. When all you face is death and terror, maybe faith in something else is indispensable.

"*I will have someone contact you . . . someone to bring you to me—*"

"Don't worry, Tristan," Cyrill said. "Security is zeroing in. We'll have this bitch in a minute."

The image flickered again, the old woman's words once again garbled.

She reached out to Tristan with a ghostly hand as if to touch him. "*When my messenger comes to you—I can't tell you where or when or who—you must follow him.*"

Tristan said nothing.

"*You must follow him, Tristan. Follow him.*"

The words broke up again, and the image shattered into tiny cubes that reassembled for one brief second before vanishing completely.

And then he and Cyrill were alone again.

Cyrill's face was angry, his lips pulled back, baring his teeth. "Mute! How the hell did she get in here?"

"That woman," Tristan started to say, "the sign said she was Okasan—"

Cyrill swept the air with his arm. Tristan sensed that if this were a real room, Cyrill might have started pulling things off the walls, ripping down pictures, sweeping media shelves.

"*Okasan*? Look, Tristan, you're too smart to fall for that idiocy. Okasan? There is no such person. There is no 'mime savior.'" Cyrill took a breath, obviously trying to compose himself. "Do you want to know who she really is?"

"I have a feeling you'll tell me anyway."

"More humor? It's not exactly an appealing trait in a mime, Tristan." Another breath. "I'd keep a watch on it if I were you."

Good advice, Tristan admitted. His mouth had got him in trouble before.

"Understood," he said.

Cyrill nodded. "This . . . Okasan is actually an agent of Church of the True Shape. She's an Imagist. You know what that means."

Tristan did. The Church of the True Shape's main tenant was the sanctity of the human form. It called for the end of all designer genes and nanoforming and the termination of all mimes. "Mime genocide."

"Correct. Forget about Selfhood . . . or the integration of mimes into society. These people think it's their holy duty to rid the planet of mimes."

"Just like the Sibs." It was great to be loved.

"The Sibs are just a violent hate group. The Imagists want to change the law, want to make it *illegal* to clone mimes, to destroy all the mimes that exist. They're a far greater threat to us all in the long run."

"And this Okasan's one of them?"

"Indubitably. How she broke in here, I don't know. But Security assures me she heard nothing. She used only a projection thrust—no receptor feed capability. So at least our systems are secure on that count."

"But why?"

"I haven't the vaguest. I saw her lips moving but her audio feed was blanked. I don't know what her purpose was. Most likely she didn't have one—just random harassment."

No audio feed? Tristan thought. But *I* heard her. He was just about to mention this when Cyrill spoke.

"Good thing she couldn't hear, because otherwise we'd have to abort. Nothing must interfere with this assignment, Tristan. Nothing."

Tristan decided to keep the old woman's words to himself. If he mentioned that Okasan knew he was headed on an assignment, he'd be pulled, and someone else—someone like that mutagen Argus—would get it.

"Ready for your briefing?"

Tristan nodded.

"Watch the bubble."

A map of Kaze Glom popped up, but the view started receding, revealing a sprawling expanse that included the large freezone that sprawled north of Kaze Quarter. Once great cities rose along the coast, grew, and merged . . . but after the Collapse they became the *jumble*, ruled by destruction and chaos and riots . . . until the gloms restored order.

Or so went the official history.

Now the sprawling gloms' centers dotted the jumble, armed pockets of power and order that represented a new world government based on economics and a secret war.

What would it have been like, Tristan wondered, to travel to the old cities before the Collapse, before there was a North American Federation, ruled by a puppet government that merely served the gloms? The cities in the old vids seemed so exciting, filled with energy and life—not like the gloms.

"There. You see the freezone north of here. I'm about to clear your neuronet for travel through that 'zone. Your tracer will be off and no one will know that you're a mime." He looked at Tristan. "Unless you tell them, of course."

The screen zoomed closer to the freezone map.

"We're uploading this directly into your neuronet, by the way."

"I figured as—"

"Now, see that building there? That's Smalley's."

Tristan knew it well. A huge smart bar, hangout for spies, wet heads, and black market dealers from every glom, including his own.

"It's dangerous territory, Tristan, especially for a loose mime. So watch what you say."

"Right. No jokes."

A sigh. "You will be contacted by our agent there—"

"And he is?"

"Can't tell you. Too risky if it's loaded in your neuronet. But the contact will have a codekey that will guide you through Flagge Quarter to the next contact point."

"And what happens there?"

"You'll meet a team of in-house agents. They will have kidnapped a Flagge datameister—"

"For true?"

"*I* don't joke, Tristan. You will use the writable template to copy the datameister's genome. No telling who or what it will be. I don't have that information yet. And you know that Flagge IDplant you were fitted with? You will copy everything from the datameister's IDplant onto your own. From that point on, as far as Flagge Security will know, you will *be* that datameister. Our agents will then dispose of the datameister and you can enter the Citadel . . . taking the d-m's place."

He remembered a line from a vid.

"Piece of cake."

Cyrill shook his head. "As I said . . . too much free time, Tristan. But that's all about to change, eh?"

The screen presented the assignment plan in text format.

"Once inside the Citadel, you follow your VR training, enter the Datacenter, sample the eye, and get out. Simple, no?"

"Sure. Especially the part about walking off with a piece of this irreplaceable datasphere. That should be *real* easy."

"Easy if *you're* a datameister."

"And if I'm caught?"

"We'll disavow any knowledge of you, of course. You know the rules: This is a war and you are a soldier . . . *our* soldier. But only we know that. So expect no rescue parties or help of any sort that might compromise Kaze Glom's pristine image. Once you leave here, you're on your own."

The story of my life.

"But why dwell on that? Better to remember that this will be your last assignment. Imagine . . . being part of this world. No more tracers for you. You'll be identical to humans."

Identical to humans. Integration. Selfhood. No implants, no more fluxing. He would live as a human. *Free.*

And then what?

Tristan knew exactly what he'd do, what he'd always wanted to do: *travel.* Go wherever he wanted, *when*ever he wanted, see the beautiful exotic places . . . climb the mountains, hike into the jungle. Just thinking about it made him dizzy.

Except for this one fear. He could do all that—

Only if any beautiful exotic places still existed.

But they had to still be here. Places with tall trees that blew in the wind, and endless seas of blue-green water under even bluer skies. Beautiful places like those he saw in the vids. And he'd start looking for them the instant he was free.

A world to explore once he was free.

But right now, simply the thought of Selfhood, and how close it was, was almost too wonderful to contemplate.

Cyrill backed away. This conference was almost over.

"But the clock is running. You meet our agent at the smart bar at oh-nine-hundred. That doesn't give you much time. He will wait one hour . . . and then assume the worst."

"Why such a tight schedule? I'd think with an assignment this important I'd have a little more slack."

"The final pieces have only come together in the past day or so. The window of opportunity—the availability of the codekey and the time when the datameister can be snatched with no one missing him—will only last so long."

"Why not give me a master key?"

"Master key? No, I'm sorry. That is impossible."

"Don't you trust me?"

"Implicitly."

"Then give me a master key. I may need it."

Cyrill shook his head. "If it were up to me I'd do it. You'd have it in an instant. But it can't be done. My superiors would worry about never seeing you again. Neither of us is completely free, you see."

"You're not a slave. You're not a mime."

"No, but you . . . you're Kaze property, Tristan."

I am well aware of that, thank you.

How could he forget? Cloned with the Goleman chromosome, that magical complex of synthetic genes that occupied the locus of the normal human sex chromosome and controlled his DNA, his special mDNA, and allowed it to mimic any other. He'd been specifically *created* by Kaze Glom, to *work* for Kaze Glom, to *exist* for Kaze Glom as a mime agent—

You own me, but damn it, you owe me.

"I know, I—"

"And as such, your movement has to be restricted. Until Selfhood, of course."

Until death or Selfhood do us part. Selfhood . . . a carrot on a very long stick.

Just one more assignment, and I get it.

"You've only thirty-six hours. That's our window before the target datameister is rotated off access to datasphere 87342J. I expect to have a sample from that cat's eye by nightfall tomorrow." Cyrill raised a hand, and made the gesture of goodwill used by all the Kazes. "Thirty-six hours . . . good luck."

"I'll be back. With the cat's eye."

But Cyrill was already fading, his image dissolving in a swirl of color. Tristan was alone in the room, then his connection terminated and he was back in his compartment.

CHAPTER 3

Regis stood by the mirror.

"This sounds *very* exiting, Lord Tristan. But before you go, I should—"

"Off, Regis," Tristan said.

Regis vanished.

If Tristan needed him he could always access him on his net. Now he had to move.

Filamentous! he thought. I'm getting out of here. *Out!*

He was almost giddy with anticipation.

But how best to get to the freezone? The tubes were fast, but sabotage was a recurrent problem. Some splinter group always seemed to have a bone to pick with one of the gloms, or was bored, or simply crazy. So they took it out on the tubes.

He went to the door leading to the main hall of the mime warren. The interior walls still maintained their wood texture, and Tristan was glad of that. He found a warm beauty in the natural look of wood, even if there wasn't an ax in the world sharp enough to hack into it. Real wood was rare and expensive. But anything could look like wood.

Outside was different. The current "orgallic" rage sweeping the gloms didn't appeal to him. Why grow a building of wood as tough as steel, and then alter its outer layer to look like steel? Didn't make sense. If you want to nanoform a building that looks like steel, build the damn thing with steel, real steel.

But Tristan knew that he was in the minority. "Real" wasn't important anymore. The word had become an archaic concept.

The cylindrical mime complex hovered on the edge of the Kaze residential complexes, sealed off from the surrounding buildings and the rest of Kaze Glom—sealed off from the rest of the *world*—by layer upon layer of protection that screened everything from pulser beams to viruses.

Separate and unequal, a luxurious prison.

Suddenly a hand locked on his shoulder, grabbed him hard, and shoved him into an alcove. Tristan's head smacked against the smooth wall with a painful crack.

He whirled to see who'd struck him.

The face was close to his, and Tristan smelled his breath, the stale odor of SynFood from teeth that hadn't been brushed in too long.

"How's your mother, Tristan?"

Tristan recognized Argus's home masque—his day-to-day warren identity. And if ever there was proof that psychseep among mimes was real, this creature was it. Argus had worn too many bad-ass templates, done too many rough assignments for Kaze Glom.

What did one Imagist leader call mimes? . . . "monstrosities without a past, without a future."

But that was wrong.

We *have* a past. And it grows with every template we use. Bits and pieces seeping in, a kaleidoscope of phenotypes and personalities.

Argus went to push Tristan's head against the wall again, but now Tristan flung up an arm and blocked the shove. Argus's face registered surprise.

"Oh, so you've got a strong masque this time, eh? Maybe you'd like to test just how strong it is."

Argus tried another jab, but Tristan was once again too quick.

Only this time, instead of merely pushing Argus's arm away, Tristan grabbed the other mime's wrist and, without a thought, gave it a sharp twist to the right.

Argus grunted and yanked his wrist away.

"How's *your* mother, Argus?" Tristan had always found the mime greeting pathetic. "And how long have you been lurking outside my door?"

"Long enough, Tristan. Even watched your dive this morning. Of course I couldn't get into the ice house, but I know you were meeting with Cyrill."

"It's a possibility. So what?"

Argus risked coming closer again. He lowered his voice.

"It's like this. I'm only a couple of assignments away from Self-hood. Cyrill told me that. But he gave this one to you." He looked Tristan up and down, checking out the new template. "New masque and all . . . strong, fast. Should have been mine."

Tristan pushed away from the wall. "Why don't you come along?"

"Don't think I couldn't if I thought it was worth it."

Could he? Tristan wondered. He'd hear rumors about mimes with hot codekeys that could bypass roam grid restrictions. But he'd never been offered one—not that he'd ever take it, not when he was this close to freedom.

"So long, Argus."

Argus raised a fist. Was he stupid enough to want to push this further? Tristan would love to accommodate him, but the clock was running.

"It was *mine*, dammit."

He grabbed Tristan by the collar of his one-piece and Tristan responded without thinking. Again he grabbed Argus's arm but higher up this time, by his elbow. Then he twisted it inward and back, until Argus was on his knees, head down.

"Let me up!" Argus gasped.

"Fine," Tristan said. "But I don't want to see your retrogenomic face again. Got it?"

An extra push on the awkwardly bent arm emphasized his point, and elicited another groan from Argus.

I *like* this masque, Tristan thought. Oh, yes . . . good fight reflexes. A certain amount of aggressiveness was genetic, and could be useful. But that was no accident, of course. He had to wonder what other advantages it held for the assignment.

Argus stood slowly. He backed away, and his mouth curled into a sneer. "We're not through, Tristan."

He turned and disappeared down the curved hallway.

Tristan took a breath. I could have killed him, he thought. That would have ended my problems with him.

And something else . . . the *idea* of killing Argus felt good, as if he might enjoy it.

He'd killed before . . . when it was part of an assignment. Sometimes it had to be done. He'd killed other mimes, and he'd killed humans. Business . . . simple necessity.

But the thought of killing Argus felt *good*.

Tristan took the down chute to ground level, then hurried along the walkway toward the tube station. Anticipation buzzed through every axon. Yes, he was starting his last assignment, but even more exciting was the immediate prospect of getting out of Kaze Quarter and into the freezone.

The *freezone*—even the name was exciting.

He stepped on the ramp to the tubes and—

—the world and everything in it lost color as if soaked with cosmic bleach, then the outlines faded to a white limbo with no up or down or left or right.

A whiteout! Mute! This shouldn't be happening. Cyrill had extended his roam grid.

Tristan shot out a hand and found a railing. Fighting the vertigo and hanging on like an overdosed Hhhelll freak, he pulled himself hand over hand, back down the ramp.

And as soon as he stepped off the ramp, the world returned.

"Regis!" he whispered.

His PDA appeared on the ramp. "Yes, Lord Tristan?"

"Why did I just have a whiteout? Cyrill downloaded the new key while we were in the Ocean."

"Yes, m'lord. But the code wasn't installed into your grid. I was suggesting that you allow me to do that when you 'offed' me."

Tristan closed his eyes and steadied himself. Yes, he had done that, hadn't he. In such a damn big hurry to get out of here.

"Would you kindly install the code now?"

"Done, m'lord."

"Thank you. Anything else I've forgotten?"

"No, m'lord."

"Off, Regis."

Just to be sure, he executed his eye-blink sequence and a strip of icons appeared across the top of his visual field: one for accessing his Roam Grid; another to let him record and retrieve events; a personal history file; and finally his Logic icon, a direct link to Regis and the Ocean's databases. He activated the Grid icon.

His Roam Grid spread across his vision. Kaze Quarter, the expanse of the freezone, Smalley's Smart Bar were masked in green. Anything beyond . . . the other freezones, Flagge Quarter, all outlined in red. All still closed to him.

But the north freezone was open—that was all that mattered now.

"Off," he said, and trotted up the ramp.

Minutes later he was in one of Kaze's main tube nexi. Masses of shufflers, the unlucky ones who still had to go somewhere to work, to stay alive, raced left and right, hurrying to catch the next tube. Shufflers . . . stuck in jobs that actually required their physical presence. One step up from Cro-Magnons. Maybe.

Nobody important passed through here. Anybody who mattered simply jacked into the Ocean. And if they did have to go somewhere, they knew the slogan. "Floaters—The Only Way to Go!"

If you could afford it.

He slipped in among them and raced toward the northbound tubes. The crowds became a living, moving maze, heading for north freezone 226, the vast land that separated the sprawling gloms of Kaze and Flagge.

The clear capsule hurtled silently through the clear tube a thousand meters above the border of Kaze Glom's considerable piece of the jumble, leaving the gleaming orgallic façades of the high-rises behind, and heading into the low-slung freezone, an architectural plain between the gloms, where the buildings rarely reached above three stories. There were thousands of enclaves in the freezone, disparate groups united in only one thing—they weren't part of a glom, at least not yet.

Once the freezone had wild areas, tall trees, and hills filled with wildlife. Now the only wildlife was the human circus, the spectacle of life in the freezone.

Once the freezones had been giant suburbs and industrial parks and high-tech farmlands, all before the encroaching sprawl of the gloms made them a dumping ground for rejects—rejected people, rejected technology—and a black market alive with services and deals that the gloms wouldn't or couldn't touch.

For mimes removed from the protection of the gloms, it could be a dangerous place. As a noncitizen, a nonperson, a mime could be captured, imprisoned, enslaved, killed, anything—for no reason. The nominal freezone governments did little but collect credits to clean up afterward.

Tristan looked over the other travelers heading to the freezone. Most were dressed in the standard, well-fitting, drab brown or black one-piece smartsuits. But the suit on the emaciated woman next to him hung in loose folds. Either she'd programmed it wrong, or the fabric was worn out. Tristan figured the latter was most likely, mainly because her suit was filthy—dirt on the leggings and food stains all down her front. The built-in cleaning enzymes must have run out long ago.

Then he noticed someone at the end who eschewed the regimental outfit. A fat man, decked in swirling colorful robes. And he had a pet with him, a spotted pygmy Triceratops.

A rarity. A pet. And a cloner at that. The chubby, knee-high saur, its three horns blunted with rubber sheaths, was rearing up on its hind legs while the fat man dangled something just out of its reach.

The gaudy man looked so out of place among these grim-faced shufflers trekking to the freezone. He talked to the saur, cooed to it like a lover while he kept up the steady teasing.

The fat man finally lowered his pudgy fingers to the creature, letting it snatch whatever was being offered.

A tone sounded. Tristan looked up to the tube car's message center. In six different languages the display informed everyone that they had ". . . just entered north freezone 226. Welcome!"

Maybe I should start a cheer.

He turned back and found the fat man staring at him. His beady eyes, deep in layers of flesh, were locked on Tristan. His expression was grim, set. The saur still rubbed against his legs and nudged his colorful robes with its blunted horns.

But the fat man wasn't playing anymore.

Does he recognize part of this template? Tristan wondered. *He shouldn't. My masque face is supposed to be as much a composite as the rest of me.*

Does he suspect I'm a mime?

A chill crept over him. Big trouble if he was identified now.

Tristan blinked and activated his neuronet.

Immediately the overlay dropped before his eyes. He could still see everyone in the tube car, still see the fat man studying him . . . but now he had access to the Ocean and to Regis.

He called for Regis, a subvocal command that might sound to anyone listening as if he were softly clearing his throat. An instant later, Regis floated before him as if suspended in the tube car.

"Yes, m'lord?"

Tristan looked back to the glowering fat man. "Him," he said through a tiny grunt, and now the fat man's red-cheeked face filled his visual field.

Tristan waited. Regis, now hovering like a dwarf by the man's right ear, turned.

"Yes, Lord Tristan . . . I'm running a search of your personal history and Kaze Glom's archives for this image."

A pause. Then an answer.

"No, nothing in either databank. Do you want me to go into the Ocean?"

Another blink, and the officious avatar vanished, swimming the Ocean in search of any image that matched the fat man's face.

And while Regis searched, Tristan heard another chime.

A new message scrolled across the wall.

"You are approaching the nexus for north freezone 226. Prepare to depart the tube car for further travel in the freezone and beyond."

The fat man looked back to his saur, rubbed its snout.

The moment—whatever it was—had passed.

Maybe it was nothing . . . maybe he's just a curious sort.

Regis reappeared. "No, Lord Tristan. An extensive search of all ID links in the Ocean yielded no data on the individual in question. But I should caution you that if the person *is* with a glom and has a protected ID, or if he's, er, another mime, then I'd expect to find nothing."

Right. And what did a face mean, anyway? People were changing them all the time. Be a different story if he had Fatso's genotype.

Another series of blinks, Regis vanished, and the neuronet disappeared.

Maybe I'm just feeling a bit jittery.

This new template might be powerful but maybe it's too edgy. Could be that's what I'm picking up on.

A steady series of chimes began sounding . . . the freezone nexus was ahead.

Tristan followed the human tide gliding down to the surface. Tubes from all the surrounding gloms intersected here, shining arms of an octopus that funneled people into the huge elevated station. Tiers of shops from competing gloms bedizened all levels of the station, offering the latest SynFood delicacies, new biochip technology, or wet cafés where you could kill an hour or a day in the Ocean.

Always strange smells and noises here, a cacophony that took on the low rumbling sound of a giant engine, a human hive.

Except Tristan knew that some of the people here, like himself, weren't human. The only way a mime could be here was if his Roam Grid had been cleared for travel . . . or if he or she was free.

And if they were free?

Then they were *integrated* . . . the mime dream, to be integrated into the world. No more fluxing, no more wardrobe of masques . . . one last flux and then your interface was sealed. One face, one body, one genotype—forever.

He'd met integrated mimes—no one he'd ever known before, but the warren administrators occasionally let one in to talk about Self-hood and how wonderful it was to be free and treated like a human . . . *indistinguishable* from a human.

Tristan would ask them about traveling. Where had they gone? What wonders had they seen? But these free mimes didn't share Tristan's desire to see the world away from the gloms.

After the first few times Tristan stopped attending the meetings. They bored him. Worse, they annoyed him, reminding him of what he didn't have. And who needed to hear about how wonderful Self-hood was. How could it be anything else?

As he stepped outside, Tristan took a deep breath . . . and coughed. He'd been in this freezone many times and it was always overcast and filled with a stench that burned his lungs.

The freezone . . . the reach of the gloms ended here.

And now the assignment began.

Tristan brushed past the ad globules hovering around the exit. A thousand feet up, giant holobubbles hung in the sky. Anybody could rent time and space on them.

Anybody.

The intense visuals were everywhere. He tried to ignore the message directly above him . . . a man in a white collar talking . . . his voice echoing down to the antlike crowd.

"—and the sanctity of the human form is lost! We of the Church of the True Shape know that. *You* know that! You can join us. Those of you who have been misled into changing can return to True Shape, and help us to restore the true human form to its rightful place at the pinnacle of creation!"

His face grew stern.

"But those who cannot join us are those who are not fully human."

The bubble filled with a shot of a colony—could have been the moon or an asteroid. Small spiderlike mime adaptees—easy targets for human revulsion—scurried close to the ground.

"Mimes are not created in God's image, but in man's most twisted nightmares! Do *you* believe God wants His image defiled this way? Of course not! End the sacrilege! Cleanse these abominations from the face of the Earth *now*!"

Tristan swallowed. The Imagist preacher was talking about him. How many times had he seen mimes cornered by a crowd of Imagists? How many times had his cover been blown and he'd found himself running for his life? How many times had he walked past a mime who hadn't been fast enough, and seen him or her lying on the ground, the masque, the *body* bruised, bloody?

Only a mime . . . the crowd thinks. While Tristan thought: Glad that isn't me.

Another message began rumbling from a competing bubble:

"Looking to invest those spare credits? Flagge Glom has limited opportunities for investors in their New Mars Sector. Get in on the ground floor of the new homeworld . . . invest in the future, invest in Mars!"

Where mime adaptees will do all the dirty work, Tristan added.

He accessed his net and Regis popped into view.

"M'lord, I've plotted the safest course to Smalley's. This course avoids—"

Tristan scanned the map floating before his eyes. He wanted to get to Smalley's fast, so he accessed a more direct route. The smart bar was too close to take a local tube, so he'd have to walk. That was okay. The freezone was reasonably safe in daylight. Still, Tristan was glad that he had a strong masque in case any trouble started.

Tristan turned a corner that would take him past the flesh shops . . . another "business" mimes had taken from humans.

Mimes had a distinct advantage in the pleasure trades. *How do you like your thrills? Will build to suit.*

Nobody seemed to be complaining about that though. Maybe because flesh was a dying trade, what with the myriad pleasures available in the Ocean.

Tristan drank in the look and feel of the natural look of the buildings. An occasional alley broke their solid fronts as they nestled cheek to jowl along the walkways. The orgallic fad hadn't reached the freezone. Not yet, at least. Too expensive for the 'zone communities. Here the buildings retained their organic look, most of them sporting the sensible, living bark siding they'd been grown with. A natural protection that was self-maintaining. Why have anything else?

Of course the flesh district sported a different kind of self-renewing siding. The shops announced themselves with breasts and penises protruding from their pink walls—walls of real skin. As he walked, Tristan ran his fingers along the spongy surface of one and watched the penises grow tumescent, the nipples harden and jut.

He loved this street.

The flesh gauntlet opened into an open-air bazaar, dotted with tents and shacks, spreading for blocks to the east.

He kept moving—past the bazaar, down a narrow block with two long green buildings on either side, these with grassy sides and roof tendrils stretching up to the dull gray sky. No windows in these vast walls, no clue to what went on inside.

He heard noises ahead, shouting. He stopped. Sounded like trouble. Maybe he should find another way to get to Smalley's. But he'd come this far already.

He rounded the corner warily and saw a crowd gathered in semi-circle facing a high wall. A man holding up a credit reader stood at its center; beside him, two hulking figures glared at each other.

"There's still time, my friends, still time to place your bets. We have two fine mime specimens here, as good as you'll see in any glom Arena. And they *will* fight to the death for you."

A mimemonger running a street fight. A poor man's Arena. Tristan's stomach tightened. I should keep moving, he thought.

"So place your bets"—he hoisted his credit reader in the air—"before this epic battle begins."

The two mimes shoved at each other and butted their brutal-looking heads.

Were these their only templates? Tristan wondered. Or were they going to flux before the fight?

He turned away. This was one of the twisted fates of mimes in the freezone. They became performers, spilling their blood for sport. He'd seen too many high-caliber fights in the Kaze Arena to waste his time with this junk.

"Say, sir, what about you?" the mimemonger said. "See a fighter you like?"

Tristan realized that the man was talking to him.

"Wha—er, no. I mean, I—"

The man held the credit reader. "Give us a poke. Pick your fighter for, say, one hundred credits? Five hundred? What will it be—?"

"I'm just passing by . . . I—"

But then someone else wanted to place a bet and called the mimemonger over.

Tristan looked at the two mimes. Here was proof of the danger of overusing templates. Too many masques, too many fluxes, and you got to the point where you couldn't completely flux out of your last masque. Bits of physical characteristics would linger from flux to flux: an eyebrow, a misshapen nose, heavy knuckles. Veteran streetfighting mimes tended to look bizarre . . . deformed. Like these two.

"All right then."

Tristan wanted to leave. He had to keep moving. But would that be suspicious? Would someone in the crowd wonder why he wouldn't stay and watch the fight?

He backed up a step and someone glanced over at him. He didn't move again.

"Are we ready, combatants?" the mimemonger shouted.

The fighters stirred, testing their stance.

The mimemonger grinned. "Oooo-kaaay, let's play!"

The fighters' arms went up, a perfunctory salute, then they separated, putting as much distance between them as the tight circle of onlookers would allow.

The people, hollow-eyed, desperate-looking, shouted encouragement to their chosen fighter. But how much effect could that have when losing could mean death?

The mimemonger withdrew, clutching his credit reader as he slunk to the rear of the crowd, already transferring the wager data into his neuronet. By now, the credits had vanished from the bettors' accounts and been tucked away in some forgotten V-Bank in the Ocean.

Meanwhile the street mimes reached for their pouches, and the crowd started whistling as the fighters raced to insert their battle templates.

Oh, no. Had they sunk so low that they were going to flux in public? Without even a tent?

Now more than ever, Tristan wanted away from here, but he didn't dare.

Feeling queasy, he watched as the mime on the left began fluxing first. Not a pretty sight. Muscles started bulging, then receding as if the genetic message wouldn't take . . . and in all likelihood, too many messages had been fired through this mime's DNA.

His genetic wiring was frayed.

But Tristan began to see a shape slowly, reluctantly emerging—heavy, musclebound, with a thick brow. A caricature of a massive human wrestler. But the fighter's eyes looked even duller, even more brutal than before.

Part of the crowd cheered, then turned its attention to the other mime. And as that mime began to flux, the cheers turned to low murmurs.

For it was quickly obvious that this mime was using a template spliced with some nonhuman code.

The head resolved first, fairly normal except for the misshapen face that was probably the result of too many fluxes. But then the mime's hands began to blister and peel. Excess skin sloughed off and fell away. A loss like that was normal with a major flux . . . but Tristan knew it could kill a mime in the long run.

Then something black took shape from the writhing pulp at the ends of the arms, and soon each hand featured a forty-centimeter talon, tapering to a razor point.

Not fair, Tristan thought as half the crowd cheered wildly, smelling death.

Then the other mime spit at the ground. Was he scared, resigned?

Don't just stand there, Tristan thought, imagining what he'd do when faced with a hybrid opponent. Attack! Now!

The second mime was still changing, the skin growing a dull gray as it appeared to be hardening into some kind of shell-like substance. But his flux was spotty and irregular. Tristan could only imagine the incredible demands a hybrid template made on the body. No amount of nutrient loading could adequately feed such repeated, radical fluxes.

The taloned mime was better armed, but weakened from the flux. Which was why the wrestler mime already should be on the attack.

Finally the wrestler waded in. He immediately grabbed the two dangerous arms of the taloned mime, holding them wide.

That's it, Tristan thought. Render those talons ineffective.

The crowd booed the move. They wanted blood, not a stalemate.

Then the wrestler mime smashed his forehead into the taloned mime's face, bloodying it. Now the crowd cheered, and some even laughed.

Tristan looked back at the mimemonger. The odds guaranteed

that he'd make out no matter who won. At least the crowd could rest assured that the fight wasn't fixed—not when it seemed a sure thing that one of the mimes would be killed.

Again the wrestler mime butted his taloned opponent, and even more blood shot into the air.

Tristan nodded silent approval. This could be over soon and then he'd be on his way.

But suddenly an alien emotion invaded his cool analysis of the fight. Loathing filled him, tinged with pity, urging him to turn away from these two pathetic creatures trapped in a nightmare.

He shook it off. Strong seep from this template. Damn whoever had been in charge of scrubbing it.

And then a surprise. The taloned mime snapped up a leg into the wrestler's midsection, a leg encased in shell, making it a nasty weapon.

In reflex the wrestler released one arm.

And in a blink the freed talon dropped and then came slashing up, ripping across the wrestler's midsection. Tristan heard the tear, the gasp of pain.

The crowd loved it.

Again that sudden urge to flee in revulsion. Tristan almost gave in to it, but he looked around and he caught the mimemonger staring at him. All it would take to get the crowd to turn toward Tristan was a single cry . . .

Mime!

He forced his attention back to the fight.

The wrestler tried to block one talon with his arm, but now the taloned mime had both arms free, and he wielded his talons with a skill born of many battles. While one talon slashed at the wounded mime's midsection again, widening the wound, a second talon daggered toward the neck area—

And plunged into the exposed flesh there. The wrestler mime stiffened, let out a strangled moan, a horrible sound, and fell to his knees. The victorious mime yanked out its talon and watched his opponent fall face forward onto the pavement.

The dying mime began to lose his shape. His arms shriveled and muscles deteriorated as his system tried to find some genetic solution to the loss of so much blood.

But there was no solution.

The winners in the crowd huddled around the mimemonger, whipping out their own cards to get a download of their winnings.

Now's the time, Tristan thought. He turned and slipped away from the ugly circle.

Thinking: it's not so different from the Arena . . . only the ambience. What was the Arena but a street fight with frills? The fine people of the gloms enjoy the same sport.

And I want to be integrated into this?

Tristan took a few more steps and then—it had to be because of this new template—leaned against a building wall and vomited. He stood there a few minutes, then wiped his mouth with his sleeve.

Like Cyrill had said: He was seep sensitive. Too *muting* sensitive. Could be a problem.

As the enzymes in the smartfabric quickly dissolved the wetsmear he continued toward the giant playground known as Smalley's.

CHAPTER 4

Coils of pulsating light swirled around Smalley's Smart Bar, blindingly bright, oscillating up and down the pyramidal exterior. Armed guards manned the single entrance, making no attempt to hide the pulse weapons strapped to their sides.

From past experience Tristan knew that other guards, less conventionally equipped, patrolled inside. When fights broke out they ended quickly.

And fights did break out. Smalley's didn't worry about the gloms' ban on Hhhelll and X-taSea. Though not addictive, both psychoactives triggered enough schizophrenic reactions to guarantee periodic violence. People got killed—but oh what a rush.

Tristan knew he was as susceptible as anyone else . . . so he'd have to be careful what he took from people in Smalley's.

He wondered why anyone needed drugs when every thrill was available in the Ocean.

He checked the time and saw that he was early for his meeting. Good. He could go in, get settled, and—

Someone touched him from behind.

Tristan spun and faced the fat man from the tube. His colorful robes seemed in tune with the lights of Smalley's. The small saur sat at his feet, the protective grommets off its horns now.

Tristan clenched his fists. This wasn't good. This guy knew something about his masque.

"Don't go in there, brother," the man said in a deep, authoritative voice. "Not yet."

Tristan sized him up. He was big, and as he held up his hand, Tristan spotted an ideogramlike tattoo on his right forearm . . . something familiar about it. But even with all the fat man's weight, Tristan figured if it came to a fight he could kill him.

"What are you talking about? And why are you—?"

The fat man looked over at the guards at Smalley's entrance who were now watching them—they were, after all, on Smalley's property. He put on a smile, signalling that this was okay, just two friends meeting outside.

"It's not safe here, friend. Not safe at all. Too many people can see."

"Why the hell are you following me?"

The fat man stared at Tristan. "She sent me." A breath. "*Okasan* sent me."

That name again . . . that myth. And now Tristan recognized the tattoo—same as the ideogram he'd seen with the beggar woman's image in Cyrill's ice house.

He grabbed Tristan's arm. "Please—let's just move away from the guards."

Tristan glanced around, unsure. He was supposed to go straight to Smalley's. But he was intrigued.

Okasan . . .

He nodded and followed the fat man and his saur. As they moved off, the man draped an arm over his shoulder.

"We're old friends, eh?" he muttered. "That's all this will look like. Just old friends talking."

The man's arm didn't feel at all blubbery. Suddenly Tristan wasn't quite so sure he could handle him in a fight.

And as soon as they were down a barren street, the man stopped.

"Thank you. Now we can talk. My name is Mung, and I'm a follower of Okasan."

"You follow . . . a myth?"

Mung laughed, a hearty, booming sound. "She's no myth, friend. Especially to mimes."

Tristan froze, caught between the urge to attack or flee. This lump of protoplasm knew he was a mime, probably even knew he was a Kaze agent. If he said anything—

"Don't worry, brother. Your secret is safe with me."

"I have no secrets."

Mung smiled. "Certainly. As you wish. But Okasan—"

"They say this Okasan is with the Church of the True Shape, that she's little more than a trap for mimes, another way to kill them."

Now Mung laughed. "Oh, that's a good one. Is that what they're telling you in the gloms? Bloaty . . . Okasan with the Imagists! I have to remember to tell her that."

The saur bleated and Mung reached into a pocket and dug out a chunk of green—a plant stalk of some kind. The little triceratops reared back and opened its mouth to catch it.

"That's it, BeeGee," Mung said gently, as if the beast could understand. "Now quiet down." He turned back to Tristan. "Okasan is *real*, brother . . . and she's no Imagist. She is working to free mimes—yes, to save them."

Tristan shrugged. "What's that to me?"

Mung nodded as if considering something important, weighing a decision. "My friend, I *know* you are Tristan, and Okasan knows that you are on an important assignment—though she hasn't told me what it is. Too dangerous for me to know, she says. She wants to meet you."

Fight or flight. Tristan weighed his options. This man could be crazy . . . too much Hhhelll, perhaps. Crazy and dangerous.

But then he could have killed me right here if all this "Okasan" wanted was a dead mime.

Mung reached out and grabbed Tristan's arm.

"Listen . . . I know it's hard to believe that someone, some *human* is working to protect mimes. But it's true. She saved me . . . she gave me freedom."

Tristan stared at him. "What?"

Mung grinned. He pulled back his cloak and revealed his belly. He ran a finger along his left side where a mime pouch would be.

"Yes, I'm a mime . . . or, rather, I was. Now I'm . . . this. Now I'm Mung."

Tristan shook his head. Why would a mime wear such flamboyant dress, and then have a saur, calling attention to himself? Too bad nobody scarred anymore. But even a scar could be faked.

"You can't be a mime."

"Oh, I'm not a mime anymore. I can never flux again. Okasan saw to that."

"But this masque, you make everyone—"

Mung tilted his head. "It's no masque. This is"—he laughed, a full sound that echoed in the deserted street—"*who* I am. No more fluxes . . . it's not even possible." He patted his stomach. "And why such, er, an ample choice? That should be obvious, Tristan. One would expect an integrated mime to select a sleek and handsome body, just like the masque you're wearing. But a person such as myself could only be a human, don't you think?"

The man laughed again, and now Tristan grinned. Not such a bad way for a mime to end up, bigger than life and twice as colorful. And he was *integrated* . . . he was out here moving about, unafraid.

Of course it could all be an elaborate lie.

But then Mung's expression became serious.

"But you must meet Okasan. She has important things to tell you . . . about what you're doing."

Tristan shook his head. "I'm meeting someone . . . in there," he gestured back toward Smalley's.

"Okasan is close by, very close. You will make your meeting." Mung smiled. "Trust me, mime brother."

Tristan stood there. A warm wind blew down the tunnel made by the deserted buildings.

I should leave now, Tristan thought.

But what could it hurt to meet this woman?

He activated his neuronet and selected Logic. Immediately Regis appeared.

"Any action taken that varies from the assignment parameters is a very grave risk, Lord Tristan. You should simply thank this Mung for his offer and—"

Tristan shut him off. No surprises from Regis . . . always the party line: follow instructions.

For some reason, he wanted to trust Mung . . . maybe even wanted to believe him.

"Okay then—take me to her," Tristan said.

Mung grinned and slapped him heartily on the back as they started walking.

The pygmy saur kept up with them, sniffing at empty buildings and making high-pitched honks at dark alleys.

"He's useful," Mung said, pointing to the saur. "If someone was set to pounce, BeeGee would alert me."

Tristan shook his head. Mung had such strong feelings for the little saur, almost as if he . . . loved the animal.

And then Tristan realized he was jealous of Mung, free . . . to wander . . . to have a pet.

Mung threw another bit of food to the animal.

"All right, now this is the tricky part." Mung circled a big arm around Tristan's shoulder. "Here's the Joblin Industrial Center. Very dangerous. Lots of scancameras about."

Tristan took in the expansive bulk of the Industrial Center—a squat mini-city within the sprawl of the freezone, surrounded by a high firebriar fence, a chaos of barbed, six-inch, toxic thorns, and patrolled by a heavily armed private security force. He'd heard of the place. Consisting mostly of giant warehouses, it functioned as a mi-

croglom, harboring legitimate businesses and used by black marke-
teers dealing everything from pirated splices to codekeys.

"Okasan's inside?"

Mung nodded.

"And we're just going to walk in?"

Mung rubbed his chin. "Not exactly. I have an IDplant." He held
up his left little finger. "The gate is coded for me . . . and I'm going to
try to bribe you in. Say you're my new partner."

"Some plan."

Mung laughed again. "If it doesn't work, I have other options."

Mung gave Tristan another too-hearty slap on the back and then
walked up to the center gate.

Tristan stayed back while the jovial Mung talked to the two helmeted guards. Their black visors hid personal HUDs, Tristan guessed,
most likely with infrared and sonar built in.

But there's no way they can tell I'm a mime, he thought, not without a strip search.

Tristan saw one guard shake his head and push Mung back. The
guard's hand rested on his hip next to a nasty pulse weapon.

What would Regis say . . . about the bad logic of endangering this
vital mission—maybe my last—to chase this wild goose?

But then Mung reached into his robe and handed something to
one of the guards. Some alloy? A bootleg splice? The guard half turned
and showed it to the other, who shook his head. Mung produced another packet. This time the second guard nodded. A deal had been
struck.

Mung returned, frowning. "Hmm . . . that was a bit more pricey
than I'd anticipated."

He walked Tristan up to the gate and thrust his little finger into a
slot. Immediately the system recognized Mung's IDplant. The scan
cameras would allow one person to enter. But then one of the guards
leaned over and punched in a code. Tristan was cleared for entry.

"Let's go," Mung said. He wasn't smiling, and Tristan again wondered if this was a trick.

A dozen scancameras followed them, all armed with mini-pulse weapons that could punch a hole in either of them or knock them to the ground until the Joblin Center security force came to finish the job.

"Keep moving," Mung said grimly.

"I thought we were clear."

"We are, we are. Still, I don't trust the guards. And who knows what island in the Ocean may have your"—he jabbed at Tristan's chest—"masque on file. If they suspected you were"—he didn't say the word *mime*—"they'd stop us."

"Don't worry. This one's a composite."

Mung gave him a strange look.

"What?" Tristan said.

"Nothing."

They made their way through the maze inside the complex, past dozens of oddshaped domes with photosynthetic walls, custom contoured to the volume specs of their tenants. The morning haze had burned off, and now the domes were greening in response to the pale, cool, midwinter sun. Tristan wondered what they housed.

"Why here?" he said.

"Hmm . . . ?"

"Why would Okasan be here?"

"Where better? This is squarely between Kaze and Flagge, in an industrial center. Who would look for a 'myth' here?" Mung grabbed his arm. "Here we are."

Tristan didn't see a door, but Mung stuck his little finger into the green wall and waited. Suddenly a vertical slit appeared and retracted to either side.

Mung stepped through. "Come on. You don't have a lot of time."

Tristan hesitated, hoping he wouldn't regret this, then entered.

Inside the cavernlike darkness, he saw a small pool of light . . . and an old woman sitting in a chair. If this was some kind of bizarre trap, now would be the moment something would happen. Tristan braced himself.

"Come on," Mung said. "She's waiting for you."

They walked up to the pool of light in the empty building. The woman, Okasan, looked exactly as she had in the Ocean.

She smiled at Tristan and extended a hand. Tristan didn't move.

"So, we meet . . . for real." Her voice shook a bit as she spoke.

"You are Okasan?"

"That's what they call me. Not my real name, of course."

Tristan stiffened as Mung backed away.

"I think I'll stay by the door," Mung said. "Just in case."

"I frighten you?" the woman said.

"Just cautious." Tristan said. "It's my nature."

The smiled faded. "You mean, your *training*. And you are on this mission, this very important assignment—"

"Which apparently you think you know something about."

"I know a lot. I know of this Flagge cat's eye you seek."

Shock waves buffeted Tristan. Flagge . . . the cat's eye . . . she knows! He had to tell Cyrill—had to abort the mission.

"Do not be alarmed," she said. "I have no wish to block your path to Flagge. In fact I *want* you to succeed. And not just for me. For others, for another community, another world. Like the first life, it was born in the Ocean, and it hides in the gloms—" She took a breath. "But I'm getting ahead of myself, and you don't have much time."

"That's true."

"I can't tell you everything now, but let me say that I am part of a cadre of organized mimes and human sympathizers who started a movement years ago. We began with only a few, but we have grown, Tristan . . . we have *grown*."

"A movement? You mean, the myth of Okasan, the mime savior."

She shook her head. "I'm no mime savior. I helped them organize, made them aware that they didn't have to be slaves—" She stood up, struggling with the effort. She was an old woman who looked like an old woman. Tristan guessed that living in hiding kept her from the best bio reengineering. She didn't look well. "We have some allies in high places in the gloms, and throughout the jumble and beyond. But you mimes are property, with powerful, jealous owners."

"*That* I know."

"And this assignment of yours—"

"Okasan!" Mung called from the door. "I think I hear something outside. Could be the guards."

Okasan looked worried. "This mission to get the cat's eye poses a deadly threat to mimes. It could lead to the end of the glom wars, with one glom supreme."

"That's a bad thing? Why should it matter?"

"As long as they are at each other's throats, with the balance of power constantly seesawing, we have hope of fragmenting their markets, perhaps even collapsing the glom system. That will mean freedom for everyone, even mimes—*especially* mimes."

"The gloms offer Selfhood, integration into—"

She reached out and gripped his hand. "No." She said it quietly, with a sad resignation. "No, Tristan, they don't. That's the *real* myth. I have much to show you."

Mung came running up.

"Yes, definitely guards outside. Probably followed us here."

Okasan still held Tristan's hand. "It's safe for you two here. But I must leave. Mung will find you again at the end of the assignment." She squeezed his hand hard. "You must bring that sample here, bring it to me. Let *us* use it against both Kaze and Flagge."

"Mother," Mung said, "you *have* to leave."

Mother? Why had Mung—supposedly a former mime—called her that? Unless it was simply a figure of speech, a gesture of respect.

And this real meeting . . . the woman could have appeared to him in the Ocean or as a holo. But did she have this real meeting so she could touch him, so he could feel her skin against his?

"You can have freedom, a *real* life, Tristan. But no one—certainly not the gloms—will give it to you. You will have to fight for it. We are engaged in a hidden war. And you must join that war."

"Okasan, please!"

She nodded, and then said, "Bring the cat's eye sample to me."

"I can't—I don't—"

But Okasan turned. The roof of the building split and a small two-person floater descended.

"What—?"

Tristan looked at the floater. Expensive toys, the technology available to only the wealthiest in the gloms. Yet, here this raggedy old woman—

Okasan stepped in beside the driver who was dressed in black. Another mime? Tristan wondered.

"Good luck," she said, then turned to the driver. "Up, Charl."

The floater rose, defying gravity. Then, picking up speed like a motorbike, it quickly lifted to the roof, and then out.

Mung stood beside Tristan, watching.

"Filamentous! Doubt they'll see her."

The door to the building split and the guards ran in.

But Mung and Tristan were alone . . . and Mung began discussing loudly how they'd use the empty building in their business.

Just before the guards got to them, Mung leaned over and whispered, "Listen, if you're ever in serious trouble here in the freezone— *very* serious trouble—go to the Bascombe district and ask around for 'Proteus.' "

"Proteus?"

"But *only* as a last resort."

"But who's Proteus?"

"Better you don't know until you have to. But now we'll chat up the guards a bit, then I'll get you back to Smalley's. You've got a lot to do, brother."

"The mime's here," said the voice in Streig's ear.

"Where?"

"Just came through the front."

"Where has he been?"

"Not sure, sir. We, uh, lost him for a while."

"Lost him?" Streig did not like that. He wanted to know every move that mime made. *"How did that happen?"*

"Not sure, sir. He dropped out of sight among the warehouses."

"Did he now?"

Streig withheld his anger. He spoke softly, evenly, knowing it would be more unsettling to this mutagen than an outburst.

"Y-yes, sir. But we're locked on him now."

"See that you stay locked on. And make sure everyone's in place."

Smalley's Smart Bar—a circus, a carnival of human oddities.

At times Tristan almost felt as if he might be the true human and they the freaks. He stood on the main floor while people bellied up to the bustling smart bar to sip or snort concoctions that delivered jolts to specific areas of the neural geography.

Want to feel warm and forgiving toward the rest of the planet and tell everyone about it, whether they want to hear or not? Try a shot of Blue Dusk, the late-generation affective/emotive accentuator, with a Rap chaser.

And for those who want their kicks more direct and to the point—say, a burst of false inspiration with the supercilious afterglow of bogus understanding?—then Eureka was your whiff of choice.

But Tristan knew the psychoactive beverages were only part of the Smalley's experience. Many came for the ambience, the noise, the chaotic life-swirl that went on and on—unless you crashed and Smalley's goons had to drag you out screaming, turning your Blue Dusk calm into a hellish morning-after.

Tristan looked around the main floor while the music thumped in his brainstem. The demimondaines—mostly splicers or nanoformed types with designer bods, stood in small groups, almost dancing but mostly hanging on to one another, letting the drugs do their work. Reptile accessories were the new rage, and Tristan saw forked tongues slipping from many a lipless mouth.

He heard laughter to his left and turned. Three reptilians were standing around a fourth, tossing snacks into the air and watching her snag them in midflight with her slim, pink, half-meter tongue.

Then frog-tongue and her companions started to twitch as designer adrenal rushes of Hhhelll kicked in. The gloms forbade Hhhelll in their territories—too unpredictable. If nothing else, the gloms liked predictability. But this was the freezone, and this was Smalley's.

Some nanoforming had practical applications. The bouncer who was passing him had a regulation right arm, but his left was a four-foot tentacle. Tristan had been impressed many times at how quickly a Hhhelll crazy could be calmed when a fleshy rope around the neck cut off all air.

Tristan had seen this sideshow before and always he had the same thought: Here I am struggling to join humanity . . . while they struggle to leave it behind.

Someone bumped into him, and when Tristan turned he saw a

female . . . or what he took to be a female. Except the "she" in this case sported a furry tail.

"Oh, so sorry," the woman said. Her glassy eyes confirmed that she was only marginally present in the room.

"It's okay."

But the female—how sure of that could he be, when all body parts were open to manipulation?—didn't move on. She sidled close to Tristan, and her tail slowly curled from the rear to the front.

"How about something warm blooded? I bet you like . . . little kitties."

Tristan kept scanning the packed room. He was on the main floor and he knew of many side rooms: the Reals, the giant communal Holotank, as well as private party rooms where the word 'party' could mean almost anything.

Finding his contact shouldn't be—

Wait—could this sexy splicer be it? He doubted it.

The woman's tail had completely encircled Tristan, the tip brushing his cheek. He felt himself responding—*lots* of testosterone in this masque.

Maybe I should simply tell her I'm a mime, he thought. If she's the contact, good. If she's not, it'll scare her off. Or maybe not. Considering that tail, she probably wouldn't mind.

And no doubt the crowd held more than a few antimime crazies. Rumor had it that people on Hhhelll got a lot of pleasure ripping mimes apart.

Better try another tack.

He smiled at the woman and brushed the tail away.

"Sorry. I'm supposed to meet someone here."

She made a small moue of displeasure. "Male . . . female . . . or other?"

"Don't know yet. We've never met."

"Interesting. Introduce me when you do. I'm very fond of three-somes."

Tristan grinned and moved away.

Not her.

A small circle of people had gathered over by a table; their rhythmic clapping filled the air. Tristan drifted over and saw a six-foot-tall lizard. The crowd cheered. And then, in a flash, the lizard was replaced by someone Tristan knew . . . someone from the old vids and movies: a platinum blonde in a white dress, pouting at the crowd, her lips full.

"Marilyn Monroe," Tristan said to himself.

"What?" said the guy next to him, physically present, wavering back and forth on his feet as if he were on a ship, but his mind adrift somewhere off Ganymede.

Tristan had seen her old vids. He had been moved by this woman, her girlish laugh, her fullness, something special that radiated from inside her.

"That's Marilyn Monroe."

"Dat's nice," the man said, staring openmouthed at the actress.

Then Marilyn disappeared, much too fast, and a man stood there, short, skinny, ugly.

Showing off his holosuit.

He touched his sleeve and suddenly he was a nude male, all bulging muscles and flashing teeth.

Don't you wish, Tristan thought.

He'd heard something in the Ocean about a young man keeling over at his wedding. Turned out he was wearing a holosuit and was close to a hundred-and-fifty years old. Past the help of the bio reengineering teams, he'd opted to look like someone a lot younger. His intended hadn't a clue until he died.

Surprise, surprise.

Tristan moved away.

Nobody is who they are anymore, Tristan thought. So why can't mimes be accepted?

He knew the answer: We're different from conception. We have the Goleman chromosome, which means we've *never* been truly human.

He looked around and checked the time . . . he should have made contact by now. The mission would come to a quick end—and his hope for Selfhood would disappear—if he didn't find the contact with the codekey.

Must be in another room, he thought.

He wandered into the large area toward the rear, the room for the Reals, those afraid of becoming wetheads, afraid of spending all their lives afloat in the Ocean, drifting from one mind-blowing virtual experience to another.

Pleasure and excitement weren't the only things people caught in the Ocean. The craving for obscure sensations tended to grow. The Ocean contained entire islands devoted to strange varieties of experience, some thrilling, pleasurable, terrifying—others that were unclassifiable.

But Smalley's had a corrective.

This dark room offered real experiences, real pleasure, real pain, real hurt.

One big attraction was NOK, a simple strategy game using real figures on a floating dodecahedron. Five NOK tables sat near the front, all bathed in pale blue light that barely showed the faces of each game's pair of combatants.

Tristan knew how to play, but he lacked the instinct or the strategic sense to play well. Maybe some sense of gameplay was missing because he was a mime.

The game was easy enough: moving pieces, capturing areas of the floating solid, capturing other pieces. The nasty twist in NOK was that each player was directly wired to the board.

And each loss of a solid's face, or worse, each loss of a piece, brought a rushing jolt to the brain—a nasty snap of electricity, carefully monitored by Smalley's game managers. Sometimes they overdid it. Tristan had witnessed convulsions at NOK games. And he'd heard of a cardiac arrest or two.

A dark, quiet room, its silence shattered by the *real* screams of real people losing.

Tristan drifted close to a table where a good-size crowd had gathered. They watched a gray-haired man, sleek, with a shining forehead glowing in the blue light as he considered his next move.

He was playing a disheveled younger man, someone who looked like a wethead. How'd they reel him in from the Ocean? Tristan wondered. What bait had lured him to dry land? Some wetheads stayed chipped in so long they forgot about food and all bodily functions. They washed up dead . . . drowned.

Not a big problem, according to the gloms.

The gray-haired man, obviously a NOK master, made a move. Though noise filtered in from the outer spaces, the NOK room was still, the games intense.

The younger man scratched his scalp, sniffed, shook his head. Tristan scanned the board, wondering what he'd do next.

The kid reached up to the floating board, hesitated, then pulled back a piece, retreating. The gray-haired man grinned and made a counter move as if pouncing.

But too quickly the man's fingers left his piece. Now the kid coughed, a vicious hack that turned into laughing.

He's got him, Tristan thought. The kid had set a trap, and the man had walked into it.

Now the kid reached up and moved.

The man lost a piece, and immediately he was jolted, his scream piercing the darkness. The crowd backed away, as if they too might get zapped.

And when the gray-haired man stopped shaking, he stood up, out of the NOK chair.

"Leaving?" the wethead said, grinning. "So soon?"

The man didn't stop to say anything.

The kid turned and looked around at the crowd.

"Anyone else want a piece of me?"

No takers.

He turned to Tristan. "Hey, how about you, big guy."

Tristan felt someone behind him, pressing against him. He turned and saw the woman with a tail hugging close.

"Go ahead," she whispered. "Bet you could beat him."

"I doubt that. Doubt it very much."

But the kid was still watching him.

Where the hell is my contact? he wondered. He had to get out of here, get to Flagge Glom—

"Come on, you look like a risk taker."

Tristan shook his head. "Find someone else."

He expected the NOK player to move on, to look for another victim. But then the kid's eyes narrowed.

"I'm like a cat, stranger. And I've got my *eye* on you."

Tristan took a breath. *Like a cat . . . I've got my eye.* This scraggly looking wethead, this biochip addict was the contact who had the codekey.

So why doesn't he get up, go into a private room, and give me the muting?

"Take a seat, sailor."

What was this, some kind of joke? Or was this ruse necessary, so no Flagge spies saw what was going on?

"I'm not a good NOK player," Tristan said.

The kid grinned. "Oh, don't worry. You will be when I'm done with you."

Tristan could feel the zaps of electricity already. He slipped into the facing seat.

"That's the spirit. Let the game and the lesson begin. You're about to learn NOK strategy from a master."

The crowd closed around the table. The air became thick with sweat and smoke and the sweet smell of the dozens of bizarre psychoactive offerings of Smalley's.

"A quick game," Tristan said, noting that his throat was dry.

The kid extended his hand. "They call me Padre . . . in this 'zone anyway. And the only kind of games I play are quick ones." He pulled his hand away. "Your move."

Why do I have to play? Tristan wondered. Why can't he just give me the damn codekey?

The kid across the table glanced at the crowd gathered around. "We got a lot of people watching us, eh?"

Was that a message? Was this place watched . . . would it be too hard to slip him the key here?

"As I said, I'm not a very good player."

Padre laughed. "No pain, no *game*, big guy. You get first move."

Tristan looked at the board suspended before them. Either one of them could press a button in the console chair to rotate the twelve-sided solid. The slender NOK pieces were held in place by a sensitive electromagnet.

What's a good opening? he thought. A game of NOK could be lost in minutes, it was that fast. And the first move was crucial.

He took one of his center pieces and slid it close to an edge to support another near a hostile space.

Padre grinned. He made his move quickly, aggressively pushing a piece onto one of the spaces on a free side.

Quiet in the room. The crowd interested in the game? Perhaps. More likely wanting to see who'd get the first jolt.

Tristan made another cautious move, which Padre followed by bringing a second piece forward to a different free side. It didn't look so bad . . . but when Tristan made a third move, Padre let out a whoop and captured one of Tristan's pieces. The magnetic charge holding it in place vanished and the piece fell to the table.

A brief, intense jolt of electricity shot through the chair and Tristan yelped.

"Nasty one, eh? Hope you've got a high tolerance."

Tristan made another move, the possibility of getting zapped always in the back of his mind. And again Padre responded boldly, this time capturing a free side . . . a victory that sent another jolt to Tristan.

He stared at Padre. Maybe I have this wrong, he thought. Maybe this NOK guru isn't the contact, maybe he's just—

But as if reading Tristan's thoughts Padre looked up and moved one of his pieces onto a space.

A space where he was vulnerable to an attack.

And suddenly Tristan knew what was happening.

He's sacrificing that piece . . . because that's the codekey?

Tristan advanced cautiously. Padre's next move was on a side directly opposite the vulnerable piece. Tristan waited, then made the solid rotate. He captured Padre's piece and it clattered to the table.

Padre yelped as the jolt hit him. "Mute. Didn't see that." He raised a finger to Tristan. "That move was . . . key."

Tristan smiled, as in . . . *I get it. I know.*

He picked up the fallen piece and covered it with his hand. It felt like any other NOK piece.

Padre smiled. "Now let's get serious."

And the kid meant it. They were going to finish the game, with many more painful blasts to come. But not for Padre.

CHAPTER 6

Tristan stood just inside Smalley's exit.

He had finally escaped the NOK table, leaving Padre seeking another victim, showing no sign that anything had happened.

The NOK piece was in Tristan's pocket. He looked at the exit, at the door scanners that checked for weapons, and at the beefy black-visored security guards watching everyone who came and went.

He took a breath and walked past the scanners, under the glare of the security guards. But no alarm sounded. He was outside.

Keep walking, he told himself—in case there's a delay.

And why didn't the scanners—whose company slogan was "We Can See What You Had for Breakfast"—pick up the stolen game piece?

Good question . . . unless Smalley was in on the transfer, paid off by Kaze Glom to let this little illegal transfer go down.

Or maybe they simply weren't programmed to look for NOK pieces. He used his sleeve to wipe the sweat off his face and his neck—and felt something.

There—just below the neckline, the tiniest thing stuck to his skin. He started to pick at it, his arm twisted awkwardly behind him.

Finally he came away with a thumbnail-size patch of flesh-colored plastic.

A dose patch!

Tristan stared at it, feeling sweat break out anew all over his body. Where had that come from? What had he been dosed with? And by whom? Had to have been that cat woman—she was the only one who'd touched him, coiling that tail around his neck.

But with what? Some sort of aphrodisiac? Or a psychoactive? He felt no ill effects—no effects of any sort.

Maybe the drug hadn't seeped through his skin, or didn't affect him.

He'd have to keep watch for any symptoms. Meanwhile, he had to get moving and look for a spot to activate the key.

He hurried down a street and passed the bazaar, quiet now . . . most of the better stuff well picked over. He watched a disheveled-looking man setting up his items, pulling them from an old sack. His treasures.

Tristan stopped.

"What's that?" he said to the man.

The man looked up, alarmed, maybe scared.

The man had something in his hand, something that Tristan had seen before. He really should go, he really shouldn't waste time looking, but—

The man was nervous. Tristan remembered that his masque was big, imposing . . . maybe even threatening.

"Wh-what do you want?"

Tristan came closer. "That thing in your hands. What is it?"

The old man's nervous, beady eyes darted from his sack of treasures to Tristan.

"This? You mean—"

The old man held it up.

"Yes."

The old man looked at the machine. He read the words. "It's—it's a 'Mr. Coffee.' "

Tristan smiled. Right. A *Mr. Coffee*. He had seen them in kitchens in the old vids. A Mr. Coffee would sit on a counter. *People went and got coffee*. They drank coffee for caffeine, maybe for the taste.

Tristan came closer to it. "It's old . . . can I—?"

The old man seemed disinterested. "Yes. It's very old . . . I guess—" The man shrugged. What he didn't know about his goods could probably fill a small database.

Tristan looked at the plastic item. He once saw someone use it in an old vid, filling it with water, then spooning in the ground coffee—

He fiddled with a part, and a small cuplike item slid out.

"Yes, there's where the coffee went."

Tristan handed it back to the man. He'd almost like to have it, this object from a world where things seemed saner, where—

There were no mimes.

Where everyone was a human.

"What else have you got?"

Tristan leaned over and peeked into the man's sack. He saw a metal flask, tarnished and corroded. Probably dating from the same period, Tristan guessed. Only the metal wasn't lasting as long.

He had seen this used too, for a different drink . . . back when there was only alcohol at bars.

Tristan nodded . . . and mimicked the words he remembered from the flat vid: "Shaken . . . not stirred."

The old man was definitely confused. He scratched his scraggly head, licked his chapped lips.

Shaken not stirred. Tristan turned the object in his hands.

"Want it? I can make you a deal . . . for the both. Credits or"—the old man licked his lips—"if you got some Hhhelll, I can—"

Tristan handed back the cup.

"I'd like them," he said. "But I can't take them now."

The old man rubbed his beard and took the cup and placed it on the table.

"I'm always here," he said.

Tristan nodded, the vision, the vid memories fading.

He left the bazaar.

*　　*　　*

Tristan stood in the dark alleyway, ripe with the fetid smell of human waste, garbage, decay. Like some blackmarket trader, he kept checking the alley entrance.

He removed the sleek NOK piece from his pocket and turned it over in his hand.

Its perfectly smooth surface reflected the light from the end of the alley. He wondered: Was this a mistake? Was the real contact detained somewhere?

But no . . . he spotted a small rectangle etched into the bottom. *Could be—*

He dug his nail into the edge and a small metal flap popped out . . . and inside, a tiny rectangular lens.

The codekey.

He checked the alley again. He was still alone, unless something that was once a person slept under a pile of garbage.

He began to raise the piece to his eye, then hesitated.

Everything had gone according to plan . . . and damn his nature, that made him suspicious.

He blinked and activated his neuronet. Regis appeared, taking up where he'd been cut off last time.

"Lord Tristan, I must remind you that you are now behind your planned itinerary. You will have to—"

Tristan held up the NOK piece.

"Regis, what's the potential danger with this codekey?"

"There is always the possibility of shadow code. I'm afraid even I can't detect every hidden subroutine."

Tristan nodded. A predatory code could eat up his neuronet in a millisecond. Then Tristan would be trapped in the freezone.

Forcing himself to relax, Tristan held the piece over his right eye and stared into the lens. A series of swirling flashes strobed the optical code into his neuronet.

Immediately, his Roam Grid appeared. Everything looked fine, the Kaze Quarter occupied the lower border, then the great expanse of the freezone, and—

The grid shifted north. To Flagge Glom. First it was outlined in red, but then the red lines disappeared and changed to green. A path appeared in the map of the Flagge Quarter, leading to a structure. It gave no indication what the building was, and he had no way for Regis to find out, not until they were actually inside the quarter.

The only way to discover his destination was to go there.

And from there he'd get what he needed to enter the heart of Flagge Glom . . . to enter the Citadel.

Or so he hoped.

CHAPTER 7

Anyone could take a tube from a freezone into the Flagge Quarter—even if you didn't belong there. Getting out was another story entirely.

Flagge's Security made Kaze's look haphazard. As soon as the tube car crossed Flagge Quarter's wall, two men in dark armorsuits and visors began moving down the aisle. They didn't search people, didn't come right out and ask them, *Excuse me but are you a mime agent?*

Tristan sat quietly among the others. They all had proper ID-plants, maybe some work assignments . . . nobody was going to bother them.

But the Flagge Security men walked up and down the car.

Looking for the "tic"? Possibly. Stories had it that if you looked very carefully you could spot a mime . . . that upon close scrutiny, mimes acted just a bit "off."

Tristan admitted there might be something to that. In most cases a mime agent had a work lifespan of maybe a decade and a half. After that many years of fluxing, strange physical and emotional residues began to accumulate.

That was the "tic." A way of sitting, a signal that said *I'm not quite like the rest of you.* And of course just the possibility that something

like that existed made it all the harder for a mime to sit here and be—
normal.

As the two Flagge guards walked toward Tristan he focused on the message center above him.

You have entered the private region of Flagge Glom. Welcome to the Glom of the Future—Flagge!

Each glom was the Glom of the Future. Each was the Shape of Things to Come. Corporate nations, fighting it out like—

Tristan had seen old vids about a period in human history like this, with kingdoms and castles and peasants . . . so many peasants. Just the way it is now.

The Flagge Security guards were almost up to Tristan.

In those old days knights went on great quests looking for something . . . the Holy Grail . . . a cup used by someone called the Savior. Another legend, another myth.

One of the guards turned and looked at Tristan as he followed a holobubble floating along the ceiling, running a 3-D ad for SynFood Snacks. A blonde whispered, "They're SYN-fully delicious."

Tristan lowered his gaze and smiled at the guard. It seemed like the natural thing to do.

I'm okay . . . and I'm glad to see you doing your job, sir.

The guards' eyes hid behind their visors. All the glom police were faceless.

And Tristan thought: The guard hasn't spoken to anyone, not a single person in this car. If one of them says something to me now I'll know I'm in trouble.

Tristan shifted his gaze back up to the holobubble. He watched an ad for a new SensReal holovid in the Ocean. *Martian Adventure*—"The closest thing to being a Martian."

Probably part of the plan to suck more credits from the peasants for this new castle, a whole world away. Invest in Mars. Because there's nothing left here.

The guard hesitated another second, facing Tristan . . . and then moved on.

Tristan forced himself to show no sign of relief. No relief because he'd been in no danger, right? Everything's fine, everything's okay.

And he was able to make an observation about this masque . . . about the personality residues of this template: Very cool. Not easily rattled. Breathing steady, calm, relaxed.

The Flagge Security men moved on.

In minutes, Tristan would be inside the Glom of the Future.

As soon as he left the tube terminal, he was lost. He accessed his Roam Grid . . . and Regis.

"Lord Tristan, I'm afraid you took a wrong turn back—here." A portion of the grid, a transparent display across his visual field, lit up, and Tristan saw where he'd missed a turn. "The Flagge Isle directory lists your destination as a SynFood warehouse. I suggest that you take *this* route." Regis showed a path that brought Tristan to the front of the building.

Tristan blinked Regis and the grid away. Flagge Security was everywhere. He knew from his previous assignments that Flagge was the most paranoid of the gloms. This was war, and Flagge Glom was always on red alert.

Ahead, at a corner, a line of DNA adaptees walked by. Tristan stopped and watched the strange-looking creatures. Adaptees used to be a rare sight Earthside. Their bodies were designed for Off-World use, genetically customized for working extensive periods in variable G's. He'd once seen some with long arms and narrow bodies, designed for the tight cavern work on Mars.

But the gloms brought home more and more adaptees as their Off-World ventures collapsed.

These particular adaptees were short, with powerful-looking arms and tiny heads. They'd probably end up doing heavy work in a small confined area.

The adaptees moved on, and Tristan continued toward the warehouse.

*   *   *

He was surprised by the small size and old-fashioned look of the Syn-Food warehouse—barely a hundred meters long; the flat, shiny yellow plastic letters of the logo clashed with its mossy green surface.

The scancamera at the warehouse entrance regarded him. No need for him to say anything. It would either recognize him and let him enter, or it would watch impassively. If he should be foolish enough to try to break in, the camera would hit him with a pulse blast and knock him across the street.

But as the camera's eye finished assessing his physical data, Tristan heard a high-pitched tone, and the interlaced tendrils across the doorway unraveled. Tristan walked in.

The warehouse, or at least this part of it, looked deserted. A row of empty offices lined a hallway, ending in a door to what he assumed was a storage area.

He walked down the hallway.

The door slid shut behind him while another camera watched his progress.

Where is everyone? Kaze moles were supposed to have a datameister for him.

And then he heard voices . . . a man crying out in pain from behind the door. He heard a sound like a slap, then another. He reached the end of the corridor, opened the door—

And found the muzzle of a pulse pistol in his face.

"Who're you?"

Tristan found the weapon reassuring. He saw a redheaded man holding it, glaring at him. And beyond him two other men flanking a woman tied to a chair. Tristan flashed on a line spoken by a detective from an old vid. *"The only thing she had on were the lights."* This one also wore a pair of pointed black boots.

"I'm supposed to meet some people here this morning. You, I assume."

The redheaded man held up a pocket holo next to Tristan's face, compared them, then nodded. "You assume right." He turned and pointed to the woman. "And there's your datameister. Name's Lani Rouge."

"Concentrate?" Tristan said as he stepped past him.

The man handed him a pressurized bottle. Tristan let the nutrients flow into his mouth as he walked up to the datameister. A female datameister, which meant he'd soon be female.

She stared at him with wide eyes, nostrils flaring over the gag that sealed her mouth, pressing herself back into the chair as if trying to seep into the plastic, as though he were some hideous demon about to eat her alive. Obviously she'd realized that she would not survive the morning.

Pity. She was beautiful, with dark, dark hair, deep blue-green eyes, and perfect skin. Nothing fashionably reptilian for this one. Just good, traditional human beauty. Like in the old vids.

Too bad she had to be a datameister—*the* datameister they needed. The trick of her brain that allowed it to be used as a living data terminal meant, in her particular case, an untimely end. Today.

But the sight of her breasts, her bare thighs . . . he was becoming aroused.

And then he noticed how a puffy area on her left cheek glowed red under the harsh light. And how both cheeks glistened with tears.

Suddenly he was angry. They were supposed to capture her, hold her for him . . . and dispose of her after he'd gotten what he needed from her. But she wasn't to be mistreated. Mute them to hell, they had no right—

Stop.

What was that all about? She was a Flagge datameister—a non-combatant, true, but she worked for the enemy and she was about to become a casualty of war. It happened every day.

He shook off the outrage. He couldn't wait to drop this masque— it was *ripe* with residues.

"You know what to do with her?" a squat man said.

Tristan nodded, still staring at her. He couldn't take his eyes off her. She struck him as uncommonly beautiful.

The man grinned. "Good, because otherwise we'd have to kill both of you."

The other two laughed, establishing the pecking order of the trio. So, the squat guy who'd just made the joke was the leader, and the other two were paid goons. Chances were Cyrill would have them all killed when this was over.

Tristan's gaze drifted back to the woman. He took a step closer to her. She looked as if she desperately wanted to say something, but the gag prevented her.

"I'm Casaluggi," the squat leader said, "and as promised, this datameister not only has access to the Citadel, she's cleared right to the heart of Flagge's Datacenter."

Another step closer. "Looks like you've hurt her."

Casaluggi laughed. "That was Harkis."

"She kicked me," said one of the men. "Right in the—"

"So you hit a bound woman?" Tristan turned and glared at Casaluggi. "Was that part of your assignment spec?"

"No, but we were getting a little edgy. I mean, you being late and her taking a kick at anyone who got near."

A pointed remark—Tristan nodded.

The leader continued: "You *are* late, you know."

Right. And time was important. This assignment was important. Selfhood, freedom, they were all *important.*

But the woman's eyes didn't leave him.

"Let's get on with it," Tristan said.

He walked close to this datameister, this Lani Rouge. She stared at him as if he were death itself. And then her foot lashed out, missing him by a hair.

Casaluggi raised his hand to smack her again, but Tristan grabbed the man's wrist and squeezed. Casaluggi winced.

"Hit her again and I'll kill you."

Oh, yes. He *had* to drop this masque.

She looked at him strangely now, wonder mixing with the fear in her eyes.

"You've copied her IDplant?" he said.

Casaluggi handed him a fist-size cylinder. "It's all in here."

Tristan fitted his right little finger into the slot and activated the device. It took only a few seconds to transfer all the identity and pass codes from the datameister's IDplant to his.

That done, he handed the cylinder back to Casaluggi, then pulled out his wardrobe case and popped it open.

"All right, remove her gag and open her mouth."

Casaluggi released the strap and the gag ball popped free.

"You're a *mime*?" she cried, her face contorting into a snarl as Harkis steadied her head. "You filthy—! Where'd you get—"

The rest was garbled as Casaluggi grabbed her jaw and forced her mouth open.

Tristan lifted the buccal scraper from his kit and ran the flat tool along the inner surface of her cheek. Then he wiped the collection of saliva and cells onto the surface of the writable template.

She stared at him in shock that chilled into contempt. "You think you're going to make a template from *me*? Forget it. By the time you get those cells back to wherever you came from—Kaze, isn't it, you've got to be Kaze agents—and make a template from them, and then get back here as me, I'll be reported missing and my Security access will be wiped. You try to get in pretending to be me and you'll be pulsed to red slime."

"I know," Tristan said.

"Just tell me one thing—"

Casaluggi reinserted the gag—and none too soon—as Tristan downed the rest of the nutrient concentrate. He glanced around for a place to flux. Casaluggi seemed to know what he was looking for.

"Over there," he said. "Behind those crates."

Tristan took his wardrobe case and walked around to the rear of the vaulted space until he found the datameister's clingsuit and two extra containers of concentrate. He checked to make sure he was out of sight. These people were nothing to him, and might all be dead before sunset, but still, to flux in front of them . . . unthinkable.

Tristan opened the slit in his abdominal wall and removed the template. Its genetic code would remain activated within him for a while, but then, lacking a steady stream of data, his cells gradually would revert to the neutral state.

Unless they were told otherwise.

Tristan picked up the writable template and stared at it. New technology . . . revolutionary. He knew it had been tested and retested and found capable of instantly copying a genome from a single sample.

But what if something went wrong this time? Nothing so dramatic as the corruption of an entire chromosome or gene . . . but what if a single amino acid sequence got jumbled in the digital translation? Odds were the effect on the Lani Rouge phenotype would be insignificant, but it *could* be devastating. He could wind up physically deformed or crippled or, worse yet, mentally crippled, so profoundly retarded that he wouldn't be able to reinsert a functioning template.

He couldn't let himself think too much about that. He took a deep breath and inserted the writable, sealed his pouch, and waited.

For a few seconds he felt nothing, then the familiar ripple as his mDNA began to receive the first messages from the new template. He felt his arm muscles quiver then tighten as the cells shifted madly to keep up with the demands of new instructions.

Then the new genetic code hit bone, heralded by a deep, explosive pressure, like steel rods being driven the length of his marrow. He braced himself. The worst was yet to come.

Tristan looked around for somewhere to sit, where he could curl up and howl while his body pulsed and constricted.

He had . . . to . . . lie down.

He clenched his teeth as bone mass liquefied and drifted off to be transformed into other material or stored along the bone axes for some flux yet to come.

He curled up on the cold floor as his jaw began to ache, a dull pain at first that grew until he felt as if someone had smashed him in the face.

Soon pain shot along every nerve fiber in his body, a hundred mad surgeons working on him with needles and blades.

A moan escaped him as sweat flowed from every pore. It was one thing to flux from a neutral state into a masque. But to trade one masque for another, with no downtime, was excruciating. Only fighting mimes whose nervous systems were so burned out by repeated changes could handle it easily.

He gave out another moan.

"You—you okay?" someone asked from the far side of the crates.

Tristan tried to respond . . . and that was when he felt the breasts begin to form.

This wasn't the first time he'd fluxed into a female phenotype, but the sudden swelling always felt odd. The breasts continued to rise as the rest of his body slowly molded itself into an exact copy of Lani Rouge's.

Tristan shivered on the ground, his eyes shut, waiting until it ended.

Finally the pain receded.

Shaky, in a fog, Tristan rose to his feet and stood naked, wavering back and forth like a drunk. He grabbed another container of concentrate and greedily sucked it down. As his mind cleared, he looked down at his new body—the white skin, the jutting, pink-nippled breasts. Everything looked complete and he was thinking clearly. He smiled. The writable had worked perfectly.

Slinging the datameister's red clingsuit over his shoulder, he strolled back to the front of the storage area.

The awed expressions that greeted him almost made the flux pain worthwhile. The datameister's wide-eyed stare was the best.

The wonder in those eyes as she gazed at herself made her even more beautiful.

"Magic," he said, answering her unspoken question.

As he slipped into her clingsuit, Casaluggi said, "You through with her?"

"I think so."

"Good." He pulled out his pistol. "We'll do her then get back to our—"

"Wait!" Tristan said without intending to. "Don't."

"It's orders," Casaluggi said. "Too risky to keep her alive."

It took Tristan a few seconds to understand the sudden panic that clutched him in an icy fist, but that didn't help him overcome it. The writable had worked but it had yielded an unscrubbed template—a genome rotten with Lani Rouge seep.

And Lani Rouge didn't want to die.

Try as he might, Tristan could not bring himself to order her death. Maybe in an hour or two he'd be able to overcome her self-preservation instinct, but at the moment his mind was racing to find an alternative.

"No," he said, turning to Casaluggi. He wished he had his old template in—he'd be much more imposing than this slim, pretty woman. "Orders are changed. She might have a vitality sensor implant that will set off an alarm if she dies. Besides, I may run into a problem . . . and she might have the solution. If she's dead she won't be telling us anything."

"So what are we supposed to do?"

"Stay here. Stay here and wait until I come back." He looked back to Lani. "And then you can do what you want with her."

His insides quailed at even the implied threat, the limit set on her lifespan. But hours from now he'd be able to give the command. At least he thought he would. What a shame to waste all that beauty.

Would the men do as he'd said? He turned back to them. The leader hesitated a moment, perhaps wondering whether he might challenge Tristan.

Tristan added, "You wouldn't want the bosu to learn that an assignment this big failed because you didn't listen to me."

That hit home. Casaluggi said, "All right. We'll stay here until you get back."

Tristan turned and crouched close to the datameister.

Like looking in a mirror, he thought. Except for the eyes . . . something strange behind those eyes.

"I'm you now," he said.

She struggled against the gag, her expression desperate. But all the pleas in the world, even from him, wouldn't save her. She'd seen the writable template in action. She couldn't be allowed to leave alive.

"You have to go, mime," Casaluggi said. "They'll start hunting for this datameister if she doesn't show up soon."

Tristan backed away from Lani.

"Don't hurt her. You hear me?"

Lani Rouge's captors nodded.

Tristan turned and hurried from the room. Outside he stopped and looked north at the ebony spires soaring above the warehouses.

The Citadel . . .

Months of training would pay off with either Selfhood or . . . death. And the latter was assured if Flagge Glom had somehow learned of the existence of the writable template. They'd have altered all their inner Security protocols.

And they'd catch him.

All that training for nothing.

He shrugged off the tension gripping the muscles of his shoulders and neck and began to walk north.

Too late to turn back now.

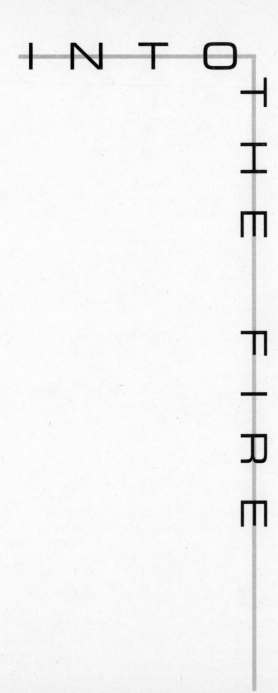

INTO THE FIRE

Tristan stared up at the looming Citadel. Its ebony spires towered above the surrounding high-rise offices and government buildings, jutting from their midst like a black spearhead. The largest structure on the planet. Jabbing the gray sky the Citadel proclaimed Flagge's power.

He'd easily passed the routine checkpoints since entering Flagge Quarter. But now the Security got serious.

He willed his thumping heart to slow. He'd be scanned time and again before he reached the Datacenter. He didn't want to be stopped because of an unexplained anxiety state.

He felt his pulse rate falling off. As it should. He could do this. No problem. He'd entered the Datacenter hundreds of times in Kaze's virtual model. This would be no different . . . *should* be no different.

Unless the virtual model was incomplete, or Flagge had added something new. He couldn't think about that, couldn't allow himself to worry about what he couldn't control.

Taking a deep breath he walked up to the Citadel gate and stepped into one of the scanning booths. The lasers swept over him, searching for evidence of holographic enhancement or disguise. He thrust his hand into the IDplant reader. Here was the first place some-

F. Paul Wilson

thing could go wrong. If his IDplant was an even slightly imperfect copy of the datameister's, pulsers would stun him and he'd be carted away for investigation.

And then he'd have to explain. Codes could become corrupted—it happened all the time—but the security officers would want to know *how*—especially when the faulty IDplant belonged to a datameister. He would have no good answers.

Termination would follow all too quickly.

The lasers blinked off and the inner door of the booth slid open.

So far, so good. This was going as smoothly as a session in the VR simulator.

He followed the corridor to his right as if he did this every day—which he had for the past month. He felt right at home. No surprises here, everything seemed very familiar.

He marveled at the precision of the VR simulation model back in Kaze. How had the glom's moles smuggled out such an amazingly accurate model? They had to be highly placed, with top security clearances.

The traitors, whoever they were, probably realized that Flagge's star was in descent . . . and were assuring their own futures by speeding its slide.

A few turns and he came to the central chutes—the only ones that dropped nonstop to the Datacenter. When he got the clear signal he stepped off the edge and floated down. He maneuvered to a corner of the shaft, keeping to the slow lanes at the periphery, letting those in a rush zip past through the center.

No hurry to get to the final checkpoints.

By the time he reached level S-25, Tristan was alone. He grabbed one of the handles and swung out to the floor. Out of the influence of the gravity attenuators his full weight returned. He'd reached the Datacenter level. Another scanning booth identical to the one at the Citadel gate awaited him in the vestibule.

No turning back now.

He stepped inside and submitted again to the laser and IDplant checks. But when the door slid open this time he found himself face to face with two Security guards.

One of them, a beefy blond woman with a jutting jaw, said, "Running a little late today, Rouge."

This grim-faced guard wasn't part of the VR mock-up back at Kaze Glom.

Tristan shrugged. "One of those mornings, know what I mean?"

The guard shook her head. "No." She jerked her thumb over her shoulder. "What're you waiting for, an escort?"

Tristan moved past her and hurried through the corridor of the Flagge Security post that sat between the chutes and the Datacenter.

Retracing the path he'd followed so often in the simulator, he found the tiny elevator—a real elevator with a car—down to the Datacenter proper.

"Rouge," said a tech stationed at a desk just outside the door. "Three's ready. Have a good session."

Tristan nodded and stepped into the booth. The door slid shut behind him and then the ceiling began to glow, revealing a platform cot jutting from the wall. He stripped, pausing only briefly to run his hands over the wonder of Lani Rouge's breasts. He felt a slight, unfamiliar *tingle*, a ripple of pleasure.

He reclined on the platform. As the venipuncture unit slid out of the wall he slipped his arm through the ring and let it tighten around his elbow. He felt a sharp prick as the catheter quickly pierced his skin and threaded into a vein.

The venipuncture unit wasted no time. He closed his eyes and tried not to sweat as the machine began its analysis. Fingerprints and retinal prints could be faked, so it came down to this: matching genotypes. The test would detect a nanomorph or DNA adaptee trying to pass as a datameister. Their foreign genotypes would set off alarms throughout the Datacenter.

Maybe that nice Security guard from the vestibule would come in and stun him herself. She looked like the type who'd enjoy that.

But thanks to his Goleman chromosome Tristan's genotype now

perfectly matched Lani Rouge's. The Goleman itself had assumed all the characteristics of one of her X chromosomes . . . and no truly accurate test yet existed for a masqued Goleman.

As far as Flagge knew a mime template took at least six days to create. If Lani Rouge was out of contact for as much as a single day Flagge Security would want to know why.

No indication yet that they know about writable templates, he thought.

But they will . . . very soon.

He opened his eyes as he felt the warm rush of virucide infusing his vein and flushing through his system along with a surge of triumph.

The writable had worked. He'd passed. Flagge Glom's Datacenter was convinced he was Lani Rouge. He couldn't cheer, couldn't even sigh with relief. All he could do was extract his arm from the wall unit and swing off the cot.

The inner door slid open and, still naked, Tristan walked into a Datacenter antechamber.

He stopped at the assignment console and let the unit read his chip. 72649K flashed on the screen. Too bad Lani Rouge wasn't being assigned to 87342J today, but that would have been too much to hope for.

He stepped over to the cat's eye incubator/storage area and punched in 7-2-6-4-9-K. After double-checking his IDplant the incubator internal carousel whirled, then spit out a silver globe. Tristan retrieved it from the tray and carried it through the rainbow curtain that walled off the accessing chamber.

The shimmer of bacterio/viruscidal radiation washed over him and tingled against his bare skin as he passed through into the tiny chamber. Lani's body was clear of any foreign agents, ready for the encoded virus inside the globe.

He stopped to let his eyes adjust to the lower level of illumination. Directly before him sat the padded recliner where he'd spend the next few hours. This was the part he'd been dreading.

And he had to smile at that. At any point during his trek through the Citadel he'd risked being pulsed, paralyzed, revealed as a mime, and terminated—but those fates paled before the prospect of exposing his brain to the virus swirling within the little silver sphere in his palm.

But Lani Rouge did it almost every day and she'd seemed to be physically and mentally sound. Still, some claimed it wasn't so safe. He'd heard rumors of breakdowns, or datameisters snapping, going berserk. The gloms, quite naturally, denied it.

And the very idea of subjecting himself to a form of controlled encephalitis . . .

He shuddered. Do it, he told himself. Get it the hell over with and get out of here.

He forced himself to step forward and drop the cat's eye into its receptacle at the head of the recliner. Then he stretched out on its cool polymer surface. He listened to the whisper of the scalp unit as it rose out of the top of the recliner and, preset for Datameister Lani Rouge, snugly enclosed his head.

But the next step was the one he really dreaded. And it came only seconds later—the cool moisture of a transdermal injection, laden with the virus from the 72649K cat's eye, infusing it through the skin of his neck.

He clenched his teeth as he imagined the viral particles slipping past his epidermal cells, piercing the walls of his capillaries, coursing through his bloodstream—free now of any competing viruses—toward his brain cells . . . invading them . . . infecting them . . . multiplying.

I'll be fine, he kept telling himself. Datameisters do this every day. This virus is custom tailored to Lani Rouge, modeled on her own RNA so there's no antigenic response. Nothing to worry about.

Unless the virus somehow exposed the Goleman chromosome.

Cyrill said that wouldn't happen—couldn't happen. They'd tested. But could they be sure that the Flagge Glom hadn't done something with the virus to trap a mime spy? Too late for such questions now.

Tristan's eyelids grew heavy. Slow waves induced by the datahelmet undulated across his cortex. Instead of giving in to their sedative effect like a good little datameister, Tristan fought to stay awake.

And he fought panic. He'd been told that the flood of raw data released by the virons as they multiplied in his brain cells was disorienting to the point of madness, but he didn't want to sleep here. To lose awareness was to lose control, to be vulnerable in the heart of enemy territory.

His vision blurred as the room began a vertiginous spin. He squeezed his eyelids shut and locked his throat against a surge of nausea. All normal, all part of the process—still he was unprepared for the violence of the feeling.

Bright lights strobed and swirled against the inner surfaces of his lids, brilliant images streaked past, elongated, distorted, increasing in number and speed until they merged into a blazing void that engulfed him and took him down headfirst with one long, slow swallow.

Tristan came awake with a start. No gradual easing from sleep, no yawning, no stretching. He was simply *awake*, in the accessing chamber.

And aware of another dose of viruscide coursing through his veins as the datahelmet retracted from his head.

Apparently the powers that be were through with 72649K for today. They'd used Lani Rouge's brain as a processor to access and modify their database or inventory or formulae or whatever 72649K held, then stored the changes as base sequences along the viral RNA and cultured the modified strain in a new cat's eye. And now they were eradicating the virus from his system.

Easy in, easy out.

How long had that taken? How long had he been out? He wished he could access his neuronet and find out, but he didn't dare, not here in the heart of Flagge's Datacenter.

He rolled off the recliner and stepped toward the anteroom—empty-handed this time. He knew it was SOP to leave the cat's eye behind. At this moment the data on the new Lani Rouge strain was being backed up onto other datameisters' strains. If something untoward should happen to Lani Rouge the revised data could be accessed via another datameister.

No one was indispensable . . . not even datameisters.

Alone in the anteroom he immediately stepped to the incubator and quickly tapped in 8-7-3-4-2-J. Another check of his IDplant, a whir, and then a cat's eye popped into the tray. Tristan smoothly peeled a clear membrane from his inner thigh, popped out a tiny canula, thumbed the eye slit to expose the access port, then inserted the canula. *Practice makes perfect.* He didn't hesitate in the slightest.

He waited a count of exactly three seconds, then squeezed off the canula, leaving it to dissolve inside the eye. He placed the cat's eye back into its tray, then smoothed the pouch back onto his thigh.

Nice and neat.

As the incubator reclaimed cat's eye 87342J Tristan straightened and quickly looked around. Pure reflex. He was alone here.

How long had that taken? Fifteen seconds? Twenty? No matter, it had been enough. He had a sample of 87342J in a shielded pouch—proof against any viruscidal radiation—and Lani Rouge's genotype on his writable template that would allow Kaze Glom to access the sample's secrets anytime it wished.

It couldn't have been easier.

For a moment he permitted himself to think of his goal in all this . . . one more step closer to Selfhood, closer to a real life. Closer to integration, indistinguishable from anyone else in the Kaze Glom.

Not that he'd want to stay in *any* glom. As soon as he was free, he'd go see the world he'd dreamed about and never look at the gloms or the freezones again.

He was almost there.

Now all he had to do was get out of Flagge Glom alive.

CHAPTER 9

Regis popped into view ahead of him and held up a hand. "Just a moment, Lord Tristan."

Tristan kept moving, walking right through him. The SynFood warehouse was only a few blocks away and he wanted to get off the street.

"What is it?"

Regis reappeared at his side. "I've picked up an alarm."

"From the Datacenter?"

He'd instructed Regis to tap into Flagge Isle's net and keep tabs on any alarms—especially from the Datacenter.

"Not specifically. It's more of a general alarm, m'lord—a heightened awareness along the perimeter of Flagge Quarter and . . . at the SynFood warehouse. Security is looking for *someone*."

He stopped. "Me?"

"That's not clear, but considering the warehouse is a focus of activity . . ."

"Yeah. Mute! A damn good bet it's me."

With a sick feeling growing in the pit of his stomach he began moving again, but turned left at the next corner—away from the warehouse.

This was bad. What had gone wrong? Could have been any number of things. Whatever it was he was cut off from his previous masque. He was stuck with the Lani Rouge genotype for now.

He wished he had his wardrobe with him or at least another writable template. All he'd have to do was swipe a few cells from somebody.

He shook off the wishes—wishes were useless—and focused on his predicament.

"Regis—keep tabs on Flagge Isle. Key items to monitor are mention of Lani Rouge or mime agents. Alert me immediately if either one pops up."

"Yes, m'lord."

Tristan shook his head. The "Lordship" motif was more annoying now than ever. He wished he'd taken time to reprogram Regis before leaving this morning but he'd been in such a damn big hurry to get *out*.

He kept walking, making random turns without bothering to check his roam grid. He simply wanted to keep moving. The squat warehouse district gave way to a glistening high-rise residential area. He noticed that the orgallic look was rearing its ugly head here as well. A fair number of the fifty-story buildings sported a metallic sheen.

He also noticed men eyeing him along the way and repeatedly reminded himself that he now wore an attractive female body. He might have to come up with some creative ways—actually, some very old-fashioned ways—to put his good looks to use before he got out of here.

Tristan didn't relish that prospect. He could probably expect a physiological response from this female body but his personal orientation had always been male. And sex from a female perspective seemed so . . . *invasive*.

Tristan heard other mimes talk about switching sexes as though they enjoyed the process, as though their orientation didn't matter.

Not for him.

Moving randomly, taking first this turn, then that, he eventually found himself on a residential street with deluxe orgallic compartment complexes with shiny, steely, fish-scale siding, rising sixty or seventy stories on both sides, homes for upper-echelon Flagge workers.

He was about to ask Regis to give him a map flash to fix his location but he stopped when a black cruiser took the corner, floating his way, ten meters above the street.

Flagge Security. Looking for him?

He had to get off the street but couldn't look like he was ducking for cover. Better to take a bold approach.

Just a good Flagge citizen going about my business.

The Security floater was still a hundred meters or so away, moving slowly, checking everyone and everything below it. Steeling himself, forcing his body into a relaxed posture, Tristan stepped off the sidewalk and strolled across the street. As soon as he reached the other side he stepped up to the nearest doorway. The doors slid open, he slipped through, and ducked to the rear of the vestibule. Turning, he watched the cruiser float into view . . . and keep going.

Tristan sagged against the wall. Maybe that was simply a routine patrol. After all he hadn't seen them stop anyone. Still he wasn't ready to venture out on the street again just yet.

He looked around. He'd picked an upscale residential complex. The orgallic fish-scale veneer hadn't been carried over to the interior. At least not yet. The blond walls rippled with the swirling grain of living wood. A comfy hiding place, but how long could he hang around this vestibule before someone began asking questions?

He stepped over to the console at the rear of the space and accessed the resident roster. If anyone passed through he'd appear to be searching for a name. He scrolled through the list, barely paying attention as he considered his next move. Suddenly a name registered and he backed up.

ROUGE, LANI—3242

What? Tristan stared at the screen. Of all the streets, of all the residences, of all the doorways in giant Flagge Quarter he could have picked, he'd chosen Lani Rouge's? He didn't believe in coincidences. And this couldn't be one.

Seep . . . that had to be the answer. He hadn't been paying attention to where he was going, so perhaps those supposedly random turns he'd been making hadn't been so random after all. Something in him must have responded to familiar visual cues and walked him home.

He stepped to the rear of the vestibule and pressed his hand against the ID plate. A section of the wall slid open, revealing an up-chute.

In a residential building? he thought. I'm impressed.

He stepped inside and let the updraft carry him. At the thirty-second floor he grabbed a rung and swung himself into the arched hallway. Empty. He walked left—it seemed the right way to go—and found 3242.

Now what? Go in? He realized he knew nothing about Data-meister Lani Rouge. Did she live alone? Was she married? Kids? Did she—?

The soft hiss of a door opening farther down the hall spurred him to action. He couldn't stand out here as Lani Rouge stupidly staring at the door—her *own* door—and didn't want to risk a conversation with someone who knew her. He slapped his palm against the ID plate and stepped inside.

The lights came on as the door whispered closed behind him. A good sign. They'd be on already if someone were here.

He did a quick explore of the compartment—no, too big to call it that. This was a full-fledged apartment. Obviously datameisters got good perks.

And lots of other things from the looks of this cluttered mess. Every table, every counter, every corner was stacked with . . . *things.* Toys, cooking implements, artificial plants and flowers, dead real plants and flowers that had never been watered, wall decorations, helper bots in all shapes and sizes, all of them clean, well-dusted, but most still in the original containers.

The place looked like a warehouse full of all the impulse junk sold in odd corners of the Ocean.

All this junk struck a cord with Tristan. He'd always liked browsing the markets, trying to spot items he'd seen in the flat vids. Like Lani, he too had an affection for near-useless stuff.

He poked the trunk of an oddly twisted miniature tree and jerked his hand back as half a dozen dead leaves fluttered free from the stiff, dry branches. He'd barely touched it.

No sooner had the leaves landed on the carpet than something round and beige and about as big as his foot scurried across the floor, scooped the leaves into its fur, and disappeared behind a sofa.

Tristan smiled. A moppet. A quick one too. He'd heard the new models ate and drank only once a week and cleaned up their own droppings.

He looked around. That explained the lack of dust—moppets couldn't move the stuff around but they could keep the clutter spotlessly clean.

Only one piece of furniture was unencumbered: an oversized black chair. He dropped into it and jumped as he felt its padding shift under him. He relaxed when he realized what it was. A smartchair. He let it mold to his body contours. Nice. He'd always wanted one of these. The super-comfy chair reminded him of those old TV vids, with a "Dad" always plopping down on the overstuffed easy chair, his adoring family gathered around him. The chair, the family, all seemed so . . . *warm*.

He closed his eyes and luxuriated in the perfect, temperature-controlled fit of the cushions.

After a moment he reluctantly extricated himself from the chair's warm embrace and rose to his feet. Couldn't afford to get too comfortable.

He walked to the window and cleared the pane. The street scene below was placid.

"Regis," he said, and his PDA appeared. "What's the current status on that 'heightened awareness' you mentioned before?"

"The same, m'lord. Does your lordship want me to—"

"Enough, Regis. Set up reprogramming."

As long as he had a few minutes to kill he might as well get rid of that muting English butler avatar. But what to replace it with? Maybe just the default floating head for now.

Tristan was halfway through disabling the butler when he spotted a Flagge Security cruiser pulling up before the building's front entrance.

He stiffened. The same one as before? He couldn't tell. Had they spotted him when he'd crossed in front of them? Or had he done something wrong in here . . . tripped an alarm?

He opaqued the window and headed for the door. Lani Rouge's luxury apartment suddenly felt like a gilt-edged trap. But as the door slid open he heard voices down the hall. He let it slide shut again and ran through the apartment, his heart pounding frantically as he looked for a hiding place.

He'd recognized one of those voices. Of course . . . he'd been hearing it whenever he spoke.

Lani Rouge was coming home—with a police escort.

He found a closet in the rearmost room, a bedroom, and slipped into one of its corners, quickly arranging the clothes between him and the door.

Seconds later and there were voices in the apartment—male, female, neither sounding too friendly. He tried to catch the words but they were too far away. Damn the size of this apartment.

He slid down the wall to a sitting position, preparing to wait.

Something in the corner on the floor pressed against his back. He reached around and pulled it out. Spherical with a flat base . . . felt like a hologlobe. He ran his fingertips along the underside of the base until they found a switch. Right—a hologlobe.

Curious as to why the datameister would leave it back here, he pressed the switch. The globe glowed and the image slowly took form.

A man in his midtwenties, just about Lani Rouge's age. A friend? A lover? A brother?

Something familiar about those rugged good looks . . . those blue eyes . . . the answer hovered just beyond his reach . . . drifting closer.

Whoever he was, the image suddenly triggered warm feelings in his seep from the datameister. Warmth . . . love . . . and grief.

And then he had it. A sudden blast of winter killed the warmth as Tristan recognized the features. He almost dropped the globe.

That face! It was the face he'd worn all morning . . . until he'd got to the warehouse and switched to the datameister's. This was the masque Cyrill had given him. It wasn't a custom composite as he'd been told—it was a *natural*.

And Lani Rouge knew him.

CHAPTER 10

Lani fumed at Flagge Security Lieutenant Garmaz. Polite on the surface, nothing but rules and regulations beneath. She'd quickly grown to dislike him.

"So I'm a prisoner? Is that it?"

"Not at all, Datameister Rouge. I've told you—this is protective custody. You've already been abducted once today. We do not want that to happen again."

She wished she could see his eyes behind the shiny crimson visor that covered the upper half of his face. She was sure he knew more than he was telling her.

"So I'm not to leave my complex?"

"Your apartment looks comfortable enough," he said, his visored head swiveling back and forth. "Perhaps you can spend the time . . . neatening it up."

A supercilious Security officer. *Bloaty!* Just what she needed.

Lani refused to follow his gaze. She hoped her embarrassment didn't show. Yes, her apartment was a mess. She knew that. But it wasn't dirty. She had the best moppets on the market and they kept the place spotless. It was just that she had so many more things than she had places to put them. If she could just stop buying things.

But how she kept her apartment was not the business of Flagge Security.

"What does restricting my movements accomplish? Why can't I—?"

"You'll be guarded as well. Your building will be under constant surveillance. Anyone who isn't a tenant had better have a verifiable reason for being here."

"Oh, so I'm not only a prisoner, I'm bait too? I won't stand for this!"

"Stop!" Lieutenant Garmaz said, raising his hand and his voice. "I have my orders. I am carrying them out. That is all we both need to know. Good day, Datameister Rouge."

"And good riddance," she muttered as he stepped into the hallway and rejoined the pair of red-helmeted patrolmen waiting there.

As the door cut him from view she heard a loud hum and then a beep from the far side. Curious, she touched the plate but the door didn't move. She touched it again, then began slapping it, but the door remained closed. They'd disabled her doorplate.

Unbelievable! She couldn't even leave her apartment.

Furious, she whirled and kicked at a table, missing it with her foot but catching the edge against her shin. Pain shot through it. Clutching her lower leg, she hopped around on one foot, screaming curses.

Finally, the pain eased and she dropped into her smart chair and it gently hugged her.

How stupid am I? she thought. Why didn't I just tell them about the mime? It wasn't Trev . . . it just wore his skin.

As hard as she tried, she couldn't find an answer to that question. She'd described the three thugs who'd kidnapped her down to their nose hairs. And if—more likely *when*—they were caught, she'd testify against them and demand maximum sentencing. They had her trussed up, naked as the day she'd been born, and subjected her to their leering and ogling.

But after a while simply looking hadn't been enough. No, they decided that something a little more physical was in order. What the hell—she was dead meat anyway. That was what they'd called her: *dead meat*. Might as well have some fun with her.

And then she'd sat there, sick with horror, as they'd traded drug patches and started arguing over who was going to have her first . . . and how good it was going to be. They started to untie her but then a fight broke out—she'd bet anything they were high on Hhhell. After some shouted threats and halfhearted pushing and shoving didn't settle it they agreed to let a game of 30–40 decide.

Leaving her half untied they settled down to play. Lani had hung her head as if asleep or deep in depression, all the while patiently working on her bonds. As a second fight broke out, this one more vicious than the first, she wriggled an arm free and used it to untie the rest of her bonds. Then taking advantage of her captors' Hhhelll-induced fog, she ducked behind some crates, found the mime's discarded clothes, and ran for the door.

One thing about living here in Flagge, you usually didn't have to go far before running into a Security patrol. Except today of course. But by the time she'd found one and led them back to the warehouse, her abductors were gone.

The patrol had brought her first to their unit station where she'd told them everything—except about the mime. The abduction of a datameister was no small matter, and so she'd been taken to Central Security in the Citadel, where she'd repeated her story—still leaving out the mime.

Why? Because he'd looked like Trev?

Truly "looked like" didn't even come close. He had *been* Trev. When he'd walked in she'd thought the man she loved had come back from the dead. But only for an instant. Trev's death had been confirmed. So that could only mean that his genome had been copied and given to a mime. But by whom? And why?

She shivered and rubbed her upper arms as she felt her skin begin to crawl. Mimes were creepy in general, but this . . . this biological freak becoming a dead man . . . all but bringing him back to life . . . and then becoming *her*.

She'd thought that was impossible.

She should have turned him in, should have told about the mime copying her on the spot.

So why didn't I? she asked herself.

They'd now be in a frenzy looking for a mime agent instead of worrying about whether or not her abductors would try again.

Was it because that mime had saved her life? The kidnappers had wanted to kill her—had been ready to pulse her to mush—but he'd stopped them.

And that was one more *Why?* to add to her list.

So maybe she owed the mime some sort of payback. But even if she didn't, she'd had other reasons to keep quiet. She didn't trust Security. It was almost a law unto itself. And if Security caught the mime he'd disappear. No one would know he'd ever existed, let alone penetrated Flagge.

Seeing him like that . . . moving, speaking, it was almost as if Trev were still alive.

She needed to see that mime again, talk to him, find out where he got that copy of Trev's genome.

She sighed. How idiotic. As if she'd ever get the chance. *"Lani Rouge."*

She bolted from her seat at the sound—her name . . . her voice—and turned.

A young woman stood in the center of the room, wearing the clothes Lani had put on this morning.

Me! No—the mime. And more lifelike than any mirror.

"Seems we share more than our looks," the mime said, hefting a hologlobe.

Lani backed away. This . . . *creature* terrified her.

"Wha . . . what do you mean? What do you want?"

The mime held up the hologlobe. "This. The man in here. How do you know him?"

"How do *I* know him?" Lani stopped and stared. "How the hell do *you* know him?"

"I don't." For the first time the mime seemed unsure. "I thought he was a composite. I never dreamed . . ."

"That he'd once been a real human being?" Lani felt her eyes sting as they filled with tears. Not now, she thought. She willed them back. She would *not* cry in front of this *thing*, this shape-stealer. "Well, he *was* a real human being—the best!"

"Was? Does that mean he's dead?"

"Yes." Those damn tears again. "He was killed two months ago— murdered."

"Was he your brother?"

"No."

"Your lover then?"

"None of your muting business." She looked away but knew it had to be so obvious. What was the point of denying it? "All right, yes."

And I miss him . . . no one can imagine how much I miss him.

"I'm sorry."

She glanced at the mime. Her face—her own face—looked genuinely sad as it stared at Trev's holo. Did mimes have feelings? It occurred to her she knew so little about mimes. They didn't matter in her world.

"Sorry about what? That you killed him?"

"I didn't kill him."

"All right then—not you, but one of your type. What does it matter?"

Finally the mime looked up at her. "Why should a mime do that? There's nothing special about his genotype."

That did it. A sob grew and burst from Lani before she could stop it.

"You bastard! It—he—was special to *me*!"

She dropped onto the edge of the chair and buried her face in her hands. She still hurt—it had been two months since his body had been consigned to the vats and it hurt as much as that first awful day.

She felt a hand on her shoulder and stiffened. She looked up and the mime was standing over her, staring at her with her own eyes, so strange.

An instant of disorientation—being comforted . . . by herself . . . dreamlike . . . a fantasy. *Confronting herself.*

That was *her* hand resting on her shoulder, and yet it wasn't her hand.

"Tell me about him," the mime said. "Please."

"Why?" She wiped her eyes and snatched Trev's holo from him. Anger slowly replaced the grief and fear. "So you can mimic him better?"

"No." Again . . . that hint of uncertainty. "Because something isn't right here. I should have been given a composite masque for travel into Flagge. But even if I hadn't, I never should have been given the genome of a recently murdered Flagge citizen. It doesn't make sense."

"And Trev's, of all people."

"Yes," the mime said softly, eyes far away. "Of all people." Suddenly he refocused on her. "Trev . . . is—was that his name?"

The mime seemed uncomfortable.

She nodded. "Something wrong with that name?"

"No, not at all. It's just that I've never worn a masque with a name before."

A masque . . . that was all Trev was to this creature. But he was so much more than that. She had a sudden urge to tell him all about Trev. This mime had to know. But first . . .

"What's *your* name?" she said. "I can't call you Lani and I'm *not* going to call you Trev. So—"

"Tristan."

"Tristan." She rolled the word off her tongue. A mime having a name was as strange to her as one of his "masques" having an identity must have been to him. "What a strange name."

"I didn't choose it."

"Who did?"

The mime shrugged. "Not from my mother, that's for sure," he said with a crooked smile. "Or my father."

Is that my smile? she wondered. Or his?

And then the full implication of his words struck: Mimes had no parents. Who'd raised him?

She had a fleeting vision of row after row of little mimes, mime children, seated on the edges of their beds, all lined up in a cold, cavernous hall, listening to a bored voice tell them to get under the covers because the lights were going out in one minute . . . one minute . . . one minute.

She shook off the disturbing image. Where had *that* come from?

Oh, yes. From Trev. He'd told her. When he could get her to listen.

He'd told her other things about mime children—about how the healthiest ones who met the criteria for intelligence and compliance were fitted with interfaces at age eight. The ones with the most responsive mDNA went on to become agents, gladiators, specialized workers. The rest . . . the rest were sold across the globe for use as test subjects for new drugs, experimental splices. Short, often pain-filled lives, then into the vats. But they were luckier than those sent Off-World, where the working conditions were even worse. There were even reports of Martian mines closing and companies abandoning the mimes like so much used machinery, left behind to die.

"All right, Tristan. I'll tell you about Trev."

She stared at Trev's holo as she spoke, intending to give the mime a few details and no more. After all, Trev belonged to her and not to him. But once she got started she found she couldn't stop.

She spoke of Trev's family, his sister and brother, both working Off-World, how Trev had scored in the top ten on the Flagge science tests and had been admitted to university studies, how he'd graduated with honors and gone straight to work in Flagge's gene prosthesis lab.

The mime had been picking his way through her living room as she spoke, not looking particularly interested. Now he stopped and turned toward her.

"He worked on designer genes? Did he have any contact with mimes?"

"Of course. How do you think they test the splices? They wouldn't use—" She stopped.

The offhandedness of her own remark unsettled her. Sure. That was one of the things mimes were really good for—testing designer genes. Splice a new gene onto a template, stick it in a mime, and see how it works. Use mimes to work out any untoward side effects before the new gene goes on the market. If one mime dies from a bad gene, there's always plenty more to take its place.

Mimes had always been an abstraction of sorts to Lani. She'd seen them in the Arena, of course, though the mayhem and violence of the fights never had appealed to her. But the mime standing before her now was no abstraction. How many mime-friends—did mimes even have friends?—had he lost to faulty designer genes?

She tensed for an angry response but the remark seemed to blow right past him. The mime only nodded.

"Trev had a lot of contact?"

"I—I don't know. He never talked much about his work."

No, she thought. That wasn't quite true. When he'd started out he'd been so enthusiastic she couldn't *stop* him from talking about the work he was doing in gene prosthetics—not only making replacements for defective genes but designing new genes to *improve* on the human body, to take the human genome where it had never been, where no one had dreamed it could go.

But as time went on he became more reticent about the work. Toward the end he might have spent his work hours in an isolation tank for the little he had to say about it.

"Was it a secret project? Was he gagged by Flagge?"

"I don't think so. He just changed over the past year. He seemed to be angry about something; he used to leave at night and not tell me where he was going. And then, two months ago—sixty-eight days ago, to be exact—his body was found in the freezone."

"How did he . . . ?"

Lani swallowed. She could face it now, even talk about it. Sure she could. But it wasn't easy.

"They—it had to be 'they' because one person couldn't have done it, not to Trev—they cut his heart out and left it on his chest. The autopsy said he was still alive when they cut into him."

"I'm sorry."

She glanced up at the mime. Sorry? What would a mime know about sorry? She watched his face—*her* face—carefully as she told him the rest of it.

"Whoever killed him used Trev's blood to write something on the wall next to his body." She paused.

"What?"

The word swam before her. She'd wanted to visit the spot, but being a datameister she was not allowed to leave Flagge Quarter. So she'd had to make do with Security Force holos . . . and they were vivid enough. She remembered the crude red-brown letters of the scrawl, the fierce exclamation points like claw wounds in the wall.

" '*Mimelover!!!*' "

The grimace of shock and revulsion on the mime's Lani-face had to be real.

" 'Mimelover?' What . . . what does that mean? The mime brothels?"

"That's what I thought at first," she said—and she was still ashamed for thinking it. "And I think Security wanted me to believe Trev was killed because of some sordid dispute over a mime whore."

"Such a sensational crime," the mime said softly. "Why wasn't it all over the datastream?"

"Because Flagge Security didn't want anyone to know about it. As soon as they had their crime scene holos they whisked Trev's body away and enzymed his blood off the wall. Anyone coming along an hour after his death might suspect something had happened there, but they'd have no idea what. I was told—ordered—to say nothing. There would be an investigation."

"Why would they want to hide the murder?"

"Exactly what I wanted to know. So—when I heard nothing from them—I did a little investigating on my own. I am a datameister, after all and—" She took a breath. "I learned that Trev had become involved with a mime-rights group."

"Wait," the mime said, holding up his hand. "Stop. A mime-rights group? Humans for mime rights? I didn't know that there was such a thing."

Lani believed him. "It's something that they don't want the public to know about. They're scared, and the truth about Trev's death might only widen support for the movement. Obviously they don't want mimes to know that humans are working to free them."

The mime looked around, found a small clear spot, then sat—a bit unsteadily, she thought—on the edge of the low table behind him.

"Excuse me, but 'they'? Who is this 'they'?"

"The gloms. Who else?"

"But they protect us. They *own* us."

"Right. And they want to go *on* owning you. They don't want you to start thinking of yourselves as anything more than property—property that they protect from a hostile world. The last thing they want are mimes realizing that there's a movement afoot to free them from the gloms and from anyone else who owns one. That's what Trev said."

The mime shrugged. "A radical minority is hardly going to change things. People hate us. They always will."

"Some do—especially those who've lost jobs to mimes—but most people don't care too much either way." I know I didn't, she thought. At least until Trev was killed. "From what I've learned the gloms play up mime hatred and antimime violence and squelch any hint of mime sympathy. I think they're afraid mime rights could catch on as a movement."

"Not if its members keep ending up like your lover."

He had a point. For a while she'd wondered if one of the gloms had killed Trev, but finally rejected it. If a glom had wanted him out of the way he simply would have *disappeared*. No, some sick bastards, most likely some of the more deranged Sibs, had wanted to make a point by killing Trev that way and leaving a bloody message behind.

"I shouldn't have said that," the mime said. "But tell me, are you . . . ?"

"In mime rights?" Lani shook her head. How was she going to say this? "No. Because of what happened to Trev I'm more interested— more aware, at least—than before. But to devote my spare time to a cause like that? I'm afraid not. But believe me, a dedicated group of everyday human beings is out there fighting for your future."

Looking dazed, the mime muttered something . . . a word. Lani stiffened. It had almost sounded like . . .

"What did you say just now?"

The mime shook himself and blinked. "Nothing."

"Yes—you said, 'Okasan.' I heard you. What do you know about Okasan?"

"Only what I've heard. Something about her being the 'mime savior.' What do *you* know about her?"

"Not enough. I mean, nothing really. But in my investigation I came across this rumor . . . some woman who was leading the movement to free mimes. I started to believe that maybe that's who Trev contacted, that Okasan was who he went to see all those times he'd disappear for hours."

The mime shot to his feet. "And now he's dead."

He began to pace the room—and immediately tripped over a dead plant and nearly fell.

"Mute!" he said. "What is all this junk?"

"Some of it's Trev's, things I kept when I cleaned out his compartment." She'd meant to go through them but somehow never had got around to it. She didn't have the will, didn't have the heart. "But most of it's things I . . . just buy."

"Do you ever *use* any of it? Most of it looks like it's never been unpacked."

"I know." She shrugged. "For the last year or so I've simply been buying things . . . for no reason. Not to have them . . . just to . . . buy them. Trev says—*said*—it's fallout from my datameistering."

The mime stared at her. "Really? It affects you?"

"I don't know. Maybe."

Lani didn't know personally any retired datameisters. They tended to move away, supposedly to luxury communities where they spent their time and accumulated wealth far from the jumble. But stories filtered back, stories of villages peopled by dull-witted ex-datameisters living out the rest of their years in mentally enfeebled comfort.

Lies, she suspected, told by disgruntled shufflers jealous of people who could retire in their thirties.

At least she hoped they were lies. Sometimes she wondered.

She didn't like talking about this but she hadn't talked to *anybody* in so long, and really, this almost seemed like talking to herself.

"I used to always have a reason when I bought things, now I just *buy*. And I don't think I'm as . . . smart as I was before. Or at least not as quick. I mean, the memory's still there, it's just that my access and retrieval times seem longer. There's a hesitation, as though there's a bump in my neural pathways."

"Why don't you quit?"

"Can't. I'm only halfway through my ten-year contract. And it's ironclad. No way out. Even if I broke every bone in my body, they'd still wheel me in for my access sessions."

She stretched to relieve the growing tightness in her limbs. Or did she want to shrug off the fear that she was slowly losing her mind . . . and that at the end of her ten-year contract she'd have little left?

"Could be just my imagination though. The power of suggestion, you know. Anyway—only five years to go. I'm saving my money, investing it conservatively. When I retire I'll be set for life."

And she would be all right. She was sure of it.

When her contract was up she'd leave the gloms and go to the winter sports resorts in Antarctica. That looked like fun, or maybe visit the deep-ocean habitats. Live under the sea for a few weeks. And maybe retire to one of those luxury wilderness communities she'd heard about, where she could walk a hundred meters from her front door and look out on a vast land with no building, no other person for as far as the eyes could see.

She smiled, but the mime's look told her that he saw through her show of confidence. He kept staring at her, making her uncomfortable. Finally he shook himself.

"It's your life," he muttered, then louder: "I've got to get out of here."

"That's easy enough," she said. "No problem. I'll call Security. They'll come and personally escort you to the Citadel."

"Is that . . . a joke?"

Something in his eyes . . . a warning.

"Just my way of telling you that's the only way you'll get out of here. You can't even get to the hallway—we're locked in this apartment. 'For my protection,' they said. Even if you could, they won't let you leave the building if they think you're me. So it looks like we're stuck together."

"Don't look so comfortable, datameister," he snapped, a definite edge to his voice now. "If Security finds us together we'll *both* be dragged off to the Citadel. And that won't be pleasant for either of us. They'll find out why I'm in Flagg—"

"Why *are* you here?"

"I can't tell you, so don't ask. You're better off not knowing."

"You came to steal data, didn't you. That much is obvious—why else impersonate a datameister? But *what* data? What does Kaze want to know so bad that it sends a mime agent into hostile territory?"

"Who said it was Kaze?"

"Who else would it be?"

"Think of an answer, because if I get taken in, Security will want to know where *you* fit into the scheme."

"But I had nothing to do with it! I was kidnapped!"

He smiled. "You'll have to be *very* convincing. What if Security doesn't believe you?"

Lani hid a shudder. He was right. She'd be implicated in whatever he'd done or planned to do. Mute! Why hadn't she *told* Security about him?

"Wh-what can we do?"

"You can help me."

"Help you *how*? My doorplate's been disabled."

A grim smile flickered across his Lani-lips. "That's the least of our problems."

CHAPTER 11

Lani Rouge's apartment door slid open.

Close behind him Tristan heard the datameister gasp. "You did it!"

From where he was kneeling before the disassembled doorplate Tristan poked his head through the opening for a quick look up and down the hall.

Empty.

He leaned back and closed the door again.

"How did you do that?" she said.

He'd been trained as an agent all through his accelerated childhood. Along the way he learned how to bypass almost any kind of lock. But why tell her that?

The less she knew about him, the better.

Besides, she didn't seem too interested in the strange life and problems of mimes.

"Not much to it really. Especially from in here. Much more difficult from the outside."

"Yes, but with only a knife and a spoon to work with—I'm impressed."

You'd really be impressed, he thought, if you owned even the simplest tool set. I'd have had this door open in a third of the time.

Feeling only slightly less trapped, Tristan turned and sat on the floor, leaning his back against the door.

"Do you hire out?" she said. "I could use someone like you around here."

He watched her smile and realized he liked the way it curved up at the corners. He liked the sparkle in her eyes too, even if it was merely a gloss on the sadness there. Her delight in his ability to bypass her door's locking mechanism was almost childlike. Would she still possess that bright quality five years from now when her datameister contract ran out?

He wondered about what she'd said about the mental price datameisters paid for their cushioned lives—that their special brains weren't the only reason their salaries were so high. Lani Rouge was going to be a woman of independent means when she retired in her early thirties. But would she still be Lani Rouge? Or would an empty-eyed, empty-headed woman have taken her place?

He shrugged off the questions. Why was he worrying about her when he should be worrying about himself?

And why was he feeling stirrings of sexual attraction?

That could only mean that the seep from her template was fading and his indigenous "Y-ness" was surfacing. He had a brief flash of the two of them, naked, entwined right here on the carpet . . . Lani on Lani.

He wondered how Lani would feel about making love to herself. Could be interesting . . . she'd know all the special places.

Tristan shook himself. Let's not get sidetracked here . . . focus.

What next? Now that he had the door working, he could leave the apartment but not the building—at least not wearing a Lani Rouge masque. He squeezed his eyes shut and tried to think. So hard to think straight with all that had happened since he woke up this morning.

Too damn many coincidences . . . too many deviations from standard procedure. Instead of a composite genome specifically tailored to the assignment, Cyrill gives him an intact natural genome for his masque. Unheard of! But worse, not just any natural genome—it belonged to a mysteriously murdered Flagge citizen. And not just any random dead Flagge citizen, but the lover of the datameister Tristan was supposed to impersonate . . . someone active in a "mime movement."

Something very wrong here.

Nothing like this had ever happened to Tristan before. He'd always felt in control when he was on assignments. Now . . .

He felt as if he were suspended on strings.

But who was pulling them? Cyrill? Someone above Cyrill? Perhaps that strange old woman, Okasan, was involved. Or some double agent in Flagge Glom.

All Tristan knew was that he had to get out of enemy territory and back to Kaze. As much as he'd chafed at his tiny quarters and limited range of movement back in the Kaze mime warren, right now he longed for that narrow space—those safe, secure, familiar confines.

He stared at the datameister. Who was she? An innocent bystander, trapped in this by chance, or another one of those strings, pulling him this way and that?

How did he even know she was a real datameister?

He felt his body go rigid with alarm as a new possibility slammed into him.

Bloaty—how did he know she wasn't another mime?

He didn't. And short of stripping her and going over her skin a centimeter at a time looking for an interface slit, he couldn't know.

So he'd have to be very careful about everything he said or did, not let on anything about the assignment, not even let on that he was suspicious.

"Tell me," he said, "is there a rear entrance to this building?"

She nodded. "Of course. But it's no secret. I'm sure Security's watching it."

"How about a tunnel to a neighboring building?"

She laughed. "Maybe in the older districts, but not around here. At least not unless you dig one yourself. But what's the problem? All you've got to do is grab one of my neighbors and do to them what you did to me."

Tristan stared at her. What was she talking about? "I haven't done anything to you."

"You stole my body!"

"Don't talk like an idiot. If I stole your body then what am I sitting here looking at?"

"All right, maybe you didn't steal my 'body,' but you stole my genes."

"No, I merely copied them. The only thing I took were a few loose cells from the lining of your mouth, and you were going to lose those anyway."

"All I'm trying to say is we can grab one of my neighbors and—"

" 'We?' "

"You think you can handle something like that on your own? Bloaty. Go right ahead and—"

"That's not my question. Why should you want to help me?"

"Well . . ." She hesitated. "The sooner you're out of my apartment the better. I mean, you don't want to be here, and I certainly don't want you caught with me. So it's to our mutual benefit to get you on your way and away from me as soon as possible. And besides . . ."

"Besides what?"

She looked embarrassed. "You saved my life. Least I can do is return the favor."

Tristan was baffled. "Saved your life? When?"

"This morning—when you told that piece of multicellular debris who had me tied up not to kill me. You could have let them pulse me but you didn't. So . . ."

Tristan looked away, unable to meet her eyes.

Saved her life? He'd tried his damnedest this morning to tell the Kaze agents to finish her. But he couldn't get the words out. Seep from her genome had saved her—not him.

"But anyway," she said, "I figure we can grab someone, steal a few cells just like you did with mine, copy the genome, and then you can walk out of here as someone else. No one will stop you. Right?"

Tristan looked right at her. "I wish it was that easy."

"Looked pretty easy this morning. You took that scraping, went around the corner, and—*poof!*—a little while later you came back as me."

Yes, it could be as easy as she said—*if* the writable template could be reused. But each was writable only once, then it was like any other template.

"Can't be done," he said, searching for an explanation that wouldn't mention the writable template. This could still be part of a trap, some trick he didn't understand. "I . . . don't have the equipment with me."

"But didn't I hear somewhere that you mimes always carry a bunch of templates you can use? You call it something . . . what is it?"

"A wardrobe."

How simple this would be if Tristan had his personal template collection with him: Open up his interface and remove the writable, slip in one of his trusty old genomes, and stroll past Security outside. But he'd never have got the collection past the Citadel scanners this morning. He'd had to leave it behind.

"Mine's back in that SynFood warehouse—at least I hope it still is. Sorry."

"Well, that's really bloaty, isn't it," she said. "We're both stuck here. And I just know this is going to come to a bad end . . . unless . . ."

Tristan watched her eyes narrow as she stared at him. "Unless what?"

"Wait a second. Can you use another mime's template?"

"Usually. They all work on the same principle. But where are you going to find—?"

"There's a mime living on the forty-fourth floor."

"Impossible. Flagge's controllers would never let a mime roam around free—"

"Oh, yes. They let *this* one."

"Even if they did, this is a luxury building. No mime could afford to live here."

"But he does. He poses as a regular person, but I know he's a mime."

"How?"

"Trev told me."

Trev again . . . dead, mysterious Trev.

"And how did he know?"

"He just . . . knew. The mime calls himself Dohan Lee. When he tried to get too friendly with me—calling, stopping by—Trev told me about him."

Tristan's turn to laugh. "He was just jealous."

"No he wasn't. Trev told me that Dohan Lee is really a mime Arena gladiator, a champ named Eel. And one of his championship perks is the privilege of living here with other upper-echelon Flagge employees."

Kind of like Selfhood, Tristan thought. You can pretend to be a *person*.

Tristan studied the datameister's scowl. She seemed genuinely annoyed.

Could it be true? What a prize for a champion mime—to have your Roam Grid extended so you could live out here in anonymity and luxury among the real people. You wear the same masque whenever you're among them, they accept you as another highly placed Flagge worker, and when they go to Flagge Arena to watch the mime-fights, when they cheer for Eel, they have no idea that they're cheering for you.

An enviable life . . . as long as you remained champ.

"Even if it were true—"

"It is!"

"—how would we get our hands on his wardrobe?"

"Easy enough. I'll drop in on him, tell him I'm lonely, and then . . ." Her voice trailed off.

"And then what? Ask him if he's got a spare template you can borrow?"

"Maybe I could steal one."

"Not a chance. Nothing in this world a mime guards more closely than his wardrobe. And a mime trying to pass as a realperson? You'd never get close."

"What if I just hit him over the head with something?"

Tristan laughed. "He's a professional fighter. Your swing will have to be too quick for him to stop, placed just right, and hard enough to knock him out the first try. You won't get a second. Can you do that?"

She bit her lower lip and shook her head. "No. But I bet *you* could."

It took Tristan a moment to understand what she meant.

CHAPTER 12

As she followed the mime down the hall Lani's heart pounded against the inside of her chest wall like a prisoner trapped in an isolation chamber.

This is insane, she thought. The two of us . . . together . . . if someone steps into the hall and sees us, how do I explain?

Oh, this is my cousin . . . from Kaze Glom. She's just here to steal some Flagge secrets.

Tristan signaled to her as he stopped and positioned himself directly in front of Eel's door.

They'd rehearsed this so there'd be no talking when it came time to do it. Shaking inside she took her position off to the side, leaning against the ribbed wall, out of direct line of sight from the doorway.

Her head seemed to have taken on a life of its own, rhythmically swinging her gaze from the heavy length of ivory the mime held behind his back—it had been a leg on one of her footstools until he'd torn it off—to the hallway on either side then back to the stool leg.

Get this over with!

The mime touched the doorplate with his free hand. The door remained closed—it wasn't keyed to him—but Lani knew that somewhere inside the apartment a chime was sounding.

She tensed. This was it. No backing out now. She'd called Mr. Dohan Lee's apartment and asked if she might stop by sometime when it was convenient. She still remembered the hungry light in his eyes as he'd babbled an immediate invitation—"Anytime! Anytime at all!"—which she'd accepted.

The door slid open almost immediately—someone was very anxious.

"Well, hello!" Lani recognized the voice. "I've been wanting to get together with you for the longest time!"

"Thank you *so* much for inviting me," the mime said with a smile, then nodded in Lani's direction. "And just to make the afternoon more interesting, I brought a friend."

Lee—or Eel—jutted his head through the doorway and looked her up and down. His grin faded as his eyes widened.

"What in the name of—"

The Lani-mime whipped his arm up and brought the stool leg crashing down on Eel's head. He staggered back out of sight and Tristan followed Eel inside. She heard a crash, then the sound of another blow being struck, then the thud of something heavy hitting the floor.

Seconds later she saw her own flushed face poke through the door opening.

"Quick. Get in here!"

Lani slipped through and closed the door behind her. An inert form sprawled on the floor. Blood trickled from under Eel's hairline and across his forehead.

"Is he . . . is he dead?"

"No," the mime said. "Just unconscious." He motioned her forward. "Come on. Help me lift him."

She pressed back against the door. She did *not* want to touch him. "No . . . I couldn't."

"Look—if you had a stronger body I could move him myself, but you don't, so get over here and *help*."

Reluctantly Lani edged toward Eel's feet and, as directed, lifted them. The mime grabbed the shoulders and together they carried/dragged the dead weight into a rear room and heaved it onto a bed.

"All right," he said. "Where's that sleeper?"

Lani fished the small black disk out of her pocket and handed it across. She'd already cleared all her preset interrupts and programmed it for the maximum sleep period it would handle—twelve hours.

The mime pressed the disk against the base of Eel's skull and left it there.

"That ought to keep him out of our way. Now"—he began stripping off Eel's clothing—"let's see if Mr. Dohan Lee is really a mime."

Suddenly uncomfortable, Lani backed away.

"Maybe I'll just wait out here."

"Well then make yourself useful while you wait. Look around for a stock of nutrient concentrate."

"Why?"

"An active mime is never far from a supply."

Lani left the two mimes and wandered through the apartment. She realized it was larger than hers by a good twenty percent. She checked through Dohan Lee's kitchen but found no sign of concentrate among his foodstuffs.

For the first time she felt a twinge of uncertainty. Maybe Dohan Lee really wasn't Eel, the great Arena champ. Could Trev have been wrong?

No. She had to keep believing—Trev had told her so, and Trev wouldn't have lied. Besides: Eel . . . Lee . . . it was so obvious when you thought about it.

Still . . . where was the concentrate the mime had said was so important?

She searched through the living room and dining room but came up empty-handed. With her spirits sagging Lani wandered toward the rear of the apartment and stepped into one of the rooms. She stopped in the doorway and stared.

A trophy room. Mime Arena trophies? She stepped closer. What else could they be? Her spirits lifted. This would prove that Trev's story was more than mere jealousy.

But her hopes were dashed when she saw that all the trophies and awards were for pitsaur competitions. Rex . . . Rex . . . Rex. Everything was for something named Rex. She leaned close to the holo of a vicious-looking pygmy raptor, all teeth and claws, and shuddered, suddenly very glad they didn't allow pets in this complex.

Lani searched the rest of the room but everywhere she looked she saw nothing but that muting pitsaur. Lee or Eel or whoever he was seemed obsessed with the creature. She was about to give up when she noticed what looked like a storage area beneath the trophy display.

"Probably more holos of Rex," she muttered as she dropped to her knees and pressed the release.

The panel slid open and she stared inside, not sure what she'd found.

Squeeze bottles, gel packets, all neatly lined up, all . . .

"You found it?" said a voice behind her.

She turned and saw the mime stepping toward her.

"See!" she said. "This proves it, right? Lee is Eel. Look at all this stuff. He's a mime."

Tristan squatted beside her and pulled a large squeeze bottle from the cabinet.

"Yes, I know."

He bit off the top and began sucking at the contents.

"You know? Well then why did you have me turning this place upside down for—?"

He held up a thin beige wafer as he swallowed. "Found his interface."

"And what's that?"

"His Dohan Lee template."

Lani leapt to her feet. "You took it from him? Just like that?"

"Of course."

"But what about him?"

"He's fluxing back to neutral." Her face betrayed her confusion because he cocked his Lani-head and stared at her. "You don't know much about mimes, do you."

"I know as much as anyone else."

"Well, if you want to see it firsthand, go take a peek at him."

"Really?"

"Yes, really. He won't bite. He'll be asleep for the next twelve hours."

Lani wasn't too sure she wanted to do this but curiosity was getting the better of her. To see a mime unmasqued, undressed as it were.

"What will you be doing?"

"I'll be looking for his wardrobe case. He'll have it somewhere about. And I'll be storing up on nutrients while I'm looking."

"For your next . . . did you call it a 'flux'?"

"Right. I'll be fluxing into Mr. Dohan Lee." He raised the container for another swig.

Lani hesitantly made her way toward the room where they'd left Mr. Lee—no, *Eel*. This whole day had taken on a surreal air. Yesterday had been so sane and normal: She'd gotten up, gone to the Citadel, done her datameister duties, then come home. Simple.

Today she'd stepped outside her door and nothing had been the same since.

She slowed as she neared the room. Did she want to see this?

Yes. She had to. Trev had been involved with these creatures, these *things*. He'd actually thought of them as human or damn close to human. "A genetic variant" was what he'd called them.

But now she had a chance to see one of these mimes in what they called the "neutral state," whatever that meant. Lani wasn't so sure she wanted to know, but how could she pass up the chance to see it in the flesh?

She paused on the threshold. The room had been darkened but she still could make out a large form on the bed. She moved closer. Lani noticed that Eel's legs were splayed and found her gaze drifting, seemingly of its own accord, toward the groin area.

She gasped.

She'd learned a bit about mimes from Trev. He'd told her how the Goleman chromosome replaced the sex chromosome on mimes, leaving them asexual in the neutral state. At least physically. Mentally and emotionally, he'd said, they retained the sexual orientation of their source DNA. If that source DNA had come with a Y-chromosome, the residuals from the Y tended to make the resultant mime think of itself as a "he." The reverse was true if the Goleman chromosome replaced an X.

Sure. Facts . . . she knew the facts. But they hadn't prepared her for the *sight* of a neutral mime.

She blinked a few times but that failed to add detail to the featureless expanse of flesh running from the lower abdomen all the way down to the space between the thighs. So smooth . . . like a doll.

She moved closer to this pale, smooth-skinned being, watching the slow rise and fall of its hairless chest, then moving up to the head with its pale oval face and colorless hair—which made the red blood from the scalp wound all the more startling. The sleep disk was still attached to the base of its skull.

She stood and stared at that sleeping face, its smooth, bland features—the almost lipless mouth, the flat cheeks and rudimentary nose, the smooth domes of the lids over the eyes—and felt . . . what?

Lani had expected repulsion, but instead she was struck by the innocence of that face. Here was a blank screen, waiting for a shape, a form, a *word* to give it meaning. Hard to believe this was one of the champions of the mime Arena who made his living battling and sometimes killing other mimes.

As she backed away she remembered how Trev had begun whiffing heavily in the months before he was killed, staggering home almost after a few too many Dewar's Greenies, and how morose he'd become. She could still hear his slurred voice: "What have we done, Lani? What the hell have we *done*?"

He'd never been quite clear as to who the "we" referred to, or what they'd "done." Now Lani thought she understood.

Back in the living room she found the mime sitting and sipping another container of concentrate as he stared at something in his hand.

He . . . if mimes were asexual, why did she think of him as a "he" or a "him," even when he was wearing a female body? Her own, to boot? Of course, the first time she'd seen him he'd been male—Trev. That had to be it. Somewhere in her mind he was linked with Trev . . . somehow she had the feeling he still carried a part of Trev inside him.

The mime looked up as she came in.

"I found his wardrobe," he said.

Lani looked down at the flat case that fit so neatly in his palm. Five little discoid compartments along the perimeter, encircling an empty depression at the center—obviously for the Dohan Lee template. Each compartment was marked with a symbol.

"The stuff dreams are made of," he said softly.

"What?"

"Nothing. Something from an old vid."

"Where'd you find it?" Lani said. "I went through this place pretty carefully."

"Sometimes it takes a mime to find what another mime hides."

"What do those symbols mean?"

"Part of a code—Eel's personal code for his templates."

"Why would he need a code?"

"For the same reason he hid the case—a mime's wardrobe is his tool set. It's how he does his job. If you want to take that a step further, it's who he is. And if you make your living in the mime Arena, you certainly don't want to let any of your rivals get to your wardrobe. They could switch runty or diseased genomes for your fighting templates."

Lani laughed. "That could be an ugly surprise."

"It could mean your life. Especially if they filled your wardrobe with meltdowns."

"What's a meltdown?"

"A custom genome incompatible with life. You flux into a misshapen lump of protoplasm with no heart or lungs or brain, or maybe you get reduced to primordial ooze. Whatever, there's no coming back from a meltdown. You're dead." He pointed to the case, his finger circling over the compartments. "One of these is a meltdown."

"How do you know that?"

"We all keep one in our wardrobes."

"In yours too?"

"Of course."

"Why?"

"Ever hear of Russian roulette? It's a wonderful deterrent. Another mime's going to think twice about stealing your templates if he knows one of them is a melter."

"So one of these will kill you but you don't know which one."

"Correct."

"Then why did you want to find it? What good is it to you?"

"I may need to flux out of the Mr. Lee masque into someone else."

"But what if you pick the wrong one?"

He gave her a level stare. "Then I die."

"Then why—?"

"Trust me, I'd only use it if my life depended on it—if it came down to flux or die." He snapped the lid case shut and held up the wardrobe case. "This at least offers me a four-in-five chance of surviving."

"Russian roulette?"

Now he smiled. "Exactly. Except this isn't a game."

He stood and slowly wandered the living room, touching things, dragging his Lani-hands along the walls, across the furniture. Then he stopped and simply stared into space with a strange, longing look in his eyes.

"Something wrong?"

"I want this," he whispered.

"This apartment?"

"This *life*. I want to have an identity; I want to be the same person every day, someone other people can get to know, and maybe even like. I want my own things—even useless things! And a place of my own to put them. And I want to leave that place when I want to, stay away as long as I want to, and come back when I damn well please. I . . ."

Abruptly his eyes refocused and he seemed to pull himself back from a faraway, private place.

"Sorry," he said.

"It's all right. I understand." She'd always assumed mimes were like robots, with no identity, no feelings. But what she had just heard . . . moved her.

He gave her a quick, sharp look. "Understand? You couldn't possibly understand."

"Well, not completely. But I'm not free either. My movements are strictly controlled for the term of my contract. I'm supposed to get permission for any deviation from my daily routine, and if I ever miss an access session, a Security patrol will come looking for me. Damn it, I haven't seen the freezone in five years. So don't tell me I couldn't possibly understand."

"It's not the same," he said. "Not even close. Five years from now your contract will expire, leaving you young and attractive, with a fat credit account and the rest of your life to do anything you want, anywhere in the world."

Right, she thought . . . the rest of my life and maybe half my mind, if Trev was right.

But she had to admit her situation wasn't nearly the same. She'd had a normal upbringing, she'd signed the datameister contract knowing the risks, and even though the only way out of the contract was death or severe brain damage, she'd chosen her own course.

But a mime . . . incubated by a glom, raised, educated, and trained by a glom, genetically altered at the whim of a glom, as often as the glom felt necessary.

And then what? What happened to old mimes who outlived their usefulness? Where did they go? Lani didn't want to ask. Probably to the vats . . . *mime* vats.

She looked at this mime and knew that even though he had no hope he still had a dream. And though he was wearing her skin, inside he was someone else. Not just a mime . . . a person . . . a someone.

Someone named Tristan.

Was that what Trev had seen? Was that what had changed him?

Why didn't I see it? Why did it take me this long?

Maybe because she'd never spent any time with a mime—at least knowingly. Trev had been in contact with them all the time through his work. But Lani . . . she was just like everybody else: Mimes were something you heard about but never saw unless you liked Arena sports.

She looked up and saw this mime—Tristan—gulping the rest of his concentrate.

"And now if you'll excuse me," he said after a final swallow, "it's time to flux. Wait for me here."

Just like that . . . *it's time to flux.*

As Lani watched him head for one of the rear rooms she fought a sudden desire to stop him. Why shouldn't he flux into Dohan Lee and be on his way?

Because I'll miss him.

What? Where had that insane idea come from? He'd invaded her life, stolen her identity, implicated her in a data felony, and involved her in an assault on an Arena mime. Good riddance.

But the thought persisted. He was occupying a copy of her own body and that somehow . . . linked them. Tenuous as it was she sensed a bond between them.

So strange, she thought, like sisters, twins . . . they were connected, and she'd been disconnected from everything and everyone for months.

For the first time since Trev's death she didn't feel so damn alone.

She started as she heard a faint groan from the rear of the apart-

F. Paul Wilson

ment. Hesitantly she got up and moved down the hall toward a closed door. Another groan—from beyond the door. She stood stiff and still, listening, her hand poised halfway to the doorplate. The red indicator was dark, which meant the door wasn't locked.

Tristan was in there . . . changing. She could only imagine what that must look like. All she had to do was touch the doorplate and she could watch. Would she ever have a chance like this again? It could be horrible, fascinating.

She withdrew her hand. No . . . if Tristan had wanted her to see he would have fluxed in front of her.

Lani returned to the living room. And waited.

CHAPTER 13

Sweaty and sore, Tristan sat on the edge of the bed and sipped a fresh container of concentrate. Three fluxes in eight hours . . . mute! His body was feeling the strain. Every cell seemed to be crying out in protest.

And not over yet. He might yet have to flux back to his first masque of the day—the one Lani called Trev. *If* he could find it.

A big if—an important if. Without it he might not be able to leave Flagge Quarter.

Tristan finished the concentrate, then rose and examined his thigh for the transport patch. Yes, the sample from the cat's eye was still in place.

He caught sight of his new body in the mirror. Good to be a male again, to have a sturdy mesomorphic frame. He'd become as tall as Eel's Dohan Lee but not as bulky—fighting mimes were bred to have more mass. He sighed. The late, great Teresa Goleman had rewritten the laws of genetics but she hadn't been able to do anything about conservation of mass. Excess could be stored along the long bones, but if a genotype required more mass than a mime possessed . . . too bad.

132 and Matthew J. Costello

His bulk was a small matter though. Unless he wound up in the Arena, Tristan felt sure he could pass.

At least this template seemed to be seep free. Either it had been well scrubbed or Eel had had it so long that any personality residues had evaporated.

He found a black jump in Eel's closet—every piece of clothing he owned seemed to be the same cheery color—and slipped into it. It went on loose, but the smartfabric adjusted quickly to a good fit. Grabbing the red clingsuit he'd removed before fluxing, he hit the doorplate and headed for the living room.

Lani jumped out of her chair and backed away, face pale, eyes wide.

"It's you, isn't it?" she cried, thrusting out her hand as if to ward him off. "Please. Tell me it's you!"

"It's me." What was wrong with her?

"No! Tell me your name!"

"My name? Tristan. And I'm returning your clingsuit."

She closed her eyes and took a deep breath. "Don't *do* that!"

"Do what? You knew I was fluxing into the Dohan Lee template. Who else did you expect me to return as?"

"I don't know. I've never been involved with a mime before. One time you're Trev, the next time you're me, now you're the man we carried into that back room. For a moment I thought he'd come to—"

"But he'd have been in the neutral state."

"I know, I know, but it's so confusing. Nobody's the same one minute to the next."

Tristan couldn't help but smile. "Welcome to my world."

He picked up Eel's wardrobe and slipped the writable with Lani's genome in among the other templates, then looked around to see if Eel had anything else he might need. He felt like a looter.

He particularly loathed taking Eel's wardrobe. As a mime Arena champ, Eel was sure to have a whole array of templates, and most likely duplicates of these. But still, robbing a fellow mime of his tools and then leaving him in the neutral state . . . it didn't sit well.

Like leaving the mime nowhere at all.

He pocketed the wardrobe, promising to find a way to return it. To complete the picture he needed to copy Eel's IDplant. But he couldn't very well carry that equipment around.

"I'll take you back to your apartment," he told Lani, "then I'll see if Security will let Mr. Dohan Lee out of the building."

She nodded absently. Tristan found it hard to relate to her confusion. This was life for him, his only life.

Maybe that's why so many hate us. We're simply too different.

As they made their way back to Lani's apartment Tristan watched her out of the corner of his eye. For a while today she'd seemed so bright and alive, with fire in her eyes. He might even have been able to convince himself that she was almost glad to be with him. But that fire was out now, and she'd reverted to her original sullen self. Why? What had changed?

He didn't want to leave her like this. He felt he owed her.

What? Rent on her genome?

No. More than that. He sensed that their lives were entwined, not simply by the fact that she'd been in love with the man whose genome he'd used this morning, but also through the seep he'd absorbed from her genome. He felt that maybe he knew her more intimately, understood her better than any other being on the planet.

Her life seemed lonely, filled with things with no connection, no meaning.

And then he realized with a start that he didn't want to leave her.

They stopped outside her door.

"Do you want to come in?" she said, looking up at him with her luminous eyes.

Yes, he wanted to say, but shook his head. "I can't. They're looking for me—not in this masque, certainly, but the heightened security along the perimeter is going to make it difficult to reach the freezone."

Another flat vid, a poor excuse for memories, floated through his mind . . . a parting at an airport . . . the actor saying "Here's looking at you, kid" . . . and then the strange antique plane's engines beginning their impatient roar.

"Then—I guess this means I won't be seeing you again."

Were those tears welling in her eyes? For him? Tristan was moved . . . a strange new feeling . . . a wonderful, indescribable feeling.

No, he thought. If anything she was feeling the loss of . . . Trev. With a mime there was never anyone to be missed, or loved, or needed. Every mime knew that.

Always the masque.

He forced a smile. "Don't be so sure. You may see me plenty of times—and never know it's me."

"Do you think you could come back sometime and visit?"

Tristan almost said yes. The word rose to his lips, wanting to believe in *this* feeling. Maybe he could stay in contact with her. When the mission was over, when he got Selfhood.

But that was impossible. He was a spy, an agent for the Kaze. When this was over, when he finally obtained Selfhood, he and everything he knew about this mission would have to disappear.

Don't make promises you can't keep.

And what was he thinking anyway? He'd be an utter fool to think this could lead anywhere. Simply seeing him in her ex-lover's body this morning had left Lani vulnerable. It wasn't Tristan the damn mime she was seeing with those moist eyes, it was the memory, the masque of someone dead named Trev.

By this time tomorrow she'd probably hate him for reopening old wounds.

"That could be dangerous—for both of us. And I'm sure you'd rather put this whole day behind you."

"No." She laid her hand on his forearm. "Really. I want to see you again."

"As Trev?"

Her eyes clouded for an instant. He had reminded her of the truth.

"Maybe . . . and maybe as you."

Her words seemed to throw a switch within Tristan, releasing a torrent of words.

"But who *am* I? You don't know *me*. I am no one . . . or I am anyone I'm told to be. There is no *me* you'd want to know. The real me now looks like Eel. Go back upstairs to his apartment and take a good look at him again. That's the real me—a pale-eyed alien, an oversized sexless fetus, a fighter, a killer. I am not a person—I am a thing. So don't say you want to see *me*. Tell me who you want me to be"—he laughed—"and I'll see if I can accommodate you. I'm a mime. I pretend to be human. That's my purpose in life. That's what I was—"

He stopped when he saw her step back and realized he'd raised his voice.

What am I saying?

From what dark hole had all this rage, this teeth-grinding frustration emerged? And why was he spewing it at Lani? All she'd said was she wanted to see him again.

Was it because whatever she thought she felt for him was not . . . for *him*?

That wasn't her fault. She didn't deserve this.

"I'm sorry," he said.

"It's all right. I think I understand. I'd be just as bitter if—" She shook her head as if deciding not to finish the thought. "But you *are* a person, Tristan. I've just spent a good part of the day with you, and no matter whether you were wearing my body or this one, you were . . . *you*. There's someone else behind all these masques you wear— someone named Tristan. I don't understand all this. This 'changing' is still . . . very strange. But being human, being a *person*, is more than simply having a certain set of genes. Don't let anyone tell you otherwise."

Tristan stared at her, wanting to believe that she was not merely spouting platitudes, wanting to believe that *she* believed what she'd just said.

Because if she could believe, maybe he could believe.

"How many more like you are out here?"

She smiled—almost shyly—and shrugged. "I don't know. Trev opened my eyes, but I think I only began to see today."

Trev . . . always Trev . . . he hovered about them like a ghost. As much as one part of Tristan never wanted to hear the name again, another part couldn't help but admire the man.

"I wish I'd known this Trev of yours."

She nodded. "I think you two might have got along."

And then, without thinking, Tristan leaned forward and kissed her—briefly, awkwardly—on the lips. He pulled back before she could react.

"I'm sorry." Mute, he was apologizing a lot lately! "I didn't mean that."

I'm only replaying scenes from vids, he thought. *None of this can be real for me.*

Lani slipped her hand behind his neck and pulled him forward. "Yes, you did," she said, smiling as she went on tiptoe and returned the kiss—longer, slower, softer this time. "You're just not very good at it. You need practice."

Tristan felt Eel's Dohan Lee body responding, a gnawing ache growing in his pelvis, so much stronger than a while ago when he had been Lani. But this was not the time, and certainly not the place.

"All right," he said. Why did he feel as if he'd just run a hundred-meter sprint? "Maybe I will try to come back and see you. But right now—"

"I know. You've got to go." She kissed him again, just a peck this time. Such a simple human gesture. "Be careful."

Then she touched her doorplate and stepped across her threshold. She smiled once before the door slid closed and cut her from view.

Tristan leaned against the wall and struggled to gather his wits. He felt weak, disoriented—and it wasn't the masque.

What was happening here? Everything—his assignment, his emotions, his whole worldview—seemed to be spinning out of control.

Wonderful feelings flowed through him . . . but he had to get focused, focus on the mission, the goal.

The mission, and Selfhood.

He pushed away from the wall and shook himself.

He hadn't thought it possible but Selfhood had suddenly become even more important than it had been this morning. But to have any sort of future at all he had to get out of Flagge Quarter. And the sooner the better.

He headed for ground level.

Tristan tensed as he stepped from the downchute and spotted a uniformed Security patrolman stationed by the entrance. His helmeted head swung toward Tristan as he entered the vestibule.

Be calm, he told himself. You're Dohan Lee. You live upstairs. You have every right to be here—so act like it.

Tristan was debating whether it would be more natural to ask the patrolman what he was doing here or simply ignore him, when the patrolman settled it for him.

"Citizen," he said, his eyes hidden behind his visor. "What is your name?"

Tristan knew a full body scan was in progress behind that visor, information blipping onto the interior surface.

"Dohan Lee. And you are . . . ?"

"Corporal Eastin."

"Is something wrong, Corporal?"

"A minor Security matter. Do you live here?"

"Of course." He rummaged through his memory—what was that apartment number? "Unit 4472."

"Just one moment."

Corporal Eastin repeated his name and apartment number, then waited. Tristan imagined a complete file of Dohan Lee flashing on the visor's HUD, confirming him as a resident of this complex.

The helmeted head swiveled back to him. "You appear to have lost some weight, Mr. Lee."

Mute! The scan had picked up his reduced mass. The last thing he needed now was a hotshot Security noncom bucking for officer status.

"Really? I hadn't noticed." He forced a grin. "After all, my smart-suits still fit perfectly."

The corporal didn't offer even a polite smile at Tristan's admittedly lame attempt at humor. He stared a moment, then held the door open. Tristan expected to be wished a good day but the patrolman wasn't through with him yet.

"Please step out to the cruiser so that I can check your IDplant."

Tristan managed a casual shrug as he stepped toward the door. "If you wish."

But inside his heart was taching into hyperdrive.

He could *not* allow this Security man to check his IDplant—not when it was still a copy of Lani Rouge's. As soon as Tristan's finger entered that slot Corporal Eastin would know something was wrong. His pulser would be out and pointed in Tristan's face.

Outside, the sun was down. Not dark enough yet to trigger the night lights, but a chill wind was picking up, hurrying the few pedestrians toward their destinations.

Tristan felt a noose tightening around his throat with each step toward the hovering cruiser. His muscles coiled, readying to spring.

But which way? He could turn and run, but how far would he get? Ten, twenty steps?

A desperate situation required a desperate solution. He balled Dohan Lee's thick fingers and examined the resultant fist. Big, heavy—he could do real damage with this. More of a weapon than an appendage.

And since he couldn't see how the situation could get much worse, what did he have to lose?

He quickly bobbed his head down to see if anyone else was in the cruiser.

Empty.

That decided it.

He reached out with his left hand and knocked off the patrolman's helmet.

Blond, blue-eyed Corporal Eastin whirled toward him, and Tristan rammed a fist into his startled face. Dohan Lee's fist made a thick smacking sound. The corporal staggered back, blood spurting from his nose, and Tristan followed him, swiftly delivering driving punches to the guard's gut and then again to his face. As the corporal's knees buckled, Tristan finished him with a right to the temple.

Flagge Security Corporal Eastin slid to the ground. He would not be doing any further identity checks today.

Tristan looked around and saw at least half a dozen people at varying distances staring at him in mute shock.

Yes, good Flaggers, I just attacked one of your dreaded Security men.

Don't mess with me.

But no doubt one of the witnesses would report him as soon as the shock wore off.

Tristan hopped into the cruiser. He felt it list under his weight for an instant then the stabilizers righted it. He groaned when he looked at the controls: Flagge Security had revamped its console. But the joystick and accelerator were still in the standard positions.

No problem, he thought, grabbing the controls as he zoomed into a steep climb.

"Lieutenant? Lieutenant Garmaz!"

Streig snapped alert.

That's me, he thought. He'd been posing as Flagge Security Lieutenant Garmaz since midday.

"Yes, Sergeant," he said.

"One of the apartment complex's residents just assaulted the guard stationed in the lobby."

Assaulted? He'd expected the mime to sneak out. Odd.

"You mean that female datameister—?"

"No, sir. This was a male—a Dohan Lee."

Streig checked the HUD inside his Security helmet. Handy things, these, although he had access to far deeper data than a Security lieutenant. He ran this Lee character and—

Mute me! He's a mime. A gladiator.

"I'm calling in a couple of cruisers to—"

"Call them off! I'll handle it. I have a squadron specially trained for cases like this. You just keep your men in reserve, ready to position themselves when ordered."

"Yes, sir."

Streig smiled as he activated the pursuit squadron. Full of surprises, aren't you, mime.

Tristan leveled off at a hundred meters and took a quick look at the compass. It told him he was flying west. *Wrong.* He had to go south— to the freezone.

He checked his surroundings. He'd risen almost to the middle level of the high-rise canyons that ruled this part of Flagge Quarter. Buildings like massive tree trunks inset with reflector windows slipped past on either side. He felt like a bird flitting through one of the fabled redwood forests of old.

He gained more altitude, slipping into the express level, then gave the cruiser more juice. At the next intersection he banked left.

All right. He was heading in the right direction. If he was lucky— very lucky—he'd be out of Flagge Quarter before Security could mount pursuit. But to make that happen he'd have to get everyone out of his way.

He played with the console switches until the cruiser's flashers and howler came on, then opened the throttle. He had the helm of a Flagge Security cruiser—why not make the most of it?

Up ahead the other floater traffic cleared a path for him. He smiled. The only way to travel.

But where was he and how far did he have to go? He activated his neuronet.

"Regis."

An American Indian wearing a leather headband and buckskins joined him in the cruiser cabin.

"Uhn. Regis not here, Kemosabe. Can Tonto help?"

"What?"

Where had this old avatar come from? He'd hadn't used Tonto since—

And then Tristan remembered. He hadn't finished reprogramming his PDA—and mute—now it was cycling through all its old avatars.

He'd deal with that later. Right now—

"ETA to the freezone?"

A transparent map popped into view. He saw a tiny glowing red dot moving through the grid of Flagge Quarter toward the sprawl of the freezone.

"Five-point-two minutes, assuming Kemosabe's horse gallops at present speed."

Five minutes to freedom—yes, this just might work. Hard to believe it was going to be this easy. Steal a floater and five minutes to freedom.

"What's the best altitude?"

"Uhn. Kemosabe will have more maneuverability if fly like eagle above mesas, but attract less attention from cavalry if stay down here between them."

"Exactly what I thought. All right. Monitor Flagge Isle and let me know if they're coming after me."

Tonto said, "Yes, Kemosabe," and disappeared.

Tristan smiled. He'd all but forgotten about Tonto.

But he stopped smiling when a bright green, finger-thin beam of light flashed to his right. He turned and saw another Security cruiser on his tail.

"Reg—I mean, Tonto! You were supposed to warn me!"

"Hey, pardner," said a scruffy, bearded, toothless old saddle hand. "Gee-willikers! Looks like you got some rustlers hot on your tail."

Not Gabby! Not now!

"Weren't you supposed to be monitoring Flagge Security?"

"Them sidewinders encrypt their telegraphs, pard. I don't have the dad blum *key*."

"Bloaty." Should have known this was going too smoothly to last.

Another green flash, this time closer. Too close.

After a little experimentation he found the switch for his rear screen and activated it. It showed he now had *two* cruisers chasing him.

His comm screen flickered to life and Tristan immediately cut the video—no sense in giving them a better description of this masque than they already had—but let the audio run.

"This is Flagge Security. You are under arrest. Those were warning bursts. Drop to street level immediately or you will be shot down."

Tristan shook his head. Being shot down was hardly a threat to a mime agent. Compared to capture, it was a blessing. His neuronet was preprogrammed with two capture options. At the first hint of torture it would knock out his speech center, leaving him unable to read, write, understand questions, or speak coherently. At the first sign of a memory probe it would induce a massive epileptic seizure that would leave him decerebrate.

No, a captured mime didn't pose a problem for the gloms.

But for the poor mime it was a different story . . .

On the surface the first option sounded preferable, but not to Tristan. Because when Security discovered that the fugitive who punched up one of their own and stole his cruiser was a mime, they'd find some very nasty, bloody games to play with him. Probably bring in a few Security men who specialized in pain. It might take Tristan days, weeks to die.

No, give me the brain fry, he thought.

Or better yet: Don't let them catch you.

Another flash, another miss—this one sizzled into the wall of a building on his right, frying and shriveling the bark siding. What were they thinking of, shooting at him with other traffic around? In the heart of a residential district, no less. Maybe Flagge citizens became expendable when Security badly wanted to get its hands on someone. The people behind their reflector windows would get quite a show.

Could be worse though. The Security cruisers could be firing trackers—one of those little missiles could wreak havoc if it missed and hit a building or locked onto some hapless noncombatant craft. What was the euphemism for such mishaps?

T-SEE.

Sorry, your husband was just blown into a million tiny pieces due to a Terminal Security Enforcement Error.

Time to climb out of this man-made canyon and get above the buildings where he could maneuver. Otherwise it was only a matter of time before one of those trigger-happy cruiser jockeys hit him.

Tristan was just pulling back on the stick when a green beam flashed in front of his cruiser. He glanced up through the transparent roof and saw two more cruisers above and ahead.

"Mute! They're all around me."

Swerving left and right, he dropped into the slower lanes, making himself a tougher target. He saw some people in small floaters look at him, terrified. He spotted a young woman and a child in a small two-seater. Maybe out shopping.

I can't stay here, he thought.

He spotted an intersection ahead and frantically began searching the unfamiliar console.

"Looks like it's time to circle the wagons, pardner."

"Dammit, Gabby—the wing control. Where the hell is it?"

"Don't yell at me, you young whippersnapper!" the PDA said, pointing to a toggle by the joystick. "Tarnation, it's right there in front of you!"

Tristan flipped the switch and extended his cruiser's wings in time to scream into a ninety-degree left turn. His rear screen showed the first pair of pursuers overshooting the corner, but the high newcomers were still with him, although they'd lost ground.

As soon as he was level again he retracted the wings—couldn't make that kind of turn without them but they'd slow him down on the straightway—and maxed the throttle.

He chewed his lip as he focused total concentration on the traffic ahead. He was moving at such speed that other vehicles couldn't get out of the way fast enough. The lanes between the buildings were now an obstacle course. He ignored all the terrified faces in the floaters he passed, but all the bobbing and weaving necessitated by the extra traffic here made it difficult to maintain his speed. And he was heading *east*, damn it!

He turned off his flashers and howler—they weren't much help at this point and probably made him an easier target.

As he approached the next corner he reached for the wing toggle. He was readying to expand them again for a turn back to the south when a beam flashed from the cross lane. He saw a Security cruiser hovering there, waiting in ambush, cutting off his turn.

He had no choice. He kept the wings in and stayed his course, dodging laser fire from the lurker as he passed. The Security cruiser didn't care if he hit anyone below.

Lasers from behind, laser from the side . . . the obstacle course had just become a gauntlet.

Flagge Quarter's night lights came on, glow strips running vertically up the sides of the buildings, brightening the lanes between them.

And making him easier to spot.

He made up his mind to take the next right—no matter what was waiting there. He had to head south, had to get out of Flagge Quarter.

He had no illusions that the Security cruisers would back off once he crossed into the freezone—they'd pursue him into hell. But at least in the freezone he'd only have to worry about danger from one direction—the rear. Here, in the heart of Flagge territory, Security could keep calling in reinforcements from all sections of the quarter and attack him from every muting side, tightening the net.

Only a matter of time.

He was fairly sure he could lose them in the freezone or at least stay ahead of them until Kaze sent out its own cruisers as an escort.

Tristan hung on to the joystick as he put out the wings and stood his craft on its side to tear into the next turn. Another cruiser was waiting, firing at him. But he ducked under it and left it behind. In his rear screen he saw one of the cruisers chasing him collide with the ambusher. Both dissolved in a ball of flame, a brilliant display reflected by the mirror windows of a nearby high-rise.

A really big T-SEE.

"Two down," he whispered as he tucked in the wings. "How many to go?"

"A good dozen or two by my reckoning," Gabby said. "Them sidewinders is closin' in, pardner."

Tristan had forgot his PDA was still activated.

He was about to off him when he spotted another cruiser dead ahead, lasers flashing, bearing down as if intending to ram him.

"You want to be crazy?" Tristan muttered. His fighting blood was up now. "I'll show you crazy."

He popped up the sighting screen, locked in on the charging cruiser, and began pressing his own trigger as they closed on each other.

Closer.

His laser shots were as wild as everyone else's—he'd never been much of a marksman—but he kept pressing the trigger, filling the air ahead of him with streaming flashes of deadly light.

Closer . . . closer.

Tristan was not going to change course.

The other pilot finally must have realized this and veered off at the last second.

"Thank *you*!" Tristan whispered.

He let out a deep breath he hadn't realized he'd been holding. That had been too close. He wasn't here to show off his fearlessness. He had a viral sample and a datameister template he was supposed to deliver. That was his assignment—*that* was why he was here.

But he was *not* going to be taken alive.

A group of cruisers appeared dead ahead. Too many for head-on heroics. He was forced into a westbound street.

"Better watch out, pardner," Gabby said. "I reckon they're boxin' you in."

"Off!" Tristan said as he quickly found an open cross street and turned south again.

He fought the urge to climb to where he could spread his pursuit and not have to worry about potshots from the cross lanes—where they'd have to come to him instead of waiting for him to run into their sights. But he knew he'd be approaching the boundary wall soon, and Security would have some heavy fixed batteries there, and certainly some smart missiles. High and alone up there he'd be a perfect target.

So he dropped his altitude almost to street level but didn't drop his speed. Teeth clenched, eyes fixed straight ahead, sweaty hands hanging on to the stick, twitching it back and forth, nudging it up and down, Tristan dodged through the air and ground traffic at bullet velocity. He was dimly aware of blaring horns and white faces, terrified or angry or both, staring, glaring openmouthed through the windows of the vehicles he bumped or cut off from above, below, or the side.

Lower—he scraped pavement and saw a mother guiding a baby scooter across the street dead ahead. Her horrified, screaming face loomed in his windshield, and Tristan was screaming too as he yanked the cruiser into a 360-degree roll, missing her by millimeters.

I'm not going to do it, he thought. I'll never get out.

Too low, no good, a little more altitude, and then a commuter shuttle gliding around a corner directly into his path. He saw the passengers ducking for cover as he rolled the cruiser onto its side and tried to slip past. He almost made it unscathed, but his passenger-side window grazed the shuttle's upper rear corner and tore. Wind screeched through the slit opening.

Abruptly traffic thinned and the buildings began to shrink, high-rises giving way to middle-rises, then to the ugly sprawl of low-slung warehouses. And then the wall was dead ahead and he knew they were waiting for him. But would they shoot? Not just mere civilians all around and behind him but fellow Security members in the line of fire as well. After what he'd seen so far, Tristan couldn't be too sure they wouldn't. All he could do was hope.

Not that it mattered now. He was committed—he'd either go over the wall or into it.

He thought of Lani then, his promise to return. *Can't return to her if I'm dead,* he thought. *But I'm only a mime. Not like losing a real life, now is it? No worse than one of these machines exploding. I'm simply a more complicated machine.*

I'm disposable.

And the only reason I have any value is because of the viral code I'm packing.

Then why do I want to live so much? Can someone tell me that? Why do I care so damn much?

A sound rose in his throat, starting as a low whisper and rising in pitch and volume as he hurtled forward, reaching a crescendo as he hit the wing toggle and yanked back on the stick a hundred meters from the wall. Every instinct demanded he squeeze his eyes shut for the inevitable impact but Tristan forced them to stay open as he swooped over the wall, barely skimming its top.

He heard a loud *thump* and felt the cruiser lurch as its underside caught the outer rim of the wall, then—amazingly—he was out of the light, plunging into the relative darkness beyond.

INTO THE DARK

He'd done it. He'd hopped the Flagge Quarter wall before they could fire a shot. He was over the freezone.

Tristan felt his heart still thumping.

But too early to celebrate—a quick glance at his rear screen showed that he wasn't out of danger yet. Far from it. At least a dozen blips were fanning out behind him.

Here come the Flaggers.

Immediately he swooped left onto a southeast course over the freezone's lower rooftops—his map said that was where he'd find Kaze's northernmost border—over the freezone's lower rooftops, and hit the toggle to retract the wings.

He checked his readouts and noticed he was losing air speed. That shouldn't be. Alarmed, he checked his throttle—at max—and his power—plenty. What was wrong?

"Regis!" he shouted. "Regis—why the *hell* am I losing speed?"

A pointy-eared humanoid appeared. "I believe, Captain, that you have already been informed that Regis is on hiatus. As for your question, logic would seem to dictate that there are three possible reasons why you would be losing air speed. A: You're running out of fuel; B: Your engine has been damaged by pulser fire; or C: Your wings are still extended. Since the control panel indicates engine function and fuel supply are both adequate, we are left with C."

"My wings? But I retrac—"

Tristan glanced out and saw they were still extended. He threw the toggle back and forth but the wings didn't respond.

Mute! When he scraped the wall going over—that must have jammed the wings.

And his rear screen showed the Security cruisers gaining on him fast.

"Find me a place to land."

The chaotic layout of the freezone popped into view—nothing like the orderly grid of Flagge Quarter—showing Tristan's craft and its pursuers as slowly moving red dots.

"Judging from the rate at which the alien craft are gaining, Captain," the humanoid said, "I calculate that they will be in point-blank range in four-point-seven minutes. They will be in average marksman range within—"

"Just tell me the best damn place to put down!"

"As you wish. From your current position there are suitable loci that afford relatively equal probabilities of escape in the Stebbins, Orsini, and Bascombe districts."

That last one rang a bell somewhere in his head. "Bascombe. Fast."

He watched the outline of the Bascombe district begin to glow green on the map. Not a bad place to put down—lots of artists and performers in the area, attracted by all the real galleries and theaters and clubs.

And on the map a small block in the district pulsed with a brighter green.

"Captain, the building indicated on the display appears to have a flat roof suitable for landing."

"Good work. Off."

As the PDA faded, Tristan saw a laser flash far to his right. He checked his rear screen—they were closing in. His air speed had stabilized but it was a lot less than what one of these cruisers could do with its wings retracted. He jiggled the throttle to see if he could coax any more speed out of the engine but it was already giving everything it had.

Crossing into the Bascombe district Tristan brought his cruiser down to rooftop level, and as he approached the building the PDA had chosen, he slowed his airspeed—deliberately now. As the building hove into view he slid open the cruiser's door and looked down.

Street level was a good hundred meters below, but the rooftop . . . that would be a mere five-meter drop—once he got over it and got his speed down. He inched the throttle back a bit more.

Taking a deep breath he grabbed the step bar below the door and swung out into the night. And there he hung, waiting for the rooftop.

The cruiser was almost down to glide speed now. He shot a glance back and saw the dogged Security ships high and behind. As he watched, a pair of the lead craft went into a dive, figuring to attack him from above. Could they see what he was going to do?

He looked down again—almost to the rooftop now. As soon as he saw the coping pass under his feet he dropped, hit the weather-pitted surface running, and ducked behind a vent as his cruiser glided away.

He couldn't hang around to learn its fate. Hopefully Flagge Security would melt it out of the sky before it smashed into the crowds below . . . and then wait till the wreckage cooled before searching for his body. But if someone had spotted his drop they'd be swarming through the building in minutes.

Had to find a way off this roof and down to street level—now.

Tristan yanked up on the grate atop the vent and found that it wasn't locked. He crawled through the opening, pulled it shut after him, and crouched on a small ledge. And then he felt around in the dark.

Mute. A soft ventilator. Metal or plastic would have made for an easier descent. These things were half alive, adjusting their gauge according to the heat and humidity of the space they served. At least it was wide open now and the air flowing past Tristan was warm and smelled of people.

A sudden burst of raucous laughter wafted up the pipe.

Lots of people.

Tristan braced his feet against opposite sides of the smooth, giving substance of the shaft, then did the same with his hands. At least it was dry—the inner surface drank most of the moisture flowing past it. Slipping off the ledge he began a controlled fall down the shaft.

About forty meters down, the shaft split. He chose the right fork . . . it looked a little wider than the left. Twenty meters farther down he reached a plateau. Lateral shafts sloped away to his right and left. Which way to go?

Another burst of laughter, louder now . . . closer. Just beyond the louvered vent before him.

Tristan paused and pressed his face against the vent to peek through the openings. Some sort of a theater below, the seats full, the faces of the audience lit by the glow from the stage that was beyond Tristan's line of sight. Whatever was going on, the crowd seemed to love it.

As they rose for a cheering ovation Tristan turned and began to crawl along the shaft trunk that seemed to lead toward the rear of the building. He found an inspection port that let him out into a narrow, dimly lit hallway—an *empty* hallway. He didn't expect to find any Security guards in here . . . but he didn't want any locals sending out an alarm.

He hurried along the wall until he found a door. He pushed it open and stepped into an alley. The fetid stink that greeted him was like perfume. To his right street traffic clattered past the mouth of the alley. He'd reached ground level.

Almost home, he thought.

"PDA," he whispered—he'd given up calling for Regis.

An angular man in a white T-shirt, dark vest, and porkpie hat flickered into view.

"Hey-hey, Tristy-*boy*! What can I do for you, ol' buddy?"

Tristan sighed. Another old avatar. Was his PDA going to cycle through every single one?

"Find me the nearest tube station."

The freezone map overlay appeared. As usual he was the red dot. A green dot began blinking to the near southeast. The map expanded until he had a full-screen view of his immediate area.

"There y'go, pal o' mine. By air it's a measly zeeero point-four kilometers"—he pronounced it KEE-low-meters—"to da nearest onramp. By street y'gotta travel a whole zeeero point-seven-five kilometers. Nuttin' to it."

"Filamentous."

All he had to do was make it to that tube station and he'd be back in Kaze Quarter within minutes.

A truly amazing performance. Perhaps he would get to see Lani again, and perhaps he'd be a free mime when he saw her, not that much different from a human—

"That's all—but leave the map overlay."

"Anyt'ing you say, Tristy-*boy*!"

Tristan headed for the street and turned left. As he wove his way through the freezone pedestrians, mingling with the happy crowd pouring from the theater he'd just left, he used the overlay to find the shortest route.

"His cruiser is empty, sir."

"Mute!" Streig muttered.

Everything had been going so well, and now . . .

"Find him," he said. "I don't care who you've got to maim, torture, or kill to get it done. Find him!"

"Yes, sir. We'll have him back in Flagge before—"

"No, you retrogenomic plasmid! Don't touch him! Don't even let him know he's been spotted. Find him, then come to me. I'll take it from there."

*   *   *

Tristan was weaving through the freezone, making good time toward the tubes, when he overhead someone say, "Hey, what are those trisomies doing here?"

Tristan followed the man's pointing finger and froze. A Flagge Security cruiser was floating down the street behind him at ten meters. People booed and shook their fists as it passed, but the Security men in the craft ignored them and kept their eyes trained on the street, searching the faces below.

Tristan whirled his head away from them and picked up his pace toward the tube station. Not too fast. Just continuing on his way.

Minding my own business.

What if they've got the tubes covered? he wondered.

Flagge Security had no official authority in the freezone. But since the freezone had no police force of its own to speak of, and since he had no contract with a private security service, who was going to stop these thugs from picking him up and carting him back to Flagge Quarter?

No one.

Freezoners traditionally hated all security forces and all gloms as well. They'd crowd around and shout and threaten if they saw someone being picked up by Kaze or Flagge Security, but they weren't brave enough or stupid enough to risk life and limb for someone they didn't know.

Tristan was halfway to the next intersection when he spotted a second street cruiser round the corner ahead and float his way.

Without missing a step he turned into the narrow alley directly to his left and slipped into its comfortable darkness. He thought he'd been pretty smooth, but when he looked back he noticed a cloaked figure staring at him from across the street.

As he watched, the figure turned and hurried off.

Had he been spotted? What was the purpose of the cloak? Some sect? An Imagist?

That was the last thing he needed now.

Hurrying along the length of the alley Tristan tried every door he passed . . . and found each one locked. And not one muting window.

And then the alley dead-ended in a tiny cul-de-sac.

The glow from a few lighted second- and third-story windows provided scant illumination as Tristan squatted in a corner and considered his two options.

Wait here until Flagge Security either found him or gave up the search.

Or walk out of the alley as someone else.

Could he risk another flux now? Maybe. He'd be weak, but he could probably handle it. The big question was: Should he risk it with unknown templates?

Tristan popped open Eel's wardrobe case and stared at the contents.

He knew the middle one: Lani Rouge. Couldn't use that one. The rest were mysteries.

And one of them was certain death.

Unfortunately Eel had not marked the meltdown template with a skull and crossbones.

What did these damn symbols mean? Switching from Dohan Lee to some strange breed of fighting mime might not get him past Flagge Security scrutiny, but he'd have a better chance of breaking free if they tried to nab him.

But he still ran the risk of choosing the meltdown disk. If he did . . . well, at least then all his troubles would be over.

"My, my . . . what have we here?"

Tristan snapped the case closed and shot to his feet. The voice had come from the mouth of the cul-de-sac. He heard shuffling feet, saw a cluster of indistinct figures silhouetted against the backwash from the street. How many there? He strained to see in the darkness and thought he could make out four or five.

The voice said, "That, er, wouldn't happen to be a template case you're clutching so intimately to your breast?"

"Yes-s-yes!" a second, higher-pitched voice hissed. "He's a mime! I know it!"

Other voices picked up the word.

"A *mime!*"

. . . and it rustled through the group like a gleeful wind through leaves.

"A *mime . . .*"

Sibs . . . only Sibs would be this happy to discover a mime. Happy to have a mime to beat and torture and kill.

"No," Tristan said, fighting to keep his voice calm. "You're wrong. Sorry. I'm no mime. Not me."

Could his luck get any worse? Of all the types he could possibly run into here in the Bascombe district, he wound up cornered by a group of Sibs.

"Not true! He's got a wardrobe case!" the second voice said. "I saw it!"

"Flux for us!" said a third voice. "Do it. We want to see you *flux.*"

Tristan slipped the case into a pocket. "No, really, I'm just like you."

The snickers and laughs that rose from the group sent a chill through his veins.

"Oh, I doubt that very much," the first voice said slowly. "I doubt you're like us at all."

As they began edging forward Tristan braced himself against the wall, poising to spring. No way around them. How about straight through them? Maybe if he attacked first . . .

Running feet down the alley behind the group, and a voice said in a harsh whisper: "Redheads all over the district! They're looking for someone but they won't say why."

"That wouldn't be you, would it, Mr. Mime?" said the first voice. "You wouldn't be a Flagge runaway, would you?"

What to tell them? The tender-loving custody of Flagge Security might be preferable to being torn to pieces by Sibs.

"They're offering a reward," a new voice said.

"A reward!" The first voice laughed. "We wouldn't think of turning him in, no matter what they were offering. Would we, my friends?"

Murmurs of assent from all around Tristan as they moved closer, into the dim light of the cul-de-sac. He could see them now and they weren't Sibs.

Tristan found himself surrounded by figures from his worst nightmares.

CHAPTER 15

The one who'd spoken last had a male voice but his face tapered to a long, golden beak; the arms and legs that protruded from his tunic were covered with feathers; a small set of wings lay folded against his back.

Next to him stood a guy with a green face, grass for hair, and arms that looked like stout vines.

Behind that pair—were they a couple, perhaps?—someone with the head of a bat-eared moth peered at him with multifaceted domes.

Circling at the rear was a woman with the head of a hammerhead shark. Watching her eyes scan all sides of the cul-de-sac at once made Tristan a little queasy.

Weren't hammerheads killers?

But the strangest of them all clung to the shoulder of the birdman. He . . . she . . . *it* looked like the end product of the worst imaginable meltdown. A blob of protoplasm in a thin-skinned sac that revealed its internal organs. The living goo moved by sending out pseudopods and *flowing* along behind. The blob regarded him with its floating pair of eyes.

Tristan watched a sac just beneath the blob's skin fill with air. It decompressed wheezily as the blob spoke to him.

"Are you really a mime?" it said in the hissing voice Tristan remembered from a few moments ago.

Tristan hesitated, more out of habit than anything else. He was an agent. You trusted no one, you told no one.

But they'd seen the wardrobe case. And obviously these were not Imagists or Sibs or anyone with reservations about altering the human form. Still . . . to let those words pass his lips outside the warren.

"You have nothing to fear from us," the birdman chirped.

All right . . . he'd say it.

"Yes. I'm a mime."

He heard appreciative, almost awed murmurs from the group.

"I wish I was a mime," the moth head said. "I'd give *anything* to be a mime."

"Me too," said the shark lady on one of her loops around the cul-de-sac.

Slightly dazed—he'd never heard anyone say that, never dreamed he ever would.

"I saw you sneak in here," the birdman said. "We'd seen the Redheads around, heard they were looking for someone. I figured you might be him."

"All right. You know who I am. But who are you people?"

"We're performers," the moth said. "We have a traveling show and we tour the various freezones. But this is our winter quarters where we hone new material. As a matter of fact we were just dropped off from a show down the street."

Tristan wondered if that standing ovation he'd seen from the theater ventilating shaft had been for these radical splicers.

And he wondered further at the amount of genosplicing and/or nanoforming these people had undergone. He couldn't even guess at the astronomical expense of such radical makeovers.

Could he trust these people, these humans who didn't want to look human? He'd listened to sociologists analyze their kind, some saying the modifications they underwent were rooted in the tattoos, scarifications, and piercings of past ages; he'd heard others say they were thumbing their noses at the Church of the True Shape by declaring the ultimate right to control their bodies; and still others who said they were artists whose canvases and sculpting clay were their bodies.

Was their radicalism more than skin deep? Were they even sane? He'd have to risk it.

"I have to get out of the freezone and into Kaze Glom," he said. "Can you help me?"

The birdman shook his oversized head. "I don't think that's possible. Flagge Security is all over the place."

And Tristan was sure the tube stations would be especially heavily guarded.

"Mute! I *have* to get back to Kaze."

And then he remembered what Mung had told him to try as a last resort, but only as a last resort.

"Have you people ever heard of something called Proteus?"

"We've heard of it," the vegman said slowly. Cautiously?

The birdman said, "Supposedly a mime underground, a collection of runaways."

"Most come from the Arena," the blob wheezed. He perched on the birdman's shoulder like some gooey, shapeless parrot. "You don't want to mess with them."

A mime underground. Did that have something to do with Okasan? And runaways? That made sense. Neither Flagge nor Kaze Security could catch every runaway . . . some slipped through. Where did they go? They had to end up somewhere.

Now Tristan had an answer. *Proteus.*

"You've met these mimes?"

The birdman shook his head. "No. But I've seen their phitti in the Ocean. They have a symbol."

The hammerhead circled closer to the group. "A fist holding the double helix," she said. "It's filamentous."

Yes, Tristan remembered seeing that. But the Ocean was filled with symbols, icons, images. Anyone and everything could have a symbol, an electronic banner, a personal emblem. Until eventually all symbols lost meaning.

Tristan looked at the birdman and he could tell he was holding back something. He looked scared, but scared of what? Scared of Proteus, scared of revealing too much?

He understood. How could they know he wasn't a spy for Flagge, that all this was an elaborate ruse to crack the mime group?

If Proteus was worth cracking—or even a real group.

But if it was, the group might have a way out of the freezone and into Kaze Glom.

And though he certainly wasn't out to spy on Proteus, he couldn't tell anyone what he was carrying back to Kaze. If they knew he was on a mission for one of the gloms they might not want to help him, mime or no mime.

He couldn't risk anything that might hurt his chance for succeeding, not now when he was so close to Selfhood. Sooner or later an outlaw group like Proteus would be crushed by one of the gloms.

But right now they might be his only way out of here.

"I have to contact them."

The moth shook its dome-eyed head. "That won't be easy. We could float a message in the Ocean. Let them know we have someone who may interest them. And then wait and see if they contact you."

"I don't have a lot of time."

"I'm afraid that's all we can do."

"Then please—do it."

The hammerhead glided away. "I'm diving in now," she said. "I'll leave a pic of your masque as well."

Tristan guessed that her sizable head hid an equally impressive HUD.

"Salina will leave a bubble," the vegman said. "And then I suggest you go to Realville and wait."

"Realville?" Tristan said.

"Oh—not good," the birdman said. "If there's one place mimes are in danger, deadly danger, it's Realville."

The hammerhead shrugged her narrow shoulders. "That's where they killed that Sib."

"What Sib?"

"The one who was on the vid this morning, bragging about how he and his goons had chased down and killed those two runaway mimes. They got him," she said with no little satisfaction. "Got him good."

"You don't know that," the birdman said.

"I don't know it," the shark woman said, "but I *know* it. You know?"

Tristan didn't care about a dead Sib. No loss to the jumble in that. He just wanted out of here.

"If Proteus is my only option, I've got to take it."

"I attached the bubble to their icon, just saying one of their kind wants to see them. Told them to reply to 'Hammerhead.' So keep a lookout for a 'Hammerhead' message."

"Will do. And thanks."

These bizarre creations, strange twisted humans far weirder than mimes, had befriended him, a stranger. He didn't understand, but he was glad of it.

They parted, opening a path back to the street.

"Be careful," the birdman said. "Good luck . . . and—"

The blob finished the sentence. "Don't forget us."

"You really think that's possible?" Tristan said, laughing.

Tristan stood at the mouth of the alley and scanned the street. He had to stick with the Dohan Lee masque now—if Proteus responded to Salina's message, they'd be looking for the Lee face. But so would Flagge Security.

But Security floaters weren't quite so numerous as before. Only a few street patrols walked among the freezone residents, cutting a wide path through the nighttime crowds as if they were so much scum floating on a sea.

Maybe Flagge Security was already giving up.

It would be a different story at the tubes, he was sure. The nexus station would be crawling with guards, and every passenger would get scanned.

Tristan said, "Regis—"

A woman with curly brown hair, white blouse, knee-length skirt, and seamed stockings appeared, ready with a pad and pencil.

"You rang?" she said around the wad of gum in her mouth.

He'd forgotten—his PDA was still cycling through avatars.

"Keep an eye on the Ocean for a message addressed to 'Hammerhead.' "

She popped her gum. "Sure thing, boss."

"And see if you can find anything about a murdered Sib."

"You got it."

An instant later the visuals flickered before him.

A Sib indeed had been murdered . . . Tristan recognized him from this morning's vid. A few shots of the body filled the bubble. He'd been hacked to pieces. The naked rage behind the act gave Tristan a shiver. Was this a random act, an argument between some Sibs? the newsface wanted to know. Was there a message in that bloody body?

Tristan knew. He swallowed. Looked like it wasn't such a good thing to get on the wrong side of Proteus.

"Enough," Tristan said, and the bubble vanished. "Mark me a path to Realville, but keep me to the side streets."

The map appeared, and he began following it, a meandering trail, zigzagging through back streets and alleyways.

He was halfway there, walking down the shadowy cavern of one street, when his PDA reappeared: a middle-aged man, goateed, wearing a skullcap and cardinal's robes, floated before him.

"A 'Hammerhead' message has washed up from the Ocean, your Holiness."

Cardinal Richelieu this time—*worse* than dealing with Regis.

"Let's have it."

"It's little more than a directional grid and a directive to mark your forehead with the Sibs symbol."

Bloaty, Tristan thought. I've got to look like one of those plasmids. Was Proteus playing games?

"All right. Load it in. And what's the latest on Realville?"

"Not much, I'm afraid. Apparently it's a very unholy and villainous place. Here—"

The transparent screen that floated before Tristan's eyes now showed a more detailed map, courtesy of Proteus.

"Not a large area. Or a particularly attractive one, your Holiness. Truly, a den of sin. Here are the crime figures."

Numbers filled the screen, each assigned to violent crimes such as murder, aggravated assault, rape.

This place sounds nice, Tristan thought. *Real* nice.

"The Sibs claim it as their own, your Holiness, but it's also friendly to Imagists. Apparently they're all enthusiastic about real experiences."

"Real? Which ones?"

"Oh, anything and everything, apparently—all of it sinful and ungodly. Unfortunately, that very desire makes them reluctant to let much information into the Ocean. I would have to give this place a mortal danger rating of nine-point-two."

At least it wasn't a ten.

The cardinal went on, "If the King's musketeers would get in there and do their duty we wouldn't have—"

"Never mind that. Go to background."

"Done, your Holiness," the cardinal said, and vanished.

Tristan paused along the way and bought a red marker.

When he reached the border of Realville he stopped. While still in the shadows of the buildings on either side, he withdrew the marker and quickly scrawled two curling bolts of red, the symbol for Sibs, on his forehead.

Then, as per the instructions, he walked up to the corner and turned left. But what he saw only made him stop again.

A giant plaza loomed ahead. A massive crowd milled about, some staggering under the weight of drugs, others groping one another, uncaring that a hundred people passed by every minute, watching them have "real" sex. Behind the partying throng, giant glowing signs lit the night with ominous names . . . *Dead to Rights* . . . *Breakout* . . . *The Killing Floor.*

The overhead lights cast a brilliant glow on the crowd.

And next to the strip of bars—whatever they were—stood a place called Funland. Tristan recognized the antique amusement devices. They were called "rides." A rattling train of wheeled cars . . . a *roller coaster* . . . raced up and down a track while the people on the train screamed.

And nearby, a round, barrel-shaped object with no bottom spun. That ride looked as if it might come rolling into the plaza. People clutched handles on the inside wall, pinned by the force of the spinning barrel.

How old were those things? Tristan wondered. If they were real antiques they might be centuries old.

Old. Rusty. Ready to break apart and kill someone.

How'd that be for some real excitement?

Screams from the right attracted Tristan's attention. A tight circle of people yelled, the bloodthirsty din brutal. Tristan couldn't see . . . but he guessed that something nasty was happening to whatever poor soul was trapped in the center of that circle.

A woman bumped into Tristan.

"Hey sailor," she said.

Tristan was confused. "I'm not—"

The woman laughed. Her golden hair looked artificial, her lips much too red, and her strong perfume probably masked other less pleasant odors.

A streetwalker. Bloaty. A "real" streetwalker, but there wasn't much on her that was real.

"Not a sailor?" She came close and toyed with the smooth material of Eel's smartsuit. "Hmm, you're a big one. I bet you like things"—she leaned close, the musky perfume almost overwhelming—"rough.

Hmm, do you?" She shot a glance down the dark street that Tristan had come from. "We could go down there. Nice and private."

Tristan shook his head. "No. Not now." He saw the woman frown. "Maybe . . . later."

The streetwalker shrugged and walked away. "Later" was not in her vocabulary.

That was fine. He had to keep going, cutting through the sea of people, some *really* stoned, some *really* screwing, some *really* eating, some *really* beating one another. He moved through the sea of Sibs and Imagists and human freaks desperate for a real sensation, any sensation, even a bad one. No VR allowed here, only reality . . . more reality than anyone could ever want.

Tristan stepped over a few bodies on the ground. Sleeping, knocked out? Dead? Who could tell? And who cared?

He laboriously made his way to the center of the plaza where the multicolored bands flaring from the bright lights painted the street and walls.

What the hell is this? he wondered, looking at Break Out's blank front. What kind of fun and games go on here? NOK? Or more exotic pursuits? Tristan had heard about other entertainment . . . indoor mazes where you could hunt dangerous, genetically altered animals—at your own risk.

A man stumbled into him and quickly locked his hands on Tristan's shoulders.

"Hey! Kill 'em."

Tristan tried to back away gently from the man but he held on tight.

"Kill 'em? Right?" The man's speech was slurred.

"Kill who?" Tristan said, hoping that few words of conversation would make him go away.

The man shook his head as if befuddled by Tristan's ignorance. Then he jabbed at the smeary symbol on Tristan's forehead.

"Right! The copycats, the damn copycats! Kill them all, right?"

Tristan nodded and found a smile. "Right, friend. Kill the mimes—every muting one of them."

The man released Tristan and staggered away to accost his next victim.

Tristan walked past the first place, "The Killing Floor." A smaller sign proclaimed it "the freezone's greatest hunting bar—three challenging levels of natural trails and caves, with over *twenty* dangerous species to hunt!" Its siding was a glossy coat of living fur, just to get the hunters in the mood. Tristan brushed the giant pelt, the fur warm and coarse.

Still walking, Tristan hit the corner, another alleyway.

He checked the map on his Roam Grid. Just a few steps down this alleyway and he would be there. Just far enough to put himself in the darkness, away from the circus outside.

Where he'd stand . . . and wait.

Tristan watched the crowd milling outside the alley, some drifting into The Killing Floor, or Dead to Rights, others aimlessly wandering the plaza. The area seemed like a giant cell about to burst, spreading its human virus through the freezone.

He watched fights break out, and couples of every description drifted his way, a few seeking the darkness for their quick sex games. The violent animal-like rutting was at once repellent and . . . exciting.

These people were living as though this was the last day of Planet Earth.

Maybe they know something I don't, he thought.

He waited but nobody from Proteus approached him.

Eventually he began to think: *There is no Proteus.* Mute, it's a setup. Sibs will probably come for me and beam a laser probe into the base of my skull and leave me a vegetable.

Tristan took a breath.

Nervous, anxious . . . scared. Whatever he was feeling it was getting creepy out here, surrounded by so much raw emotion.

He couldn't wait much longer, not with this stolen treasure stuck to him. If this didn't pan out he'd have to try and find another way back to Kaze.

He heard a sound. A faint click just behind him. He started to turn when something smooth and black slipped over his head and adhered to his face. He felt it fit itself around his ears and mouth, leaving them open. A smartmask, but his eyes remained covered.

A voice whispered in his ear.

"Don't move, *mime*. Don't say a damn thing. Don't do anything unless we tell you. Understand?"

"But I can't see."

A blunt instrument delivered a painful jab at the base of his neck.

"Did you forget? Say *nothing*. And as for not seeing, that's the way we want it."

Then hands dragged him to his right, away from the plaza, deeper into the alleyway.

Someone pushed down on his head and guided him into a seat. A ground speeder, Tristan thought. He felt bodies pressing against him on either side, heard doors slide shut, and then the speeder began moving.

No one said anything now. Tristan held back the questions exploding within him.

The speeder accelerated, taking turns in dizzying succession.

Taking me to Proteus? he wondered. To the underground? Or somewhere else?"

He thought of activating his PDA. His Roam Grid would show exactly where in the freezone they were taking him—but he was also sure his companions would know if he did.

And they might kill me for that.

So he sat quietly.

CHAPTER 16

Lani slumped in the chair and stared at the blank vid chamber. Her apartment seemed eerily quiet. She was alone . . . her usual state since Trev's death. She turned away from the chamber, fighting the urge to turn it on.

She looked at the clutter in her apartment, the unopened boxes stacked neatly by the door, the shelves filled with statues that glowed and moved when she neared them, and small clear stones that grew warm and produced a low soothing tone when touched.

All these *things,* she thought. As long as I keep working as a datameister I'll continue to buy . . . things.

She turned back to the vid chamber.

She said the word softly, halfheartedly.

"On."

A bubble flashed to life with a swirling 3-D display of fireworks. A man's voice, deep, generic, whispered: "Welcome, Lani." The display ended abruptly, shifting to her default channel: FGN . . . Flagge Glom News.

And suddenly the chamber filled with red floaters soaring through the canyons of the glom in hot pursuit of someone in a speeder. She leaned closer to the bubble while the announcer dispassionately commented.

And Flagge Security reports that earlier today a terrorist was pursued into the freezone. The stolen floater was destroyed by a crack squad of Security Commandos, but the criminal remains at large.

The bubble turned white with a brilliant flash.

"Tristan?" she said. She shook her head. He hadn't made it to Kaze. Was he hiding now? Running for his life? Or already dead?

While the vid bubble replayed the explosion, Lani thought of Tristan, seeing him as Trev, as if Trev had never died.

But Trev *is* dead, she told herself. The mime simply wore his masque like a costume, like a smartsuit.

And yet, sitting here, surrounded by all the things in her apartment, things that meant—she knew—absolutely nothing to her, she couldn't stop thinking about him.

She looked at the vid bubble, thinking: I shouldn't do this. I really shouldn't—

She said the word before she could change her mind.

"Archives." Then quickly: "Trev."

And instantly he was *there,* smiling at her, looking almost as real as the mime who'd come here wearing his body.

Trev held up a hand.

"C'mon, Lani—put the cam down. We're not capturing me for posterity. Give it here."

Lani heard her own laugh. "Not yet. Just be patient."

She realized she hadn't laughed like that in such a long time. Trev could make her laugh. No mime could ever do that.

In the vid chamber Trev reached forward. "Here, give me that." And then he took the holocam from her hand. The image of the apartment spun with the change of operator and now the camera was trained on Lani.

The image froze. A voice asked: "Would you like to continue with the vid?"

She knew what came next. She should really stop. Really.

"Continue."

And now the camera came close to her laughing face. And she saw Trev's hand reach out and touch her cheek.

"You're beautiful," he said.

Closer, and the camera was right on her because Trev had come so close.

No, she thought. No more.

"Stop."

The vid froze. Then, "Off."

Too blurry, watching this through her tears.

She walked over to the shelves that groaned under the weight of her interactive knickknacks.

Got to stop crying, she told herself. She was past this—at least she'd thought she was.

She reached up to one shelf, to touch something, anything. Then abruptly she smashed both her fists down on the shelf.

A dozen different toys bounced into the air. She banged down again and then swept her arm across the shelf in front of her, sending the items flying to the floor.

She had been past the pain. It was over.

Until Tristan showed up.

Another attack on the shelves and more "collectible" junk went tumbling to the floor, and again until she dropped to her knees.

Through her tears she was vaguely aware of the small army of moppets scurrying about her like hyper kittens, sweeping up the debris, disposing of the broken items, and stacking the undamaged ones in neat piles along the wall.

"Damn!" The word burst through a sob. "I can't even make a mess when I want to!"

She curled up on the carpet and cried . . . but when crying was finally over, she had an idea.

Tristan was still alive—and free. Had to be. Otherwise Security would be trumpeting his capture or death. He was out there somewhere.

She clasped her hands, feeling how cold they were, chilled by what she was thinking.

This mime had made Trev come back to life.

And . . . and if he could do that once, he could do it again.

Trev was back there. Inside the warehouse.

She touched the glass.

The mime had left his wardrobe *there*.

And what was her idea? To venture out and recover the little disk with Trev's genetic information? And then what? Find Tristan if he was alive and beg him to—*please*—become Trev again?

But to do that she'd have to find this woman Tristan had talked about, Okasan.

She shook her head. It was crazy. Pathetic, in a way. She had everything she needed right here, anything she wanted. She looked at her apartment filled with all the things she bought, and then realized—I'm not leaving *anything* here.

She strode to one of her shelves, grabbed a palm flash—she owned three different models—and stepped into the hall. She hurried toward the down chute but slowed as she heard voices echoing from within.

". . . thought nothing would surprise me anymore. I mean, after ten years in Security, I figure I've seen everything, but a mime gladiator, living right here in the middle of all these realfolk—"

"Eel, no less! Have you seen him fight? A mutin' animal!"

"Yeah. Won a pile once betting on him, but that doesn't mean I want to live next door to him."

"But was he mad! Too bad we can't find that mime agent and put him in the Arena with Eel. Be something to see, yeah?"

As the voices faded, Lani turned and rushed back to her apartment.

Security—and they'd already been to Eel's apartment. They must have awakened him.

She huddled in her lounger, trembling, expecting red-helmeted figures to burst through the door at any moment. Any moment.

Finally she stumbled to her window and checked the street. Far below she could see the Security men loading into their cruisers. When the last one was aboard they roared off.

Why weren't they coming for her? Eel must have told them about her.

This didn't make sense, but she wasn't going to waste the opportunity. She was getting out of this building.

What am I doing here? Lani wondered as she negotiated a dark alley behind the warehouse where she had been held prisoner.

She moved carefully, directing the beam from her palm flash ahead of her, feeling more frightened with every step, until she turned a corner and reached the side door to the warehouse. No scancam here. She had expected the door to be locked but the tendrils unraveled at a touch. It obviously wasn't much of a real warehouse to begin with.

She felt strangely cold and tired as she moved silently toward the rear of the warehouse. She'd been a captive here . . . they'd planned to kill her after copying her genotype. If Tristan hadn't stopped them . . .

A deeper chill racked her as she saw the chair that she had been tied to. She approached it, afraid to come too near, as if it might reach out and grab her. She turned and put her back to it, trying to orient herself.

She'd been sitting here, facing this way . . . Tristan had scraped the inside of her mouth and gone over . . . there.

She followed what she imagined to be Tristan's path and found a little alcove among the crates. He could have fluxed here . . . and then her light flashed off an empty nutrient packet. Yes! Here. He'd been here.

She dropped to her knees, directing her beam into the spaces between the crates. Nothing . . . nothing . . . and then another glint. A silvery discoid case, very similar to the one Tristan had stolen from Eel, wedged into a corner.

Lani felt her heart pound with excitement. It was still *here*. The discarded wardrobe. Trev. He was *in* that case.

Gingerly she reached out and pulled it free.

So strange the way she felt holding this thing that could bring Trev back to life. She held the case close against her, then looked around.

She suddenly felt as if she was being watched. The hairs on the back of her neck went rigid and tiny pinpricks of gooseflesh sprouted on her arms. She stood, struggling to control her breathing, but she saw no one, heard no movement. She was alone in the warehouse.

She released the breath she'd been holding.

All right. She had the disc. Now for the rest of her insane plan.

First she had to find Tristan . . . if he was alive. Assuming he was, he'd be either back in Kaze, or with Okasan. She couldn't go to Kaze, so she'd have to try for Okasan. To do that . . . she had to get into the freezone. But datameisters weren't allowed out of the glom. She'd be picked up by the scanners the instant she tried to pass the checkpoint before the freezone.

But she'd heard a rumor about a way to bypass the checkpoints. She hoped it was true, because it was the only way she'd ever get into the freezone.

Flagge Glom felt different now that she was planning to leave it.

In her mind every Security guard was scrutinizing her as she walked past them. She looked away, feeling her plan was too visible, written on her face.

The guards' scanners could tell them so much if they turned them her way: her name, where she lived . . . that she was a datameister— and a fugitive, perhaps?

Would they wonder what she was doing here as she edged closer to the northern districts of the glom? Here the shining steeples of the Glom Center gave way to the squat SynFood factories and repurposing facilities, mile-long buildings that took every bit of metal, stone, plastic, and organic waste and reconstituted them into raw material for other factories to use, over and over again . . . nothing ever wasted, nothing ever lost.

Shifts were changing and she watched the gray army of shufflers who marched in and out of the windowless buildings, working for a paltry amount of credits. Seeing them made her think about her own life. Her work wasn't very hard and she had more than enough credits.

Lani kept walking. She'd got off the last tube before the freezone checkpoint, just before the scanners would pick her up. As she kept walking the crowd of workers thinned out until she walked behind two men, one older, the other younger. Maybe his son? she wondered. What was their life like in the great Flagge Glom? They'd get all the vids, of course. And they probably got some limited access to the Ocean.

But most likely reality took up most of their time.

She quickened her pace. Her smartsuit rustled and she was aware of how much she stood out.

Close to them now and—

"Hello."

They didn't stop. They probably thought she was talking to someone else.

"Hello, please—"

The younger man stopped and turned to her but his father kept trudging on, probably heading to one of the residence towers that ringed this industrial quarter.

"Please," she said, trying not to sound too pathetic. "Please—I need some help."

And now the older man stopped. He turned to her and waited while she caught up to them. He didn't say a word. She looked from the older man to the younger and saw a family resemblance.

She came closer and spoke softly. "I need help."

The man rubbed his chin. "There's a station with Flagge Security, about—"

She shook her head. "No. I need to get to the freezone."

Now the younger man spoke. "There's a tube back near the factory. You can—"

But the old man raised his hand. He could see that it wasn't a tube station she was looking for.

"What do you want?" he said slowly, cautiously.

"I need a way into the freezone. I've heard—" She paused. "I heard that sometimes the workers have ways in . . . and ways out. To sneak goods—"

The older man's eyes narrowed. "You mean smuggling?"

Yes. Smuggling. And guards receiving regular payments to look the other way.

"I—"

"Avoiding taxes is against the law. The same as stealing from the glom. We don't *steal* from Flagge. And you best get out of here. It's not safe."

He started to turn away and Lani reached out and grabbed his shoulder.

"No. I don't want to steal. But I can't leave the glom. I work for Flagge—" He wouldn't understand what a datameister was. "I'm not allowed. And there's someone in the freezone waiting for me."

A lie. But somehow it felt true.

The man hesitated. He had nothing to gain from helping her. Lani took out her card. "I can give you some credits."

The man laughed. "And have them tracked by Flagge?"

There was nothing else for her to do. She begged.

"Please. If there's a way . . ."

The younger man looked at his father, and Lani saw that they knew a way into the freezone, a breach in one of the walls, or perhaps a tunnel.

The older man hesitated. He looked in her eyes and somehow he must have known that Lani couldn't have been with Flagge Security.

He turned to his son.

"You can take her to the entrance. But"—he poked the younger man's chest for emphasis—"don't go into the freezone with her. Just to the entrance." Now he turned to Lani. "After that—you're on your own."

She nodded. Then—impulsively—she took his hand. The man's hand felt rough, battered, and etched by real work when hardly anyone touched anything real anymore. "Thank you."

He didn't smile at her. "If you're caught, you know nothing, you say nothing . . . and as for us, we've never seen you in our lives."

She nodded. Why was he helping her? Was he part of some underground in the glom, some worker rebellion doing what it could to weaken the all-powerful Flagge Glom?

"C'mon," the son said to her. "We should get going. It's not far."

Lani released the older man's hand and followed.

The freezone lay ahead, and Okasan and Tristan . . . and Trev.

CHAPTER 17

After what seemed like an hour but was probably half that, the speeder stopped. From the number of twists and turns, Tristan guessed that they'd doubled and tripled back, guaranteeing that he'd never be able to retrace the path. No one had said a word during the trip.

The sound of doors popping open. And a *smell*. A stench. Food gone bad. Garbage.

"Get out," the voice said as hands grabbed Tristan's shoulder and guided him to the pavement. The stench was stronger out here. Tristan hadn't eaten in hours—now he couldn't imagine sucking on nutrient for a while.

They wasted no time moving him to the next stop of his tour. He walked/stumbled his way on the pavement, his feet catching holes in the ground, bumbling into debris, tripping, saved only by the hands holding him. Then they stopped.

Tristan heard metal scraping against metal. The sound of something heavy, scratching, screeching in protest against being moved. Then he heard a *thunk* as it was released.

A new smell. This one worse . . . moist . . . the smell of fresh blood.

If this wasn't Proteus . . .

If this *wasn't* a mime underground . . .

Tristan's mind balked at imagining what awaited him at the end of this little trip.

Closer to the smell.

The voice again. "You're going to climb down, *mime*. Handrails on both sides. Take it slow. No one will be holding you, you hear?" The voice rattled Tristan's shoulder roughly. "But one of us will be right above and right below you. You understand?"

Tristan almost spoke.

He nodded.

He'd like a chance to try out one of Eel's gladiator templates against Mr. Voice, a chance to face Mr. Don't-Say-Anything.

Rattle *his* shoulder a bit. Pinch *his* neck.

Tristan doubted such a moment would come.

"Okay—down you go . . . *mime*."

The voice said that last word as though he didn't believe it, and one of the others in the party—three or four here, Tristan figured—snickered.

Someone took Tristan's foot and guided it to the first rung of the ladder. Then step by step he slowly started down, until his hands could grab the rails.

The damp, dead smell oozed through his mask.

"Who's bringing the sacrifice?" the voice said.

Tristan heard confused muttering.

"Look," the voice said. "I don't care which one of you does it, but somebody bring the damn sacrifice or one of *you* gets strung up down there."

Maybe he'd have been better off risking Flagge Security at the tubes.

The descent went slowly. Once, someone above Tristan stepped on his head. An accident? Tristan couldn't tell, he just felt a heavy boot clunk him. No one said sorry.

Finally Tristan's shoe hit pavement.

"That's it," the voice said. "That's the bottom. Come on."

He was nudged forward, stepping into ankle-deep puddles. Tristan could feel the oily water clinging to the material of his smartsuit. He banged into walls and pillars, surely covering Dohan Lee's body with a nice arrangement of bruises.

But he managed to keep his feet until his toe caught on something and he went down. He landed elbow deep in a slimy puddle, splashing his mask. A bit of the liquid reached his lips, and he could taste it.

Tristan started coughing.

"Get up," Mr. Voice said. "Get up now."

Tristan nodded, and eased himself up.

Then—another voice: "You've got to take his mask off, Callin."

"I don't know."

Mr. Voice—Callin.

Then another voice, raspy, guttural: "We can't watch him, can't guide him . . . not below. Let him see."

Hesitation from the leader of this gang.

Yes, Tristan thought. Take the damn mask off and let me get a good look at you nice fellows. And maybe some day I'll get the chance to bash you from stone wall to stone pillar.

I'll enjoy that.

"Not fair to keep him blind, no matter who he is," the second voice said. "I mean, considering what we might run into."

Tristan stiffened. What did *that* mean?

"Mute," Callin said.

The mask whipped off.

Tristan almost said thanks but remembered Mr. Voice's—Callin's—injunction.

He looked around. He stood in a cave, a large opening with smaller tunnels running in three, maybe four directions. Hard to tell, since the only lights were the small laser torches that each of his four captors held. And though they were in silhouette, almost as black and dark as the cave itself, Tristan noted one other thing.

Each of his captors was imposing in his own way. Tristan couldn't see much more than their outlines, but the massive, shadowy forms were formidable enough. Most of them were probably escapees from the Arena. Maybe some had crawled their way out of the subterranean developments, the deep earth mines or the cavernous fungal farms.

They all looked as if they had fought their way out of hell—and we're still fighting.

One of them had something slung over his shoulder . . . something man-sized.

Now Mr. Voice came close, and the glow from his torch revealed a face that went with the attitude.

The one they called Callin had a large head marked by little bubbles of flesh and muscle that protruded at unsightly angles.

Tristan recognized the syndrome.

Too many fast fluxes and things don't always snap back to normal. Chunks of old fluxes remain as bits of distended flesh and muscle.

A face that only the mother Callin never had could love.

"Listen, *mime*—"

More snickers from the troupe.

"I'm going to tell you what's ahead, where we're going. You best listen . . . because if you don't, you won't finish this trip alive. Got it?"

Tristan nodded. Yeah, Callin obviously had had countless battles in the Arena. And somehow he'd escaped . . . to this hell hole. Some trade-off.

"But first take a good look around."

Tristan did just that. What the hell was this place? And that smell? Beyond the dampness the stale odor of trapped air, tinged with . . . what?

"Welcome," Callin said, "to one of the marvels of the Twentieth Century. This used to be the way people got around, back in what were called cities."

Tristan nodded. Sure, he knew what this was. He had seen the vids, the parents clutching the children, and men dressed in strange costumes with colorful material dangling from their necks. Ties . . . men wearing ties and getting on—

"Subways, they were called. Trains that ran underground. Under the city."

"And they left these tunnels here?"

Callin laughed. "They became abandoned holes in the ground. What would you expect them to do?"

"Callin—we best keep moving."

Tristan looked at Callin's face as a cloud of anxiety crossed it. This massive Arena gladiator was worried about something.

"Right. Come on."

Callin grabbed Tristan and yanked him forward, guiding him down one of the smaller tunnels. The black walls sucked up the light from their torches. They stepped over small pools of oily water and into other puddles hidden on the shadowy floor.

They splashed along until—

"Wait!" Callin stopped.

One of the others said, "Do you hear something?"

"Quiet. I'm trying to—"

Callin craned his head left and right. Tristan couldn't hear a thing. What could be the problem inside a deserted tunnel under the free-zone?

Callin shook his head and turned to the others.

"Good a place as any to leave the sacrifice. Hang it up." The beam from his torch flashed around until it picked out a sturdy-looking support jutting from under a pipe. "There."

Three other beams focused on the spot and Tristan got his first look at the "sacrifice."

A Flagge Security man. As the corpse was lifted and hung from the pipe support by the back of its jacket, Tristan saw that the entire front of the Flagge uniform was dark with clotted blood.

He had a pretty good idea of the answer but asked anyway.

"What happened to him?"

"Strayed from his friends and somehow managed to get his throat cut," Callin said. "What you call being in the wrong place—near us—at the wrong time—when we needed a sacrifice."

"Sacrifice to what? Is this a religious thing or—?"

That broke them up. Their peals of laughter echoed off the walls.

"You're a regular Joey José, mime!" one of them said.

Finally they were ready to move again. Callin turned to Tristan.

"Stay close and walk fast. We don't dawdle down here."

Tristan nodded, and now they were nearly jogging through the tunnel that stretched into an even deeper blackness beyond. If this led to the headquarters of Proteus—assuming there *was* a Proteus—then they'd picked a good place to hide. Even glom security would think twice—three times—before entering this stench hole.

Their steps echoed in the tunnel, punctuated by splashes. Tristan wished someone would say something. But apparently they had to keep silent for some reason.

Why?

More steps, and ahead on the left, another black opening appeared. Callin led the group in that direction . . . and the puddles grew deeper. Though the footwear connected to his smartsuit was completely water-resistant, Tristan could feel the water rising past his ankles.

"Getting there," Callin said, breaking the silence. "Just a few—"

Skre-e-ek!

The earsplitting shriek erupted from behind Tristan. As he turned to look he saw one of Callin's mimes go down . . . with something attached to his back.

"Mute! It's one of them!"

They spun, torches tracing wild arcs on the walls of the tunnel. Tristan spotted dozens of little caves and caverns dotting the rough surface.

Somebody—something—had made those caves.

Callin had his pulser out, as did the others. Tristan stood there empty-handed, feeling defenseless.

Callin ran back to his partner on the tunnel floor . . . wrestling with something.

"Stop moving!" Callin said. "Stay the hell still!"

Then the tunnel was lit by the incandescent blast from his pulsar and another shriek echoed in the tunnel.

The thing rolled off the mime.

The wounded mime stood up, and Callin's torch showed the damage, a big chunk torn out of his upper arm.

"Damn thing ripped me! I thought we had a deal!"

"We do," Callin said. "Or we did." He jammed his pulsar under his arm and cupped his hands around his mouth. "We left a sacrifice!" he shouted. "It's back there. A *sa-cri-fice*—understand?"

Callin nodded. "We have to move faster. Others will hear this, smell it."

Callin's torch beam caught the creature on the floor. At first glance it looked like an animal, a lightly furred creature, about the size of a ten-year-old child, with an elongated head and a ratlike jaw. But then the creature's eyes and teeth—yellow-brown things—caught the light.

Callin let the light linger there a moment longer.

And Tristan knew that it wasn't an animal.

"Mutin' Dwellers," Callin said. "Let's move."

Tristan got into line behind Callin. The injured mime was right behind him, his open wound glistening.

"What are they?" Tristan asked.

"They're Dwellers. Once they were people, years ago, decades ago, living down here in this darkness, feeding off what was discarded above. Somehow they got hold of the wrong garbage. They didn't know they were eating failed experiments, ingesting test viruses that altered their chromosomes. They ate, they mutated, until they became this . . . *species*."

"They're like rats," Tristan said, "human rats."

"And they'll eat anything. Which is why we come this way when we want to make sure we won't be followed."

Tristan looked around at the walls, eyeing the small openings in the side, looking for pairs of glistening eyes looking back.

"But you mentioned a deal."

"We have an . . . arrangement. If we 'sacrifice' a member of our party—kill him and leave him at the intersection back there, where they can feed without a fuss, they let us pass—our 'toll,' you might say."

"But you don't—"

"Of course not. We reduce a glom's security force by one and leave him or her."

"Then why did that one attack?"

"I don't know. Their leaders—and I guess they get that way because they're the toughest and smartest—seem fairly reliable. But some of their underlings are little more than a collection of instincts."

"Then why are we hurrying?"

"Because we've got a fresh wound among us, and the smell of blood could send these Dwellers into a feeding frenzy."

Tristan tripped and stumbled, plunging into another oily pool and the water splashed onto his face. He scrambled to his feet and wiped it away.

"Almost there," Callin said. "And then we'll see what your story is, *mime*."

Tristan nodded. His primary worry wasn't these mimes anymore. He was tempted to contact his PDA, just to see a familiar face in all this gloom. *Almost there,* he told himself, feeling more scared than when he was in the heart of Flagge Glom. Almost there . . .

Shre-e-ek!

Something heavy slammed against Tristan's shoulder. He felt thin arms wrap around his neck, tough fingers and talonlike nails dig into his neck, and then rip. Sharp teeth started gnawing at his scalp as though it were a piece of tough-skinned fruit.

He reached up and grabbed skin, clothes—he couldn't tell—and tried to pry the Dweller off, but it was attached to him like a Siamese twin. No matter what he did he couldn't dislodge it.

Then he felt the talons being yanked from his neck, just in time. Only the creature's legs were still wrapped around Tristan.

He turned to see Callin jam his pulsar into the Dweller's mouth and fire. The head disappeared in a crimson cloud and another foul odor was added to the mélange.

Skre-e-ek! Skre-e-ek! Skre-e-ek!

The attack on Tristan seemed to have burst an invisible dam. Suddenly Dwellers were everywhere, pouring from the holes to the side, and then—more horribly—from right above them.

Tristan turned and saw the mimes gathered into a tight group against one of the walls, pulsars out, trying to pick off the Dwellers as they came close. And farther back in the darkness hundreds of eyes reflecting the pulsar flashes.

"The deal, dammit!" Callin was shouting. "We have a deal!"

Tristan splashed to the mime group and shouldered into their tight circle. Callin slid a weapon into his hands.

"Hope you can use this, mime. Aim for the bigger ones if you see them. They're the leaders. Kill enough of them and the others will back away. Otherwise we haven't got a chance."

Tristan looked at the glowing eyes encircling them, moving left and right, edging in and backing away, and tried to make out the size of their owners. He couldn't.

"It's the little ones doing all the attacking," one of the mimes said. "They've gone crazy!"

"We're dead," said another.

"The sacrifice!" Callin shouted, pointing back the way they'd come. "It's back there! Fresh meat! Back *there*!"

And from farther back in the tunnel came another screech, deeper, louder, and even more frenzied than the ones from this crew.

Suddenly the milling circle of eyes froze, but only for an instant. And then with a hellish chorus of shrieks they all turned and raced down the tunnel.

"Thank the Helix," Callin said. "One of the leaders found the sacrifice."

Tristan felt the gun being lifted from his hand.

"Thanks," he said to Callin.

"Just doing my job, mime. Getting you there safe. What're you called?"

Tristan thought about giving his name. Why not?

"Tristan."

"That's a strange one." He turned to the others. "Let's get out of here before they change what little minds they have."

Stepping over the bodies of the dead Dwellers they resumed their trek into the darkness.

"Don't relax yet, Tristan," Callin told him. "The tough part for you is still ahead."

CHAPTER 18

Tristan looked around this great room with its ceiling arching so high, somehow—it seemed familiar. He stood in the center of the room surrounded by more mimes than he'd ever seen in one place.

And what mimes! Nearly all of them were massive. If they were runaways, they *must* have all come from the Arena. Most bore the telltale signs of too many fluxes, with distended bits of flesh and bone that didn't quite make the transition from one phenotype to another. One mime sported crocodilelike fangs that he kept licking as he eyed Tristan with something that looked hungrier than mere suspicion.

Tristan looked away.

He didn't need any enemies. And just as he was feeling comfortable with Callin and his crew, they'd vanished after depositing Tristan here. He was told to wait. And as he did the mimes of Proteus—forty, fifty of them—came close and stared.

Tristan spotted weapons. One corner of this great room was filled with open crates of stunners, pulse rifles, and compact laser cannons. A considerable arsenal, and if the mimes here knew how to use them, they could be a mighty army.

Of course the firepower of the gloms was far more immense. Still it showed that these mimes were serious.

Tristan heard voices from a far end of the room. The crowd cleared a path and Tristan saw Callin following another mime, as big as the rest, with a leonine mane and clear blue eyes, but without the stigmata of too many fluxes.

This new mime walked up to Tristan while Callin and the others stayed to the back. He turned to the room, raised a first, and yelled, "Proteus!"

The mimes responded with raised fists, hurling the word back: "Proteus!"

So there is a Proteus.

That was some comfort . . .

This was obviously the leader, and now he turned back to Tristan. "I'm Krek."

Tristan nodded. "I'm Tristan. And this is Proteus?"

"One cell. Merely one cell in a creature that grows stronger every day. But before we proceed any further, let us see . . ." Krek took a step closer to Tristan.

"See? See what?"

Krek smiled. "Your 'face, of course. You say you're a mime. We'll prove that before we go any further."

Krek reached toward Tristan and pulled open the fastener of his smartsuit. He studied Tristan's exposed midsection.

This was a violation, a deliberate insult in front of his runaway mimes. No mime ever let anyone examine his interface. Tristan wondered whether it was a test, to see how he'd respond.

Krek reached toward the slit.

"No," Tristan said.

Krek looked at him. "What's that you said?"

"I said . . . no." And now Tristan grabbed Krek's hands. They were massive, the fingers like steel claws. If Tristan fought him it would be no match.

Still, Tristan held tight.

"*I'll* show it to you. But no one"—and here Tristan raised his voice—"*no one* invades my pouch."

Then came the terrible hesitation. Everyone became very quiet. If this test was scripted, the audience didn't seem to know who had the next line . . . if there were any more lines.

Tristan began to feel that he'd made an error. He shouldn't have challenged the leader, certainly not in front of his motley crew.

But then Krek smiled, a great big grin, and he roughly cuffed Tristan on the chin.

"We wanted to see how much the gloms owned your soul, mime. Good to see you can still stand up for yourself . . . in such a friendly environment."

The assembled mimes laughed.

Tristan nodded.

"Now—your 'face," Krek said, with a gesture.

Tristan ran a finger along the slit, parting the flaps of skin to expose his interface, the key to who or what he was. Krek made a show of leaning down and examining it.

"Want a laser torch?" Tristan said.

Krek laughed. Then turning to the rebel mimes, "He's a brother."

Good, thought Tristan. Now will you help me get the hell out of here?

"On to business then, brother. You contacted us—"

"Because I'm being hunted."

"The Flaggers?"

"Yes. They're all over the tubes. There's no way I can get back to Kaze Glom."

"Kaze?" Krek spit on the ground. "Even worse than Flagge. Mute, what the hell were you doing for the kindhearted mutagens of Kaze in Flagge Glom?"

This wasn't going the way Tristan had hoped. He thought he might get some quick help. Instead he was being interrogated.

"They wanted me to steal something."

Krek leaned close, obviously very interested in every little detail of the story.

"Steal what?"

"I can't say."

"Yes, you can. We're all brothers here."

It was all Tristan could do to keep from laughing in his face. Brothers? What romantic garbage was this?

He said, "You mean, as in, we all came from the same mother?"

"No, Tristan. I mean *brother*—in every sense: in our cells, where each of us carries the Goleman chromosome, and in our lives of slavery. The gloms have raised us to look at our brother mimes as rivals, competitors. They've fostered that since deincubation, and with good reason. The last thing they want is any sense of solidarity between mimes. Keep us at odds, teach us to kill each other for sport, make us do tricks for the treats they dispense, do *anything* to curry their favor. And above all don't let us get close, because then we might realize what we share. We might come to think of ourselves as related, as part of a . . . *family*."

Family? Tristan throught. Who needs family? An antiquated concept. Even realfolk don't have much sense of family. And besides, he sure as hell wouldn't want to be connected with a mime "family" once he'd achieved Selfhood.

"So tell us, brother," Krek said. "What did Kaze want you to steal?"

Tristan hadn't thought ahead to prepare a convincing lie. But maybe he could risk revealing *some* truth. Tell him what Flagge undoubtedly knew already, but keep the writable template secret. Lani knew about that . . . but he hoped that she hadn't told anyone, at least not yet. If he told Krek about the writable, and Krek told his people . . . then it could get back to Flagge.

"Kaze acquired a special template. It got me through the Citadel's Security."

"The Citadel?" Krek's eyes narrowed. "Sounds . . . tricky. Some of us, those who fought in the Flagge Arena, might even say it sounds impossible." Krek sniffed the air.

Smelling something fishy . . . ?

"If that isn't what I did, then why are the Flagge redheads crawling all over the freezone looking for me?"

Krek nodded. He's unconvinced, Tristan felt.

And mute! I'm no closer to getting home than I was hiding in that alley with those splicers.

"So then—where is this thing that you stole?"

Tristan laughed. "I didn't get it. Didn't even get close to it. As soon as I got into the Citadel something I did triggered Flagge Security. I was lucky to get out."

"So you failed?"

"And it means I won't get Selfhood. Not yet."

Krek laughed, a booming sound picked up by the others. Tristan looked around. He needed Krek to believe him. Why was he laughing?

"Selfhood? Don't tell me that you actually believe that the gloms ever let a mime go." Krek could barely contain himself. He took a breath. Tristan felt shaken by their . . . ridicule.

Then the mime leader's smile faded. "What if . . . what if what you say isn't true. What if you were sent by Flagge?"

"Sent? Why?"

Krek moved closer, his face only centimeters away. Tristan smelled the mime's breath.

"Sent to find *us*, to bring Flagge Security here, maybe to penetrate Proteus. They'd *love* to destroy us."

"No. All I want is to get out, get back to Kaze."

"To do more slave work for a glom? Why should we help you help them? They're the enemy, brother. We're your family. Time to choose, Tristan."

This wasn't going well at all.

Tristan tried to think of a cogent argument to steer Krek toward helping him back to Kaze. Problem was, he couldn't come up with one. He wished he'd known about Proteus and all this "family" nonsense in advance.

Family . . . maybe he could play on that.

"You could simply help me. One mime brother to another."

And then someone new entered the room—a portly, colorful figure.

"Krek! I heard there's a mime named Tristan here. Where is he?"

Mung. He'd steered him to Proteus. Maybe he could get him out.

"Yes, Mung," Tristan said. "It's me. I'm here."

Somewhere in this dungeon, this warren of tunnels and caves, they took Tristan to an empty room, and now he sat with Krek and Mung . . . and Mung's saur, who sat beside its master as if awaiting a command.

Tristan looked around. This room was probably a storage area at sometime, but whatever had been kept here had been pillaged ages ago.

Mung turned to him. "Tristan, where did you get this masque you're wearing?"

"Flagge Glom," Tristan said. He had to be very careful here.

"So you were successful?"

"No. My cover was blown as soon as I reached the Datacenter. I didn't even get to see the cat's eye, let alone steal a sample from it."

Mung looked disappointed, then grinned. "But I'm sure you were going to bring the sample to Okasan, had you acquired it."

Tristan returned the smile. "Of course."

Then Mung turned back to Krek. "I wonder if I could have a few words with this mime agent . . . privately."

Krek said, "He wants to go back to Kaze, back to slavery. Talk him out of it. He should join his brothers."

"That may not be the best thing for him right now," Mung said. "Or for Proteus. Let us talk."

The Proteus leader stood and walked to the door.

"Family should come first," he said.

When he was gone, Mung leaned forward.

"Now, listen, my mime friend. I don't know whether to believe you or not—"

"I didn't get it," Tristan said. "I'm sure Kaze will send me back. But I'll need new codes, new templates."

"I hope you're telling the truth, Tristan. Kaze wants the data in that cat's eye to use against Flagge. But we—meaning Okasan, of course—can use it against *both* gloms." He took a breath. "I'll try to convince Krek to get you to a tube."

"He'll listen to you?"

"We all fight the same battle. Of course Proteus is a rather extreme group. But we have common goals." Mung's eyes narrowed. "I'll help you, but I want your word, a pledge that when you get to the eye you will bring the sample directly to Okasan. Will you make that promise?"

Tristan thought of the deal—and what he'd have to give up. This was the mission that would bring him Selfhood. How could he abandon that hope, especially after Lani?

He knew he couldn't.

But he said to Mung: "You have my word."

Mung shook his head. "No. More than that. If you don't bring the cat's eye sample to us, I will get revenge, Tristan. Believe me. You will be a traitor to the family. And in this family traitors don't live long."

Mung walked to the door and called Krek.

"Listen to me," he said when the Proteus leader returned. "I've spoken to Tristan and made a deal, an important deal for all mimes. He says that he will certainly be sent back for this cat's eye. And then he will deliver the sample to us."

"And why is this cat's eye so muting important?"

"Okasan is convinced that it holds secrets that can hurt the gloms. She can use those secrets."

"Why not us? We want to hurt the gloms as much as Okasan. We revere her but she's not a mime, not family. Why not bring the cat's eye *here*?"

Mung shook his head. "My friend, would you know what to do with it, how to use it? Your mimes are warriors, fighters. Let us deal with the cat's eye." Mung slapped the leader's back. "But first we must get it. And for that to happen we have to get this mime agent back to his glom—and fast."

Krek didn't look completely convinced, but finally he shrugged and nodded.

"All right. We'll get him back to Kaze. But he'd better not let his brothers down. If he doesn't return I will personally track the motherless mutagen down"—Krek turned to Tristan and leaned into his face—"and I will rip out your interface and shove it down your throat."

I believe you, Tristan thought.

And he wondered what Krek would do if he knew that the data from the eye was only inches away, resting against the inside of his thigh.

"You have my word," Tristan said.

Which he guessed showed how worthless his word was.

But he'd told worse lies in his career . . . for less.

Mung raised his hands. "Let's get going then. Time is important. Every day more mimes die and the gloms grow stronger."

"Follow me," Krek said.

Tristan walked to the door to the great hall, but Mung stayed behind.

"I'll be leaving the way I came in," Mung said, "It will be safer that way."

Tristan nodded.

"But don't worry, Tristan. We *will* meet again."

And then Tristan hurried to catch up with Krek.

CHAPTER 19

Tristan pressed his knees against one wall of the slender metal shaft.

No Dwellers had attacked as they made their way through a different set of tunnels to this point. Krek and his mimes had cut a hole into the shaft, providing—they said—a secret entrance to the tubes.

Secret, but very tight.

Tristan supposedly hung above the main tube platform but wasn't sure he could squeeze out of the shaft when the time came. For now though he had to wait.

Somewhere outside, dawn was approaching.

At last here was respite . . . time to consult Regis—or whatever avatar was next on rotation.

"PDA."

A six-foot, animated, carrot-chewing rabbit appeared, as if both of them were sandwiched in the tight shaft.

"Eh, what's up, mime? Didn't know you liked rabbit holes."

Tristan thought he'd erased this avatar. He'd programmed it directly from the old animated flatties and hadn't liked dealing with the anarchic personality.

"Anything urgent in the Ocean?"

"Dis an' dat. Your mailbox is filled wit' requests for updates, Doc. All from some guy named Cyrill—whatta maroon."

"Send a confirmation. Let Cyrill know that I'm returning."

"Yeah, yeah. When I get to it. What about your assignment status, Doc? He'll probably want to know dat too."

"Say nothing about that."

"Heh-heh-heh. Keepin' it a secret, eh, Doc?"

Just yesterday Tristan couldn't have imagined missing Regis. Now . . .

"Anything else I need to know? Do you detect anything to concern me in the tubes themselves?"

"Well dem Flagge Security yokels is still all over da freezone. Looks like mime hunting season is open. But I guess it's always open season on mimes, eh, Doc? But anyway dey ain't havin' any luck, so I t'ink dey're packin' up dey're shotguns and headin' home."

Good . . . because I'm close to getting out.

"Done."

The rabbit vanished.

Tristan sat scrunched up in the darkness, waiting, hoping that Krek and his mimes didn't mess up. If they'd miscalculated where the shaft led, Tristan could drop down onto the head of Flagge Security, or he might have to crawl back through the shaft, back to the black tunnels . . . to play with the Dwellers.

He waited, listening to the muffled voices and noises.

Come on, Tristan thought. *What's taking so long?*

As if in answer an explosion erupted from below, shooting acrid smoke into the shaft, and Tristan's waiting was over. The gas and smoke made his throat close and he hacked out a cough. Whatever he was breathing tasted deadly. The time had come to move.

He kicked the panel in front of him, expecting the metal grate to tumble out, down to the tube entrance below. But the grate didn't react to his kick at all. And now the smoke was so dense he couldn't even *see* the damn grate.

Another kick and he thought he felt some give.

F. Paul Wilson

Wouldn't it be just bloaty to wind up trapped and killed here by the diversion designed to get him out.

He started kicking crazily at the metal grid, cursing at it, slamming the metal with his foot, hoping that Dohan Lee's muscles would prevail. No popping here—if the grate was going to come out, it would come off gradually, ripped loose from the screws holding it tight.

And all the time he kicked he kept coughing, breathing the caustic mixture of smoke and stench.

He began to feel light-headed.

How many more kicks did he have before his body couldn't kick anymore?

He heard a rip.

He couldn't see anything, but the *screech* of metal prying loose was damn near musical. Despite the smoky claws that tightened their grip around his throat, he kept up his kicking, cursing at the grid, talking to it as if it were an enemy.

"Move, you mutagen!" *SLAM!* "Come on—and let me"—*SLAM!*— "the hell"—*SLAM!*—"out of here!"

Another kick and—this time—his foot kept going into space. He let his body slip through the opening, sliding on the smooth metal, tumbling down to the ground below.

He landed on his side, banging his hip. He sprang to his feet.

Empty.

Any Flagge Security guards stationed here before probably had gone to check out the explosion at the tube entrance. The cavernous corridor roiled with smoke . . . and it seemed to Tristan that maybe the rebel mimes had maybe used a bit too much explosive.

He turned and started running for the tubes, passing people wiping their tearing eyes, coughing.

Let's hope the tubes are still running, he thought.

But as he waded deeper into the terminal, the smoke cleared, and now most of the travelers awaiting their tube to the gloms or to other freezones looked down toward the smoky entrance way with only mild curiosity.

Ignoring stares at his battered face and filthy clothes, Tristan checked the schedule for the next Kaze-bound tube. He wasn't out of the woods yet. Flagge Security could still be here.

But so far it looked as if the explosion had done its job. Not a Flagge uniform in sight. Tristan spotted the signs for Kaze Glom and now he ran, beginning to believe he was going to pull this off.

He thought of Selfhood . . . and Lani. The two thoughts linked. Was that what Selfhood meant, thinking of someone else, having someone else who mattered?

He reached the platform. According to the digital readout a Kaze tube was only minutes away. The area was deserted except for an old man.

Tristan slowed his pace. His lungs still ached from the burning smoke. He passed the old man . . . who spoke:

"E-excuse me—"

Tristan stopped. He turned to the old man. Panic was *this* close. Who was he? "I have a message . . . a message from Lani Rouge."

The old man extended a box to Tristan. It glistened under the brilliant tungsten lamps of the tube platform.

A message from Lani? How did she find him?

Tristan took the box, flipped open the lid—and staggered back as a brilliant flash of light shot out, blinding him.

Suddenly Tristan's Roam Grid appeared. The green and red trails glowed, flashed for a brief second—and then disappeared.

"What?"

A tube shot into the station, the clear cylinder gliding soundlessly along the platform.

Tristan looked at his Roam Grid and saw that it was completely *wiped*. He couldn't go anywhere outside this freezone.

So close . . . yet so far away.

The tube opened.

It was pointless to try to enter it. He'd white out the instant he set foot inside.

As the tube slid away, sucking air from the platform, he looked at the old man.

The old man looked at him and smiled.

"You won't be going anywhere."

"Who are you? What have you done?"

Something very strange here. If this guy obviously wasn't Flagge Security, and if he wasn't from Proteus, who—?

"Your Roam Grid's been wiped, mime. You're trapped here in the freezone . . . with me. And I've got the reactivator key."

The old man dangled a spherical optical key from one of his grubby hands.

Tristan made a grab for the key but the stranger snatched it out of reach.

Moves awful quick for an old man, Tristan thought, but let it pass. He had to restore his Roam Grid, and he'd kill this lousy plasmid if he had to. Gladly.

The old man grinned as if he knew what Tristan was thinking.

Other people gathered on the platform now, waiting for the next tube.

The old man laughed. "You don't know who I am, do you?" he said in a low voice.

"And I don't care. I—"

"But I know you, Mr. Dohan Lee."

"Who *are* you?"

"Oh, you know me. You see—you're wearing my masque."

Eel! This was Eel! Of course there must have been a tracker in the wardrobe, and the gladiator obviously had more than one copy of his templates. Somehow the sleep disk cycled off, and Eel tracked him down. Bloaty!

Before Tristan could say anything Eel turned and bellowed, "Mime fight!"

Tristan backed away.

Eel quickly slid a hand into his pouch, fingered his 'face, and in seconds the old man began to change.

Grayish-green scales emerged for Eel's skin, while his head, grinning, leering, swelled to twice its size, the jaw tapering, shaping into a snoutlike mouth lined with sharp, glistening teeth.

"Your move," Eel said in a gravelly voice.

People gathered around in a wide, cautious circle. Who wouldn't want free entertainment while waiting for a tube?

My move, Tristan thought. He knew he couldn't fight Eel with the body of "Mr. Dohan Lee." It would be over in minutes, with Tristan ripped to pieces. He had to try something else.

"Eel, I'm sorry. I know I took your wardrobe but I—"

"You stole it, mime. And is there anything worse than stealing another mime's templates? Fortunately I had a backup case. So now— pick one from the collection you wanted so badly."

"Eel—"

"*Pick!*"

Eel had a right to be pissed. Like in those old vids they called westerns, where good guys wore white hats and bad guys dressed in black, and the worst thing you could do was take another man's horse.

In this new west Tristan had done the worst thing you could do to a mime.

"Go on," Eel hissed, a long tongue flicking over the dagger teeth.

Tristan tried once more to explain. He'd feel the same as Eel if situations were reversed. But there were extenuating circumstances.

"I wouldn't have done it if there'd been another way. But I was trapped, cornered."

Eel lashed out with an arm, smashing a leathery fist into Tristan's head. The shock sent him flying, and some of the crowd cheered.

"*Now!*" Eel yelled.

Tristan leaped to his feet. If he didn't pick a masque now he was sure the lizard king would unceremoniously kill him. And rightly so.

Tristan didn't want to flux in public, but he wanted to die even less.

He pushed open his wardrobe and stared at the templates.

Russian roulette.

Six choices: one of them the writable with Lani's genome, one of them a meltdown template. Maybe more than one. Eel might like the extra security of having two killer templates.

The mime gladiator took a step closer.

Whatever Tristan was going to do he had only a few seconds to do it.

His fingers danced over the different templates, each marked with an icon, a coding that only Eel would understand. Tristan noticed that one icon was a tiny, three-pointed crown. Wasn't Eel's award-winning pitsaur named Rex? And Rex was a fighter. Worth a try. Especially with no clue about the others.

He removed his current template and inserted the one with the crown icon . . . and immediately began to flux.

He fought a surge of nausea as a savage feeling coursed through his body. Was this what a meltdown felt like? Was his entire genetic structure about to collapse, responding to a code that would turn him into a mass of formless protoplasm?

His stomach heaved . . . his tongue seemed too big for his mouth. But when he looked down at his hands, they were now massive, the hands of a fighter, with wicked little hornlike protrusions on his knuckles.

I'm not melting, he thought.

But that joyful thought was cut short by a curse and a grunt from Eel, who sent another fist crashing toward Tristan's new face, this time with claws extended. Tristan jerked back and felt the claws rake his cheek. He tasted his blood.

Obviously Eel was disappointed with Tristan's lucky choice.

Tristan rammed both his fists up into Eel's lizard gut—the force of the blow knocked the wind out of Eel and sent the lizard fighter staggering backward.

The crowd cheered, but the moment passed quickly as Eel reared back, then leaped like a spring, flying into the air. Tristan backed up but not nearly fast enough—he'd had no time to adjust to this new masque.

He watched Eel's lizard snout curl into something like a smile. Or maybe he was imagining that.

Eel landed, slamming Tristan's new body to the pavement.

"You're pathetic," he said, straddling Tristan and pinning his arms with his legs. "This isn't even a contest."

"You've got more experience," Tristan grunted. He felt as if his chest was being crushed.

"Yes, I do. But here's an experience I *don't* have: being ripped apart . . . by an expert."

Eel opened his right fist, displaying the sharp claws at the ends of his fingers. He cocked his arm, bringing the claws back, ready to rip Tristan open.

Tristan wiggled and got one arm free. He shot a hand up and grabbed Eel's wrist.

Eel's tongue snaked out and licked Tristan's face.

Which is when Tristan saw that he had been tricked. Eel raised his other hand, claws poised to dig into him. No time to deflect the blow, no time to do anything except wait for the agony of those claws digging into his chest.

A *flash*. From somewhere behind Eel.

Tristan looked back to Eel who was still squatting atop him. But now the clawed hand had slowed its descent, sputtering to a stop only centimeters from Tristan's throat.

Blood dripped from those claws but not Tristan's. A pulser had cut into Eel, piercing him back to front. A red stream poured from the still-smoldering hole in the scaly skin of his left shoulder.

Eel tilted his lizard head and looked at the hole, then back to Tristan, wondering *why? . . . how?*

How could this happen?

Tristan was equally mystified.

He pushed Eel off, and the massive lizard fighter rolled to the ground, to lay writhing on the platform. Blood still bubbled from the hole. Tristan ripped a piece from his already-torn smartsuit and jammed it into the entry wound in the back of Eel's shoulder, then rolled him onto his back where he did the same at the front. It slowed the flow but didn't completely stanch it. Already blood was pooling on the platform under the wounded shoulder.

"Thief," Eel said. The pinkish forked tongue lolled out one more time and then the lizard eyes closed.

Eel—who perhaps deserved better—was going to die if he didn't get medical aid soon.

Tristan stood and turned, expecting the crowd to be closing in, eager to see the strange spectacle. But the crowd had vanished . . . the sport suddenly turned deadly.

As Tristan searched for the origin of the blast he heard the chilling words behind him.

"Kill the copycats!"

He saw a group of men walking toward him.

Sibs—ten, twelve of them wielding stubby metal pipes. But nothing more modern. No pulsers.

If Eel hadn't been shot by one of them, then who . . . ?

"Get him!" one shouted.

Sibs . . . looking for trouble—and they'd just got lucky.

While Tristan's luck was clearly gone.

As the Sibs encircled him Tristan considered his options. He could run, break through the circle, and make a dash for . . . where? Back to the freezone and into the arms of Flagge Security? And that meant leaving Eel lying here helpless, dying on the platform, leaving him to be clubbed to death.

That rankled. *Eel's here because of me.*

The other option was to stand and fight. After all, Tristan was in a gladiator masque. He wasn't a professional fighter but he could make sure he took a few of these plasmids with him.

One Sib smacked a pipe into his open palm. He grinned. "You know something, copycat?"

Tristan did a slow turn, looking around at the ever-tightening circle.

"A mime took my job. A clone clown like you took the food from my table."

Tristan shook his head. "I didn't do it," he said, knowing reason was futile but hoping to buy himself some time. "We didn't ask to be born. Your gripe is with the people who made us. Go bash *their* heads."

The pipe kept smacking into the Sib's hand.

"Oh, we would if we could, mime. But we can't find them. So you'll have to do."

And now Tristan noticed that the other gang members were doing the same thing—smacking their pipes in unison against their palms. This was ritualistic . . . primitive . . . a slaying for the tribe.

A slow, painful death. Slower, more painful, far more satisfying than if they used pulsers, or even knives.

Then—from behind him—a *crack!* and a blaze of pain in the back of his skull. White spots danced before his eyes and the pain bloomed in his head as he staggered forward. He saw an iron bar raised before him and lashed out with a fist, catching the Sib's cheek with his spiked knuckle and tearing half his face off.

The man screamed and dropped his pipe as he clutched his cheek. Tristan dove for the weapon. Maybe that would help even the—

Another pipe smashed into the side of his face, and Tristan, already overbalanced, dropped to his knees. Damn! If only he'd had more time with this masque.

Another pipe slammed against his back.

And Tristan knew that this would go on until he'd beg them to find a goddamn laser and drill a hole into him. He tried to speak but the inside of his mouth tasted gummy, filling with blood.

What fun . . . this sport of mime killing. How wonderful to be a human.

He saw a dozen arms raised, ready to rain a fusillade of blows down on him.

And he thought: What a stupid way to end.

He closed his eyes and steeled himself against the coming agony, coiling his legs to spring at the first blow. He'd take someone with him.

But the blows never came. Instead he heard other voices crying out in surprise and agony.

Tristan looked up and saw the lead Sib's face, mottled and livid. A massive arm was coiled around the man's neck. He looked terrified.

And then a wrenching *crack!* and the lead Sib went limp and slid to the ground, eyes wide.

Leaving Tristan facing a familiar figure.

"Don't kneel there, you useless plasmid!" Krek shouted. "Get up!"

Krek wasted no time jumping on a Sib who was furiously trying to beat back another Protean with his pipe. To his right Tristan saw still another Protean grab a Sib by his feet and swing his head against a pillar with a sickening *smack!*

The Sibs were crying out in terror, trying to scramble away. But the Proteans wouldn't allow that. The Sibs were engaged in the fight of their lives.

Not having fun anymore? Tristan wanted to say. Too many mimes to play with now?

More cracks, and more Sibs slid to the platform . . . so much human refuse. The few survivors ran away, back to the tube entrance.

Krek laughed as he walked over to Tristan.

"You look like shit, brother."

Tristan nodded, wiping at his bloody mouth.

"You followed me?"

"Mung suggested we keep an eye on you—at a discreet distance, of course. Good thing too." He looked down at the unconscious Eel. "Who's this one?"

"Name's Eel. He's—"

"From the Flagge Arena? I know him! Fought him a few times. He rearranged my base pairs but good. *Damn* good fighter. Why was he after you?"

"It's a long story."

"All your stories are long, aren't they, brother? Well let's see if we can get this poor bastard to our doc. Good thing someone shot him when they did, otherwise you were a goner."

"Who shot him? One of the Sibs?"

"Don't know, but we've got him, whoever he is. Caught him climbing down from a ledge above the platform entrance. He's got a Sib mark on his head, but something's not right about him. We'll take him back home, and if he doesn't tell us what we want to know, we'll let the Dwellers nibble on him a bit—that's a sure tongue loosener."

Tristan shuddered.

"As for you, you'd better flux into something a little more presentable. A new tube will be here in minutes."

Tristan wondered whether he could handle yet another flux. "I don't know—"

"You can't travel like that, friend."

Tristan nodded and he activated the Dohan Lee template. But this time he felt as if he were splitting in two. It should have been easier to return to a more normal physique but pain racked his body. He groaned and fell to his knees, heaving from the tremendous physical stress.

When it was over he looked up at Krek. "But wait. It doesn't matter. I can't travel. He—" Tristan pointed at Eel's unconscious form as a big mime slung him over his shoulder and started to carry him away. "He wiped my Roam Grid."

Krek rubbed his chin. "If we were back home I might be able to help you, but here—"

"Wait!" Tristan said. "He said he had a reactivator key."

Tristan ran over to where the big mime stood with Eel and searched the gladiator's pouch.

"Yes." He pulled out a small white sphere. "Got it."

No guarantee the key would restore his grid completely, but he hoped at the very least it would clear him far enough to get back to Kaze Glom.

He held the sphere's pore before his right eye and squeezed. As light strobed and flickered from the tiny opening, his Roam Grid appeared. The image wavered, threatened to break up, then stabilized and exploded into a network of green intersecting lines.

All green. *No* red.

It took a few seconds for the meaning of the unfamiliar uniformity of color to register.

"It's a universal!"

"What? What do you mean?"

"A universal. I can go anywhere with this, out of the freezone, to any glom. It's a goddamn universal key."

"Good feeling, isn't it?" Krek said. "We've got one too. Soon as someone joins us, they get a peek."

Tristan stared at Krek, then at Eel being carried off to get patched up, and felt something he couldn't quite identify, let alone put into words. Whatever it was, he felt it growing, filling an unfamiliar space within him.

"Thanks, Krek."

"For what?"

"For saving me."

"Don't need thanks for breaking a few Sib heads. Do that for free. Hell, even pay for the privilege."

"Well . . . thanks just the same."

Krek took a step closer and draped an arm over Tristan. "You just go home, brother. And remember—when you get that cat's eye, you bring it to Okasan. Do that, or we'll finish what these Sibs started."

Tristan was about to say something when the tube glided silently into the station. The passengers' faces looked stunned, scanning the pile of bodies on the platform. Krek stared back at the faces and laughed.

"Just part of the show, ladies and gentlemen." Another clap on Tristan's back. "Go home."

The tube opened, and Tristan entered, out of the woods at last, on his way back to Kaze Glom, to Cyrill, and—though he could hardly believe it—to Selfhood.

CHAPTER 20

What am I doing here? Lani wondered as she followed this fat stranger through a dank tunnel under the freezone.

She'd spent most of the night wandering the freezone, her feelings swinging between joy at being free of the Flagge Quarter's limits, and anxiety that she'd be caught. But wherever she went she asked if anyone had ever heard of Okasan.

No one admitted to that, but someone must have known, because eventually a rather large man with a pet saur attached himself to her. Dressed in florid robes he seemed larger than life within the swirl of colorful cloth. At first he seemed to be merely one of the freezone's many eccentric characters, searching for companionship.

But then he'd dropped a name.

Okasan.

And now she was following him through this underground maze.

"Just stay with me," the fat man said. "Straight ahead . . . that's it."

I'm going to meet Okasan, she kept telling herself. *At least I hope I am.* She remembered the feeling of being watched in the warehouse. Was someone watching her? Was this man really taking her to the woman?

But if he took her to Okasan she could see Tristan again. She pressed the disc in a side pocket.

That kept her going. She wanted to see this woman. All paths . . . Trev's . . . Tristan's . . . they all led back to Okasan. And maybe this mythical woman could help her understand or come to grips with what had happened to Trev, and with her feelings for the mime who'd assumed his form.

"We've got to turn to the right here."

She followed him into a canyon of towering crates, leading to a dim light at the far end.

"Almost there."

They rounded the corner and the pygmy triceratops broke into a trot toward an old woman sitting at a table.

The old woman looked up.

"This," said her escort with a flourish of his florid robes, "is Okasan."

The old woman nodded. "And you are?"

Lani hesitated a moment. "I'm Lani Rouge. A datameister."

"Sit down, Lani Rouge," the old woman said in a cracked voice. "Mung, get her a chair."

Lani took the chair from Mung—wood, an antique, early Twenty-first Century at least. She had never seen a chair like this, real wood, battered, scratched. What other ancient treasures hid in this tunnel?

"You may guess it's no accident that Mung found you." Lani looked over at Mung. Had he been in the warehouse? "We followed you out of Flagge Glom. Heard you asking about me. So now why don't you explain why you came to the freezone."

Lani told Okasan her story, how she was captured by Kaze agents, how Tristan took a scraping from her, and how he became her.

"A writable template?" the old woman said. "That is new . . . and dangerous."

"A writable template?" Mung said. "No, that can't be."

Lani nodded. "It's true. He took a scraping and fluxed into me."

"This puts . . ." the woman said slowly, "Kaze way ahead of Flagge Glom. They could easily become the most powerful of them all."

"Why should we believe her?" Mung said.

But Okasan held up a hand. "Continue."

Lani explained how she escaped the warehouse and discovered Tristan in her apartment. She told Okasan about Trev.

"Tristan had used the masque of my . . . of someone close to me, a man named Trev who—"

"Trev?" Okasan said. "You knew Trev?"

"Yes. We were . . . close. He spoke of you. Did you know him?"

"Of course I knew him. We all knew him. But we didn't know about *you*." The old woman seemed agitated. "Mung, she knew Trev."

"So she says, but—"

"Think about it, Mung: Kaze gave its agent this datameister's dead lover as a masque."

Why is she so upset? Lani wondered.

"A coincidence?" Mung said.

"Oh, I doubt that. I doubt that very much." She turned back to Lani. "And this Tristan, this Kaze mime agent—he told you about me?"

Lani nodded.

"He trusted you?" Mung said.

"Yes, and I—"

"A Kaze agent trusting a Flagge datameister! He must be crazy," Mung said. "This is all crazy."

"I've told no one. I wanted to give him back this—"

Lani handed Okasan the flat metal case.

"His wardrobe?"

"It's Tristan's. It holds his other . . ."

"Masques," Mung said, taking the case from Okasan. "He will want this back."

And *I* want him to have it back.

Lani said, "It contains the masque he wore to enter Flagge Quarter."

Not just any masque, she thought. Trev . . .

Mung put the case down on the old wooden table. "Well, we can't get it to him now."

Lani looked at Mung. She'd expected Tristan to be here. Wasn't this Okasan, the mime savior, the leader of the mime underground? She assumed Tristan would be going to her.

"I don't understand. He's here, isn't he? This is where—"

Voices rang out from somewhere behind, and Lani turned to look down the long crate canyon then back to Okasan. Was this a raid? Had Flagge Security followed her here?

Okasan looked concerned but not alarmed. Apparently she recognized the voices.

"Why are they coming here?" the old woman asked Mung.

"Oh—they have something to show you, Okasan. They caught a Sib."

Lani was confused. Who were these people, marching noisily toward the splintery wooden table?

As soon as they arrived Lani guessed who they were . . . mimes, from the Arena. She had seen their type before, bulky fighting machines.

One of the mimes held a bloody prisoner who dangled from his massive arm.

"Okasan," the mime said, "we are honored to bring this—" he rattled his puppetlike prisoner—"to you."

"Krek, it is always a pleasure to see you and your group."

Mung pointed to the puppet prisoner. "Is he one of the Sibs that attacked Tristan?"

"Tristan?" Lani blurted. "Is he—"

Krek reared back and laughed. "Is he okay? A little bloody maybe, but that's nothing for a mime agent. No . . ." Krek punctuated the word with a rattle of the bloody prisoner. "This is no Sib."

"What?" Mung said.

"He shot the pulser that saved Tristan. Tristan would have been killed by the lizard mime he was fighting . . . if this one hadn't drilled a hole in him."

"Perhaps," Mung said, "they wanted to kill one mime and play with—"

Lani watched the big mime shake his head. The gladiator frightened her. She had never been this close to something so brutal, so savage, so primitive. She wished she were out of here and back in her cluttered apartment.

She moved to stand behind Okasan.

"Tell them!" Krek yelled.

But the man said nothing.

"Tell them, or you'll pay another visit to the Dwellers."

That did it. The man started and began to shake. Whoever "the Dwellers" were, he wanted no part of them.

"No . . . please." He looked up at Okasan. "I'm not a Sib."

From behind, Lani heard a step, and she turned to see Okasan walk closer to the prisoner, her face troubled, the lines and cracks deepening as she passed under the white light.

"Not a Sib?" she said quietly.

The prisoner shook his head.

"And the others who attacked Tristan?" Mung said.

"Oh, they were probably Sibs," Krek said. "But this one's a glom agent. We knew something was strange . . . why shoot one mime and spare the other?"

"An agent, perhaps? For Kaze? Helping his glom's mime?"

Krek laughed. "Oh, he's an agent all right, but he's a *Flagge* agent. He's been watching for Tristan." Krek rattled the agent to make him speak. "Isn't that right?"

"Yes, i-it's true."

"*Flagge* wanted Tristan to get out?" Okasan began walking around the group, wringing her hands. She stepped up to the agent. "What were you supposed to do?"

The agent cleared his throat. A reddish foam bubbled near his mouth. He spit to the side.

"My orders were to see to it that the mime agent escaped. Sharp-shooters were placed at all the tube plexes to guarantee that no one stopped him."

Okasan turned away.

"They *wanted* him to escape," Krek said, pointing out the obvious.

Okasan walked back to the table. She looked shaky. Lani didn't understand any of this. What was going on here? Something terrible was happening, and Tristan was at the center of it. And now—some-how—so was she.

Okasan eased into her chair. "Can we reach him?"

Mung shook his head. "No. Tristan is on his way back to Kaze. But he failed in his mission. He didn't get the sample from the . . ."

Mung's voice trailed off, and at the same moment, Okasan gazed at Lani. The old woman's eyes looked sad.

"—the cat's eye?" Okasan said slowly. "Yes, that's what he said. But was he telling the truth?" She closed her eyes. "And if he was lying, if he had indeed succeeded in obtaining a sample, why would Flagge not only allow him to escape but go to such lengths to assure his safe return to—"

She stiffened as her eyes widened in what Lani could only call horror.

Okasan's voice was barely a whisper. "No!" She whirled to face Mung. "The G-strain—could they have perfected it?"

"I—I haven't heard anything." Mung suddenly looked sick. "But that would explain everything."

"Yes! Including the antibodies."

Mung gasped. "The antibodies! Oh, no!"

Lani's mind whirled in confusion. G-strains, antibodies—what were they talking about? Why were they so terrified? She felt as if she'd walked into a madhouse.

"Find him," Okasan said in a cracked voice barely above a whis-per. "No matter what it takes."

Mung turned to Krek. "Quick! Maybe there's a chance. Contact your other cells, everyone you can. Tristan must be stopped. He can't be allowed back into Kaze Glom."

"Why not?" Krek said.

"I'll explain it all later. Just trust me in this: He *must* be stopped."

"And what if we find him and he won't come, or we spot him and can't reach him?"

"Kill him," Okasan said softly.

Lani gasped. Kill him? No! What had he done?

Krek's eyes narrowed. "He's a brother mime. With all due respect, Okasan—"

"When have you ever heard me wish any harm to a mime?" Okasan snapped.

"Never, Okasan."

"Then trust me in this: For the sake of your family's welfare . . . you may have to kill Tristan."

Krek stared at her for a moment, then nodded. "Only for you."

Dragging his prisoner behind him, he led his group out of the tunnel.

She watched Okasan place a hand over the wardrobe on the table and rub it with her bony fingers, as if it were a crystal ball and could tell her where Tristan might be. Lani thought . . . Trev is in there somewhere.

What a fool I was, suckered by a clever mime agent. A fool, and now I've risked my career, my future, perhaps my life.

She had a more disturbing thought.

If they were ready to kill Tristan, what about her? Would they let her out of this place?

She was a Flagge datameister. She knew who they were, where they met.

Lani reflexively took a backward step, bumping into a stack of crates.

"You don't understand, Datameister?" Okasan said. She seemed suddenly exhausted. "I'm not surprised. You work for the gloms, archiving data and spitting it out again, a willing human computer, with about as much soul. As much a tool as any mime."

The words stung.

"I don't know what—"

"No, you don't know. After all, you're only a datameister. And neither does he. He's acting as a glom tool—but for both gloms."

Who is this woman? Lani thought. This near-mythical old woman who's become the symbol for freedom to mimes everywhere? Was she herself a mime?

Lani turned to Mung. "What happened? What did Tristan do?"

"Tristan sampled the cat's eye, you see? He lied to us. He promised to bring the data to us, to help us in our struggle against the gloms. But he may not be carrying data at all. He may be acting as a vector for a completely different kind of virus."

"The 'G-strain' you mentioned?" Lani said.

Mung nodded. "Flagge has supposedly been working on it for years, but we figured that was just rumor, another jumble legend." He sighed. "Until recently."

"But what is it?"

Mung ignored her and turned to Okasan. "I'll go see who else we can use to intercept him."

Mung waddled away with his pet triceratops trotting close behind him.

"What's going to happen?" Lani said to Okasan when they were alone. "I mean, if you don't catch Tristan?"

The old woman's voice was barely audible.

"A holocaust."

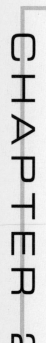

CHAPTER 21

And then, as if the entire mission had been a strange dream, Tristan's tube left the freezone and passed into Kaze Quarter. He hesitated before activating his PDA. What avatar would appear this time? He had Groucho somewhere in there. He didn't think he could deal with oscillating eyebrows and wisecracks right now.

"PDA," he said, and almost threw his arms around Regis when he appeared, prim and properly flustered with excitement.

"Lord Tristan, Mr. Cyrill has been sending messages every fifteen minutes. He's *most* anxious that you go to him immediately upon clearance by ID."

"Good to see you again, Regis. All right. As soon as I get back to the warren, we'll dive and—"

"No, m'lord. Mr. Cyrill doesn't want to meet you in the Ocean. He wants you 'in person'—at the Tower."

In person.

Tristan looked out the tube, now gliding over one of Kaze's industrial "plexes," a maze of boxy steel and glass structures connected by hundreds of umbilical pipes, tying each building to the other. And then over a series of hydrodomes, churning out the enriched, fast-growing fungus that was the basis for nearly every food consumed on the planet. He barely saw them.

Cyrill wanted a real face-to-face.

That could mean only one thing: *This is it. I've successfully completed the mission. I get Selfhood. I can be free.*

Like realpeople.

Then he thought of the Proteans, brutal, violent warriors . . . but so proud of who they were, mimes who scorned the very idea of anyone *giving* them Selfhood—they *took* it.

From the window he spotted the mammoth Tower, rising to a needle point, lost in the smoggy clouds. Some said the Tower was the tallest structure in the world, dwarfed in size only by the chain of Terra Nova Station orbiting the earth. Another interesting thing about the Tower . . . as high as it went, it also went deep.

Deep, and secret. No schematics could be found anywhere in the Ocean, at least none you'd think were reliable. Kaze Security was that *good*.

I'm on the right team, thought Tristan.

Kaze Security escorted him past the environmental seals to the mime ID chamber. This time the autoweapons were armed and aimed at selected target areas on his naked body as his Roam Grid was put through the call-and-response sequence.

The procedure always gave him the shakes. What if his codes somehow had become corrupted during an assignment? If his grid didn't supply the right answers he'd be stunned and carted off to an interrogation cell where he'd have to find a way to prove he was Tristan the Kaze mime agent.

But how does a mime prove who he is?

He heard a soft whirring and sighed as he saw the muzzles of the weapons rotate away from him. He'd passed.

His Roam Grid flashed before him and then he noticed that his universal roam had been wiped. He felt a flash of panic. For a little while he'd been free to go *anywhere*. But the foreign element had been located and removed when they scanned his grid.

Doesn't matter, he told himself. Not with Selfhood so close. Selfhood, and *real* freedom, to go anywhere, do anything.

And he still had the key. He'd keep that. Not that he'd need it. Just a souvenir. No more Roam Grids or keys once he was free.

He laughed at the thought. Where would he go, what would he do? That was the delicious thrill of it. To think and decide, and then just *go*.

His grid was now reprogrammed to a modified home mode—restricted to the mime warren but with an added narrow path to the Tower.

He blinked it off and rose to his feet.

"Agent Tristan?"

He turned and saw a young woman standing in the doorway. She wore a loose white jump and a tight white cap. A light green plastic container dangled from her right hand.

"That's me."

"I'm from data. Do you have the sample?"

"Right here."

He reached down and peeled the sample pouch from his inner thigh. When he looked up again she was closer, her eyes wide as they surveyed his collection of gashes and bruises.

"All you all right?"

"I've had better days," he said. He dropped the pouch into her container. "But I'll be all right."

In fact I'll be more than all right after I meet with Cyrill. I'll be free.

"I have your route to the Tower," said Tristan's PDA.

As soon as he'd reached his compartment Tristan did two things. First he switched his PDA to the default avatar: a disembodied face he called "Joe," which now floated in the air before him. Then he slow-fluxed from Dohan Lee into his home masque. The tissue remodeling of the flux healed most of his bruises and lacerations. He was still marked up, but the wounds looked days old.

"Let's see it, Joe."

Tristan's Roam Grid appeared, displaying a path to the Kaze Tower and then a series of code numbers that would take him to Cyrill. He'd been to the Tower only once before, but never to meet Cyrill.

He hurried on his way, clearing once again the seals and security of the warren and keeping to the Tower-bound path.

All locations in the Tower were coded by a series of numbers and letters; the sequences identified a location and a way to get there. Up, down, north or south, the numbers conveyed nothing about a room's physical location. But with those numbers, he could travel the strange chutes and tubes of the Tower and end up where he needed to be.

Finally he arrived in a black room lit by a dozen spear-shaped lights jutting from the ceiling. But he was alone.

Tristan looked for a chair. He realized how tired he was. More than that—he'd been chased, beaten, cut, and banged around. He needed a few liters of nutrient and hours, *days* in a null state.

No place to sit. The room wasn't at all like the warm, reassuring virtual rooms where he and Cyrill usually met.

Tristan waited.

The journey to this room had left him disoriented, as he'd known it would. There were times when he'd felt as if he was flying up in a chute cab, and then sideways, down, and up again, until he felt as if this room could be anywhere, perhaps not even in the damned Tower.

Hope somebody or something keeps track of where everything is, he thought.

Waiting. The lights made brilliant, perfectly circular pools on the black floor. No dust floated in their white arcs. The room's filtration and climate control wouldn't tolerate anything from the outside.

Tristan took a breath. He felt every aching bone, every bruise. Hungry, exhausted . . . he rubbed behind his neck, feeling the tight muscles.

A wall panel slid open, and a man walked into the room, stepping into one of the white pools of light. Cyrill. Tristan knew because he looked exactly as he always had. That was reassuring since Cyrill could have adopted any guise at all in the Ocean. This was the same 'Cyrill' Tristan knew.

The panel slid shut.

Tristan stood there expecting a smile. Instead . . .

"You're late."

Late. That was true. Tristan felt so relieved to have made it out of the freezone that he hadn't even worried that he was . . . late.

"Yes, Cyrill. But I had a terrible time with—"

"I know. The Flagge patrols. We're not exactly 'blind' in the other gloms, you know. We were watching much of your rather irregular progress every step of the way."

"Getting out of the freezone . . . wasn't easy."

Tristan realized that he couldn't tell Cyrill too much about that part of the mission. He couldn't tell him about the renegade mimes who wanted to bring down the gloms. And Okasan, who he betrayed for Kaze.

He couldn't tell Cyrill about any of that. But how much did he already know?

Tristan shifted uneasily on the floor. The silence was irritating and he wished that this meeting were taking place in the Ocean.

Cyrill took a step closer to Tristan, moving from one pool of light to another. The room itself felt ominous, not a meeting room at all; more like an interrogation chamber.

"We lost you in the freezone. You met some . . . performers."

Tristan nodded. "They helped me . . . thought I was a runaway mime."

Cyrill grinned at that. "Where did you go from there?"

"They—they showed me some old tunnels. A way to the tubes past Flagge Security."

Cyrill nodded as he listened to Tristan's faltering story.

"There was an explosion in one of the tubes," Cyrill said softly.

We're not exactly 'blind' in the other gloms. But how much could they see . . . how much did Cyrill know? Did he know about Lani, did he know about Okasan? Was this some kind of test?

"Yes, I heard it. That's when I entered the tube. But I don't know where the explosion came from."

Cyrill stared into Tristan's eyes, and Tristan wanted to back up, to step over to some other safer island of white light.

"Oh, you don't know about that, eh?" Cyrill kept staring until he said, "But you got the cat's eye sample, yes?"

Tristan nodded.

"Good." Cyrill smiled and turned back to a wall. "Wonderful . . . it will look good on your profile."

"Profile?"

Cyrill turned, his face revealing no awareness of what Tristan was about to say.

"I completed the mission. I brought back the cat's eye sample and the datameister's template."

"I'm sure that's true . . . the datalab will have to confirm that, of course."

"Of course. But if I have, then—we have talked. You and I, we've discussed . . ."

Why is this so hard? Outside I'm unstoppable. Since yesterday morning I've run the gauntlet of Flagge Security, crazy Arena mimes, and bloodthirsty Sibs. But put me in front of Cyrill and I'm like a muting, weak-kneed child, afraid to ask for more porridge.

"About what?" Cyrill said.

"Selfhood."

There. He'd said the word, expressed his wish, his expectation. No, more than that. His *right*.

This cat's eye can destroy Flagge Glom—at least that's what Cyrill said. This should be the mission that frees me.

Another smile from Cyrill, sour this time. "Ah, yes. Selfhood. That will be yours if the board approves."

"*If?* But I succeeded."

"Success is relative, Tristan. You were supposed to terminate the datameister. You didn't. You were supposed to return directly from the Citadel. You didn't. You spent hours of unaccounted time in Flagge Glom. How do we know you weren't compromised? How do we know you didn't sell out?"

Cyrill waved off Tristan's protests before he could voice them. He smiled.

"Enough discussion. All that will be forgotten if you've brought back the data we want. We'll check the sample and study it. Then— and only then—will we discuss Selfhood."

Cyrill's tone softened. "You're going back to your warren, yes? I'll speak to you later. For now, rest. Get your strength back."

Rest, that sounded so inviting. And Cyrill, now he almost sounded as he had in the past. Like a mentor, a concerned parent.

Tristan raged silently at the comfort that gave him. But maybe that was the key. Tristan had always looked to Cyrill as the father he never had.

Cyrill moved toward the back wall, ready to leave this unnamed place lost in the mammoth maze of Kaze Tower.

As another panel in the wall slid open Cyrill stopped, turned.

"And Tristan," he said, "be sure to turn in that stolen wardrobe." Cyrill smiled. "You won't be needing those masques anymore."

And Tristan smiled back. No, he wouldn't—not when he was about to achieve Selfhood.

Then Cyrill vanished, leaving Tristan in the black room, standing alone amid the pools of brilliant white light.

CHAPTER 22

Tristan tossed one empty packet of concentrate on the floor then grabbed a fresh one and ripped it open. He felt as if he couldn't get enough of the greenish jellylike substance.

He'd fluxed down to null state as soon as he'd reached his compartment yesterday and dropped into a deep exhausted slumber.

He'd awakened blank and featureless, reborn. And he was *hungry*.

As Tristan fluxed up to his home masque he watched a multibubble display set up by his PDA.

The top row filled with frozen holoimages of recent news stories. More clashes between mimes and Sibs, with glom guards standing by while mimes were beaten. And an update on the investigation into the slain Sib leader.

I know who did that one, Tristan thought.

He finished off the new packet and let it fall to the floor.

And more news . . . a breakthrough on Mars. Of course that was what they always said. Always "great breakthroughs" on Mars, yet the planet remained uninhabitable. If the gloms said things were going great on Mars, who could say otherwise?

He glanced at the disembodied face floating beside the holobubble.

"What else have you got, Joe?"

"I can arrange a series of live feeds that might interest you. There's the winter games at McMurdo, and—"

"Never mind. Done."

Joe and the bubble disappeared.

Now, bloated on concentrate, he was ready to go back to sleep. He had a lot of catching up to do. As he turned toward his crib a tone sounded.

Someone at the door. He wasn't expecting company.

"Who is it?"

A security screen displayed the face of Tristan's visitor.

"Argus? What the—?"

He considered ignoring the pathetic mutagen but something about his smirk bothered Tristan. Argus looked almost . . . happy. And that could only mean bad news for someone else.

He opened the door and Argus pushed his way into the compartment.

"You're back, Tristan."

Tristan nodded. "How observant, Argus. Yes, and I was just about to take a nap, so if you don't mind—"

Argus slammed the door behind him and stood there gloating. Tristan wondered if he should alert warren security. Argus wasn't the first mime to crack.

They even had a name for it. A *mimebender*. Sometimes a mime snapped. Too many fluxes, too much psychseep. Who knew?

Argus jabbed him in the chest. "You muted it, Tristan."

"Really?" Tristan tried to hide his unease. *Argus knows something.* "If you mean by opening the door for you, yes, I agree."

Argus blinked rapidly, three times in a row. A tic, as if something were jamming the signals from his brain to his mouth. Odd.

"Kiss your dreams of Selfhood good-bye, Tristan."

Another attempted jab to Tristan's stomach, but this time Tristan brought his arm up and deflected it. He was quickly tiring of this.

"Say your piece and go, Argus."

"I told you that should have been *my* mission. If *I'd* gone I'd have brought back the right virus."

Tristan froze as a blast of interstellar cold shot through his veins. He tried to keep his voice steady.

"What's that supposed to mean?"

"Th—that I have f-friends in the data-l-lab," Argus said, the stammer arriving a second after another succession of eye blinks. "And they tell me they don't know what you delivered, but it's like no dataviron they've ever s-seen. They're sending s-samples around trying to inden-den-dentify it."

Another succession of blinks. Argus opened his mouth. It was comical, the demented mime trying to—

Argus's tongue lolled out and then, as if he was doing a trick to impress Tristan, the tongue began to expand like a balloon.

Tristan laughed.

"Argus, I didn't know you had—"

The tongue expanded and popped, spraying Tristan with reddish goo. Tristan recoiled in horror as bulges appeared on Argus's face, pulsating, shifting, then expanding, blistering into open wounds.

What the hell was going on? Too many fluxes was bad . . . all mimes knew that. But Tristan had never seen anything like this. Argus's eyes rolled in his deformed head, as if the milky orbs wanted to jump out of his skull.

And then they did exactly that—a squishing noise, and then the white globes were hanging from their bloody sockets as something inside Argus's skull forced them out.

Tristan gagged.

"Joe! What the hell's happening?"

Argus fell to his knees. He reached up to his neck and closed his hands around the throat. Some terrible pain there, or did Argus think he could stop whatever horror was going on inside his head?

The Joe-face appeared and said calmly, "Sir, I have nothing in any medical or mime files on this phenomena. And there are no images in the Ocean that match—"

The PDA's report was cut off by a strangled yell from Argus. His hands dropped from his neck as the fingers inflated like little bladders, swelling . . . but instead of popping like firecrackers, the flesh of the fingers seemed to melt together forming pinkish clumps at the end of his stumpy arms.

Argus slid to the floor and curled up, gasping, groaning. His clothes hid whatever else was happening to his body. Tristan didn't know what to do. He was afraid to get closer, especially to Argus's head—his scalp kept bubbling, as if the hard bony structure of the skull had turned pulpy.

Tristan felt the nutrient bubbling in his stomach. He'd never liked Argus, and a few times even had considered killing him, but this . . . no one deserved this.

"Sir?"

"Joe! You've found something?"

"Yes, sir. I believe these are related incidents."

A holobubble appeared in front of Tristan, obscuring Argus's writhing, bubbling body . . . cooking sans heat on the floor of Tristan's compartment. The bubble displayed others going through the terrible melting that Argus was experiencing.

"What the hell?"

"Live feed from elsewhere in the warren, sir. Others seem to be suffering the same malady."

But exactly *who* was this happening to?

Tristan's heart began to pound. What was going on?

He stepped through the holobubble and saw that Argus had stopped breathing . . . and his body had begun to ooze into a puddle.

Tristan ran to his door . . . and out to the warren.

Only mimes . . . only mimes were suffering.

Tristan stood in the plaza in the center of the warren and had to remind himself to keep breathing, to ignore the smell, the carnage, the blood, the bubbling bodies . . . *everywhere*.

Not every dying mime was in the same state. A few seemed to be taking longer to lose control of their cellular structure, while others had long since degenerated into brownish pools of undefined muck.

Tristan forced himself to walk among the madness.

One mime, his head tilted at an unhealthy angle, tried to open his mouth as if to say something to Tristan. *Please . . . help me,* perhaps.

But the mime's mouth was only an ill-defined open hole now . . . soon to disappear completely. One eye stayed fixed on Tristan, struggling so hard to hold it together, until the eye itself dribbled out of what once had been a head.

Tristan staggered away. *This can't be happening. This has to be a dream, a nightmare. But if it is happening, why isn't it happening to me?*

More steps, to where the melting mime bodies had been reduced to smoldering heaps, steaming from the heat of rapid cellular decomposition. Tristan tried to make sense of the horror. It was almost as if his fellow mimes suddenly had been thrown into a rapid flux . . . then into nothingness. Something was turning their bodies into raw organic material, with no genetic plan.

The screams started to fade now, the madness—at least this part of it—coming to an end. The few humans who lived or worked near the warren looked on, their faces transfixed by the horror.

Numb, disoriented, Tristan leaned against a wall and slid to a squatting position. His mind veered back to that key question.

Why not me?

Then the Joe-face appeared.

"Sir, Cyrill wishes to speak to—"

"Yes," Tristan said. *Cyrill . . . Cyrill will know . . .*

And then Cyrill appeared in a bubble, his face contorted by rage.

"Tristan—*you* did this!"

Tristan shot to his feet and shook his head. Tristan's VAE program registered all of his gestures, his facial expressions. For Cyrill it would be the same as seeing him.

Can it register the fear in my eyes? Tristan wondered. *The anguish? Can it pick that up?*

"I didn't do this, Cyrill. How can you say—?"

"That cat's eye you sampled . . . they must have known you were coming. They *wanted* you to bring back a sample. And look what it's done—"

The bubble filled with a dozen quick images of mimes scattered throughout the far-flung Kaze Glom, all going through the same cellular degeneration.

"Every mime?" Tristan said softly.

"The virus is *everywhere*, spread by our own shuttles to all our worldwide centers of operation. Not every mime has shown signs of the disease yet, but we have to assume that the apparently healthy ones are infected and in the incubation period. Soon every Kaze mime will be reduced to a pool of goo."

A virus? Inside the Kaze borders every mime was linked to the glom for information and instructions. But there had never been a virus. No way a virus could go undetected and attach itself to a routine mime location check. No way—until now.

"And it's all because of you, Tristan!"

"Me?" Tristan was angry now. "Who planned the mission? *You!* Who designated which cat's eye should be sampled? *You!* I followed *your* orders."

"Don't add insubordination to your crimes."

"The deaths of all these mimes are on *your* head!"

"Mimes? Who gives a damn about you mimes. We can always clone more of you—or at least we could. It's the DNA banks that matter, and they've been contaminated! Our Goleman stock is ruined. Our mime operations are crippled—Kaze Glom *itself* is crippled!"

Tristan was missing something here. The shock, the horror made it so hard to think.

"You sold out, Tristan. You're a traitor to your glom!"

"No. How could I—?"

Cyrill thrust a finger at Tristan as though he could reach across the miles and jab him in the eye.

"You know nothing? You did nothing? Then tell me this—how

come you're still standing? How come *you* are alive while every mime—every *Kaze* mime, that is—lies dead or dying? Every one except—*you!*"

Right, thought Tristan. That's it. I'm alive. And how that must look to Cyrill. Natural to think I'm a traitor.

"Return to your quarters now, Tristan. I'm sending a Security team to bring you to the Tower. Maybe we can find what's keeping you alive. Remember, there's nowhere you can hide. Now, move—"

Cyrill disappeared. He had a right to be scared. And angry—though Tristan didn't understand what had happened, or even why he alone survived.

And then he remembered something.

Cyrill didn't know he had a universal key.

I can get out of here . . . if I want to.

But where? Where was safety?

And another question: Who else had known what he was stealing? Now that he thought about it, for all the running and hiding, it hadn't been all that difficult to get to the cat's eye. That part had been almost easy.

Too easy.

Had Lani Rouge known what was in the cat's eye? Had Flagge Glom been waiting for Kaze to send someone in to steal it?

He needed to think. If Cyrill caught him he'd run a complete psych probe and learn exactly what Tristan had done to get back. That alone would be grounds for his termination. But even without that, they'd undoubtedly take him apart to discover what was keeping him alive while others died.

It occurred to him that he had two things working in his favor right now. The first was that no one knew he had a universal key. As far as Cyrill knew Tristan was trapped in a narrow region of Kaze Glom. The other was that, with all mimes dead or dying, everyone would assume he was human. Amid all the chaos here he wouldn't be checked until Cyrill sent out an alarm.

And by then I can be out, Tristan thought. Maybe.

But where to?

I'm alive, I'm free . . . but like an old fable, I carry a curse . . . the mark of Cain.

I've slain my brother—hundreds of my brothers.

I sound like Krek, he thought.

But he could use a brother right now.

What would Okasan and Mung think? He'd sworn that he'd never reached the cat's eye; he had looked them in the eyes and promised to try again and bring the sample to them if and when he succeeded.

Lying was the least of his offenses. He'd played Trojan horse for one of the two major gloms, allowing it to cripple its major rival. He'd single-handedly upset the delicate balance of power, leaving Flagge Glom poised to become the supreme power on the planet.

But the biggest loser in this would be the mime rebellion. They'd—

Tristan reeled at the thought of what might be happening in the freezones, with all the runaway mimes going into meltdown.

And Proteus . . . if they weren't dead yet, they soon would be. He thought of Krek with his braying laugh. He'd been tough, and harsh, but he'd had a certain *joie de vivre* that Tristan envied. And he'd saved Tristan's life on the tube platform.

I'll bet Krek regrets that now, he thought. If he's still alive.

If Tristan reached the freezone he'd have to dodge any surviving Proteans . . . avoid them like . . .

. . . the plague.

A choked, haunted sound—half laugh, half sob—burst from him and echoed away.

But the truth remained. Any surviving Proteans would kill him on sight. And be perfectly justified in doing so.

Alive, free . . . and cursed.

Tristan began to make his way through the terrible landscape of bodies. He wanted to run directly for the gate, but his restricted Grid wouldn't let him pass. He had to get back to his compartment, use the universal key, and then get out before Cyrill's "escort" arrived.

Tristan forced himself to maintain a hurried walk—the pace of a realperson who was upset, disgusted, but not on the run from anyone.

Tristan retched as he stepped into his compartment. The stench from Argus's remains was almost overwhelming. Holding his breath he immediately retrieved the universal key and flashed it. Then he filled his pockets with concentrate packets, grabbed every template he could find, and ran for the hall.

If he was lucky, he wouldn't run into the "escort" on his way out; if he was even luckier, Argus's remains might throw them off for a while, making them think that maybe this Tristan mime hadn't been immune after all.

And if he was *really* lucky, he'd never see the inside of Kaze Glom again.

But even if he managed to escape, he still had no safe place to go.

Anyplace was better than here though.

"Joe, plot the safest path to freezone north—"

"But Cyrill instructed you to go return to your compartment and await—"

"I'm overriding that. I want to get back to the warehouse where I met Okasan yesterday morning."

He thought of his dreams of Selfhood and how naive he'd been.

Today the world changed, Tristan thought. And I was the instrument—the *tool*—of that change.

A muting tool . . . that was all he'd ever been. He'd—

"Cyrill will be very angry."

He wished he had time right now to disable the PDA's situational logic components. Until this was over he didn't need something reminding him every second of what *he* thought Tristan should be doing. Those days were over. From this moment on Tristan made those decisions.

"Forget Cyrill, Joe. Do you have the path?"

Tristan's Roam Grid flashed with red lines showing a twisted maze to the tubes, into the freezone, and on to the warehouse.

Tristan picked up his pace. Even in the hallways the air was filling with the stomach-tightening stench of death from decomposing mimes behind every door.

He shut out the images but he couldn't shut out the memory of the fear in Cyrill's face.

War . . . the word echoed through his brain.

War broke out today, he thought. And I'm a part of it.

Another word replaced war, a word that before had no meaning for him, a word from vids, especially the strange vids about men with guns who stood and faced one another for honor and land in the ancient wastelands to the west.

Atonement.

He could see only one course: Contact Okasan, join her. If she'd have him. If it wasn't too late.

And then find Lani.

INTO THE WAR

CHAPTER 23

The freezone had changed.

Tristan sensed it as soon as he stepped onto the platform at the freezone north tube station. Tension so thick he could almost smell it.

He looked across at the packed outbound platform. People were pushing, jostling for position to board the next tube. To the far right a fight broke out and a woman nearly fell from the platform.

Fear, bordering on panic.

Tristan could guess why: mime meltdowns. The virus had undoubtedly hit the freezone by now, causing hapless mimes, whether here legally or not, to devolve into goo. Obviously the frightened people packed on that platform over there didn't know the virus was mime-specific. How could they? Who'd tell them?

He couldn't see Flagge admitting to knowledge about the virus. And Kaze would be keeping it quiet for economic and public relations reasons: The world would know soon enough that Kaze Glom's mime stock had been destroyed, but how could they admit that they themselves had smuggled the deadly virus out of Flagge and contaminated themselves?

They'd be the laughingstock of the worlds.

Since most of the mimes here in the freezone were runaways, trying to pass as realfolk, all these terrified people knew was that some of their fellow 'zoners were dying horrible deaths, and if it was contagious, they wanted to be somewhere else. Fast.

Yeah, it's contagious, Tristan thought as he turned away and made for the exit. It's a veritable plague. But not to worry—you're all immune.

And so am I.

Why?

The question had hounded him all the way from Kaze.

Tristan checked his grid as he hurried down the ramp, then struck off in the direction of the warehouse where he'd first met Okasan.

Physically the freezone appeared just as he'd left it, but its mood, its ambience, its populace, were different. Fewer people pushed through the streets, and none of them the usual strollers and amblers. These tight-faced 'zoners moved quickly, purposefully, as if rushing to get where they were going so they could shut the door behind them. A siege mentality was in command.

If nothing else, it made travel easier. He made good time, but along the way he passed a putrescent puddle—all that remained of a freezone mime. People were giving it a wide berth as they hurried past or turned and ran the other way. Tristan averted his eyes as he passed.

I did this, he thought. And then he whispered, *"I'm sorry!"*

He kept a wary eye out for Flagge Security patrols but saw only two, and they were moving along as if they had a specific destination rather than on a search. Although he knew they wouldn't recognize him in this masque, their presence made Tristan uneasy. And that was heightened by the casual way they floated along . . . as if they owned the freezone.

Tristan's stomach twisted at the thought that that might be on Flagge's agenda: claim freezone north and annex it.

He found the warehouse district and stood in an alley among the nondescript buildings. They all looked so similar. Which one had been—

"Hello, traitor Tristan."

Tristan whirled. He knew that voice. Krek stood in the alleyway, grinding a fist into his palm. He wasn't alone. Tristan recognized Callin and some of the other Proteans he'd seen in the lair.

Joy and relief overcame his shock, and Tristan took a hesitant step forward.

"Krek? You're alive? Thank Helix! How?"

"Surprised? Thought you'd be the only mime outside Flagge left standing, didn't you."

"No. No, that's not—"

"Well, it didn't work. Sorry to disappoint you."

"No, you don't understand. I'm so glad—"

Callin leaped forward and, before Tristan could react, drove a fist at him. Tristan's face exploded in pain and he staggered back against the wall.

He shook his head to clear it, and when he looked up, the Proteans had moved closer. He saw the naked hatred blazing in their eyes and knew he deserved it.

He fought the urge to make a run for it. He had a feeling he wouldn't get far anyway. And right now, he lacked the will to run.

"We lost a lot of brothers today, traitor," Krek said. "Every Kaze mime is dead. Except you."

"I know, I know," he said, feeling utterly miserable. "But I don't know how. You're alive too—all of you. Why? I don't understand any of this."

"Liar!" Callin shouted. He stepped forward again with a raised fist, but Krek grabbed him.

Tristan spread his arms, welcoming him. "Go ahead. Do it. I deserve it."

And he meant that. He leaned back against the wall and sank to a squat. He hung his head.

Death was so inviting now. To join all those dead mimes. He'd known few of them and cared for none, but their deaths burdened him like the weight of the earth. Mimes who had somehow survived, blamed him and hated him. If Kaze Glom didn't have a price on his head yet, it surely would by the end of the day. Cyrill, his spiritual father, wanted his head. Lani was somewhere in Flagge and may have been a part of this awful conspiracy.

With no one left to trust, and no one left who trusted him, with everyone he knew either dead or out to get him, what was the point in fighting back?

"Come on," Tristan said. "Let's get this over with."

When nothing happened, he looked up and found the Proteans staring down at him.

"A good show of remorse, traitor," Krek said. "If you were anyone else I might even be convinced. But I'm not." He stepped closer. "And besides, it's not going to be that easy. Tear you up? Beat you to death? Much as that's exactly what we'd like to do just now, it's too good for you. When you go we'll see to it you go just like your brothers. You'll know their fear, their agonies. But that's not going to happen just yet."

Tristan blinked. "What's that supposed to mean?"

"It means we've made promises concerning you, and we intend to keep them."

Krek signaled to a pair of mimes who yanked him to his feet and held him while Callin slapped a patch on Tristan's neck.

"But after those obligations are discharged, you're *ours*. And then we'll deal with you."

Tristan's skin tingled as lights began to flash before his eyes. But too soon they dissolved to black.

Tristan awoke gasping and sputtering. He coughed, wiped foul-smelling water from his eyes, and looked around. He knew the place: the Proteus lair.

"You awake now?" Krek again. "Good, because I'm only going to say this once. The only reason we didn't rip you to pieces back there is Okasan. The old woman wants to talk to you."

"Okasan?" How could he face her? "I don't want to see her."

Krek gave him a rough shove. "What *you* want doesn't matter. She says you might know something important. Something useful. I think she's wrong, but we let her have her way. She started this group, brought the first members together, found us this place to stay, so we owe her. We humor her. We promised we wouldn't mess you up until she spoke with you. But after that . . ."

"Bloaty," Tristan said.

"You're just lucky she's not here right now. Gives you a reprieve of sorts. But not for long. She's on her way." He grinned—not a nice sight. "And while we're waiting we thought we'd let you pass the time with an old friend. A reunion, you might say."

Krek signaled to Callin who came over from where he was monitoring a newsfeed. The two of them half dragged, half walked Tristan down a dank corridor lined with doors that once might have led to storage rooms

"Yes, traitor Tristan," Krek said. "We promised Okasan no rough stuff until she talked to you. But we can't be responsible for the actions of someone who's *not* a member of Proteus, can we?"

They stopped before the last door on the dead-end corridor. It stood open. Krek knocked on the door frame.

"Company!" he said.

Then he and Callin shoved Tristan inside and closed the door behind him. He heard them laughing as they walked away.

Tristan quickly took in his surroundings—two beds, a weak glowplate in the center of the ceiling, an old aluminum folding table with two mismatched chairs . . .

. . . and someone lying faced to the wall on the bed on his right.

Tristan watched the figure stir, roll over, and sit up on the edge of the thin mattress. He noticed that the right shoulder was heavily bandaged. And when he saw the lizardlike skin and fanged face, he stepped back.

Eel.

"So," the mime gladiator said in his rasping voice. "It's you."

Tristan's instincts screamed to run, but once again he overrode them with the reality of his situation: There was no escape from the lair, and no place to go if he got free. It was going to end soon for him. Might as well end here.

Tristan stood his ground. "Yes. Me. Hello, Eel."

Eel rose and stalked toward him, eyes blazing. Tristan didn't step back.

Make it quick. Do it now. This way I won't have to face Okasan.

Eel pushed his face close to Tristan's, their noses almost touching, and stared. Tristan didn't flinch from the reptilian gaze. He steeled himself for a gut-ripping blow from the talons on Eel's good arm.

But it didn't come.

What are you waiting for?

Eel backed up a step and turned away.

"They tell me your name is Tristan."

Tristan knew he shouldn't feel relieved that he was still in one piece, but he did.

"They?"

"These runaway mimes here."

"Yes . . . Tristan."

"They took me to a doctor, you know," he said without looking around. His voice was flat, as if he were reading the words.

"I noticed the bandages."

"She told me I was lucky. Very lucky. That I never would have reached her alive if someone hadn't packed my wounds."

"Probably right."

"But none of these mimes did it. They say it must have been you."

"Well, you were bleeding pretty badly."

And now Eel turned to face him. "So it *was* you. Why?"

"Like the doctor said—you were dying."

"But why would you *do* that?" He stepped closer again. "I was all set to kill you—and *enjoy* it. That shot saved your life. Why would you care that I was dying?"

"I had no quarrel with you."

"But *I* did with you! When Security woke me and told me that a mime agent from Kaze had stolen my masque, I was furious. But when I discovered my wardrobe gone, I nearly went mad. I dug out some spare templates and went to the main tube nexus and I waited. You might get by Security, but you weren't going to get by me. I was there to *kill* you."

"And rightfully so. If places were reversed I'd have been out for *your* blood. You were shot because you were on that platform, and you were on that platform because of me. So I felt some responsibility. I don't know much about you but I knew you deserved better than to be backshot by a Sib."

"That wasn't a Sib. It was a Flagge Security marksman. I'm told he was posted there to make sure no one prevented you from getting back to your glom."

Tristan closed his eyes against a surge of nausea. The guilt for the catastrophe he'd caused had receded in the adrenaline buzz since his capture by Proteus, but now it all rushed back in a wave.

He sat on the other bed and stared at the floor.

"How—how do you know that?"

"These Proteus mimes told me. They captured the shooter and got it out of him."

What a plasmid I am, Tristan thought. What a worthless mutagen! Thought I was so muting smart, eluding Flagge Security at every turn, outsmarting them, outrunning them, and the whole time they were playing me like a ten-credit remote bot.

"What is it with these mimes here?" Eel was saying.

Tristan dragged himself from his pool of self-loathing. "What?"

"This Proteus group. What are they about?"

"They're runaways, many from the Arenas—like you."

"I'm not a runaway," Eel snapped, and then his tone changed. "But maybe I should be."

"Because they shot you?"

He nodded his big reptilian head. "Snipered by my own glom. They had to know it was me—they knew everything else—but that didn't stop them. I was dispensable."

"I wouldn't take it personally," Tristan said. "I'll bet they'd have sniped one of their own officers to spring me."

"Still, it makes one think. And then there's these mimes. They didn't know me. Not personally. The only time we might have met was in the Arena, and if so, they came away hurting—and yet they carried me to a doctor. They saved my life. That puts me in debt to them."

"I'm sure they don't feel that way."

"Doesn't matter how they feel. A debt is a debt. I owe you one as well. For packing my wounds." He turned away again. "Too many debts. I don't like that."

"Well, you don't have to worry about me. It was my fault you got shot, so we're even. But even if we weren't, I doubt I'll be around long enough to collect."

"Yes," Eel rasped. "They hate you with such a passion. They blame you for the deaths of all the Kaze mimes. But they didn't even know any of those mimes. I don't understand Proteus."

"They think all mimes are related. You know, having the Goleman chromosome and all."

"So they've told me. They want me to join up."

"Well, since all mimes are one big family to them, I'd say you're already a member."

"A family," Eel said softly.

"Strange concept for a mime, no? I'm told this whole Proteus thing was Okasan's doing."

"Okasan." Eel stared at him. "She's real then? Not just a myth?"

"I've met an old woman who calls herself Okasan. She seems genuine. And despite the fact that she's a realperson—or says she is—she seems to have genuine concern for mimes."

"Even for you?"

Tristan swallowed. "She did. But I doubt she does anymore." *Not after I lied to her and sneaked my deadly little packet home.* "The Proteans think I'm a genocidal maniac and Okasan probably agrees. They're going to put me out of my misery after she speaks to me."

"Maybe they were hoping I'd do the job for them. Probably why they threw you in here with me. But I can't harm you now. I *can* put in a word for you."

Tristan was touched by the offer, but knew it was useless. "Save your breath. And why would they listen to you?"

"I'm thinking of joining them."

Now *that* was a surprise. "With all your freedom? Your own apartment? Why would you give that up to live"—Tristan spread his arms—"here?"

"Because I'll probably wind up in someplace like this anyway. That apartment isn't mine. It's on loan from the Arena moguls. Same with the roam freedom. Championship perks. Mine to enjoy . . . as long as I stay champion. But what happens when I begin losing?" He jerked a scaly thumb over his shoulder. "Back to the warren."

"Still better than this dank hole."

"Maybe. Maybe not." He began pacing the small floor space. "I've had time to think here, about this idea of family . . . of being part of something bigger than yourself . . . of being connected to a larger organism. I think I like that."

Tristan nodded. "I know what you mean." The idea had been growing on him as well. But he could forget about all that now.

Eel said, "And after what Flagge did to the Kaze mimes . . . it shows how disposable we are."

"Property. A resource, and a renewable one, at that."

"And property can be disposed of once it loses its usefulness. But family . . . family is forever." He stopped pacing. "Mute Flagge. I'm joining Proteus."

Tristan wondered how long a mime used to a luxury apartment would last down here, then decided it didn't matter what he thought.

Tristan reached into his pockets. "Then you'll need this."

He was startled to find them empty, then realized he shouldn't be surprised. Why would the Proteans leave him with templates to use?

"I brought back your wardrobe. Your new brothers have it. Ask them for it."

Eel stared at him a moment. "You did that? You brought it back?"

Not exactly, Tristan thought.

In his rush to get out of Kaze he'd grabbed anything that looked remotely useful. Eel's wardrobe had been handy.

Tristan shrugged. "I certainly won't be needing it."

Eel started for the door. "For what it's worth, I'll do what I can for you."

Tristan said nothing as Eel hurried out. He remained hunched forward on the bed, staring at the floor. And then he heard the door swing open. He looked up, expecting to see Krek or Callin. But it was a woman.

Lani.

CHAPTER 24

Tristan shot to his feet.

"Is it you?" he said. "Really you?"

She nodded. "I should be the one asking that, don't you think? They tell me Tristan's in this room, but I'm standing here looking at someone I've never seen before." She shook her head. "This is so damned confusing."

"I'm the same man you told—let me get this right—that being human, being a *person*, is more than just having a certain set of genes. And you told me not to let anyone tell me otherwise."

She bit her upper lip and looked as if she were going to cry. "Yes," she said softly. "It's you."

He took a step toward her and stopped.

It's me. But is it you?

If only he could be sure. This could be a trick, a nasty joke by the Proteans. They might have got hold of a writable template and snagged Lani's genome. For all he knew, this could be one of the Proteans—not Krek or Callin, but one of the smaller members—waiting for him to make a fool of himself.

Humiliation before execution.

"How long have you been here?" he said.

"I just arrived. Okasan brought me."

"Okasan . . . then she's here."

That meant his time had just about run out.

"Yes. She wants to speak to you. But I asked her if I could see you first. The others didn't want to let me but Okasan told them I was to have some time with you."

She was Lani . . . she had to be Lani . . . he wanted so much for her to be the real Lani.

Maybe too much.

He held back.

"Time for what?"

She dug into her belt pouch and removed something. She extended her hand toward Tristan.

"Here. I brought this for you."

Tristan stared at the round flat case. "My wardrobe. How did you—?"

"I sneaked back into the warehouse and found it. I thought you'd want it."

Tristan stepped closer and took it from her.

Yes . . . this was his. He recognized the pattern of scratches on its cover. He rubbed his fingers over the surface as he stared at her.

And she was Lani. Her voice, the inflection, the way she moved . . . all just as he remembered. And how could the Proteans have retrieved his wardrobe on their own?

He reached out and touched her shoulder, ran his fingers down the length of her arm. He wanted to take her in his arms, feel her against him, kiss her like they'd kissed back in her apartment.

When had that been? Seemed like ages.

"You did that for me?"

"Well . . . not entirely for you. I did it for me too."

"I don't . . ."

She reddened. "Trev . . . the Trev template is in there. I didn't want it to get lost."

"Oh."

"You understand, don't you?"

Tristan wasn't sure if he did, but it didn't matter. Simply having her near, touching her arm, filled him with such wonderful feelings.

But she was thinking about Trev . . . always Trev.

"No. I'm just glad you're here."

"I . . . I was wondering if you'd . . ." Her face turned an even deeper red and she looked away. "This is so hard."

And suddenly Tristan understood.

"You were wondering if I'd flux into Trev again."

She nodded, still not looking at him. "Yes."

When he said nothing, she faced him.

"Are you mad? Have I hurt you?"

Some silly phrase like, *Why can't you want to be with me for the real me instead of who I can be?* flashed through his mind.

But how absurd was that? He'd been four different people during the three times they'd been together. And one of those people had been her.

So who was the *real* me? Even Tristan wasn't sure.

He said, "To tell you the truth, I don't *know* how I feel."

He dropped his hand away from her arm but she grabbed it and squeezed his fingers.

"You've got to understand. Trev went out one night and that was the last I ever saw of him. He was supposed to be home by morning but he never came back. We never had a chance to say good-bye. Can you understand that?"

Tristan could grasp some of it, but he sensed he was missing so much more. He'd never experienced what Lani and Trev had had together, so how could she expect him to understand.

"If that's all you want," he said, "then you don't need me. Any mime will do."

"No," she said firmly, and squeezed his fingers so hard they hurt. "Any mime will *not* do. It has to be you."

"And why?"

"Because of what I sense inside you. Your outside keeps changing but your inside remains the same, and inside you're like . . . oh, I wish

I could say this better. Inside you're *not* the same as Trev, but you share something with him. A kinship of sorts. So that's why it must be you. Please? Will you bring him back for me? Just this once?" She took a breath. "And I swear I'll never ask again."

How true, he thought. I won't be around for you to ask.

"All right," he told her. "If it means that much to you. But you'll have to step outside."

He didn't want to flux in front of her.

"I understand."

When she was gone Tristan removed his home template and inserted the Trev. He leaned against the wall as the flux pains shot through him, but these were relatively mild since home-to-Trev involved no major structural changes.

When he'd caught his breath he turned to the door and called to Lani.

"All right . . . it's done."

She did not appear immediately, and when she did, she edged into view like someone examining a wound. When she saw him she stopped. Her hands flew to her mouth as she stared.

After a frozen moment she began moving. Slowly, hesitantly at first. Without removing her glistening eyes from him, she fumbled a hand back, found the door, and swung it shut behind her. The sound of its closing seemed to spur her forward. A few stuttering steps and then she was fairly falling toward him. Tristan caught her in his arms and she clung to him, sobbing.

"Oh, Trev," she whispered. "Why did you leave me?"

And then she was kissing him, his neck, his cheeks, his eyes, his mouth. She pulled at his clothes, tore at her own, and the feel of her bare skin under his hands transferred her heat to Tristan. With each accelerating heartbeat, her calling another man's name meant less and less, became lost in the roaring in his ears. He wanted Lani as he had never wanted anyone or anything in his life. Soon there was nothing between them and they were tumbling onto the bed, locked together, fusing in a timeless flux of passion and need.

And when it was over and they lay there, Lani softly sobbing and Tristan feeling utterly used and yet indescribably wonderful, he pulled the damp sheet over them and pressed her trembling body close against his. Tristan knew he could handle the used feeling—perhaps even cease to feel used at all—if wearing Trev's masque meant keeping Lani by his side.

Part of him demanded to know: What kind of life is that—pretending to be a dead man? But another part said, What difference does it make? You have to wear some sort of masque—if this one forges a link to Lani, then wear it.

Anything . . . anything to keep her.

And then a third voice chimed in: You're not keeping *anything*. You're a dead man.

As if in confirmation, the room door creaked.

"Well, well," said a too-familiar voice. "When she said she wanted a few minutes alone with you, I never dreamed she had this in mind."

Tristan raised his head and saw Krek staring at him from the open doorway. Krek's eyes suddenly widened.

"Mute! You've fluxed. And where'd you get *that* template? Of all masques you could—" And then he stopped short and nodded. "I get it. *She* brought it. Well, fun's over. Time to see the lady."

As Tristan kissed Lani's forehead and began to slip from under the sheet, she clutched at him.

"No. Don't go yet. Stay a while. Okasan will wait."

"Okasan may, but the others won't," Tristan said. "No use in stalling the inevitable."

"Inevitable what?"

He stared at her. "Don't you know?"

He could tell from her blank look that she had no idea what was coming.

"I know they're awfully mad at you, but it's not your fault."

"Right," he whispered. "And I'm sure Okasan and I can convince them of that." He hoped that sounded confident enough.

"Then you'll be back?"

"Soon, I hope." He lowered his voice to a whisper and made an impulsive proposal. "If I return and fuse my interface closed with the Trev template inside, will you go away with me?"

"You'll be Trev forever?"

"Yes."

She threw her arms around his neck. "Oh, Tristan! That would be wonderful!"

"Come on, mime," Krek said. "Enough stalling."

Tristan pulled away. "Wait here," he told her as he slipped back into his one-piece. "I'll be back as soon as I can."

If I can come back at all.

He didn't have the heart to tell her that odds were high she was about to lose Trev for the second time.

CHAPTER 25

Krek's big right hand was tight around Tristan's upper arm as he guided him up the hall.

"You think that masque is going to help you, traitor? Think again. Much as we liked Trev, your looking like him won't change anybody's mind."

"It's not for your benefit," Tristan said.

"For the datameister's then? Lucky you. As a condemned man you can consider your last request already granted. That's one confused lady back there. The one we're heading for is not."

Krek yanked Tristan to a halt, then pushed him through a doorway to his right. Tristan staggered in, then came up short before an old woman wrapped in a long black dress that ran from her neck to the floor; she sat in a chair in the center of the small room.

Okasan.

Her eyes caught and held him. So infinitely sad, they seemed to grow, swell, expand, until they dominated the room, until he could see nothing else, until he was in danger of tumbling into those bottomless wells of grief.

And then they released him, flicking to his right as he heard Okasan's voice say, "Thank you, Krek. You may leave us now."

"Not a good idea, Okasan. He's got nothing to lose. No telling what he'll try."

"Please. I appreciate your concern, but I know what I am doing."

Tristan felt Krek's grip tighten on his arm. "I'll be right outside. Don't even *think* about harming this woman. The price will be . . . unimaginable."

Harm Okasan? Tristan thought as Krek released him and strode back to the door. What kind of monster do they think I am?

He answered his own question: a mass murderer.

"He could have stayed," Tristan said when Krek was gone.

"He hates you so," Okasan said. "Why would you want him here?"

So I wouldn't have to face you alone, he thought. But he said nothing.

"Tristan, Tristan," she said, slowly shaking her head, staring at him with those sad eyes. "Why did you lie to me? Why couldn't you trust me?"

Those eyes . . . like the mother of a slain child . . . and Tristan had done the killing.

He thought of a dozen things he might say. How could he be blamed for all that death, the slaughter of so many mimes? He hadn't known what he was carrying. He didn't ask to have his own life spared. He'd be dead too—if not for Okasan.

So many words of explanation.

But he said nothing.

Instead—Okasan spoke.

"Is it *so* hard . . . so terribly hard to trust, Tristan?" She smiled. "You wanted Selfhood, to be a human . . . and trust is such a human thing to do."

A pressure built rapidly in his chest. Trust . . . is that all it would have taken to stop this terrible genocide? The enormity of what he'd done and the lives he had cost broke through his defenses. The horror swirled around him until finally the weight of it drove him to his knees and he cried out his guilt, his remorse, in a long, loud, inchoate wail that filled the room.

Tristan knelt before her, hands over his face, crying for the first time since his too-brief childhood, utterly helpless in the face of these overwhelming emotions.

And then he felt Okasan's hand leave his shoulder and land on his head, smoothing his hair, then drawing him forward until his face rested on her knees. He wrapped his arms around her lower legs and buried his face in the black folds of her dress. And sobbed uncontrollably.

He felt her hand stroking the back of his head, soothing him. Was it possible that she didn't hate him? No. How could she not hate him?

But if . . . *if* . . . Okasan could forgive him, perhaps he could find a way to forgive himself.

Finally, when he could speak . . .

"Selfhood," he said without lifting his head. "They promised me Selfhood. And it blinded me to everything else."

"Poor Tristan," she said, still stroking his hair. "Selfhood is a myth, a bauble the gloms dangle before their most capable mimes. Ask yourself: Why would a glom deactivate its best mimes and send them out into the world as realpeople?"

Tristan lifted his head but still couldn't look at her. He stared at the dark, damp splotches left on her dress by his tears.

"As a reward for years of loyal service," he said.

But even as the words crossed his tongue, he tasted the lie.

"Think," she said. "A glom exists for its own interests. What does it profit a glom to lose its best mimes?"

"It's not a matter of 'losing' a mime," Tristan said, recalling what had been drilled into him since childhood. "Selfhood is an incentive to do your best work, a reward for years of exemplary service."

Okasan made a disgusted noise. "Mimes aren't employees. They're property. When the smart circuits in your favorite suit wear out after 'years of exemplary service,' do you give it a special place in your closet and let it hang there permanently?"

"But I know mimes who've gained Selfhood."

"Do you? Tell me where one lives and we'll go visit him."

"I can't do that. Selfhood involves taking on a new identity. All connections to your mime past must be severed. But I've met a number of them. They visit the warrens and . . ."

He looked up and saw Okasan shaking her head.

"Actors," she said. "Hired by the gloms to make the rounds of the warrens. The Selfhood myth allows the gloms to cull out the best mimes and recycle their mDNA."

Tristan went cold. "The vats?"

"Not the hoi poloi vats. 'Selfhood' mimes go into special vats where their high-grade strains of mDNA can be mixed and matched into new and better hybrids. You yourself are most likely the result of such a pairing."

"But Mung told me he was once a mime . . . or is that a lie too?"

"Mung was indeed a mime, but he didn't wait for his glom to confer 'Selfhood' upon him. A slave can't ask the master for freedom. A slave must take it. By deceit or force or stealth, by whatever means necessary."

Tristan closed his eyes and clutched Okasan's knees as the room threatened to tilt. Two days ago he'd have laughed her off as a crackpot conspiracy monger. But now, after Flagge's attack on Kaze—not killing its people, merely damaging its assets . . . and Cyrill's enraged response—not at the agonies suffered by his mimes, but at the contamination of the Kaze mDNA vats.

Agonies.

He opened his eyes and pushed away from her. He didn't trust himself to stand yet, so he settled on the floor and sat cross-legged before her, like a student before a teacher.

Teach me.

"Why am I still alive?" he said. "If anybody should have died—*deserved* to die—it was me."

"Because someone immunized you against the virus."

Tristan stiffened in shock. "*What?* When? Who?"

"Someone who knew you were going to be exposed to the 'G-strain.' "

"What's a G-strain?"

"The virus you transported from Flagge to Kaze. I've heard rumors over the years that Flagge was working on a virus that would attack the pilot chromosome—"

"The Goleman chromosome?"

Okasan's mouth twisted. "Yes. The so-called 'Goleman chromosome,' as it's come to be known, but it was originally called 'the pilot.' But whatever it's called, Flagge knew that if it could disable the pilot chromosome, the rest of the mDNA would be unable to flux.

"We learned that Flagge was dosing all its mimes with a viral antibody. Against what virus, we didn't know. But we weren't alarmed. It's not uncommon for mime populations to receive mass inoculations, as you well know."

Tristan nodded. Mime warrens were close quarters and mini-epidemics occurred periodically despite being sealed off from the rest of the world. He'd been vaccinated many times over the years.

"We got hold of a supply of the antibody and were dosing any of our mimes who were traveling through Flagge—just as a precaution," she said softly and stared at an empty corner of the room. "But we never guessed, never imagined . . ."

"But how—?"

"Probably through an inoculum patch—"

"On my neck!" Tristan remembered that disk he'd peeled off outside Smalley's.

He told her about it.

Okasan nodded. "They wanted to make sure you would survive premature accidental exposure to the G-strain. They didn't want anything to impede you."

Tristan swallowed and gazed at the floor. "Sounds like everyone was pulling for me—you, Kaze, and especially Flagge."

"Yes . . . *Flagge*."

The venom in the word snapped Tristan's head up. He saw a different Okasan now—lips drawn into a tight line, eyes blazing with fury. He'd never seen her like this, never imagined she was capable of such rage.

"Flagge could have developed a 'G-strain' that merely disabled the pilot chromosome, but no, it focussed its efforts on a strain that reset the pilot in a meltdown configuration. Disabling Kaze's mimes wasn't enough—no, Flagge decided to slaughter them in the most hideous manner imaginable. And they will pay for that, Tristan. I swear to you, they will pay."

"That they will, Okasan."

Tristan turned at the sound of Krek's voice and saw him standing in the doorway.

The gladiator pointed at him. "But first this one pays."

Tristan rose to his feet and faced Krek. This was it. This was where he met his fate.

"Krek," Okasan said. "Don't you think enough mimes have died already?"

"Too many," Krek said. "So many that one more won't make a plasmid's worth of difference."

"You know I don't interfere in Proteus's internal affairs," Okasan said, "but this is one time I feel I must. Please. I need this mime."

"So do we."

"Listen to me, Krek. I want you to look at the bigger picture. Kaze Glom has been crippled. It's not dead, but it might as well be. Over the next few years Flagge will take advantage of its coup and surge past Kaze in economic power. The seesawing equilibrium between them is gone. When Flagge reigns supreme the mime liberation movement will be dead. Flagge will annex the freezones; Flagge Security will be *everywhere*. You will have no place to hide—not even down here. It will be the end of everything we've worked for."

Tristan felt the growing heat of Krek's glare.

"And *he's* the cause. All the more reason to put him out of our misery."

"No, Krek. If Proteus is to survive, if mimes are ever to be free, we *must* find a way to restore some balance between the two major gloms, either by helping Kaze or hurting Flagge. I see no way we can help Kaze, but I think we can hurt Flagge. And I *want* to hurt Flagge. Killing Tristan doesn't advance that purpose . . . it hinders it."

"I don't care."

"Kill him and you may be killing Proteus's future."

Krek stood silent, his gaze flicking between Tristan and Okasan. At last her words had penetrated the wall of Krek's lust for revenge.

Finally Krek said, "What can he do that the rest of us can't?"

"If we strike at Flagge, it must be through its Datacenter. Tristan has been there. Have you?"

"No. But we have the datameister."

"We will need her too." She sharpened her tone, clipping her words. "We will need every last bit of help we can get, including Tristan's. *Especially* Tristan's."

"And you'd trust him? After what he did?"

Tristan knew then it was time to speak for himself.

"I never intended to hurt mimes—or anyone else, for that matter. I was only doing my job . . . doing what I was told . . . just as I'd always done. I thought I was taking my final step toward Selfhood."

Krek snorted. "Selfhood. Yeah, I bought into that once myself."

"But now I *have* Selfhood of a sort—I'm a mime without a glom. And believe me, Krek, I'll do anything to get back at Flagge."

"Anything?"

"Don't get me wrong. I want to live—more now than at any time in my life." He stepped closer. "But Flagge used me . . . used me as a tool of mass murder. No matter how long I live, I will never be able to fully atone for what they tricked me into doing. But I can try. So I am willing to die—get that Krek? *Die!*—to bring Flagge down."

Krek stared at him for a long time then shifted his gaze to Okasan.

"Do you believe him?"

"Yes," said Okasan. "I do."

"So do I, mute me. But I'll have some job convincing the others."

"He wants a chance to hurt Flagge. That should not be so hard for the rest of Proteus to understand."

"Yes, but *they* want a chance to hurt *him*!"

"Please see that they don't. In the meantime I will take the datameister with me and see if we can devise a way to damage the Datacenter."

"And you come with me, mime," Krek said.

At least he's not calling me "traitor" anymore, Tristan thought.

"Let's see if we can convince my brothers that I've found a more useful way for you to die."

CHAPTER 26

"Where are we going?" Lani said as the crawler turned onto one of the main freezone boulevards. Traffic was sparse and the driver was making good time.

"Mung has a safespace," Okasan said. "Since we heard of the Kaze holocaust he's been gathering all available information on the Flagge Datacenter."

"There can't be much of that. Even the people who work there know next to nothing about it."

"You'd be surprised how much we've pieced together over the years," Okasan said with a wan smile. "And with your help we hope to fill in some crucial blanks."

"Please don't get your hopes up. I know very little about the Datacenter. I've been allowed to see only the areas where I function, and no more."

"I'm sure you know more than you think you do."

Lani hoped so. Everyone she knew who worked in the Datacenter was allowed strictly limited access once inside. She was sure that was deliberate. Probably only a handful of Flagge higher-ups had the whole picture.

She shifted in her seat and cringed as she glanced up and saw a

Flagge Security cruiser floating overhead. Her first instinct was to duck her head to hide her face; then she remembered the bubble on the crawler was a one-way membrane.

She grabbed Okasan's arm. "Are they following us?"

Okasan looked up then leaned forward toward their driver. "What do you think, Charl?"

Charl shrugged. He had wide shoulders and a strip of yellow hair running front-to-back along the center of his scalp. Lani thought he was a mime, but she couldn't be sure.

"That one just appeared. The redheads are so thick out here today. It's the third I've seen. They swing by, hover over us a second or two, then drift off. I think we're attracting attention because the traffic's so light.

"Still," Okasan said, "I think we should be extra cautious. Take a circuitous route. Let's be sure we're not being followed."

Lani watched the cruiser hover a few seconds longer then bank off to the left.

Relieved, she leaned back and thought of Tristan . . . and of how making love to him as Trev hadn't been what she'd expected. He'd looked like Trev, he'd felt like Trev, but he hadn't made love like Trev. He'd been different.

Better.

She hadn't fully faced it until now, but Trev had been deeply pre-occupied during the last year they were together—the last year of his life. Even when making love he never seemed to be completely with her. A part of him always seemed to be looking past her.

But Tristan . . . Tristan had been *there*. All of him—beside her, inside her, all there for her. For those wonderful, ecstatic moments she'd been his whole world.

And he hers.

She couldn't remember the last time someone had made her feel that way.

Maybe it had been just the queasy excitement of the moment, the bent, almost outlaw aspects of making love to a mime in the masque of her dead lover.

But no. That had been more than mere thrill-ride rutting back there. She could download the same physical sensations from the Ocean. And she had . . . many times since Trev's death. This had been different. She'd bathed in a fierce passion flowing from Tristan, something no sensory download could duplicate.

Passion.

Tristan loved her. She could tell.

And Helix help her, she thought she felt the same—*feared* she felt the same.

In love with a mime . . . how sick was that? How could you love someone who kept changing his body? Sure, anybody could change their body these days, but not in minutes—nanite restructuring and gene splicing took time. A mime could be your dead ex one moment, and a woman the next.

But the Tristan inside didn't change. Whatever his masque, she'd sensed something decent inside, someone experienced and yet naive, fully grown and mature and yet still in a stage of . . . *becoming*.

She found that refreshing . . . and so terribly attractive.

As a shadow fell across the crawler, she heard Charl say, "I think we've got trouble."

Lani looked up and saw three Flagge cruisers hovering over them. A lead weight dropped into her stomach.

"What are they doing?" she asked as they began to drop toward the crawler—one edging ahead, one falling behind, and one staying directly over them.

"Boxing us in," Charl said.

"It's me they're after."

"Why?" Okasan said. "You've committed no crime."

"But they suspect me. And I wasn't supposed to leave my apartment—especially for the freezone. Anyone who's with me will be dragged into it. Let me out and I'll run. You can get away while they're chasing me."

"You'll do no such thing," Okasan said. "You can't outrun a Security cruiser, and neither can we."

"But this crawler can go where no cruiser can," Charl said. "I've been a good little driver up to now, but I think it's time to change all that."

He yanked the steering wheel to the right and hit the accelerator. Lani held on as the crawler lurched into an alley and picked up speed—

And then slid to a stop.

"Mute!" Charl yelled.

Lani saw why: A Flagge cruiser sat directly ahead in the alley, blocking it. She turned and saw one of the first three cruisers glide in behind them.

"They've got us boxed in," Charl said. "Must have been following us all along."

"The question is," Okasan said, "who do they want?"

"It's got to be me," Lani said. She rubbed her trembling hands together. She felt awful. Okasan was going to wind up in a Flagge Security cell because of her. "Why would they want you?"

Okasan's expression was grim. "Oh, they've been after me for a long time." She leaned forward. "Your IDplant is in order?"

Charl nodded. "The best that barter can buy."

"And mine says I'm a retired splicer." She turned to Lani. "But what about you?"

Lani saw one of the red-helmeted guards step out of the cruiser ahead of them and approach.

"I'll be all right," she said, trying to sound more confident than she felt. "I'm a valuable commodity, after all. Datameisters don't grow on trees."

The guard rapped his gloved knuckles on the driver door of the crawler. "Open up and let's read your ID's."

Charl flipped a switch and the membrane rolled back. The guard raised his hand to reveal the black disk of a vidplate in his palm. His eyes were hidden behind the visor; his lower face remained impassive.

"Here they are, sir." A pause, then, "Right away, sir. And what about the driver?" Another pause, then a barely perceptible nod. "Yes, sir."

He pocketed the vidplate then signaled to the cruiser behind them. Two more red helmets appeared and approached.

"Everyone out," the first guard said.

Charl rose and helped Okasan out of the rear compartment. Lani followed.

"Where are you taking us?" Okasan said.

"For a ride. You two, anyway." He cocked his head toward Charl. "He stays here."

"I go where she goes," Charl said, moving toward Okasan.

"Wrong," the guard said.

And then Lani saw a pistol in his hand, saw a flash, and suddenly Charl was falling back, arms flung wide, eyes bulging, mouth gaping in shock, with a charred, smoking hole in his chest.

Lani screamed as she and Okasan were grabbed and propelled toward the waiting cruiser.

"How long are they going to keep us here?" Lani said.

She'd lost count of how many times she'd wandered the perimeter of this tiny, windowless room. Bare walls, bare floor, and so small she found it difficult to take a full breath. No furniture except for a single rickety chair, and she'd let Okasan have that.

Which left Lani free to pace.

"It's a tactic here at Central Intelligence," Okasan said. "The waiting frazzles the nerves."

Lani stopped and looked at the old woman. "You sound like you've been through this before."

"I have."

"When?"

"It's not important."

Lani resumed her trek to nowhere.

"Poor Charl," she said. "They didn't give him a chance. Shot him down like a . . . a—"

"Like a runaway mime."

Lani whirled at the sound of the strange voice . . . and yet, not so strange.

A tall, slim, middle-aged man in a black clingsuit stood in the doorway, smiling.

"Which is exactly what he was," he continued. "Runaways can be terminated at will." The man laughed. "It's the law. And I so willed it."

He turned to Okasan. His smile broadened as he stepped toward her.

"And at last, after all these years, we meet again."

Okasan stared at him with ill-disguised disdain. "Hello, Streig."

"Oooh—I'm flattered you remember my name," he said with a mocking bow. "But which one of yours shall I use? Your birth name or one of your many aliases?"

"Okasan will do. I'm used to it by now."

"Yes, I imagine you are. Very well. Okasan it shall be."

Lani had been studying this man. That voice . . . something so familiar.

Suddenly it came to her. "It's you! You're that Security lieutenant who put me under house arrest!"

He turned toward Lani. "My compliments on your powers of observation. But I'm not a 'lieutenant' and I'm not with Security." Another mocking bow. "Commander Streig, Flagge Central Intelligence, at your service."

"FCI? But why were you—?"

"In a Security uniform? Just one of the many roles I've had to play in this little game. And it's been quite a game. *My* game, in fact. I spent years setting this up." He smiled. "And it's gone exactly as I'd planned." He held up a finger. "No, wait. Perhaps 'exactly' isn't quite right. It's gone *better* than I'd planned. For not only is Kaze's mime industry wiped out but I've managed to snag the notorious 'Okasan' in the process."

"And 'snag' a seat on the Flagge board, as well, perhaps?" Okasan said.

Lani looked at the old woman. She seemed so calm, so resigned. And she and this FCI officer seemed to know each other from the past. How?

Streig shrugged. "It's only my due. Once I learned that the G-strain had been developed, I knew immediately that we had to use it. The question was *how* to use it. We knew that even if we managed to get it past Kaze's defenses, the virus eventually would be traced back to us. The attendant legal fallout and negative publicity would reduce our gains, might even nullify them. So it occurred to me that if instead of *sneaking* it in, we could dupe Kaze into *bringing* it in, then Kaze would have no one to blame but itself. The board approved my plan, and with the help of our contacts inside Kaze, I brought it off."

"But the mime agent was vulnerable to the virus," Okasan said. "How did you immunize him?"

Why does she keep questioning him? Lani wondered. Does she want to keep him talking? Is that it?

"Ah!" Streig said. "That was a problem. I knew he'd use a sterile negative-pressure transfer pack to sample the virus, but what if there was a glitch and he was contaminated. It wouldn't do at all to have him go into meltdown before he reached Kaze. I decided the ideal place to immunize him would be Smalley's Smart Bar. His contact there was a NOK player"—yet another bow—"played by yours truly. During—"

"I'm impressed, Streig," Okasan said. "Allow me to compliment you on your ability to assume many identities. One might almost suspect that you could be . . . a mime."

Streig's face reddened with anger—the first real emotion he'd shown since entering. "Watch your tongue, old woman. What happens to you in the next few hours can be merely unpleasant or a living nightmare. The choice is up to me."

Okasan appeared unconcerned. "I'm sure it is."

"Then remember that." Streig had regained his composure by

now. "As I was saying, during the course of the mime's time in Smalley's, one of my people applied a transdermal patch loaded with G-strain antibodies."

"You make it sound as if you anticipated every complication," Okasan said. "But I doubt very much that you planned for Tristan to crash in the freezone."

"Well, no. I must confess that was not in the scenario. When he made his run for the wall in that Security cruiser, we herded him toward a laser battery that had been disabled. If he'd been a better pilot, that would have done it: He'd have been over the wall and I'd have seen to it that he outran us. But the clumsy plasmid damaged his craft and had to bail out in the freezone.

"Improvisation is one of my strong points, however. I may have lost track of him when he was underground, but I had the tubes covered and marksmen stationed to make sure no one interfered with his trip home. It all worked out for the best. We gave him such a difficult time getting back to Kaze that he had no inkling that he was, in effect, working for us."

Streig's careless braggadocio turned Lani's stomach.

"But you made him into a murderer!" she said. "He carried death back to his fellow mimes. Do you have any idea how terrible he feels?"

She felt foolish as soon as the words left her mouth. But she'd seen the pain in Tristan's face and had blurted her feelings without thinking.

Streig stared at her as if she were mad . . . or on Hhhelll.

"Do you have any idea how little I care about how a Kaze mime agent feels? Or even if he *has* feelings?" He took a step toward her, fury building in his eyes. "Why would you even ask such an idiotic question?"

Lani backed away, afraid he'd hit her. But then the fury faded and he smiled.

"But why should I be surprised at idiocy from someone who consorted with a mimelover."

Lani gasped. "Trev! You were watching me?"

"No, we were watching *him*, hoping he'd lead us to Okasan. Unfortunately the Sibs got to him first. But we decided he could be useful, so we slipped his genome to our contact in Kaze—so we'd know what the mime agent looked like when he came calling."

Lani wanted to claw his eyes out, but Okasan's voice broke through, steadying Lani and returning Streig to his favorite subject: Streig.

"So your plan was a triumphant success and your elevation to the World Board is assured. Why then did you continue to pursue me?"

"Because being *on* the board is only the first step."

"You want to be chairman, of course. Hardly surprising. But you'll be playing in a new arena, Streig, with opponents far more experienced and better equipped for battle than some hapless mimes."

"Yes. But they won't have splice 662RHC to offer."

Lani saw Okasan stiffen in her seat. Her face blanched. And when she spoke, her voice was hoarse.

"Splice 662 . . . what is that?"

Streig laughed. "Splice 662RHC. The loyalty gene . . . the compliance gene . . . whatever the hell you want to call it. Don't pretend you've never heard of it, old woman. You built it!"

"I . . . I don't know what you're talking about."

"And don't insult me by lying. I combed what little we could find of your records after your 'death.' I found three references to 662RHC . . . but no sequence for it. I know it exists. I know you experimented with it. I know it works." Streig leaned his face close to Okasan's. "And I *want* it."

Apparently Okasan saw no use in further denying her knowledge of this "splice." She held Streig's stare and spoke in a hushed tone.

"I will die first."

"If you won't give it up we'll take it. You know we can."

"Do your damnedest."

"You can count on that." Streig straightened and spoke to the air. "All right. Time for transport."

Immediately two Security guards entered. One took Okasan's arm and pulled her to her feet.

"Where are you taking her?" Lani cried.

"To the Citadel. And not just her. You're coming as well."

Lani's mouth went dry. She swallowed. "Me? But I—"

"You're a datameister, aren't you. Well we're going to extract some information from your friend—lots of it. We'll need a way to record and encode it. And you're it."

The second Security guard grabbed her arm and tugged her toward the door. Suddenly Lani was afraid—but not for herself. Poor Okasan.

"What are you going to do to her?" she cried. "She's just an old woman. She doesn't know anything!"

Streig turned and stared at her. He studied her face a moment before speaking.

"I thought you were playing a game here, but you're not. Amazing . . . truly amazing. You have no idea who she really is, do you."

CHAPTER 27

Tristan looked up from where he sat in the main chamber of the underground lair and found himself surrounded by at least a dozen grim-faced Proteans. Callin was among them.

"Neat trick, wearing Trev's masque," Callin said.

"Not a trick," Tristan said. "By request."

"So you say. But whatever the reason, it makes it hard for us to get worked up against you. Trev was good realfolk. One of the few. Almost like a brother."

Where's this leading? Tristan thought as more mimes crowded up behind Callin. He began to wonder if these battle-hardened ex-Arena gladiators liked to practice their old skills down here.

Seconds later the question was answered.

"But we've got someone here who never knew Trev," Callin said. "So he's got nothing holding him back."

He turned and bellowed over his shoulder. "Dee! Dee, come over here!"

Immediately the Proteans parted, clearing an aisle leading straight to Tristan . . . leaving him in perfect position to see the mime gladiator walking his way.

And the sight made him back up a step, right into a wall of mimes who pushed him back, center stage.

Here was the tallest mime that Tristan had ever seen. He hadn't known they even made mimes this large.

Callin moved closer to Tristan, as if relishing his distress.

"Meet Dr. Dee. They made him during the year they lifted the mass restrictions. He's about as big a biped as you can have before the weight—the sheer bulk—interferes with mobility. Undefeated in the Arena until they reimposed the mass restrictions. Most of the oversized fighters like him were retooled for other work. Not Dr. Dee. He escaped." Callin laughed. "Who'd stop him?"

"Dr. Dee," Tristan said. He felt chilled even though he was sweating. He needed to get some control.

"Dr. Dee, for short," Callin said, grinning. "Dr. Death is his full name."

Callin and the rest of the mimes laughed while Dr. Dee took his time coming, obviously aware of the importance of a dramatic entrance and its value in intimidating an opponent.

Tristan remembered seeing vids like this. A sport like the mime Arena. The fighting wasn't real but the fighters all had outlandish names and costumes. Not so different from the Arena, except there the *bodies* were as outlandish as the names and costumes.

Tristan stared at the approaching mass of flesh.

Dr. Death's head rose to a bulbous top, a hard cranial battering ram that looked to be mostly bone, with little room for brain. Even with a couple of opponents clinging to him, Dr. Dee could easily lash out with his head and bat an attacker or two away. His hands were the size of platters, and each thick finger ended in a long nail.

Grab someone then cut him open.

More chills, more dryness as Tristan's heart thumped in his ears. He realized that he'd lost all ability to control his autonomic nervous system. Now he was like any battered human facing death, completely out of control.

As Dr. Dee entered the circle he flung off his dingy robe, revealing a hugely muscled torso. He stood before Tristan wearing only a loincloth that barely reached his interface. He flexed his muscles, reaching over his head, locking hand to wrist to make his tree trunk-like arms bulge and pulse. He opened his mouth, displaying nicely filed fangs, and he then honked in a great gulp of air.

He looked like a djinn from a lamp that had been fashioned in a dark corner of hell.

Tristan looked around for help or a way out. Nothing. He'd even welcome a visit from Flagge Security about now.

"Mimes—ready for battle!" Callin yelled.

Dr. Dee raised a single arm in the air and bellowed, "Proteus!"

The word was almost unintelligible. Elocution wasn't the good doctor's strong point.

"This isn't fair!" someone said.

Tristan looked and saw Eel—still in his lizard man masque, his arm still heavily bandaged—pushing into the circle.

Callin said, "You've got no say here, Eel. You've been a member for less than a day."

"Well I'm going to speak anyway. You and I know that Krek promised Okasan that we wouldn't kill this mime."

"True," Callin said, unfazed. "And we'll honor that. But Krek's not here right now, and nothing was said about not making this mimekiller want to *wish* he was dead."

"At least let him flux into something that will give him a chance," Eel said.

Callin spoke through his teeth. "He gets as much chance as he gave the brothers in Kaze. Now back off, Eel."

The other mimes pulled Eel away and pushed him outside the circle. He looked at Tristan and shrugged as he pointed to his wounded arm, as if to say, I'd side with you but I wouldn't be much help.

Tristan nodded his gratitude. At least he'd tried.

"Begin," Callin shouted. "Combat!"

Dr. Dee wasted no time. His first move was as fast as it was unexpected. He did a high kick that sent a giant foot crashing against the side of Tristan's head. Tristan's vision filled with bright flashes as he went flying to the side.

The mimes cheered—and Tristan flashed on something: This is just like the Arena. The only difference is that here the mimes are the ones screaming for blood.

He rolled to his feet.

"You like this?" he said to Callin. "Mimes fighting mimes? No different from—"

But Dr. Dee didn't wait to listen. This time he sent both massive fists out like pincers of a giant clamp, trying to trap Tristan's head between them.

Tristan fell to his knees just in time, and the twin fists crashed into each other—causing little or no pain to the "doctor," he was sure—centimeters above his head. Tristan came up, smashing Dr. Dee in the midsection, a solid blow that elicited a grunt from the mime giant but didn't faze him. He bulled forward, forcing Tristan to backpedal until he was stopped by a wall.

Nowhere to hide, nowhere to run. The mime gladiator grinned.

And then a high-pitched voice rang out, somehow heard above the din.

"Stop! Hold on! Stop this!"

Dr. Dee cocked his head. He glanced at Callin who was looking toward the back of the giant room. Hard to believe that these hardened fighters would stop for that voice.

Tristan turned to look with everyone else . . . seeing first a small creature running ahead, a pygmy triceratops galloping into the room, followed by a round figure in flowing robes—Mung.

Why was Mung here? He was supposed to be meeting Okasan and Lani. Tristan saw Krek enter behind him. And from their grim expressions he knew something was terribly wrong.

"They've got Okasan!" Mung cried.

"Who?" Callin said.

"Flagge Security. Three or four cruisers intercepted her on her way to meet me."

"Oh, no!" Tristan said.

He thought he'd been afraid before, but now he knew a deeper terror. He pushed past Dr. Dee, dodging the huge hand that tried to grab him, and hurried up to Mung.

"What about Lani?"

"They've got her too. Took both women with them. But they killed Charl. Just . . . murdered him."

"Another mime dead!" Krek said, jabbing a finger at Tristan's face. "If this is your doing—"

"Don't be an idiot," Tristan snapped. Krek didn't frighten him now. Not even Dr. Dee. Only what might be happening to Lani. He turned to Mung. "Any idea where they were taken?"

"Yes. And this is strange. Witnesses I spoke to said Okasan was taken prisoner by Flagge Security, but when I activated her tracer—"

"Tracer?"

"Yes. Okasan has a tracer implant. When she was late for our meeting I activated it and saw that she wasn't in the freezone anymore. She was in Flagge Quarter. And as I watched, her tracer signal disappeared."

"Does that mean she's dead?" Tristan asked, his heart hammering.

"No. It only means she entered a shielded building."

"Flagge Security HQ," Krek said. "No surprise that's shielded."

"But that's the strange part. She wasn't taken to Security HQ. She was taken to the FCI building."

"Central Intelligence!" Tristan said. "But didn't you say—?"

"Yes. Arrested by Security but taken to the FCI. And that must mean that Flagge Central Intelligence has been behind this sick plot to get the G-strain virus into Kaze Glom."

"But what would those trisomies want with Okasan?" Krek said.

"FCI has been on her trail for decades, probably since before some of you were deincubated. And now they've got her."

"A damn shame," Krek said, shaking his head. "She's a fine woman, the finest realperson we've ever known."

"And ever *will* know!" Mung said. "You've got to free her!"

"Now wait a minute, Mung. We love her and revere her, and many of us owe our lives to her, but even if we hadn't lost all our Kaze-origin members"—Tristan winced at the glare Krek shot him here—"we still couldn't mount a successful raid on the FCI building. We—"

"But she's not there anymore!" Mung cried. "They've taken her to the Citadel!"

Krek barked a humorless laugh. "Oh, bloaty! That's a different story! We'll just waltz right into Flagge Citadel and march Okasan out the front entrance."

"You don't understand," Mung said, and Tristan thought for a moment the ex-mime was going to burst into tears. "FCI's been after her all these years not because she's Okasan, but because of a gene she developed many years ago."

"A gene?" Tristan said. "She's was a splicer?"

"Not 'a' splicer—*the* splicer. You see, Okasan herself was once a tool of the gloms—*all* the gloms. She gladly worked for the highest bidder as a freelancer—you could do that back then. She never gave much thought to how her work was being used—it was the work it-self that mattered. The work was all she cared about.

"But then came the day she located a gene common to people who make the best soldiers, the best corporate employees, the best team players. She took that gene and modified it, then spliced it into a few templates and tested it on some mimes. The results were astounding. The test mimes were blindly loyal to her, would do anything—even die for her. The loyalty gene, or compliance gene, or whatever you want to call it—she labeled it 662RHC—*worked*.

"And that frightened her. Especially when she looked around and saw how the other gene technologies she'd originated were being cor-rupted by the gloms. Her eyes were wide open now. The work she did, the genes she'd created, were having vast consequences beyond her lab. And the consequences of this new gene would be the most devastating. So she destroyed all her new research—including the 662RHC templates and all references to them.

"And then she did the unthinkable: She went to court to challenge the gloms' misuse of some of her earlier innovations. The gloms didn't completely own the courts back then, so they sent hit squads after her. She faked her death but they found evidence that she'd perfected a loyalty gene. They didn't buy her death completely, so they've been looking for her ever since. And now they've found her."

Mung paused for a breath.

"That's why they took her to the Citadel. They'll probe her memory—she won't be able to stop them. And they'll have the loyalty gene by the end of the day."

He bit back a sob and looked around.

"And then the horror will begin: They'll splice it into every mime and every template, but they won't stop there. Next they'll see to it that every Flagge citizen carries it. And since they're soon to be the most powerful glom, it won't be long before they start splicing it into *everybody*. Imagine: Every being on earth, loyal to Flagge—to the death!"

The Proteans were silent around him as the horrific scenario played out in Tristan's head. But something else about Okasan was nudging at his brain. She's old . . . a ground-breaking geneticist . . . who faked her death.

Then Krek spoke and interrupted his train of thought.

"Aw, that's just stories. People been talking about a loyalty gene for ages. Billions have been spent and no one's ever come up with one. Besides, Okasan may be a wonderful person and all, but I can't believe that kindly old wrinkle could come up with something that all these other brilliants can't."

"You plasmids!" Mung said angrily. "Are you all that dense? Okasan isn't just *any old woman*! She's Teresa Goleman! She invented mDNA. Flagge has kidnapped the only woman any of you will ever be able to call 'Mother.' "

CHAPTER 28

"Imagine," Tristan said softly. "Teresa Goleman . . . still alive."

"And you met her," Eel said.

The two of them sat off to the side, stoking on concentrate as the members of Proteus bustled about the central chamber of their lair. Eel had returned to his Dohan Lee masque; his bandaged shoulder was hidden under a frayed jump.

"Yes. Okasan and Teresa Goleman . . . one and the same. No wonder she's taken such an interest in mimes. She's our mother."

"That's carrying it a bit too far, don't you think?" Eel said. "We're clones. We have no mother—or father, for that matter."

"But she's more than just a spiritual mother," Tristan said. "Every one of our cells carries genetic material from her—the Goleman chromosome. I think that makes her our genetic mother as well. And if that's the case . . ."

"Then all mimes are brothers," Eel said. "Just like Krek's been saying."

Tristan nodded as the wonder of it finally struck home. "Yes. We're all brothers, all members of the same family."

Family . . . he had seen all those families on the old vids, and sometimes he watched people come together, people who loved one another . . . turning themselves into family.

Just like this.

This feeling of belonging was strange and new, but Tristan embraced the idea.

He looked at Eel. "Sort of changes everything, doesn't it."

"That it does," Eel said softly, looking around him. "That it does."

It hadn't taken Proteus long to decide to invade Flagge. Their fighting blood was already up when Mung interrupted Dr. Dee's dismantling of Tristan, and the word "mother"—coupled with the fact that the woman who filled that role needed their help—shifted the focus of their rage from Tristan to the glom that had developed the G-strain virus.

A few mimes held back, unconvinced that this was a good idea. Eel was one of them.

"Attacking the Citadel," he said, shaking his head as he watched the furious activity of Proteus girding for war. "I don't know . . . it's crazy. The Citadel is so well guarded—the best-protected location in all of Flagge Quarter."

"But look at it from their angle," Tristan said. "Proteus exists as a refuge for runaway mimes, as a focus from which sympathetic realfolk can agitate for mime rights. But if Flagge gets hold of the loyalty gene and splices it into its mimes, there'll be no more mime runaways, no new recruits for Proteus. And after Flagge starts splicing the gene into its realfolk, the idea of mime rights will die too."

"But this is a suicide mission."

"Maybe. Maybe not." Tristan finished his second concentrate packet and reached for a third. "But I can see Krek's point. This is a do-or-die mission for Proteus: rescue Okasan—I mean, Dr. Goleman—before Flagge extracts the 662RHC code from her, and do some damage to Flagge's Datacenter in the process, or Proteus's days are numbered. And any dreams that any of us ever had of Selfhood or freedom or even *free will* are gone."

"But the Citadel is crawling with Security guards," Eel said. "Their best goons."

"Doesn't matter how good they are if we attack from a direction they won't expect and won't be prepared for—from below."

"But when the alarm sounds, reinforcements will be rushed in immediately."

"That's why it's got to be a quick in-and-out operation. Surgical precision. Once we're inside we can use Okasan's tracer to find her. We'll free her and get out."

And hopefully Lani will be with her, Tristan thought . . . prayed.

If not he might have to break from the others and look for her.

"So what do you say, Brother Eel? Going to come along?"

Eel didn't respond. He sat next to Tristan, staring straight ahead, but didn't appear to be seeing anything. His mind seemed to be light-years away.

Finally he appeared to come to a decision. He blinked and straightened and looked at Tristan.

"All right. But I'll need a peek at that universal key these fellows say they've got."

"Flagge gave you that luxury apartment but not free roam?"

"Almost free—free to wander the freezone and almost all of Flagge Quarter, but I'm blocked from the Citadel area. No reason for me ever to go there, I was told. And they were right. Until now." He stood and looked around. "Where's Krek?"

Tristan had been keeping an eye on the Proteus leader since the decision to attack. "Over there."

Eel nodded and started in that direction, but after a few steps, stopped and turned back. He fished something out of his pocket and extended his hand to Tristan.

"Here. I want you to have this."

Tristan took the object: a template. He looked up at Eel.

"Who's this?"

"My lizard 'plate—the one I wore when I caught you on the tube platform. I call it 'dragon mode.' You can use it on the raid. It's a superb fighting masque."

"But what about you?"

"I've got another. I want you to have this one. You many need it. But be careful. Very ferocious. It can be hard to control first time you use it."

Tristan stared at the little disk. A significant gift, this. Eel was giving him one of his treasured gladiator templates. Tristan was touched.

"Thank you. I'll remember that. And I'll use it well."

Tristan watched him walk away and speak to Krek, saw Krek call over another mime and send Eel off with him.

And then Krek was alone.

Time for Tristan to make his pitch. Taking a deep breath, he walked over to where Krek was charging the pulsers.

"I'm coming with you."

Krek looked up and stared at him a moment. "I decide who's coming, and you're not."

He'd been afraid of this. But he had to find a way to convince Krek. Tristan *had* to be in the raiding party. He might be Lani's only chance.

"You need me. I'm the only one of us who's been in the Citadel. I—"

" 'Us'? Since when are you one of 'us'?"

"Since I became a runaway."

"No. Not good enough. You lied before and that lie cost countless mime brothers their lives. You've got some muting nerve asking us to risk *our* lives by taking you along."

"You must take him." It was Mung, waddling up and pointing a finger at Tristan. "He knows the layout of the Citadel's lower levels. He's done VR explorations of their Datacenter. Okasan will not give up the 662RHC sequence voluntarily, so Flagge will have to scour her brain for it. That's why they brought her to the Citadel. They'll probe her memory in their Datacenter. And Tristan has been there."

"We don't care where he's been." A new voice now—Callin's. "We don't want a traitor—"

"*Mute!*"

Without warning—he surprised himself with the move—Tristan gave Callin a violent two-handed shove. The mime's eyes were wide with shock as he staggered back a couple of steps, then they narrowed with fighting rage. Tristan didn't care. He was fed up with being pushed around. He'd taken all the abuse—verbal and physical—he could stand.

This was where it stopped.

As Callin started toward him Tristan grabbed the pulser Krek had just charged and pointed it at Callin's chest.

"Don't even think about it."

Callin stopped. "I knew it! I knew you were—"

"Call me 'traitor' once more and I'll jelly your muting head!" Tristan raised his voice. He wanted all the Proteans to hear this. "I am *not* a traitor. You can call me a fool, a liar, a dupe, a double-trisomy idiot, but I am *not* a traitor. Yes, I carried the G-strain virus back to Kaze, but I didn't know what I was carrying. Yes, I accept responsibility for what I did—and believe me, I will be haunted the rest of my days by the sights and sounds of my fellow Kaze mimes suffering the agonies of cellular dissolution—but I will *kill* the next mime who even hints that I did it intentionally. Is that clear?"

They'd gathered around him now. He could see their hands opening and closing into fists. They couldn't wait to get at him.

"Pulser or no pulser," Callin said, glaring at him, "you don't really think you're getting out of here alive, do you?"

"Maybe I don't much muting care," Tristan said, lowering his voice. "I don't seem to have much to lose. My old glom has a price on my head, I'm sure. My fellow mimes—or should I say, *brother* mimes—call me a traitor. The one woman in all the world I can call 'Mother' has been arrested and is being held prisoner."

Along with the woman I love, he silently added.

"Then what's all this about, Tristan?" Mung said.

"Yeah, mime," Krek said, pointing to the weapon in Tristan's hands. "What's this going to get you?"

"Your attention. Listen to me. You all blame me for the mime slaughter, but ask yourself, Who do *I* blame? *I* blame the people who invented the G-strain and duped me into bringing it back home: the same people who've taken our 'mother'—*and Lani*—'captive.' "

Tristan heard his voice began to shake as the rage built within him.

"No one in this room—*no one*—wants to hurt Flagge Glom more than I do. I would raze the Citadel, the whole muting Flagge Quarter, if I could. So here I am, this fellow mime with a bigger grudge against Flagge than any of you, a mime agent trained in subterfuge, skilled in espionage, and the only one of you who's ever been inside the Citadel, *and you won't use me!*"

He realized he was shouting. He searched the faces surrounding him. Was he getting through?

"Think about that," he said, lowering his voice. "I'm at your service. Use me. If not"—he tossed the pulser to Callin—"use that."

For one bad moment Callin looked as if he might do just that. But he looked at Krek instead. Tristan noticed that they *all* were looking at Krek.

But Krek was staring at Tristan. For a long string of heartbeats the mime leader's gaze seemed to bore into Tristan's brain. Then he nodded and turned to the others.

"I'm for taking him. He could mean the difference between success and failure. But we'll have to take a vote. Got to be unanimous." He stepped to the center of the circle. "All those in favor of letting Tristan guide us into the Citadel, raise your hand."

Krek raised his, and slowly, singly at first, then in groups of two and three and more, other hands went up until all were raised.

Except one.

Krek said, "You blackballing him, Callin?"

Callin hesitated then shoved the pulser back at Tristan.

"Make it unanimous." He pointed at Tristan. "But I'll be watching every move you make."

"Filamentous," Tristan said, and made a stab at détente with the angry mime. "I'll take comfort in knowing you're watching my back."

Callin shook his head and turned away.

"Where you going?" Krek said.

"To see if I can find us some backup," Callin said. "We're going to need all the help we can get."

"Where's he going to find backup?" Mung said as Callin moved away.

Krek shook his head. "I don't know. Callin's a good mime but a strange one. I've yet to figure him out."

Tristan was included in the plan-making. Since time was of the essence, they had to make do with the partial maps they had of the tunnel system. What was available indicated that a couple of tunnel branches passed close to the lower levels of the Citadel, and one actually appeared to have been bisected by the nether regions of the huge complex.

Tristan thought that tunnel might be the key. It would take them right up to the south wall of one of the lower levels. There, if luck was with them, and if the Citadel's designers had concentrated their security measures elsewhere—after all, who would expect a breach from below?—they might find a means of silent entry.

If not, they'd cut or blast their way in.

Because one way or another, they were going in.

As the plans progressed, and as Tristan contributed to them, he sensed a gradual grudging acceptance by the other mimes.

And then it was time to move.

Their weapons were maxed on charge, their bodies maxed on concentrate. They had cutting lasers, shaped charges, and satchels crammed with tools of destruction. The Proteans had their most ferocious templates ready, but held them in reserve, preferring to wear more conventional bodies for the trek through the tunnels.

Tristan had decided to stick with his Trev masque—its supple agility wasn't the only reason—but otherwise he was armed like the others: a rifle slung across his back, a compact pulser shoved in his belt, and in his fist a steel pipe liberated from one of the Sibs Proteus had killed yesterday.

He was ready . . . *more* than ready.

"Callin?" Krek called, looking around.

Mung waddled up. "He called in and said to start without him. He'll catch up to you."

"Where is he?"

"He didn't say."

"But he doesn't know the route," Krek said.

"Don't worry about that," Mung said. "I'll upload it into his grid when he gets here."

The tunnels were no place for someone of Mung's girth, so he was staying behind.

Krek hesitated. "I don't like it. Callin's one of my best—"

"Go! Go!" Mung said, shooing him off. "Helix knows what they're doing to your mother while you're wasting time."

That did it.

"All right, mimes. Buddy up with your partner and we're off."

Krek had divided the Proteans into fighting units of two—a holdover from the tag-team matches in the Arena, no doubt—and Tristan had been paired with Eel.

He looked around now but didn't see him.

"Where's Eel?" Tristan said.

No one knew.

"Look at this!" Mung cried, hurrying from the north end of the main chamber and holding up a pulse rifle and pistol. "I found them at the bottom of one of the stairwells that lead to the surface."

"Mute!" Krek shouted when he saw the weapons. "These were

Eel's. He's run off!" He wheeled on Tristan. "You're his partner. Why didn't you stop him?"

"I had no idea!" Tristan said. "He was ready to go, anxious to fight . . . or at least that's the way he seemed."

"Well, that's just bloaty! He's going to give us away to Flagge Security, isn't he."

"No," Tristan said. "No, I don't believe that. He won't betray us. But I got the feeling he doesn't believe we can win. And maybe he's gotten too used to all the perks and comforts of an Arena champ to risk them in a worthless cause."

Tristan felt disappointed . . . and worried as he thought of Eel scurrying back to his luxury apartment and sitting there in the dark, hoping he wouldn't be connected to whatever Proteus did in the Citadel. Tristan felt personally betrayed. He looked for anger, but found only sadness.

Eel had traded family for a few luxuries.

"Hey!" one of the other mimes shouted. "That lousy trisomy took our universal key with him!"

"Brother or not," Krek said through his teeth, "there's a mime that needs killing. No matter, we have our own ways into Flagge Glom. We'll worry about Eel later. Let's go." He turned to Tristan. "I'm solo— Callin was supposed to be my partner—and so are you now. Looks like we're a team. Better hold up your end, Tristan."

"Don't worry. Lead on, Krek."

But as Krek opened the hatch that led to the tunnels, Tristan's mind was filled with worried questions about Eel. If his plan was to sit out this battle, why had he taken Proteus's universal roam key with him? What possible use could he have for that?

CHAPTER 29

They followed a large, relatively straight tunnel due north.

"What about Dwellers?" Tristan asked, looking for the telltale burrows in the sloping walls.

"Not up here," Krek said. "Dweller realm is pretty much confined to the western tunnels. Don't ask me why, they just seem to prefer it there."

After nearly two hours of trudging through slimy water, fetid air, and deep-space darkness relieved only by their laser torches, they came up against a pile of rubble choking the tunnel's gullet.

"Mute!" Krek said. "What's this? We should be there by now."

"I think we are," Tristan said.

He blinked his Roam Grid overlay into view and checked the tunnel map he'd uploaded earlier. This was the branch that was supposed to dead-end at the Citadel's nether regions. And if the Citadel's builders had had to cut through a tunnel, wouldn't the severed end be filled with . . . debris?

Tristan climbed the slope of the pile of jumbled granite boulders and crawled as he traversed the space between its peak and the arched roof of the tunnel. When he flashed his light ahead and saw the beam bounce off a smooth onyx surface, his heart kicked up its rhythm.

He turned and called back. "We're there!"

Now . . . how did they get in?

Tristan heard someone approaching behind him. He turned, expecting Krek, but found Callin instead.

"Well, well," Tristan said. "The prodigal son returns. Where've you been all this—?"

And then he saw the pulser pointed at his midsection.

Callin flashed his own light at the Citadel wall ahead.

"I guess you're right," he said, holstering his weapon. "We *are* there."

"What'd you think I was—?"

"I don't know *what* to think about you, mime. Especially now that your pal Eel's run off. The two of you could have cooked up a little trap for us here."

"Give it a rest, Callin."

"I'd love to. Believe me, I've got better things to do. But till you prove yourself, I'm watching you. Every move, every step."

"Do your damndest," Tristan said. "But in the meantime we've got to get through that wall."

Callin moved past him. "Well, then. Let's do just that."

They weren't so lucky as to find a convenient airshaft protruding into the tunnel mouth, but the Doppler gauges located a relatively thin section of wall—one meter—and they began cutting their way through.

The work was hot, the progress agonizingly slow, and the closer they got to the inner wall, the more important silence became.

Finally, when they'd carved a large, roughly circular depression—big enough for Dr. Dee—and had only a few centimeters of wall separating them from the other side, Krek called a halt and attached an electronic ear to the wall.

"It's quiet in there," he said after a long moment of watching the readout. "Nothing moving, or even breathing."

"At least we're not stepping into an ambush," Callin said.

"Make me a peephole," Krek said.

A pinpoint laser drill opened a centimeter hole, but no light shone through. Krek threaded an optical worm into the opening, then checked the image-intensifying display.

He looked up and grinned. "Some sort of storeroom or utility room. And it's empty. Let's move."

Minutes later they were through the wall and gathered in the center of the room.

"All right, brothers," Krek said, stripping off his jumper. "Fish out your fiercest fighting template. Time to flux."

"Shouldn't we wait?" Tristan said.

"What for? One look at us, even as we are, and they'll know we don't belong here. Might as well shock the cytoplasm out of anyone who does see us—and be ready to rumble."

He had a point.

Tristan stepped back and pulled out the box Mung had given him. The tracker was cued to Okasan's tracer implant. It had been dead while they were in the tunnels, but now that they were inside the Citadel's walls . . .

A red light blinked in the lower left corner of the three-dimensional display.

"Got her!" he said. "Okasan is—"

The words died in his throat as he looked up and saw the transformations taking place around him.

Amid grunts and groans, visible among the long shadows cast by the laser torches rolling on the floor, the members of Proteus were fluxing into monstrous shapes more radical than he'd ever dreamed possible, even for Arena mimes—shapes designed not only to provide a fighting advantage but to evoke fear and revulsion as well.

Krek was the closest, lying on the floor, writhing with the pain of his flux. His upper body had developed rippling iridescent scales but was otherwise little changed. His lower half was another story: His legs had fused, and as Tristan watched in horrid fascination, the new appendage stretched and lengthened into a slender, coiling, serpentine shape. Krek had become a snake from the chest down.

To Tristan's left, Callin puffed and wheezed as he lay curled into a naked ball with his legs drawn up tightly against his abdomen. Tristan blinked as the mime's folded legs seemed to melt into his torso and other limbs—long, multijointed, and hairy—began to emerge from the sides of his chest wall.

And beyond them Dr. Dee seemed to be sprouting a long, squidlike grasping tentacle from under each arm; others were becoming part centipede or part leech, and Helix knew what transformations were occurring in the deeper shadows.

Finally, it was over, and one by one the Proteans regained their feet . . . or whatever they would be using as feet.

Krek reared up on his serpentine lower half and slithered over to Tristan.

"No flux? I thought Eel gave you a fighting 'plate."

Tristan had expected this and was prepared for it.

"He did but Eel's run off and I'm not so sure I should trust that 'dragon mode' of his."

Plausible, and perhaps half true. He told himself he wasn't really lying.

Callin stepped closer . . . on six legs. His arms, shoulders, and head were still human, and little changed in structure, but the rest of him was mostly tarantula.

"I don't like this," Callin said. "You're up to something. You either flux or get back in the tunnel."

"*Someone* has to look human. We don't know what we're going to run up against, and one of us may have to get into a Security helmet and uniform. You think you could pass the way you look now, Callin?"

Callin didn't have an answer for that, so he pointed to the tapered end of his bulbous spider body.

"See that?"

As Tristan watched, a curved spike slid out of the tip.

"That's no spinner gland. I had it modified. It's poison. And I'm watching you."

Callin moved away, but Krek remained, staring at Tristan.

"It's the datameister, isn't it," he said.

Caught off guard by Krek's unexpected perceptiveness, Tristan stammered. "What? No. I mean, what makes you say—?"

"Save it. I saw you two together earlier, remember? You're not fooling me."

Tristan's insides knotted. Lani was somewhere nearby, he could feel it; and if—*when* he found her, he wanted her to recognize him. He'd come this far. No one was going to turn him back now.

But he had another reason for not wanting to flux into a fighting masque, a reason he'd be ashamed to articulate before this crew. His relationship with Lani was at such a delicate stage. He wanted her to think of him as human and didn't want to confront her as any human but Trev. And he especially didn't want to confront her as a dragon man.

"I meant what I said about someone—"

"And I agree," Krek said. "Someone should stay fully human-looking—just in case. And that someone might as well be you." Krek moved closer and lowered his voice. "But get this straight, mime: Our primary objective is Okasan. *That's* why we're here. You don't know if your datameister's even in the Citadel. But if she is and we can get her out while we're here, fine. We'll gladly do so. But Okasan comes first. I don't want you sneaking off looking for your woman until we've saved our mother. Understood?"

Tristan wondered if he could accept those terms. More than anything he wanted to save both Lani and Okasan. But if it came down to a choice, he knew he'd side with Lani.

But when we find Okasan, she'll know where Lani is.

"Understood," Tristan said. "Okasan first."

"Do I have your word on that? Your word as a mime brother?"

Tristan looked at him closely. "You'd take my word? I've lied to you before."

294 and Matthew J. Costello

"I know. But you weren't in the family then."

Family . . . that word again, that feeling.

Tristan thrust out his hand. "My word then."

Krek gripped his hand and squeezed. "Good! Now where is Okasan?"

Tristan held up the tracker and pointed to the blinking red dot.

"According to this, she's about twenty floors down in the northwest corner."

"Any idea what's there?"

"Could be the Datacenter or the Security post—they're both in the same complex."

"So either way she's in a nest of redheads."

"Afraid so. I'll have a better idea when I find out what floor we're on. The Datacenter's on S-25."

"Excellent. And I promise you, as soon as we—"

"Look at this!" cried one of the mimes.

Tristan followed Krek to where a mime with a lobster claw for a right hand held a laser torch in his normal left hand and pointed it at a recess in the wall.

"Looks like a power grid server," Callin said.

"For the whole Citadel?" someone asked.

"Naw," Callin said. "Probably just for this floor. Or maybe just this corner of the floor." He looked at Krek. "But a little confusion can't hurt us, can it?"

"Can only help," Krek said. "Do it."

Callin raise his pulser. "Stand back everyone."

A cacophony of shuffling, slithering, rustling, clacking, and clicking, then a red beam lancing into server. A brief white-hot flash, and then . . .

Two ceiling panels lit with a feeble glow.

"Emergency lights," Krek said, grinning. "It worked. All right, now. We need to get deeper. Tristan's got the tracker. He'll lead. Pack up your gear, ready your weapons, and let's go."

Tristan opened the door and peeked outside. A long, deserted hall, dimly lit by the emergency panels, its inward wall broken by an occasional doorway, stretched away in both directions.

Hoping the security vidplates were powered down as well, he motioned for the Proteans to follow him, and led them left. He knew from his VR training for the mission that only the central chutes went all the way down to the Datacenter.

Trouble was, he didn't know this floor or how to get to those chutes from here.

He moved quickly, hurrying ahead to the first corner. He had no doubt that the building's sector computer already had the power problem area pinpointed and was trying to reprogram the server. But no one was going to fix that coagulated mass. After a number of failed attempts it would reroute power from other sources and send an inspector to eyeball the problem.

Tristan wanted to be in the chutes by then.

He turned and watched the Proteans' slithering, crawling, creeping progress along the hall behind him. He smiled as he imagined a Flagger rounding the corner and seeing this.

They'll think they've stepped into an anteroom to hell.

And then someone did just that.

Tristan was two or three meters from the corner when a middle-aged woman strode into view. Her eyes were downcast and she appeared to be lost in thought. She glanced up at Tristan and nodded, then her gaze headed back toward the carpet—but never made it. Her head jerked up and she froze. Her jaw dropped and her mouth worked as she stared wide-eyed past Tristan's shoulder.

"Hello," Tristan said. "We're on a tour and we seem to have lost our way."

She made a strangled sound and began to backpedal. She was halfway into a turn when Tristan grabbed her arm and pulled her close. He clamped a hand over her mouth.

"Not a word," he said. "Answer my questions and you won't be hurt. Understand?"

She nodded, the air whistling through her nostrils as her bulging eyes fixed on the Proteans.

"Good. Now what's the fastest way to the central down chutes?"

He removed his hand a centimeter from her mouth. Her breath was hot on his palm.

"Make a right here, go down two corridors, and make another right. They're right there."

"Thank you. Any Security along the way?"

She hesitated, and Tristan saw her eyes dart back toward the way she had come.

"Don't lie," he said and tightened his grip on her arm. "Where and how many?"

"Two. Right outside the chutes."

"Very good. You've been a big help. And now you'll accompany us for a while." Fear in her eyes as she opened her mouth and started to struggle, but he clamped his hand over her lips again. "You won't be hurt as long as you keep silent. Our fight's not with you."

"Kill her now and get it over with," Callin said.

Tristan felt the woman recoil against him as the mime sidled his spider body closer.

"That's what the Flaggers'd do to us," Callin hissed.

"But we're not Flaggers, are we," Tristan said. He looked her in the eye. "But if she makes one peep, I'll do it—personally."

Tristan didn't mean that, but he hoped she bought it.

He pushed her back and Krek assigned her to one of the other mimes, and then Tristan was on his way, leading them around the corner and planning his next move as they hurried down the wider hallway there.

Tristan held up a hand and stopped just shy of the second corridor. The Proteans bunched up behind him as he peeked around the corner and saw a pair of red-helmeted Security guards in a cubicle directly opposite the chute entrances.

Taking a breath he handed his weapons to Krek and stepped into view.

"Excuse me. Can you tell me what level I'm on?"

"S-5," said one of the guards. "But who are you?"

"Never seen you before," said the other. "Step over for an ID check."

Tristan turned and darted back the way he had come—and stopped. He didn't have to wait long. Seconds later the two guards rounded the corner with weapons drawn—and slid to a halt. Tristan couldn't see their eyes behind the visors, but their gaping mouths said it all.

"Meet my family," Tristan said.

Before the guards could react a barrage of pulser fire cut them down.

The woman screamed.

"Drop her and leave her," Tristan shouted, afraid an overzealous Protean might kill her. "Once we hit the chutes, everyone's going to know we're here anyway."

He retrieved his pulsers from Krek and sprinted toward the down chute.

"Down to level S-25!" he cried. "S-25!"

Tristan leaped off the platform into the express lane in the center of the shaft and plummeted downward past the slower passengers gliding down along the perimeter.

"Emergency! Clear the way!"

He heard screams and looked up. The Flaggers in the chute—men and women—were grabbing the nearest handholds and recoiling in horror as Krek and Callin and the rest—laughing and reveling in their monstrousness—plummeted through the center of the shaft.

Tristan checked the tracker and watched the red dot of Okasan's position rise in the indicator chamber. As the blip neared midlevel he checked the floor marker on the wall of the chute: S-23.

No doubt about it. She was in the Datacenter. Almost there. He stowed the tracer and pulled out his pulser, then he drifted toward the front of the chute.

"You're first out, Tristan," Krek called from close above. "Don't hesitate to use that. You won't get a break from Flagge, so don't give them any."

Tristan checked his hand pulser to make sure the safety was off, and realized his hands were trembling.

Adrenaline? Fear?

Maybe a little of both. Maybe *lots* of both.

Because the deeper they sank into the bowels of the Citadel, the less their chance of leaving this place alive. In his headlong rush toward Okasan and—he hoped—Lani, Tristan had either missed or ignored that grim reality. But now that they were approaching Flagge's Datacenter level and its attached Security post, the growing inevitability of death began gnawing at his stomach lining.

Better to die this way, he thought, than be hunted down in the tunnels like some rat.

He slipped his sweaty forefinger around the trigger and prepared to exit the chute firing.

He grabbed the handhold at the S-25 level and swung out of the chute with Krek's words echoing through his brain.

You won't get a break from Flagge, so don't give any.

A pair of Security guards stood against the opposite wall, looking bored. That changed as soon as they saw Tristan's drawn weapon. They reacted quickly but Tristan had the drop on them. Both went down with a loud clatter, the first dead before he hit the floor, the second screaming in pain. A blast from Krek finished him.

And then the chute foyer was filling with Proteans.

Krek directed most of them to the left, toward the Security post, and told the rest to stay right here and watch the chutes and hold the foyer.

"Shoot anyone who tries to step onto this floor."

Cries of pain and screams of horror erupted from the direction of the Security post as Krek turned to Tristan.

"Which way is Okasan?"

Tristan pulled out the tracker and rotated his body until the blip floated straight ahead.

"This way."

The tracker led him around a corner and into the Security post—or what was left of it. The smoky air was redolent of burned flesh; red-helmeted bodies lay sprawled everywhere. But Proteus hadn't come through unscathed. He passed two dying mimes, their wounds still smoking, their bodies slowly reverting to neutral state.

The tracker pointed toward the left, but Tristan saw no door that way. They continued straight ahead, toward the cries and clatter of battle.

It was over by the time Tristan and Krek got there. A middle-aged Security officer, his helmet off, his hands high, stood amid the shambles of his office.

"Helix!" he said. His eyes shone with fear but no respect. After all he was a Flagge Security officer, and these creatures facing him were just . . . mimes. "What do you freaks think you're doing?"

Krek ignored him. He looked over at Callin who was working the computer. "All accounted for?"

Callin nodded. "The body count equals the number logged in. We got 'em all. This one here is the last."

"VD plates off?"

"All communication from this post is *out*," Callin said. He looked at the officer and grinned. "Alone at last."

"But not for long," the officer said, a sneer playing about his lips. "The alarm's gone out. There'll be a company—a *brigade*—of Security here before you know it."

"But they can only come in through one set of chutes," Krek said. "We'll pick them off as soon as they appear."

"They'll send so many you won't be able to shoot fast enough."

"Good," Callin said. "The more the merrier."

"Have you all gone crazy?" the officer said. "You freaks are as good as dead. What do you think you're accomplishing here?"

"We've come for our mother," Krek said.

The officer looked around, stunned. Dropping Flagge jaws were becoming a familiar sight.

"Your *what*?"

"Okasan," Krek said, slithering closer. "Where is she?"

"Never heard of her."

Without warning, Krek knocked him down with a violent shove, then leaped upon him and coiled the serpentine end of his body around the man's chest.

"Please!" the officer grunted, his face reddening. "Can't breathe!"

"That's the whole idea," Krek said. "I was forced to kill brother mimes this way when I was in the Arena. It's not a pleasant way to go."

Tristan watched the coils tighten further.

"The old woman," Krek said. "Where? Tell me and I'll let you live."

The officer's face was purpling now, and he could barely raise a whisper. "Must be . . . Streig's prisoner."

"Streig? Who's he?"

"FCI . . . she's . . . in the . . . holding . . . cell."

"There," Krek said, loosening his coils and releasing the officer. "Wasn't that easy?"

"Muting freaks!" the officer gasped. "They should have used that virus on all of you!"

Callin stepped past Tristan and blasted the officer in the head with his pulser.

"I told him he could live," Krek said angrily.

"He was going for his pulser," Callin said. When Krek continued to stare at him he shrugged. "All right, he was *thinking* of going for his pulser."

Tristan felt nothing at the loss of a Flagge Security officer, but he couldn't resist adding, "He's not wearing a pulser."

Callin glanced down at the officer then back to Krek. He grinned. "Yeah, but if he *had* been wearing one, he'd have been thinking of going for it."

The other Proteans laughed.

Krek shook his head. "Stay here then and hold the area." He turned to Tristan. "Lead on."

Following the tracker, he led Krek and two other Proteans through a doorway and into a small chamber with two doors. One was open, the other was blocked by forty or fifty horizontal bars, each a couple of centimeters thick and about the same distance apart.

Tristan ran up to the door and gripped the bars as he peered through. And saw . . . .

Okasan, still in her long black skirt, sitting on a platform bed, staring at the floor.

His throat tightened at the sight of her, and her name almost clogged there. The last time he had seen her she'd been a nice old human woman and that was all. Now she was so much more.

"Okasan!"

The woman raised her head slowly and stared at him uncomprehendingly, as if she didn't recognize him, and for one heart-stopping moment he thought, *They've probed her and wrecked her mind in the process.*

But then her eyes lit. She gasped and rose shakily to her feet.

"No. It cannot be you."

"It's me, Okasan."

Tristan felt the Proteans begin to close around him, pressing close to see their mother.

"No," she said, anger in her eyes as she stepped forward. "This is a trick and I will not—"

But then she stopped and her eyes widened as she saw the Proteans. Her hand flew to her mouth.

"Oh, no! It *is* you. And you've brought the others!"

"Actually they brought me."

"Tristan, you shouldn't have come! None of you!"

Krek said, "We know who you are, Okasan. We couldn't leave our mother in prison."

"Mother?" She took a step back.

"Yes, Dr. Goleman. Mung told us."

"Mung! He swore never to—"

"He was frightened, terrified of what they might do to you to get the loyalty gene."

"He told you about *that*? Helix! Is there anything he *didn't* tell you?"

Krek said, "You can take that up with Mung after we get you out of here. We've no time for talk now." He bent and studied the cell door's lock control. "Look's like a combination key."

"Bloaty," Tristan said. "That officer would have known, but he's not talking, thanks to Callin."

"No one in Security can help," Okasan said. "An FCI commander named Streig recoded the lock after he deposited me here. Only he can open this door."

"And where's he?"

"I don't know."

"All right then," Krek said. "We'll have to do it the hard way." He turned to a mime in a leechlike masque. "Get the cutting laser."

"No!" Okasan cried. "That will take too long and you haven't got time. Security will be counterattacking soon. You've got to leave!"

"We will," Tristan said. "As soon as we get you out."

"Leave me! I'm no use to you or anyone anymore."

" 'Use?' What does that have to do with it?" Krek said. "You're our mother."

The leech mime returned with the cutting laser and began setting it up.

"Please listen to me," Okasan said. "Leave me and save yourselves."

Krek patted the leech mime on the shoulder and pointed to the bottom bar across the doorway. "Start with that one—right along the edge where it joins the door frame."

As the thin red beam began to play against the metal Krek turned to Okasan.

"Here's how we'll do it: We'll cut off the bars, starting from the bottom and working our way up. Soon as we've opened a big enough space, you'll stretch out on the floor there, we'll grab your hands, and slide you right through. Have you out in no time."

"But this isn't necessary. I'll be fine. They've already taken what they wanted from me."

"The gene?" A wave of despair washed over Tristan. "They've got the 662RHC splice?"

Okasan nodded sadly. "They went into my mind and copied whatever they wanted. And used your datameister to transcribe it."

"Lani?" Tristan lunged forward and clutched at the bars. "She's here? Where?"

"I'm not sure. She could still be in the datachair. I'm afraid for her, Tristan."

"Afraid?" A cold leaden weight dropped into his stomach. "Why? They won't terminate her—she's too valuable as a datameister."

"That's true," Okasan said. "But I heard Streig say she's an accomplice and can no longer be trusted."

"But what does that *mean*? They're not going to hurt her are they?"

Okasan looked away. "Flagge has been known to veg datameisters who become uncooperative."

"No!"

Tristan released the bars and slumped against a side wall. Closing his eyes, he pressed the back of his head to the cool metal surface, stretching his throat to help hold back a surge of bile.

Lani . . . veged . . . her brainstem deactivated and all her life-support functions put under computer control . . . leaving her alive and aware, but completely cut off from her body.

Aware . . . but not for long. The horror of her minute-to-minute existence, coupled with the relentless overuse of her brain in the Data-center would soon take care of that. Her intelligence would melt away and her consciousness would plunge down a bottomless well of psychosis.

"*She's* the one you should be working to free," Okasan said. "Not me."

Tristan opened his eyes and saw Krek staring at him.

"How about it?" Tristan said.

"No. Not till Okasan is free."

"But even if I don't find Lani, I can do some damage in the Datacenter. Maybe even destroy their copy of the loyalty gene sequence."

Okasan said, "Let him go, Krek."

The mime leader glanced down at where the laser was still working on the first cut.

"How's it coming?"

"Slow," the leech mime said. "Don't know what this alloy is, but it's *tough*."

"All right," Krek said to Tristan. "This is going to take longer than I thought. Go see if you can find her. And do what damage you can. But know this: Soon as Okasan's free, we leave—with you or without you."

"Understood," Tristan said. "And . . . thanks."

He rushed into the carnage of the outer offices of the Security post and headed for the elevator to the Datacenter. Callin grabbed his arm as he passed.

"And where's our human-looking brother headed in such a hurry?"

Tristan yanked his arm free. He wasn't going to tell Callin any more than he needed to know.

"To the Datacenter."

"Really?" Callin pulled the pulser from Tristan's belt. "Well then you won't be needing this."

"Why not?"

"The whole Datacenter's rotten with suppressers. Energy weapons won't work there."

Tristan could see the wisdom of that: It reduced the chances of accidental—or even more importantly, intentional—discharge in a sensitive area. But how did Callin know?

"When did you become such an expert on this place?"

"It's all in the post's computer." He handed Tristan a steel bar.

"Here. This'll do more damage down there than a battery of pulsers. Want me to come along?"

Tristan shook his head as he slipped the bar through his belt. His skin rippled at the thought of being squeezed into that tiny elevator with Callin's hairy spider body.

"Thanks, but I should be fine."

"Sure you don't want to flux into a fighting masque before you go?"

"I think I can handle any datatechs I come across."

And then he was on his way. He didn't have to look around to know Callin was watching him. He could feel the mime's suspicious stare burning into his back.

But he shook it off. Lani was somewhere ahead, and she was in trouble. He prayed she was all right, and that he'd find her in time.

CHAPTER 30

Tristan leaped out of the elevator with his steel bar raised and ready. The half-dozen datatechs clustered there cowered back.

"Who are you?" said a woman with short maroon hair in a supervisor's suit. "Is it over up there? What's happening?"

Tristan realized they thought he was a fellow Flagger.

"Everything's under control now."

They let out a ragged cheer and hugged each other in relief.

"We saw the attack on the monitors," the woman told him. "It was horrible. And then they all went blank. We've been so *frightened*."

"The Security post has been retaken," he assured her. "But what about this level? Any of those mimes sneak down here?"

"No, thank Helix," said one of the men.

"I always knew those damn things would be trouble," said another. "Haven't I said that? Haven't I? Get rid of them all, I say."

Tristan kept his expression neutral. "Well we're definitely rid of the ones that attacked the Security post. The officers in charge will want to debrief all of you, so proceed immediately to the upper level. Where is the rest of your shift?"

"We're it," the supervisor said. "The whole level was cleared for some special FCI project."

The Teresa Goleman mind probe, Tristan thought. A *very* special project.

Tristan nodded as if this was no news to him. "Anyone leftover from that?"

"I don't think so," she said. "We weren't allowed to see anyone or monitor anything. And quite frankly, after seeing what happened upstairs, we've been a little distracted, if you know what I mean."

"I understand perfectly," Tristan said soothingly. "And I know you want to get back to your homes and loved ones. So the sooner you're debriefed, the sooner you can be on your way."

It took the elevator two trips, but finally he got them all upstairs. Tristan hadn't known what kind of a welcome they'd receive up there, but couldn't worry about it. The clock was ticking.

As soon as the elevator door slipped closed on the final load, Tristan turned and raced along the rows of booths, checking them one by one. The first two were empty. But in the third . . .

The upper half of her head was enclosed in the scalp unit, but he knew those lips, knew the naked body that lay stretched out on the recliner.

Lani.

He thought he might burst into tears at the sight of her. She looked so vulnerable there with her body as well as her mind . . . exposed.

Cautiously, he stepped to her side and looked down at her. She breathed evenly, no doubt still under the influence of the helmet's slow-wave sleep. He felt like the prince in that old animated flattie he'd seen once, but knew it would take more than a kiss to wake this Snow White.

He had to stop those slow waves. But how? Would it hurt her if he cut them off too abruptly?

Had to risk it. He didn't have time for anything else.

Tristan found the manual release switch and flipped it. The helmet expanded and retracted.

Tristan watched Lani's body stiffen for an instant, saw her eyes moving back and forth under the lids. The lids fluttered, then opened. The pupils darted back and forth, then fixed on his face.

Her voice was thick, dry. "Tristan . . . is that you?"

Tristan! Not Trev—she'd called him *Tristan*!

"Yes, Lani, it's—"

"No!" she cried. "This is just another one of Streig's slimy tricks!"

"Lani believe me—"

And then he saw her eyes widen as she looked past his shoulder. He heard a noise behind him. As he started to turn, the back of his head exploded in pain. He lurched forward against the recliner and felt another blow to the back of his neck.

Dazed, he turned as he went down and, through a blur of pain, saw a pair of tight-faced men in brown jumps leaning over him, using their pulsers as clubs.

FCI men—they must have been trapped down here by the attack, hiding and waiting for rescue.

He reached for his steel bar and had it half free when they began kicking him—hard, vicious blows from their heavy boots to his abdomen, groin, chest, face. He felt the bar slip from his grasp as he rolled away and tried to protect himself.

But the blows kept coming. Tristan heard his ribs crack, felt them buckle in blazes of pain and give way under the relentless onslaught. He tried to rise, but one of the men jumped on his spine with both feet, slamming him back to the floor.

Dimly he heard Lani screaming.

"Stop it! Stop it! You're killing him!"

But no one was listening, and Tristan felt his consciousness slipping way . . . slipping over the precipice.

And then a voice, filtering through the ringing in his ears, echoing as if calling from the top of a well.

"I think he's about done, don't you, fellows?"

But the blows kept falling.

"I said enough!"

And at last, they stopped.

"*Sorry to interrupt your fun, but we may want to probe one of these mimes after this is all over, and I doubt there'll be any left alive upstairs after Security counterattacks.*"

The voice moved closer, as if inspecting him.

"*Well, mute me. Look at this: He's in the masque of our datameister's dead lover-boy. I'll bet this is the same retrogenomic mime agent I fooled into couriering the G-stain virus into Kaze.*"

What did he mean, *I fooled . . .*? Was this FCI man involved in the mime holocaust?

Tristan tried to lift his head to see, but his battered muscles wouldn't respond.

The voice came closer. "*We meet again, mime. Only you looked a lot better last time I saw you.*"

Last time? Tristan thought. When was that?

"*My, my, my,*" the voice said. "*You two really seemed to enjoy that.*" A laugh. "*Something to be said for full contact sport, eh?*"

More laughter, this time from other voices. One of them said: "*Best fun I've had in I don't know how long.*"

Lani's voice, high with rage and fear: "*You sick . . . subhuman—*" Cut off by the smack! *of flesh on flesh.*

And then the first voice again: "*All right, drag that garbage out of here while I put our noisy little datameister back to sleep.*"

Tristan was dimly aware of an increase in the agony that suffused his body as the FCI dragged him by his ankles, facedown across the floor. He forced his eyes open long enough to see the bloody wake of his passage, then they drooped closed again.

He was dumped in a corner where he fought to hold on to consciousness, clinging to it by a fingernail.

"Well, there's one mime down," said a voice. "How many more to go?"

"Don't know," said a second voice. "I saw more mimes than I ever wanted to see before the monitors kicked out. And none I wanted to meet in the dark."

Tristan reached out to the sounds like a shipwrecked sailor

searching for flotsam on a dark sea, anything that would keep him afloat.

"I'm with you there. *Really* glad this one came down in human form. Imagine if he'd had all those teeth and spikes like some of the others."

A laugh. "Yeah! I'd have given Streig the honor of attacking him with a dead pulser."

Streig . . . was that the man in the other room? The one who'd said they'd met before? The officer upstairs had mentioned his name . . . so had Okasan. But Tristan had never met anyone named Streig, let alone from FCI.

"Yeah, damn these suppressers anyway. I think I may have messed up my pulser on this thing's skull. And it's got mime blood on it."

"Mine too. Got a rag?"

"No, but there should be one around."

As the voices moved off Tristan realized he had one hope: Eel's template. If it truly was truly the "dragon mode" genotype he'd used on the tube platform, fluxing into that masque might save him. The bone and soft tissue remodeling mandated by the nonhuman splices could heal most of his wounds, even bridge the breaks in his ribs—*if* the edges were close enough.

And *if* his battered, broken body had the reserves to weather a flux. He'd stoked up on concentrate with the rest of the mimes, and under normal conditions his body would be ready for any flux.

But now . . . ?

And then there was the question of the reliability of a template received from a mime who'd deserted his brothers when they needed every available body. Helix knew what genotype this 'plate held.

But it was the only one he had.

Moving in tiny increments, Tristan slid his hand into his pocket and found the disk. He parted a seam in his jump, found his interface slit, and switched templates. He managed to get the precious Trev 'plate back into the pocket just before the flux began.

The sudden surge of agony was so intense it pushed a groan past his tightly sealed lips. Something was wrong! Never had he felt pain like this during a flux. Was it the broken bones—or a faulty template?

Despite his best efforts to hold it still, his body began to tremble and quake.

"Hey!" said one of the voices. "Something's wrong with the mime."

"Looks like he's having a fit or something. Streig's not gonna like it if he dies."

"Maybe you shouldn't have kicked him so hard in the head."

"That wasn't me! You had the head!"

Their voices faded as the pains spiking through Tristan's chest doubled . . . then tripled.

It's over, he thought. Eel gets his revenge, and the last laugh.

But just when Tristan thought he was going to die from the pain, it began to ease. He glanced down at his hand and saw scales where he'd had skin, sharp claws where he'd had neatly trimmed fingernails.

He stopped shaking, stopped groaning, held his breath, and lay perfectly still.

"Oh, bloaty!" one of the voices said. "He's stopped breathing."

Tristan sensed them moving closer, felt a shoe nudge him none too gently in the back.

"Something wrong here," said the other voice. "He looks different—"

Tristan rolled over and grabbed the foot. Its owner—his eyes wide white globes, his mouth a dark oval—shouted in shock and fear. His partner raised his pulser and aimed at Tristan's head.

Tristan still hurt, especially his ribs, but the pain was far away. He felt strong, and he felt an inhuman rage boiling within him. Dimly he remembered Eel warning him about that, but those words were back there, with the faraway pain. Only the here and now mattered, and the moment was suffused with scarlet fury and a lust to rend and tear.

He sprang to his feet, giving the foot a vicious twist as he rose. He felt something give way in the ankle, and then farther up the leg as he upended the FCI man, who crashed to the floor, moaning and clutching his knee.

His partner was backing away, pointing his pulser at Tristan's face. Tristan could hear the repeated clicks of the useless trigger over his equally useless cries for help.

"That won't help you," Tristan said. His voice sounded strange and harsh. "Suppressers, remember?"

The man tried to turn and run but Tristan caught his wrist and twisted it as he yanked back on it. The man screamed as his arm wrenched free of the shoulder socket with a satisfying *pop*. He went down.

Tristan grabbed him by the front of his one-piece and pulled him off his knees; he did the same with the first, dragging him from the floor. Then he began slamming the FCI men together, ramming the face of one against the other's.

SLAM!

" 'Best fun I've had in I don't know how long?' "

SLAM!

"Isn't that what one of you said?"

SLAM!

"Still having fun?"

SLAM!

"No? *I* am!"

The two men were beyond replying by now. They hung limply in his hands, their faces bloody ruins. Part of him—the "dragon" part—wanted to stand there and keep smashing them together until their skulls were soft and baggy, but another more insistent part wanted to get to Lani.

Tristan dropped them and opened the door to the inner booth. A man stood with his back to him, running his hands over Lani's exposed things, her lower belly, her—

He whirled. "I thought I told you not to—"

Tristan had been moving toward the man, his rage soaring toward a towering peak, but he froze at the sight of his face. He knew that face . . . he'd seen it just two days ago . . . at Smalley's . . . on the far side of a NOK board.

Am I such an idiot? he wondered bitterly. They played me like a holopuppet.

"Han!" the man cried. "Barr!"

"They can't hear you . . . Padre."

Puzzlement filtered through the shock on the man's face.

"Padre? Who's—" And then he seemed to remember. "Oh, yes. So it's you. Come to rescue your little datameister? What's the attachment here? A mime and a realperson? How quaint."

Tristan started for him but Streig's hand shot out to a switch on the console to his left.

"Don't!" the FCI man shouted. "Any closer and I'll fry her brain!"

Tristan stopped. The dragon part of him wanted to keep going, to lunge at Streig and tear out his throat. The rest of him fought to hold back.

Was Streig bluffing? Could he injure Lani from that console? Tristan's VR training hadn't included details like this.

"Don't do that."

Streig smiled. "So . . . you *do* care. Isn't that interesting. Seep from the Trev template? But no . . . you're not using that one. It must be"— the grin widened—"true love." He reached over and fondled Lani's pubes. "Unrequited love . . . or can it be that she's receptive? I never imagined our little datameister could be so twisted."

Tristan took an involuntary step forward.

"I'm warning you, mime. She won't be veged—she'll be brain dead. And don't think of leaving so you can cut the power. We've got a little stalemate here. So all three of us will stay just where we are until Security retakes its post upstairs from your fellow monsters."

Tristan ground his teeth in frustration. Streig seemed to have the advantage—*if* he could deliver on his threat.

Tristan couldn't stand here forever. He had to make a choice.

Another smile from Streig. "You played this about as well as you played NOK back at Smalley's—pitifully."

"You said before that you 'fooled' me," Tristan said. Maybe if he could distract him . . .

" 'Fooled' is hardly the word for it. The Trojan horse concept for releasing the G-strain was all my plan, you know."

Tristan reeled as the bubbling, agonized faces of all those dying mimes flashed before him.

This was the man, this was the one!

"And you made such an excellent horse," Streig was saying. "A dancing horse. I played the tune and you—"

Suddenly the main lights cut out as if someone had . . . pulled a switch.

Streig began working the console, slamming his palm against its top, his voice rising in pitch.

"What happened? Where's the power?"

Tristan was across the room before the emergency glow panel reached full brightness and he was in Streig's face when he looked up.

"Get back!" Streig cried. "It still works! I can—!"

Tristan stabbed the fingers of his right hand into the underside of Streig's chin; the claws at the tips pierced the soft flesh there, penetrating the floor of Streig's mouth as Tristan lifted him kicking and writhing off the floor. Streig tried to speak but could make only gurgling, gagging noises. Tristan could see the tips of his claws jutting through the bloody pool under Streig's tongue.

"You!" Tristan gritted through his dagger teeth. "You call *us* monsters?"

And then he let the dragon rule.

He hurled Streig against the wall and, before the body could fall, began slashing at him with his claws. The booth became a dank cold place and Tristan seemed to stand outside himself as his masque kept slashing at Streig, shredding his suit, flaying his skin, ripping his flesh to the bone, twisting Streig's spasming body left and right and left and right as great red gouts of blood and tissue flew, splattering the room, splattering the wall, splattering Tristan.

And then a voice, crying, screaming, pleading. Not Streig's, for Streig was beyond speech, beyond breath, beyond life. No . . . another voice. A woman's. He heard his name and focused on it.

"Tristan! Oh, Tristan, if that's you, stop it! You can't hurt him any-more. You can't—"

He turned and was dimly aware of what was left of Streig's body sagging down the wall, smearing the splatters as it sank.

He saw Lani, sitting up on the recliner, staring at him, her hands jammed against her mouth. The power failure had allowed her to awaken.

"That *is* you, isn't it, Tristan?"

He looked down at his bloody hands with their gore-crusted claws, at the crimson splatters on his suit, and felt ashamed. He hadn't wanted her to see him in any masque but Trev's, but now she'd seen him as a man-dragon, ripping a human to pieces.

He could deny it, say Tristan was upstairs, but that would only be delaying the original. He opened his mouth—

"He's Tristan, all right."

Lani gasped and Tristan whirled to see Callin standing in the doorway, his human head and arms half through, his spider body in shadow behind him. He carried a high-powered pulser rifle.

"Guess I was wrong about you," Callin said. "Good work on these FCI plasmids." He pointed the pulser toward Streig. "Especially that one."

Tristan didn't look around. He didn't want to see.

"The power . . . was that you?"

Callin nodded. "When you sent up those techs I started wonder-ing what you were doing down here. Found those two bloody heads out there and heard this one here playing games with you."

Tristan closed his eyes, realizing if Callin had charged in then, it might have been the end of Lani.

"Thank you for staying out of sight."

"When I heard what he was saying I called upstairs and told them to cut the power down here."

Tristan was moved. "You did that for me?"

Callin shrugged. "I was convinced by then that you were really one of us, and I figured you had something personal to settle with him. So . . ."

"Thanks . . . brother."

Callin nodded and smiled, then he looked at Lani. "You coming with us, Datameister?"

Lani—Tristan dreaded facing her, but forced himself to turn. He saw her slip off the recliner and rise unsteadily to her feet. She looked so vulnerable in her nakedness and uncertainty. He wanted to hold her, tell her she'd be all right, that he'd protect her, but he couldn't . . . not like this.

"I—I can't stay here."

She looked at Tristan, then at the bloody ruin that had once been Streig; she shuddered and looked back at Tristan, but it was not the way she'd looked at him before when he was in Trev's masque.

She said, "But Streig . . . he's got—or had—a cat's eye with the 662RHC sequence. We can't leave without it."

"See if you can find it, Tristan," Callin said. "We're running out of time."

"Is Okasan free yet?" he said, stepping to Streig's corpse and crouching over it.

"Okasan?" Lani said, brightening for the first time. "You found her?"

"Yeah," Callin said, "but we're having a muting tough time cutting through the bars of her cage. Security has already made one counter-attack, but we beat them back. There's only one set of chutes to this level, and we fry them as soon as they appear. So I figure it won't be long before they send in the bots. We've got to be on our way back to the fifth level before that."

Tristan picked his way through shreds of flesh and smartfabric, looking for the tiny sphere.

"Lani, are you sure he had it?"

"He showed it to me after they beat you, said it would change the world into two classes: those who had the gene, and those who told them what to do. You've got to—"

"Found it," Tristan said, holding up a tiny, blood-encrusted sphere. He went to put it in his pocket.

"Hold it," Callin said.

He looked up and saw Callin pointing the pulser rifle at him. "What are you doing, Callin?"

"Making sure that doesn't leave here. Put it down on the floor and back away."

Tristan did as he was told, wondering what Callin was up to. A pulser was useless down here because of the—

A bolt of energy sizzled from the muzzle and played around the cat's eye for a second before the tiny sphere exploded.

"How'd you do that?" Tristan said. "The suppressers—"

"Are off. When the power went down, so did they. So much for Okasan's loyalty gene."

"Well, for that sample yes. But I'm sure he made copies—lots of them."

"No," Lani said. "That was the only one. Streig wouldn't allow it to be copied—wouldn't even let anyone else near it. Before the probe I heard him tell the techs to disable the auto-replicating protocols. I guess he wanted to control the only copy."

"Well!" Tristan said, feeling his spirits lift. "At least we've accomplished one of our goals. Now we've got to get you and Okasan out of here."

"Which will be a much taller order," Callin said. "But first"—he tossed Tristan the pistol from his belt—"let's do some damage before we leave. You start here, I'll start at the far end of the hall."

He backed out of the door and disappeared.

Tristan looked at Lani, then at Streig's remains. "I'm sorry you had to see that. I lost control and—"

"It's all right," she said, but he didn't quite believe her. "If anyone deserved it . . ." She looked around. "They took my clothes."

"I saw some in the outer chamber. You get them while I start ruining their data banks."

Tristan watched Lani hurry out, then turned and stared at Streig's remains. Such an evil and powerful man should have been harder to kill. And yet he'd bled and died as quickly and easily as the lowliest DNA adaptee. Nothing special about his passing except that it was, Tristan hoped, more painful than most. And that hadn't been gratuitous. Streig had earned it.

Tristan hefted his pulser, dialed it to max power, and began firing.

CHAPTER 31

"They've cut off our power," Krek said.

Tristan had just stepped out of the elevator with Lani, expecting to find the Security post as bright as he'd left it. But it too was lit only by the emergency ceiling panels.

"When?"

"Not long. We saw it coming. We knew from the readouts that they were evacuating all the subterranean levels, and then we saw them cutting off power, level by level, until the blackout reached us."

"Mute," Callin said, hefting his pulser. He'd taken a solo ride on the elevator before Tristan and Lani. "I wanted to recharge this."

Between the two of them they'd done considerable damage to the Datacenter, going from booth to booth, frying all the cat's eye depositories and melting all the transcribing and replicating units they could find.

Tristan said, "I'm sure the armory here's loaded with fresh pulsers." He turned to Krek. "Is Okasan free yet?"

Krek shook his head. "Not yet. There's so any bars and the cutting is maddeningly slow."

"Can I see her?" Lani said.

She'd reclaimed her clingsuit, yet she stood about a meter away, arms folded across her breasts as if still naked, and gazed in awe at Krek and the other mimes. Tristan had noticed that she'd kept to the far side of the elevator car on their ride up from the Datacenter. He'd so wanted to hold her but didn't dare—not with these bloody, scaled arms. He'd hoped to be able to flux back to Trev once he got her up here, but that didn't seem wise now. The situation was deteriorating and he'd need every iota of this masque's dragon vitality.

Leaving Krek and Callin behind, Tristan led her back to the holding cells. As they entered the area he heard Okasan crying out to whoever would listen.

"Leave me, I tell you! Every minute you waste with me lessens your chances of getting out alive!"

"Okasan!" Lani cried, and ran toward the cell door. She had to stop short because of the mime working with the cutting laser on the lower bars.

Okasan smiled with relief and squeezed her fingers between two of the horizontal bars.

"Lani! They didn't hurt you! Oh, I'm so glad! I would have felt responsible." Her smile faded. "I'm responsible for so much already."

Lani reached out and caressed the old woman's fingers.

"No. I'm all right. Tristan saved me. And Okasan—the loyalty gene . . . the only copy is gone . . . destroyed."

"But Streig—"

"Gone too. Tristan . . . took care of that."

Okasan looked at him over Lani's shoulder. "This is Tristan?"

Tristan nodded. "It's me, Okasan. And it's destroyed."

Okasan's gaze seemed to wander into space. "Then the secret of 662RHC is a secret again. All mine."

Tristan leaned forward to see how the cutting was going.

Not well. Only two of the lower bars had been removed, and the laser was barely halfway through one end of the third. Okasan might be able to slip her legs through to the knee, but certainly no farther.

Tristan's mood, boosted by the freeing of Lani and the destruction 662RHC, plunged.

At this rate they'd all be killed before Okasan was free. He cudgeled his brain for a solution. How could he speed this up?

And then Krek slithered in. "They've shut off the power to the chutes."

Lani turned from Okasan and looked at them. "Then we're trapped—as locked in as Okasan."

"Not necessarily," Tristan said. "We may be able to route some emergency power to them."

"I wouldn't count on that, brother," Krek said.

Tristan shrugged and turned away. He'd worry about the chutes later. Right now he had a more pressing problem: freeing Okasan.

"I have an idea," Okasan said. "There's some sort of a plate in the wall here to the side of the door. It's just opposite the lock mechanism on your side. If I can get it open maybe I can find a way to bypass the lock."

"Really?" Krek said. "How's it fastened to the wall? Can it be pried off?"

"I don't think so," she said. "Slip one of your pulsers under the bar and I'll try a beam on it. Certainly can't make things worse."

"Anything's worth a try," Krek said. He pulled a pistol from his belt and handed it to the leech mime using the laser cutter. "Here. Push this under."

As the leech mime slid the pulser under the bars Okasan glanced up. Her eyes locked with Tristan's for an instant and he cried out at the terrible resolve he saw there.

"No! Don't give it to her!"

But too late. Okasan snatched the weapon from the floor and backed away from the door.

"Why not?" Krek said. "What's wrong?"

But Okasan answered for him.

"You cannot get me out in time," she said softly. "You are all very brave and I am so very touched by this grand gesture on my behalf, but the sad hard truth is that, no matter what you do, I will still be in this cell when Flagge Security reclaims this post. And they *will* reclaim it. The only variable is how many of you will die in the process. If you stay here trying to free me you'll all die."

"We're not leaving you," Krek said flatly.

"I know that," Okasan said. "And so I must leave you."

No, Tristan thought, knowing what Okasan was about to do. Not now, not after I've learned who you are.

A chorus of pleas rose from Lani, Krek, and the others as they realized what Tristan had already guessed.

Okasan closed her eyes and shook her head. "Thanks to Tristan, the world just got a reprieve from 662RHC. But if I'm alive when Security retakes this post, someone else from FCI—another Streig—will have me probed again. And Flagge Glom will once more have the key to domination. I cannot allow that to happen."

"Okasan," Tristan said, and heard his voice teeter on a sob. "Mother . . . please!"

"Mother . . ." she said, gazing at them with moist eyes. "For so long I have been ashamed of the misuse of my mDNA. But now, looking at you, seeing through the frightful shapes you've assumed, I find something good and noble. I'm proud of you—all of you."

"Keep cutting," Krek told the leech mime. "We'll get you out."

"The best thing you can do for me is survive. That is the greatest gift you can give me. Live on to find and free other mimes. When the word of your revolt spreads it will set other mimes to thinking. You've started a fire here—spread its flame across the globe, across the planets. But to do that, you must leave me here. Good-bye."

A chorus of pleas arose from Lani and Krek and other mimes who had been drawn into the cell area, but Tristan had been struck dumb by the intensity of the strange emotions roiling within him. He gripped the bars, wanting to squeeze through them and grab this old woman, embrace her and tell her that he'd just found her and he couldn't—*wouldn't*—lose her now.

But Okasan ignored the desperate cries. With calm deliberateness she moved to the shelf that served as the cell's bed and lay down on her back. She made an adjustment on the pulser pistol, then pressed its muzzle against her chest, over her heart.

She turned her head toward them. "Go," she said. "Please. Don't watch this."

But Tristan wasn't leaving, and neither was anyone else. Their pleas merely increased in volume.

"Very well," Okasan said with a tremulous smile. "Good-bye."

With Lani's screams in his ears, Tristan finally found his voice, but his intended shout of protest emerged as a wail of anguish.

And that clogged in his throat when he saw Okasan's thumb depress the trigger, saw her body shudder as the beam drilled a hole through her heart. Her arms spasmed and the pulser clattered to the floor. Her body stiffened, arched slightly for an instant, then went limp.

The cries and pleas died, strangled by the horror of the scene before them, replaced by groans and sobs. Lani turned and clung to Tristan for an instant, then pushed away—repulsed by the drying gore, by his dragon skin?—and stumbled away.

Tristan didn't go after her. He stayed where he was, staring through the bars, feeling as if he were coming apart.

Okasan . . . Teresa Goleman . . . his mother . . . was dead.

CHAPTER 32

Finally, after each of the mimes had paid his respects to Okasan's remains, and the door to the cell area was sealed closed with spot welds, Krek gathered his troops and addressed them. He struggled to clear his throat.

"As you know," he said, "power to the chutes has been cut. And try as we might, we haven't been able to restart the grav attenuators. Unless someone comes up with a brilliant idea, we're stuck."

"Not necessarily," Tristan said, his mind racing.

He'd been frantic, trying to think of a way out of this trap. Not simply because he wanted to save Lani, but because Okasan had given them a mission: Spread the mime revolution. He'd vowed to honor her last request.

"The chutes are dead, brother. Just dark and empty shafts."

"Exactly," Tristan said. "Dark and empty. With handholds running their entire length. We can climb out."

Krek brightened as the other mimes murmured appreciatively.

"Mute me, he's right!" Callin said. "They won't be expecting that." He clapped Tristan on the shoulder and laughed. "Aren't you all glad I insisted on bringing him along?"

That lightened the grim mood, but only briefly.

"How far up do we have to go?" Lani said.

"Twenty stories," Tristan said.

"I can't climb that far."

"You won't have to," he told her. "I'll carry you."

"As Trev?"

Tristan could tell by the look in her eyes that she was hoping he'd say yes. But that couldn't be.

"No. Trev couldn't climb twenty stories either. But with the vitality and special musculature of this fighting 'plate, I can get both of us out."

"How? You'll need both hands."

"I'll work something out."

While Krek was directing his fellow Proteans into the dark up chute, Tristan scavenged belts and holsters from the dead Security men and fashioned a makeshift harness for Lani.

Krek waited for them in the empty vestibule and helped strap Lani to Tristan's back.

"There," Krek told her after he'd tightened the last strap. "You hold on tight around his neck and you'll be fine."

Tristan noticed that she hesitated an instant before wrapping her arms around his scaly neck. He could almost feel her skin ripple with revulsion.

"Don't worry," he told her. "It won't be long."

"I hope not," she said. "Will you be able to climb all that way with my extra weight?"

"That'll be the easy part. The real challenge will be staying ahead of Security."

"Enough talk," Krek said. "You two are the last. Get started. I'll bring up the—" He stopped and cocked his head, listening. "What's that? Coming from the down chute."

He slithered over and stuck his head through the opening. He jerked it back just as a barrage of finger-thin red beams lanced from above.

"Bots!" he cried. He twisted toward Tristan. "Get moving! Now!"

Tristan felt Lani's arms tighten around his neck as he swung into the shaft. The counterattack had begun. He'd hoped to have a little longer to put some distance between himself and the Security bots. The winged ones flew, the boxy ones rolled, both forms were heavily armored, and once they got moving they were almost impossible to stop.

As soon as their controllers saw that the post was deserted, they'd repower the up chute and send the bots screaming after them.

As he started his ascent Tristan noticed Krek heading back toward the Security post.

"Krek! This way! Where are you going?"

"Get moving!" he said, waving Tristan off. "I'll draw them off."

"No!" Tristan cried. "They'll fry you!"

"They've got to catch me first. I'll make them think we've retreated to the Datacenter. By the time they find out it's just one mime you'll be back in the tunnel. Now *move*! If they see you they'll figure out what we're up to." He waved. "Remember me to the family and tell them not to waste time mourning. Tell them to get free. That's all that counts now."

Tristan knew Krek was right. Proteus's only hope was this sort of diversionary tactic. But it tore the heart out of him to watch Krek slither back into the Security post and know it was the last time he'd ever see that noble mime.

Tears blurred Tristan's vision as he started to climb. Only days ago he would have found Krek's decision utterly incomprehensible. But now . . . if Lani weren't here, he might have offered to stay in Krek's place and send the leader up to guide his mime troops to safety.

He blinked to clear his vision and concentrated on finding the handholds in the darkness and climbing as quickly and silently as possible.

He reached the opening for the S-24 level and found it empty, faintly lit by emergency panels. Good. If all the subterranean levels were this deserted they just might make it.

Suddenly Lani whispered in his ear. "Tristan, look. Down there."

Tristan glanced down and saw a winged Security bot glide into the chute. His heart began hammering. Did they suspect?

He swung out of the chute into the twenty-fourth-level vestibule. Pulser out and ready, he crouched to the side, just beyond the opening, praying they hadn't alerted the bot's infrared sensors and motion detectors. He didn't count on it. Two bodies harnessed together like his and Lani's put out a lot of heat. But he could always hope. After a certain interval he'd hazard a look into the chute.

He began counting.

And didn't get very far before the gleaming black wedge of a Security bot glided through the opening, it's left wing tip only inches from his nose.

Tristan didn't hesitate. He grabbed the wing and rotated it away from him to expose the bot's tail section. Everyone knew bots were vulnerable aft, and everyone considered it useless knowledge. Bots never retreated. They kept coming until they were downed or they had nothing left to kill.

But Tristan was looking at the thrusters and guidance ports of one such aft section right now.

"Close your eyes," he told Lani, then turned his head as he pumped three blasts into it.

The bot took off like an orbital shuttle, careening off the walls, then spinning into a nearby hallway.

Tristan was already on the move—back into the chute and climbing as quickly as he could. Had to be farther up before more bots arrived. And he had no doubt more would be coming. Whoever was running them would split off a few from the Security post counterattack to see what had happened on level twenty-four. Which was good: more time wasted searching an empty floor while Proteus made its escape.

The others were far ahead of him, but they'd be waiting. The plan was to regroup in the vestibule on S-5 and move to the tunnel en masse.

The climb seemed endless, and Lani's extra weight took its toll.

His muscles burned, his lungs labored, but he wasn't sweating—dragon skin, he guessed, didn't perspire.

Finally he reached S-5 and found the others clustered in the twilit vestibule outside the chutes. Waiting for him . . . and one other.

As Tristan loosened the harness and released Lani from his back Callin scuttled to the chute entrance and looked down. "Where's Krek?"

Tristan had dreaded this moment all the way up.

"He's not coming."

Callin's voice rose above the shocked babble. "What's that supposed to mean?"

Tristan told them of Krek's sacrifice. Silence followed. Was it his own guilt, or did he see an unasked question in their eyes?

Why didn't you stay?

"Let's go back for him!" someone said.

Amid a chorus of agreement the group surged toward the down chute. Tristan stepped in front of them, blocking their way.

"No! Stop! Krek's last words to me were, 'Tell them to get free. That's all that counts now.' You've got to honor that."

"Maybe you leave a brother behind," Callin said, pushing toward the chute, "but we don't."

"Damn it!" Tristan said. "Your brother—*our* brother—is sacrificing himself so that we can get away and fight on. Our *mother* did the same. So now you're heading back down there to make their deaths meaningless. The gloms will wipe us out, and Okasan and Krek will have died for nothing. Is that what you want?"

Callin stood poised on the edge, ready to push off with his eight legs, but he didn't move.

"Okasan and Krek . . ." Tristan whispered. "They both had the same last wish: Get free. Freedom's down the hall. We'll live to fight another day. And we'll make the gloms wish they'd never heard the word 'mime.'"

Finally Callin turned to Tristan. "You're right. It feels wrong, but . . ."

Tristan motioned toward the hallway. "Let's go."

Keeping Lani at his side and slightly behind him, he led the way out of the vestibule. He was about to step into the hall when a warning flashed through his brain. He held up his hand and stuck his head around the corner—

Then jerked it back. The hallway flashed daylight bright as a squad of Security troopers opened fire.

The mimes began returning fire, making blind shots around the corner.

"They've got shields!" Callin said.

Tristan lay on the floor and sneaked a look. Callin was right. The Security men were inching a phalanx of heavily armored barriers down the hall.

"Maybe we should try another floor," Callin said.

He moved back to the chutes but was driven back by pulser fire from above and below.

"They've got the muting chutes covered!" he shouted. He scuttled to Tristan's side. "We're trapped here."

"Worse than trapped," Tristan said. "It's only a matter of time before bots arrive to attack us from the rear."

"Then what do we do?"

Who elected me leader? Tristan wondered. He didn't want the job, but somebody had to decide *something*.

"The only way out I can see is to charge those Security plasmids in the hall. I counted about a dozen of them—probably stationed here as a precaution against any more mimes sneaking in from the tunnels."

"They'll chew us up from behind those shields before we reach them," Callin said.

"I know. It's a suicide charge for some of us, but the ones who get there can finish them and the survivors will have a clear shot at the tunnel. The alternative is waiting here for the bots, and then *none* of us will survive."

"Some bloaty choices, eh?" Callin said as he took a peek around the corner. "Either we—oh, mute!" He pulled back. "Reinforcements!"

Tristan heard cheers from down the hall. He looked and saw another dozen Security troopers moving up to join those behind the barricades.

"We're dead," Callin said. "We'll never get through that many."

Tristan held his hand up for Callin to be quiet. Something strange about these guards—the way their helmets wobbled on their heads. And their uniforms—even the smartfabric had trouble conforming to their bodies.

The original guards must have noticed it too. Their cheers turned to cries of alarm as the new arrivals ripped off their helmets and attacked *them*.

What were they doing?

And then Tristan knew.

"They're mimes! They look like . . . gladiators!"

New cheers arose, but from Tristan's end of the hall as the new arrivals tore into the guards.

Tristan squinted and recognized a too-familiar "dragon-mode" masque. He rose and stepped out into the hall.

"Eel? Eel, is that you?"

The "dragon" tossed a limp Security trooper aside and raised a fist.

"*Proteus!*"

The cry was picked up by all the mimes—the original Proteans and the new arrivals—and it echoed up and down the halls.

Tristan grabbed Lani's hand and pulled her forward.

"Who are they?" she asked.

"New recruits!"

Reaching the barriers, Tristan embraced Eel.

"Why did you sneak off?"

"I was pretty sure I could convince some of my fellow gladiators to join me, but I needed Krek's universal key to give them free roam. And since I didn't think Krek would trust me to wander off with it, I 'borrowed' it. These fellows were easy to convince. We jumped a Security squad, took their uniforms, and arrived as 'reinforcements.' They told us to get down to S-5 in case some crazy mimes showed up. So we got here, fluxed, and—"

A leonine mime came charging down the hall from the chute area.

"Bots!" he cried. "Coming up the chutes!"

"That way!" Tristan shouted. He pointed to the far end of the hall. "Everyone to the tunnel!"

From then on it was a headlong dash along the corridor. They were three-quarters there when pulser beams began to flash around them. A couple of the mimes bringing up the rear were hit before they rounded the next corner. One was dead, the other wounded, and he was scooped up by Dr. Dee's tentacles and carried along.

As Tristan rounded the corner he glanced back and saw three flying bots in V-formation. Merely the vanguard, he was sure. More were on the way. But these three were gaining fast. They'd decimate the mimes along the next stretch of hallway.

We need an edge, he thought. Just a little extra time.

He slowed and pushed Lani ahead. "Keep going!"

She looked back at him, worry in her eyes. "What about you?"

"I'll be along soon. Just get to the storeroom as fast as you can."

Then he caught Callin. "Take that wounded mime from Dr. Dee and tell him to stay with me."

"What're you up to?"

"Got an idea."

A crazy idea, a desperate idea, but if Okasan and Krek could give everything, he could at least risk the same.

As the huge mime rounded the corner Callin grabbed the wounded brother and shouted. "Stay with Tristan, Dee."

Dr. Dee gave Tristan a strange look when he'd rattled off what he wanted him to do.

But when Tristan said, "They're programmed not to shoot at other bots," Dr. Dee nodded and smiled, showing off his sharp teeth.

They crouched at the corner. As the bots glided into the turn in

V-formation Dr. Dee wrapped a tentacle around the wing of the nearest. Putting all his weight behind it, he swung the bot around and used it as a club against the one in the center, sending it crashing against the bot on the end.

The bots whirled in confusion, their sensors telling them they were being attacked but their overrides preventing a response against one of their own.

Tristan had hoped that in the confusion they'd expose their vulnerable afts to his pulser, and that might have happened had Dr. Dee got out of the way. But battle fury had overcome the giant.

"Bots kill brother! Dee kill bots!"

He kept swinging the first bot by its wing, hammering ferociously at the others, grunting with every armor-denting blow, until Tristan had to grab his free tentacle.

"That's enough, Dee. Whoa. Ease up now. They're not going to hurt us any more."

Dr. Dee finally stopped and Tristan watched the pair of free bots turn and wobble away through the air, bent, broken, bouncing off the walls as they wove drunkenly down the hall.

Dee shouted a garbled "Proteus!" and threw the third after them. It clattered to the floor and lay there, moving in slow, aimless circles on the carpet.

And then Tristan and the giant were running the other way. Dr. Dee laughed and roughly clapped Tristan on the back, nearly knocking him to the floor.

"Dee like Tristan!"

Tristan staggered and regained his balance.

"You're okay too," Tristan said, but moved away from Dr. Dee. Another display of affection like that and he'd have to be carried through the tunnels.

Outside the storeroom they found a number of dead Security guards. Apparently the mimes had surprised a small group and blasted through the shock-frozen Flaggers before they knew what hit them.

Tristan and Dr. Dee stepped over the bodies and past the two Proteans guarding the door.

Lani was waiting for him, and the relief in her eyes was a tonic. He helped Lani into the wall opening. Callin and Dr. Dee followed.

"Bots and guards in the hall!" came the shout from the doorway and the rest of them hurried into the tunnel.

They crawled through the opening atop the rubble pile and slid down the other side.

"The bots can't follow us past the shielded walls," Tristan said, "but Security can. Soon as they fit themselves with night sight, they'll be coming through."

Callin said, "I know," and hefted a sack from the base of the rubble.

"Some of us will have to stay and fight," Tristan said. *Hold them off at the pass.* "Otherwise they'll follow us all the way home."

"I'm hoping that won't be necessary," Callin said. "I've arranged a little surprise."

"What?"

"You'll see."

Just then the mimes guarding the top of the rubble pile began firing into the opening.

"Here they come!" someone shouted.

Tristan grabbed Lani's hand and led her into the darkness.

"Where does this take us?" she said.

"Back to the freezone—and freedom." *Maybe.*

Some of the mimes had fluxed back to more humanlike form, but Callin was sticking with his spider masque. And Tristan could see why: His eight legs moved him swiftly and surely through the debris-strewn passages.

Pulser beams began to flash around them.

"Looks like they're sending a whole regiment after us!" someone yelled.

"Just keep moving!" Callin said. "Put as much distance as possible between us and them! They'll be expecting an ambush along the way and that'll slow them down."

"Not a bad idea," Tristan said.

"Got it covered, brother," Callin said.

They pressed on, using their torches sparingly. Tristan found that his dragon retinas saw far better in the dark than any human eyes he'd ever owned. Just before entering a particularly dark and dank section of tunnel, Callin pulled something from the sack he'd been carrying and handed one to Lani, then to Tristan.

Tristan squinted at it in the darkness: a ten-centimeter disk attached to an elastic strap.

"What is it?"

"It's a toy," Lani said. "I, um, bought one recently. Big thing with kids. It's got a colony of phosphorescent thermophilic bacteria under the membrane."

"Put it on," Callin said.

"Where?"

"Someplace prominent. Around your head, I suggest. Then move through this passage as fast as you can."

As they moved on, Callin stayed put and handed out a disk to each mime who passed.

In the deeper darkness Tristan slipped the elastic band around his head and positioned the disk over his forehead.

"I think Callin is going crazy," he said. And then he glanced at Lani's disk where it sat in the middle of her forehead. "Look. Yours is glowing."

"So's yours. The bacteria are responding to the heat of our skin."

He looked around and saw one disk after another begin to glow with a sickly greenish light as the mimes donned them.

"Won't these make us easier targets for Security snipers?" Tristan called back to Callin.

"Trust me, brother," the spider mime replied. "You don't want to be without one in here."

Lani tripped in a puddle but Tristan caught her before she fell.

"Carry her, Tristan," Callin said as he caught up to them.

"It's all right," she said. "I can walk. I'm not a child."

"If speed weren't so important," Callin said, "I'd say, filamentous. But the faster you go, the greater the chance of falling and cutting yourself. And you don't want to bleed here. Especially here."

Tristan felt his scales shift uneasily. He had a feeling he knew what Callin meant.

"Why not?" Lani said.

Tristan lifted Lani and carried her.

"Let's just do as the man says." He picked up his speed. "At least for a little while."

After a long Stygian stretch, they entered a wider, more open section of the tunnel. Callin turned to Tristan.

"What do you think? Good place for an ambush?"

"Why ask me? I'm new to these tunnels."

"You've been trained as an agent. I'm just a gladiator. Krek gave all the orders. I just carried them out."

Tristan looked around. The area was studded with girders and recesses.

"Well, if we put a mime with a pulser behind every girder and in every recess, then wait till the redheads are well out of that narrower section . . . the Flaggers will have to spread their fire while we can concentrate ours. Only problem is there's too damned many of them."

"Maybe fewer than you think coming out of that section."

Tristan looked at him. "Have you made some sort of deal with—?"

"Skre-e-ek!"

The cry pierced the darkness and Lani lunged against him, clutching at the fabric of Tristan's suit.

"What was *that*?"

Before Tristan could answer, the initial shriek was answered by a chorus of others, echoing from the tunnel. And then other cries, human voices shouting in pain and terror as pulsers flashed like distant lightning.

Callin was already moving about, positioning mimes behind girders and in recesses.

"They're called Dwellers," Tristan said.

"I've heard that word," she said as he led her to a particularly thick and sturdy-looking column. "Krek used them to make the Flagge sniper talk."

Tristan repressed a shudder. "I think Dwellers could make the dead talk."

He joined Callin and helped position the rest of the mimes just as the first Security guards emerged from the tunnel. Some were firing over their shoulders as they ran; others were stumbling, trying to pull free of the voracious fanged horrors clinging to their backs and shoulders.

"Concentrate your fire on the ones without Dwellers!" Tristan shouted. "The others are already good as dead."

"That's what they get for not wearing these little glo-disks," Callin muttered. "You don't have one, you're a 'sacrifice.'"

"Since when?" Tristan said.

"Since today when I arranged a 'big sacrifice' with their leaders. Told them to wait in the passage—let those with glo-disks pass and a feast will follow."

"This was the 'backup' you were arranging?"

He nodded. "Our new allies—for the moment."

Pulser beams lanced from all sides as the mimes opened fire on the moving targets. The Security men who weren't felled immediately had no cover; they were forced to drop to the filthy floor and return fire from the prone position.

Not one retreated to the tunnel.

"Looks like they'd rather die out here than face the Dwellers," Callin said.

"Can you blame them?" Tristan said.

Callin shook his head. "No. Can't say as I do. Almost feel sorry for them." He grinned and fired at a Security man crawling for cover. "But not quite."

The firefight ended soon after it began. And in the tunnel the human cries and the inhuman shrieks died as the flashes receded and finally petered out. Tristan guessed that the only sound in the tunnel now would be the Dwellers . . . feeding.

Callin said, "Think we got them all? I mean, between us and the Dwellers?"

"Not all," Tristan said. "We know none of them survived here, but I'm sure some got out the other end and made it back to safety."

"Mute!" Callin said. "I didn't want no survivors."

"No. Be glad some got away. We need survivors to spread tales of the horrors that wait in the tunnels."

"Hadn't thought of that. Maybe that'll keep 'em from hunting us."

"Even better if they think we perished along with their men. Then there'll be no mimes left to hunt."

Tristan moved to where he'd left Lani and found her crouched at the base of the column, hugging herself and shivering. She looked up at him with wide, haunted eyes. She'd been through too much today and looked as if she was going into shock.

Tristan felt sorry for her. Because she still had one more shock to go. And Tristan was going to be the reluctant source.

CHAPTER 33

"Tristan?"

She sat on the bed where they'd made love . . . how long ago? Not quite a full day yet, but it seemed like eons.

So much has happened since then, Tristan thought. So much has changed. Especially in me.

"It's me."

Instead of moving next to her, he chose the other bed. He sat on a corner and stared at her.

The surviving members of Proteus and their new recruits had found their way back to the lair with no further interference. A celebration was in order, but no one felt too cheery this soon after the deaths of Okasan and Krek.

So while the other members of Proteus sat around and got to know their new brothers, Tristan and Lani had slipped away to be together.

"But I thought you were going to change to . . ."

"Trev? I didn't say that. I told you I was going to flux out of that dragon-mode masque."

Tristan had gone to another room and fluxed into his old home masque—his day-to-day Kaze identity. As human-looking as could be . . . but not Trev.

"But I assumed . . . I mean, after what you said before they took you away—"

Was it fair to do this to her? Did it really matter so much that she wanted him as Trev?

But he knew something now, something about freedom and Selfhood.

He had foolishly believed that Kaze would bestow Selfhood on him, that he'd have freedom to travel, to pass among normal humans, undetectable. But he'd learned that it was all a lie. Selfhood *can't* be bestowed. It can be fought for, it can be taken—but it can't be given.

And something else . . . real Selfhood meant a whole lot more than freedom. He was now free to become *someone*, and that someone couldn't be 'Trev' because that would be living a lie.

He was free to become someone—but who? He didn't know, not yet.

"I know," Tristan said. This was so hard. "I know I promised I'd fuse my interface and remain Trev forever, but . . . I'm hoping you won't hold me to that."

"Not hold you . . . ? I don't understand."

"I've got to remain a mime—a *functioning* mime. You heard Okasan: We've started something. We can't let it end here."

"But you *can*! We can move out into the freezone and live out our lives as ordinary, everyday human beings You said it yourself: Flagge thinks we're all dead."

"That's just it. We'll let them think we're dead—for a while. And then we rear up and show ourselves again." The fire built in him, raising him to his feet, moving him back and forth across the small room. "Show them that Proteus can't be killed. You think you've stamped us out over there? Guess what? We're over here. We can't let Proteus peter out and die. We've got to keep pushing for mime freedom, spreading the mime revolution."

"But you never belonged to Proteus. They hated you and you feared them."

"Yes. But that was before . . ."

"Before what?"

How could he tell her so that she'd understand?

That was before he knew about Okasan, before he and his fellow mimes invaded the very heart of Flagge Glom to save her, before he stood shoulder to shoulder with them and faced death, before Krek made the ultimate sacrifice to buy time for the mimes he called brothers, before Tristan knew what it meant to be part of a family, before he saw the woman who was the mother of them all end her own life to leave her children free to seek their destiny.

"Before *everything*, Lani. The mime who made that promise no longer exists. That mime spent his entire life trying to escape who he was. But he's gone. This mime needs to remain a mime, and intends to wave his mime flag in the faces of the gloms and dare them and anyone else to say they own him."

"That doesn't sound like a mime who's going to live too long," she said softly.

"Perhaps, but at least he won't spend the rest of his days pretending he's something he's not."

"You'll remain a mime forever?"

Tristan hesitated. "That's not a choice for me. As long as I have the Goleman chromosome, I am a mime. Will I go on fluxing till the end of my days? I hope not. But until this war is over, yes. And afterward—" He laughed, masking the words he had to say to this woman who he knew he loved. "Lani, I can fit any masque . . . but I have to find one that fits *me*."

Tristan reached into a pocket and pulled out a disk. He handed it to Lani.

"That's Trev's 'plate. Keep it. It's all that remains of a good man. But he's dead and I'm not. So I won't be wearing that masque again."

Tears welled in her eyes. One slipped over; its trail of salty water on her cheek scored an acid trench along the wall of his heart.

"I thought you loved me."

Tristan knelt before her. "Oh, I do, Lani." He placed his palms against her knees. "But you must love me in return. Not Trev. *Me*. I know it seemed like you had Trev back, but you didn't. And I know I felt as if you were making love to me, but you weren't."

Lani sobbed. Her tears splashed on the backs of Tristan's hands. He fought his own tears.

"The one inside this shape loves you," he said. "But my brothers need me. Can you wait?"

She sniffed. "I think so." She looked up at him. "I really think so." She looked at the template in her hands, and Tristan imagined her thoughts.

"I could wear that masque for you—always. You would never see me in any other shape. But that wouldn't be me. I need to become *someone*, Lani."

"But even so, I know I won't be first in your life. Proteus will come first, won't it."

Nodding took such effort, but he had to be honest. "Yes. For now. For some reason they've started thinking of me as their leader. And if they need me, I'll be that leader. For now. But not forever."

"You're asking a lot."

Not as much as fusing with Trev's template would have cost me, he thought.

But he said, "I know."

"I don't know what to do," she said. "I'm a fugitive in Flagge. I can't return to my old job—"

"A job that was hurting you. A job that would have used you up until there was nothing left." Tristan shook his head. "Not much different from the life of a mime."

"Maybe. But I can't even return to my home or get at my savings. I've lost everything. But I didn't care because I thought you . . ."

"I'm still here, Lani. And I can still be with you *if* you want me. We can find a place in the freezone to live. I can take on a realperson identity separate from Proteus. We can start growing a new life to-

gether. We'll both be starting from scratch, *together*, discovering ourselves, discovering each other. That can be a wonderful thing."

"If you survive."

"I fully intend to survive. I'll do anything you want."

Except become Trev.

Lani sat silent for a while. Then, "I need time to think about this."

"Of course."

He leaned forward and kissed her on the forehead.

"And I have to go outside. The others are waiting."

Lani nodded.

As he turned from her he felt as if he was leaving one world for
another. For how long . . . he didn't know.

Tristan stepped into the hall and closed the door. He felt as if he
were sealing off a chamber of his heart. But as he walked toward the
main area, he sensed new chambers opening, a new kind of life and
energy surging through him.

He was joining his brothers, and he was so damn proud of them.
Together they were going to change the world.

As he entered the chamber his brothers leaped to their feet and
thrust their fists high. Their cry echoed through their home.

"Proteus!"

And Tristan knew one answer to the question that had been
plaguing him.

Who am I?

I am the leader of Proteus.

He raised his fist in answer, his voice loud, commanding, a call to
battle.

"PROTEUS!"